THE SUMMONING GOD

BY KATHLEEN O'NEAL GEAR AND W. MICHAEL GEAR
FROM TOM DOHERTY ASSOCIATES

THE FIRST NORTH AMERICANS SERIES

People of the Wolf
People of the Fire
People of the Earth
People of the River
People of the Sea
People of the Lakes
People of the Lightning
People of the Silence
People of the Mist
People of the Masks

THE ANASAZI MYSTERY SERIES

The Visitant
The Summoning God

BY KATHLEEN O'NEAL GEAR

Thin Moon and Cold Mist
Sand in the Wind
This Widowed Land

BY W. MICHAEL GEAR

Long Ride Home
Big Horn Legacy
The Morning River
Coyote Summer

THE SUMMONING GOD

BOOK TWO OF THE ANASAZI MYSTERIES

KATHLEEN O'NEAL GEAR

W. MICHAEL GEAR

A TOM DOHERTY ASSOCIATES BOOK

NEW YORK

THE SUMMONING GOD

This book is printed on acid-free paper.

Maps © 2000 by Miguel Roces
Scene ornaments by Ellisa Mitchell

A Forge Book
Published by Tom Doherty Associates, LLC
175 Fifth Avenue
New York, NY 10010

www.tor.com

Forge® is a registered trademark of Tom Doherty Associates, LLC.

Library of Congress Cataloging-in-Publication Data

Gear, Kathleen O'Neal.
The summoning God / Kathleen O'Neal Gear, W. Michael Gear.—1st ed.
p. cm—(The Anasazi mysteries ; bk. 2)
"A Tom Doherty Associates book."
ISBN 0-312-86532-5 (hardcover) (acid-free paper)
ISBN 0-312-87639-4 (first international trade paperback edition) (acid-free paper)
1. Pueblo Indians—Fiction. 2. Archaeologists—Fiction. 3. Serial murders—Fiction. 4. New Mexico—Fiction. I. Gear, W. Michael. II. Title.
PS3557.E18 S85 2000
813'.54—dc21

00-028015

First Edition: July 2000

Printed in the United States of America

0 9 8 7 6 5 4 3 2 1

To Drs. Calvin and Linda Cummings for forty years of hard work,
documenting and protecting the rich archaeological resources
of the American Southwest.

Thanks, folks.

Without you two, there would be a lot less to write about.

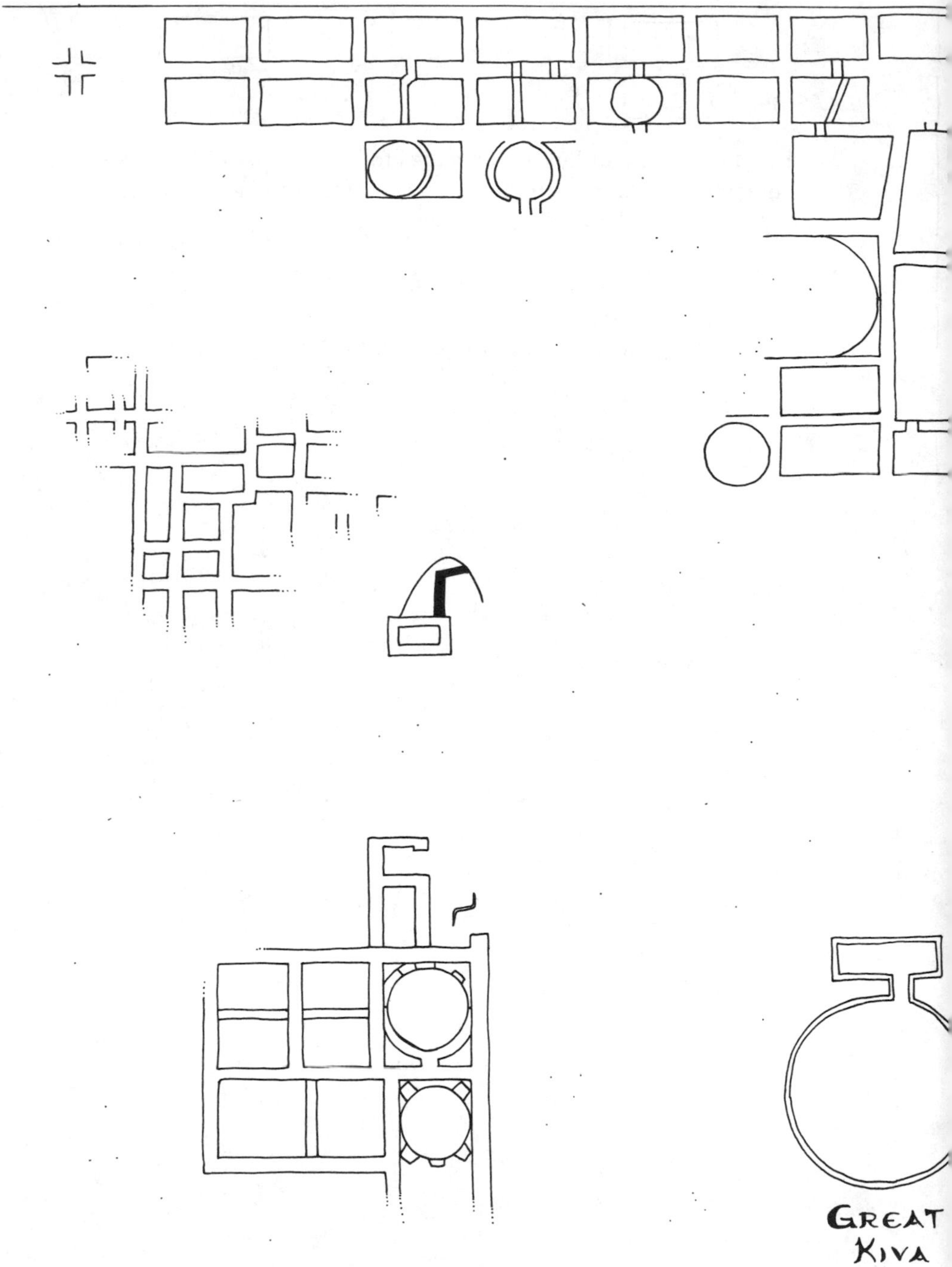

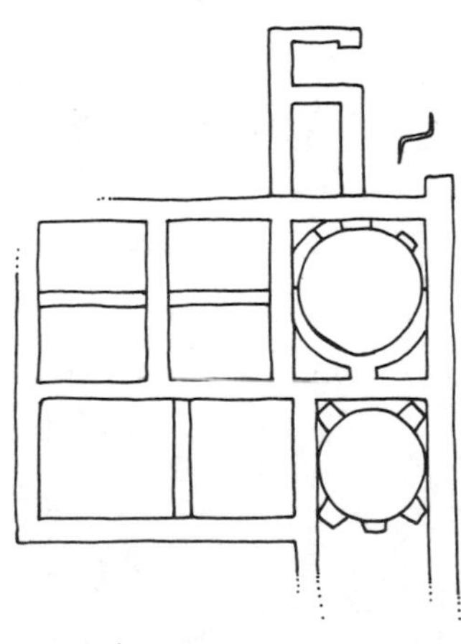

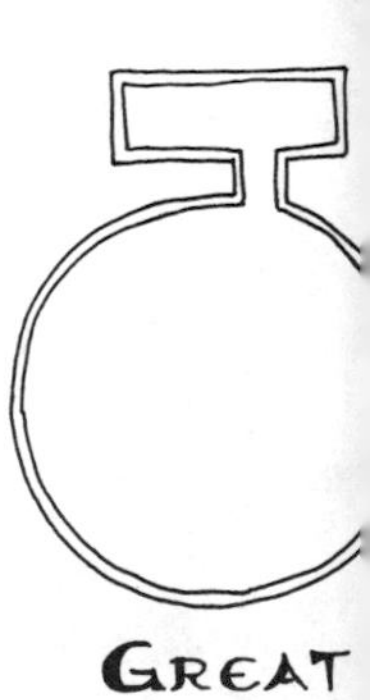
GREAT
KIVA

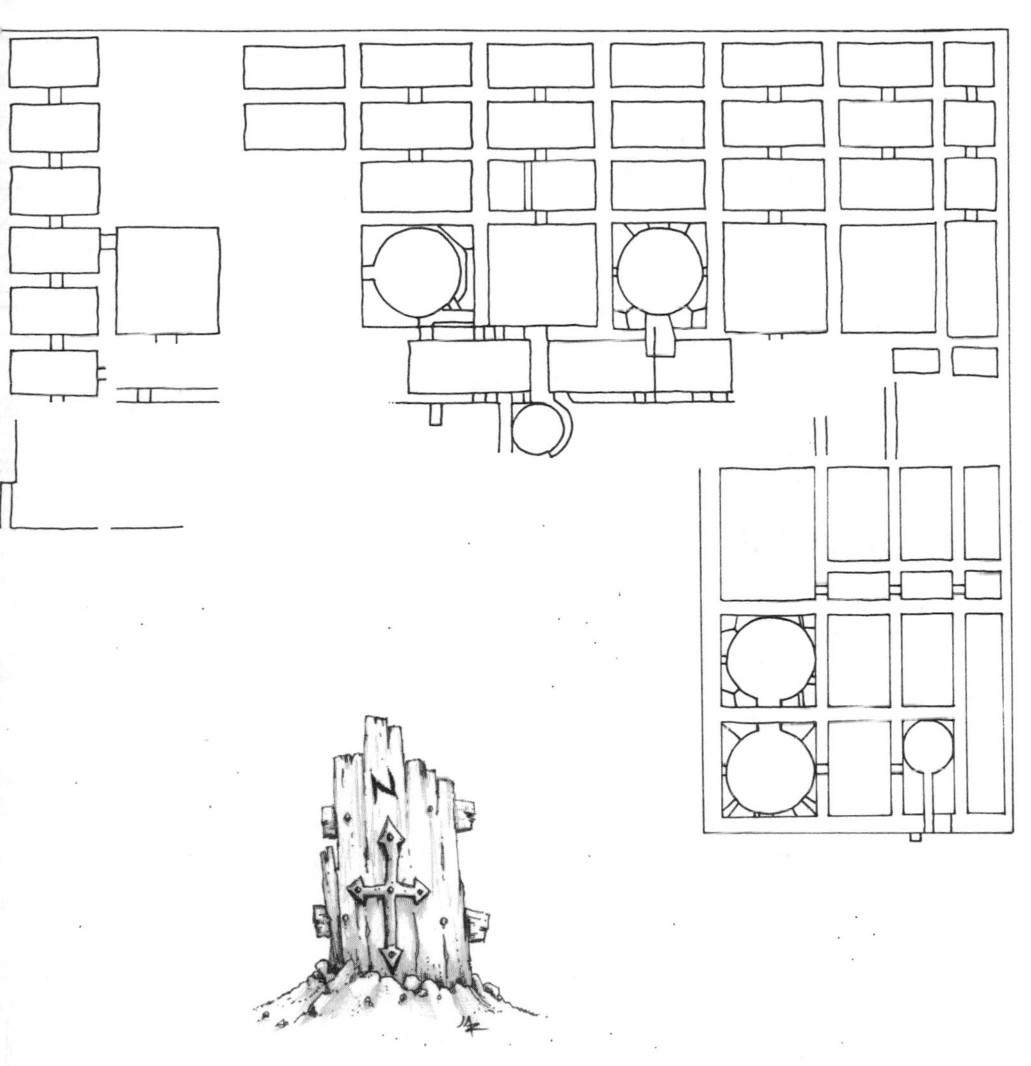

THE SUMMONING GOD

The Rise and Fall of the Anasazi: Why Should We Care What Happened to Them?

During the eleventh century, a high desert valley in northwestern New Mexico named Chaco Canyon became the cultural center for a people we call the Anasazi, or Ancestral Puebloans. Their culture encompassed over 115,000 square miles and included approximately 100,000 people. The Anasazi built five-story buildings with over eight hundred rooms in them; they charted the solstices and equinoxes, the cycles of stars, even the 18.6-year cycle of the moon; they established far-flung trade routes that brought them scarlet macaws and cast copper bells from Mexico, seashells from the Pacific Ocean and Gulf Coast, and buffalo hides from the northern plains; and they engineered a road system that would be unequaled in North America for seven hundred years. But by A.D. 1400, they had all but vanished.

Perhaps the two questions archaeologists are most often asked are: "What happened to the Anasazi?" and "What do they have to teach modern people?" Though both questions are linked, the latter is the more important, because the answer bears directly upon the survival of our own civilization.

Around A.D. 1130 the climate began to change. In Europe it would become known as The Little Ice Age, but the Anasazi knew only that a new drought had begun. Not in their wildest imaginations could they have guessed that the period of deep cold and reduced rainfall would last for more than three hundred years. The count of tree pollen in the archaeological record drops dramatically during this period—meaning they cut down every tree they could find to clear fields for crops, to build their homes, cook their food, fire their pottery, light their kivas, and keep warm during the bitter winters. When the trees ran out and the soil became depleted, they imported many of the basic items of their lives—wood, pottery, food, and animal hides. But, in the end, not even that would save them.

To understand what was happening to the Anasazi, we need to look no further than our own lives. Since the arrival of Europeans in North America we have cut down 90 percent of our forests. Most of the wood we use to build our houses comes from forests hundreds of miles away. We import a great deal of our meat, fruits, and vegetables, often from distant places like South America and Hawaii. Much of the oil that fuels our automobiles and heats our homes is shipped in from the Middle East. Why? Because we, too, have over-utilized our resources and are now relying upon trade to provide us with many of our most basic needs. But the parallels to our own time do not end there.

In 1900, 80 percent of the people in the United States lived in rural areas. Today, 80 percent live in cities. In the 1200s, as the shortages grew and the climate deteriorated, the Anasazi abandoned their small towns and moved to large pueblos. Let us make this point clearly, before A.D. 1150 there were hundreds of Anasazi settlements, small and large, scattered across the Colorado Plateau. By A.D. 1400, *there were three:* the Hopi villages in Arizona, and the villages of the Zuni, and Acoma, in New Mexico. The rest of the traditional Anasazi homeland was a vast no-man's-land.

How could such a thriving and sophisticated culture be reduced to a mere handful of survivors? Despite the romantic image that the Puebloan peoples were peaceful farmers, we have abundant archaeological evidence to demonstrate that during the thirteenth century the Anasazi were engaged in brutal annihilation-oriented warfare. Massacres, scalping, slavery, torture, and even cannibalism occurred.

The vicious cycle that led to the rise and fall of their civilization has become clear as a result of the excavation of hundreds of their towns: the rise began with a warm wet climatic episode that resulted in a period of affluence and scientific achievement. With the affluence came swift population growth. In the process of feeding their people, they exhausted the soil, cut down the trees, over-hunted the animals. Then the climate changed. When their crops wouldn't grow, they expanded their trade routes. When their trade routes were cut, they turned to warfare to keep them open. When they couldn't keep them open, they took what they needed from their closest neighbors. They must have next fought to protect their homes from their victims' wrath, then the fight became a struggle just to stay alive.

We leave it up to you to decide where in that cycle our modern civilization stands, but several things are clear: we've over-utilized our resources, the climate is changing, and we've already begun to "fight."

CHAPTER 1

Sun Cycle of the Great Horned Owl
The Falling River Moon

I WAKE WHEN a twig snaps, but I do not move.

I lay still in the brush, barely breathing, listening to their whispers.

Pine needles crackle. Clothing rustles.

They each have their own way of walking, one a little faster, another very slow. The leader has wide shoulders that hiss against the brush. There are four of them. But the last in line, the female, is the most dangerous. She is as silent as mist.

I ease my head from the ground, and my nostrils tremble, smelling them. A growl tightens my throat, but I don't let it out. Scents of woodsmoke, urine, and old blood cling to their clothing.

After they pass, I raise myself on all fours and peer through the weave of brush—they resemble ghosts, gray and floating. Muscles bulge on their heavy bodies. A lot of meat.

I creep out of the brush and trot behind them for twenty breaths, until they stop to look out over the rugged canyon.

Then my fingers reach for a limb, and I climb at the speed of a pine marten, silently swinging from branch to branch, until I can crouch on a limb overlooking the warriors.

I lift my nose to the wind again, but I can't smell them; the scent of pine resin is too strong.

They hiss to each other, their voices like coiled snakes, then they spread out, hiding behind trees as they work their way toward the village.

I slip over the branch's edge and hang by one arm, watching, listening. Satisfied that there are no others coming, I let go and silently fall onto the trail. Pine duff rises beneath my feet.

I scamper forward into the closest shadows. And wait.

THE MOONLIT NIGHT breathed silence.

Browser, War Chief of the Katsinas' People, braced his back against the dark smoke-colored trunk of an enormous pine and listened to the faint echo of his warriors' footfalls. The scent of their sweat drifted through the trees, dank, filled with fear.

Browser got down on his belly and crawled the rest of the way to the canyon's edge. One thousand hands below, water splashed over rocks, and shafts of moonlight danced along the eroded cliffs like leaping ghosts. His fist tightened around his war club.

Silver owl eyes sparkled on the ledges of the massive sandstone cliff across the canyon, and he could hear their faraway hoots as the owls called to each other.

To his right, jumbled boulders stood like dark giants, their tops smoothed and rounded by a thousand summers of thunderstorms. Aspen village sat to his left, tucked into the cliff wall. Two stories tall, with forty chambers, the huge scooped-out hollow in the cliff dwarfed the village.

Freshly painted images covered the village walls. The katsinas had not been there three days ago when he and his war party left to scout the canyon rim. Now they appeared to be the only thing alive. The katsinas had human bodies but animal heads; unearthly smiles curled their fanged muzzles and jet black beaks.

Browser slid closer to the edge. Baskets of corn sat around the plaza. A deerhide lay staked out on the ground, drying. Two looms with half-finished blankets leaned against the wall. There were no dogs. No torches.

He rubbed his mouth with the back of his hand as he thought. Had Matron Eagle Hunter become frightened and ordered her people to abandon the village? The matron was the village decision maker, the leader of the clan. Perhaps she had seen or heard something and believed that they had no choice but to leave.

Five days ago, a Trader named Old Pigeontail had come to tell Browser that warriors calling themselves the Flute Player Believers had been seen massing in the forests near Aspen village. The Flute Player was a very old god, a Creator deity. The "Believers" said his music had conjured the world from black emptiness. Matron Eagle Hunter had feared her village was about to be attacked by the Flute Player warriors. Flame Carrier, the Matron of the Katsinas' People, had ordered Browser to help them. He and Catkin, his deputy, had run for two days straight to get here. They'd stumbled into Aspen village, exhausted and starving, and found most of the inhabitants in their beds, desperately ill with the coughing sickness.

But he heard no coughing tonight. No crying children.

Browser had left eight healthy warriors to guard the village and formed two scouting parties from the remainder. His own consisted of four warriors, and the other party, led by War Chief Running Elk, had five men.

Browser had seen nothing that would signal enemy camps, no fires sparkling along the rim, no shadows of men moving about in the moonlight.

His gut knotted.

Many villages had converted to the Katsina faith in the last sun cycle, including Aspen village. Browser looked down at the great kiva in the village plaza. The kiva, a circular ceremonial chamber dug into the ground about twenty hands deep, was not a place of this world. It existed outside of human time. The kiva was a womb of Beginning Time—the moments before the First People climbed up through the underworlds to reach this world of Father Sun's light. The architectural levels in the kiva—the floor, the bench, the roof—represented the three cave worlds through which the First People had climbed. Each time a person climbed up out of the kiva, he was reliving the sacred journey, moving from darkness to light, killing the child of darkness that lived inside him, and being reborn as a gleaming creature of brilliance.

Is that why Aspen village had been attacked?

Just last moon, Matron Eagle Hunter had ordered her people to replaster and repaint the great kiva. They had covered up the old images of the Flute Player and the gods of his time, and in their places painted enormous, magnificent katsinas.

The katsinas had always existed, but they'd first shown themselves to a human about one hundred sun cycles ago. The great priest, Sternlight, had seen the Wolf Katsina Dancing down from the clouds, using the raindrops as stepping stones. The Wolf Katsina's thunderous growl had called lightning from the clouds, and as the bolts flashed across the sky, the glorious faces of all the other katsinas had been revealed to Sternlight.

As the Katsina faith spread, the devotees of the old gods grew more and more angry. Three moons ago, Browser had heard a Flute Player Believer whisper that the Katsinas' People were witches. He said they changed themselves into animals by jumping through enchanted yucca hoops and loped through the darkness breathing evil, witching others to make them pledge themselves to their wicked half-animal gods. Every time something went wrong, if the rains didn't come or the spring was too cold for planting, the Flute Player Believers blamed the Katsinas' People for witchery.

Catkin, Walker, and Bole crawled up behind him. They kept their heads down, but their eyes flashed when they gazed at Browser.

Over his shoulder, he whispered, "Catkin?"

She slid forward. Moonlight gilded her beautiful oval face and turned-up nose. Her long black braid lay across her back like a glistening serpent. The fringes on her red leather shirt fluttered. When she looked at him, he could see the softness in her dark eyes. She had loved him for over a sun cycle—three hundred and sixty-five days—a love he had never been able to return the way she wished.

Catkin whispered, "How bad?"

"I don't see anyone."

"No one?"

He shook his head.

Catkin's face slackened. Very bad.

Walker and Bole muttered. They had wives, parents, children here. Their fears showed in the hard set of their jaws.

"Walker?" Browser called to the sixteen-summers-old youth lying next to Catkin. Shoulder-length black hair blew around his young face. A streak of soot cut a diagonal line across his right cheek.

He pulled himself forward on his elbows. "Yes, War Chief?"

"Catkin and I will go around to the eastern trail. Wait for my signal, then I want you and Bole to follow the western trail into the village. Take care. We know nothing yet. Your clan may have grown anxious and left, but that does not mean the village is empty. Do you understand?"

Walker wet his lips, and his eyes widened in fear. "Yes. I understand, War Chief."

Even if the villagers had fled, the people who'd frightened them might still be inside.

Browser nodded to Catkin and crawled away on his hands and knees. They rose in a small grove of junipers. The berry-laden branches filled the air with a sweet, tangy fragrance.

Browser examined the towering pines with painstaking care, making certain no one hid in the shadows. He'd thought he'd heard something earlier, a *shishing*, like fur brushing against branches.

His eyes narrowed. None of this made any sense. If the village had been attacked, they should already see evidence of it: belongings dropped when people tried to run, thrashed brush, overturned rocks, dead bodies. Warriors generally burned conquered villages. The scent of smoke should be acrid and strong.

Moonlight sheathed Catkin's large dark eyes and full lips. "I'm not sure that separating our forces was wise, Browser. If our enemies are inside—"

"I doubt they are, Catkin. I just said that as a precaution. A warrior who secretes himself in a room is asking to be trapped there when the owners return. It is more likely we will find our enemies behind the trees and boulders on the trail. Or even up here in the forest. That is where I would hide."

Catkin did not blink. She gave him a stony look. "And I would be inside the village where I could shoot my bow from a protected position."

"Yes," Browser said with a nod, "but you are like Badger. Bold and confident that your claws are sharper than anyone else's. Most warriors, including me, are like Packrat. Always afraid. We have to know there is a back way out of our hole."

Catkin tilted her head and her dark eyes seemed to probe his souls. "Which type of warrior do you suppose is more dangerous, Browser?"

He shifted his weight to his other foot. They generally viewed the world differently, which made him value her opinions all the more. He was cautious, prudent, a War Chief. She thought like an assassin. Because of that, she had saved his life many times. And he hers.

"Let us hope that tonight I am right." Browser gestured for her to follow him through the forest.

A billowing flock of Cloud People gathered before the face of Sister Moon, and the night turned black and unnaturally silent. Browser's sandals crackled on the old pine and juniper needles that blanketed the forest floor. He stopped every three paces to listen. Wind Baby whistled in his ears, but Browser ignored him. The evil Spirit child often tricked people, blowing a warrior's scent to his enemy just before he could release his arrow, or singing through a bowstring at exactly the wrong instant.

Catkin stopped. Browser stopped.

Ten hands wide, the eastern trail to the village had been beaten to dust, but brush lined the way over the rim and down into the canyon. He glanced up at Sister Moon. As the Cloud People drifted off to the south, the corner of her face appeared and silver light flooded the canyon. The trees and boulders gleamed.

At moments like this, cowardice always reared up and did a dance in his belly. What was he doing here?

Browser had joined the Katsinas' People four summers ago because his wife threatened to leave him and take their infant son away if he did not join. He hated the katsinas. They had been Ash Girl's gods, not his. But Ash Girl had been dead for nine moons, along with his precious son, Grass Moon. Why didn't he go home to his own people? Warfare raged across the country. Most of his clan had been driven out of the northern mountains and taken refuge with other clans in the desert regions to the south. They needed him.

Though I doubt they want me.

He had just passed his twenty-ninth summer, but he felt old. Old and afraid. The constant sun and wind had turned his skin as brown as old leather. White strands sparkled in his black hair. And by now his family would have heard that he'd killed his own wife.

Catkin eased up beside him and her face tensed. "Look." She pointed to a large boulder thirty paces ahead.

The painter had splashed white on the rock, then carefully filled the center with the black silhouette of a hunched beast.

"What is it?" he whispered.

"I can't tell."

Something about the image struck him as menacing. It didn't seem to be painted on the stone, but rather *attached* to it. Browser walked forward.

Behind him, he heard Catkin's steps, then she whispered, "Blessed Spirits."

Wisps of long gray hair clung to the mummy's desiccated scalp. She had been laid on her side at death, her knees lifted and elbows bent. She had dried in a fetal position with her skeletal hands curled beneath her chin. Long ago her eyes had rotted away, leaving dark empty sockets to stare up at them.

Catkin recoiled a step. "Look at her mouth." Stubby brown teeth filled her gaping jaws. "She must have screamed at the end."

Browser studied the rope that wrapped the mummy's waist and looped over the top of the boulder. "Someone hung her here for us to see."

"A warning not to take the trail down to the village?"

He looked out at the fallen trees and rocks that loomed in the darkness. "Perhaps, but a mummy is a poor substitute for freshly mutilated bodies."

Catkin glanced around, then stepped closer to look at the mummy. "Where do you think she came from?"

"Many of the dry caves in this region contain burials." He gestured to the dark hollows that pocked the cliffs on the opposite side of the canyon. "They could have stumbled upon her while sneaking up to get a better look at Aspen village."

"And carried her away?" Catkin scoffed. "I do not think so. War parties travel fast and light. She would have been a silly burden."

"Warriors are often silly, Catkin. They do unfathomable things when they are tired and hungry."

The quartzite cobble on the end of Catkin's war club lowered to the woman's right wrist. "Her arms were broken. It looks like she used them to block blows."

The bones had not mended correctly and stuck out like knobs on old limbs.

"But not blows from fists," he said. "Something that could snap bone. An ax or stone-headed club."

Catkin's war club moved to the mummy's head. "Her arms weren't the only things they struck."

The skull undulated like the surface of a rotten melon. The numerous small dents meant the woman's skull had been cracked by a master, a man who knew how to strike hard enough to injure, but not hard enough to kill.

"And look at this," Catkin said.

Browser knelt at Catkin's side and saw the tattoo. Black spirals decorated the mummy's chin. Three or maybe four. A cold sensation filtered through him. His grandmother and all of her people had proudly worn spirals on their chins. He did not know what the spirals stood for, but . . . it seemed odd that this ancient corpse would carry the same symbol. Could she be one of his distant relatives?

Catkin whispered, “Isn’t that the same—”

“My great-uncle, Stone Ghost, has three black spirals on his chin. My grandmother had four. I don’t know what it means.”

His gaze landed on every human-shaped shadow on the trail below. Pine needles glimmered. Boulders wavered in the moonlight. Had someone expected him to be here? Perhaps known he would be here? No. Many people wore tattoos. Many tattoos included spirals. This was coincidence. Nothing more.

The sun-bleached shreds of cloth that hung from the mummified body fluttered in the wind. Browser looked at the darker splotches, brown with age. He used his club to push the cloth aside and saw the wide slit in the abdomen. “They cut her open.”

Catkin shifted to look, and her eyes widened. “Gods. I wonder how long it took her to die?”

Browser shook his head tiredly. “A person can live for days with a belly wound. I remember once when I and four of my warriors were captured by the Fire Dogs. They sliced Mug’s gut open and slowly pulled out his intestines. He screamed for three days.”

Catkin reached for the dead woman’s necklace, but halted when she noticed that skeletal fingers twined in the brightly beaded strip of rawhide. Alternating chevrons of turquoise, shell, and coral covered the hide. Magnificent work. Catkin backed away.

“Browser”—her voice had gone tight—“she deliberately grasped the necklace before she died. It must have been very important to her, like a Power bundle or sacred pendant.”

Browser studied the delicate fingers that clutched the hide. “Are you sure it’s a necklace? Or is it a collar?”

She gave him an incredulous look. “No one would waste such beauty on a slave.”

Browser pulled the mummy out from the boulder to examine her back. “A necklace would have laces. The woman might wish to take it off. This is sewn together. And look here.” He indicated the scar tissue beneath the necklace where the flesh had been rubbed raw and healed. “The rawhide must have been wet when they sewed the collar together. It shrunk tight to her throat. Too tight. She must have had trouble breathing.” Browser met Catkin’s gaze. “A slave, but a very highly prized one.”

Catkin frowned for a long moment at the fingers in the collar. “Gods, Browser. She’s not holding the hide. It’s wrapped around her fingers, as though she used the collar to cut off her own air.”

Browser touched the hide. It felt dry and as hard as rock. Despite the tightness of the collar, the woman had managed to slip two fingers beneath it and twist the hide into a loop. Her mummified fingers remained locked in the twist. She hadn't let go. Not even at the end, when panic must have set in.

"What a brave woman. I wonder who she was?" Catkin asked. "A clan matron?"

"Or maybe a great warrior."

Catkin got to her feet and looked at the woman's belly slit. She straightened and her mouth fell open. "Did you see this?"

"What?"

Catkin held something up. It tinkled.

"A bell?" he said in surprise.

She held it up to the moonlight. The bell shimmered and twinkled. "A bell worth a village's ransom."

Catkin handed him the cast copper bell, and Browser turned it over and over in his palm, awed by the sight. They were rare and beautiful. The Feathered Serpent People who'd made them had died out long ago. They had lived far to the south, but had traded with the legendary First People of the Straight Path Nation.

During the Age of Emergence, the First People had bravely climbed through a series of dark underworlds to get to this world of light. On the second day, the Creator decided the First People were too few and needed help to build the world. He had turned a variety of animals into humans: badgers, buffaloes, tortoises, ants, wolves, and other creatures. Hence, they were "made" people. The First People had never liked the Made People. They had considered them inferior, and had enslaved and tortured them. Fortunately, First People only married other First People, and their blood weakened over time. When the Power began to dwindle, the Made People rose up and made war on them. The last of the First People had died more than a hundred summers ago, and the Made People had celebrated for a full sun cycle. Browser's people, and all people alive today, were Made People.

The bell might have been an offering, placed inside her wound by the people who'd buried her. In that case, they had either been very wealthy, or they'd sold everything they had to possess it.

He said, "Whoever buried her loved her very much. No one today would squander such wealth on the dead."

Browser put the copper bell into his belt pouch. His village, Longtail village, had been raided six times in the past nine moons. They could trade the bell for enough food to feed their children through the winter.

"No, Browser." As she turned, moonlight gilded the smooth dip in her nose and splashed her broad cheeks.

"What do you mean?"

"That bell was loose in her belly. If it had been placed there when she was buried, it would have melted into the drying flesh and become part of it. I would not have been able to just pick it up. Someone put it there tonight."

"But why?" he whispered, and slowly rose to his feet. "Whoever hung the mummy here must have known the first traveler who came by would take it."

Catkin pinned him with dark moon-glazed eyes. "I'm sure they did. They probably also figured they would get it back when they killed us."

Browser turned to search the trees and cliffs for any sign of an ambush. Wind Baby whimpered through the boulders on the slope below.

"Maybe, but I'm still going down. We have to know what has happened. I wish you to stay at the top of the trail where you can see the trees."

Catkin nodded, but her gaze remained on the mummy. The corpse's stubby teeth gleamed. Moments ago, she had seemed to be caught in a final scream. Now she looked like she was laughing, a great deep belly laugh.

Browser's skin prickled. *Your shattered souls are playing tricks on you, you fool. The mummy hasn't changed.*

"Shout to me if anyone comes out of the forest. I will return as soon as I know what's happened."

"Go. I will guard the trail."

Browser cupped a hand to his mouth and gave the melodious call of a raven in flight, *kloo-kloc-kloo-kloc,* to signal Walker and Bole to start down the western trail.

Then he headed down himself.

Aspens grew in the spaces between the boulders. The trembling autumn leaves appeared white in the pale light, but he remembered that in the daylight they glowed a brilliant luminous yellow.

Browser silently skirted a large boulder and navigated the first bend in the trail. He lost sight of Catkin. Wind Baby gusted across the cliff, rattling the fringes on his knee-length shirt. As the trees blew, splotchy wind-spawned shadows danced over the slope.

He'd never had much love for solitary heroics. He preferred a large and conspicuous war party at his back. But he had no choice tonight.

He proceeded slowly, on the balls of his feet, until he came to a fallen tree where he crouched and gazed at the village no more than half a bow shot away. They'd built in a secure but difficult location. The huge rain-eaten hollow in the stone swallowed the small two-story village. Just a few body lengths beyond the plaza, the sheer cliff dropped seven hundred hands to the canyon bottom. If a person slipped, it meant his doom.

Where were Walker and Bole? Inside, searching from room to room? The faint trace of smoke clung to the air. Someone had lit a fire today, but he saw no glow of flames in any of the windows or doors. Aspen village appeared dead.

Browser turned when he heard a sound.

He whispered, "Walker?"

No, the soft scraping couldn't be an adult. A child's moccasins on gravel? Claws working at stone?

He could not identify it yet, but some other scent twined with that of the smoke, a tang that clung to the back of his throat like pine pitch.

Browser moved only his eyes.

There, on the ground two paces away, lay another copper bell.

He stared at it.

It had been polished until it glowed. Browser walked over and picked it up. The velvet feel reminded him of the skin of a young woman. Sensuous. Too smooth to be real. He tucked it into his belt pouch and regripped his war club. His palms had grown sweaty.

The quiet ate at his insides. The very emptiness of the village held threat. Every dark window and doorway seemed to watch him.

Another copper bell lay just ahead.

He could not believe his eyes. He grabbed it and shoved it into his pouch. Right here in front of him lay enough wealth to . . .

Three more bells. In a line.

The trail led to the kiva, the circular chamber ten paces away.

Browser's gaze darted over every shadow. He had captured wolves this way, by dropping pieces of meat just far enough apart that the wolf could see the next one. The last piece of meat always rested on the disguised roof of the killing pit. By the time the wolf got there, his mouth dripped saliva, eager for the tasty bite. When the wolf leaped onto the roof to get it, the roof collapsed and sent him plummeting twenty hands straight down. Hunters with bows could walk up and shoot him with little effort.

A tingle moved from the base of Browser's skull, down his arms, and into his belly. They wanted him in the kiva. Why?

He turned in a slow circle, seeing nothing. No one.

The clawing continued.

"Walker? Bole?"

They might have come down, found the village empty, and gone back up the trail to search for him and Catkin.

Browser walked to the edge of the kiva. The only way in or out was by ladder through the entryway cut into the middle of the roof. The ladder had been pulled out and the entry covered with thick buffalo hides. The ladder rested on top of them. If someone was imprisoned in there, no one would ever hear his screams.

The owner of the bells wanted Browser to look into the kiva. He was betting that once Browser looked, he would have to climb down, and then . . .

Browser backed away and turned to the village.

The katsinas had been lovingly painted. The teeth in the Wolf Katsina's muzzle gleamed. The white spots of stars on his black arms and legs fell in perfect rows. The spear in the Badger Katsina's right hand shimmered as though made from a fine glassy obsidian.

Perfectly rendered. Except that each katsina had a gaping white hole in the middle of its chest. A kill hole. The Fire Dogs did the same thing with Power pots. They believed that such pots had souls, and that by knocking a hole in the bottom they released the soul to travel to the afterlife with its dead owner.

Had the invaders sent the katsinas' souls to the afterlife with their dead followers?

Browser walked to the first doorway and pulled aside the leather curtain. "Matron?" He had been in this room three days ago. "Matron Eagle Hunter?"

All of her belongings lay as he remembered. Baskets stood stacked in the corner to his right. Black-and-white pots lined the wall to his left. Her bedding hides lay rolled in the rear of the chamber. If she had run away in fear, she would at least have taken her bedding.

Browser backed out. Moonlight flashed from the cliffs and the tattered Cloud People that drifted over the rim. The katsinas vanished, then reappeared in a sudden wash of light and wavered . . . *Dancing*. He could see it. Awe swelled his heart. They slipped from light to dark, their white kirtles swaying as though they'd lifted their sacred feet to Dance the world out of existence. Browser could almost hear their animal voices calling to him, delicate and birdlike, tinged with a panic that echoed his own.

His thoughts leaped from one possibility to another. Perhaps the mummy had been left by the fleeing villagers, not by invaders. Maybe it hadn't been a warning, but an offering. The mummy had been precious to someone. Matron Eagle Hunter? One of the other villagers? If so, she'd given it up, left it for . . . whom? Had the attackers threatened the village to obtain the mummy? Then why hadn't they taken it with them when they'd gone—if they'd gone?

He trotted the length of the village, ducking into doorways, peering through windows. Everything appeared normal. If these people had left in a hurry, he could see no sign of it. The more chambers he searched, the more certain he became that they'd all packed up and left for a few days, perhaps to attend a nearby celebration, a marriage, or burial feast. Clearly, they had planned to return. Perhaps the people who'd painted and then desecrated the katsinas had come in after the villagers were gone.

When he reached the western edge of the village, Browser looked up the trail. Cloud People had covered Sister Moon's face again; he didn't have enough light to see tracks, but he searched for them anyway. He had ordered Walker and Bole to come down this trail. There should be some evidence of their descent. Overturned pebbles, scuffed soil, snapped twigs.

Browser walked halfway up the trail before he found the place where one of the men's moccasins had slid and grooved the soft dirt. He turned around.

The copper bells winked at him. Taunting. Calling to him.

Browser marched down the trail and across the plaza to the kiva. As he stepped onto the roof, the scent of smoke grew stronger. Smoke and something else.

Browser knelt beside the dark brown buffalo hides. He jerked off the ladder and dragged the hides away from the square hole. A wave of warm air bathed his face, and the sickening coppery tang struck him like a blow to the stomach.

"Matron Eagle Hunter?" he called, his voice frantic now. "It's Browser! I would speak with you. Are you down there?"

The kiva seemed to exhale suddenly. A gush of warmth blew over him. Had someone moved? Perhaps disturbed the air?

Browser reached for the ladder and almost missed the marks. Long dark streaks covered the roof. They might have been soot or mud, but they looked more like the claw marks made by bloody fingers.

He touched them, matching them with his own fingers, then jerked his hand away.

"Matron! I'm coming down."

He lowered the ladder through the entry and it hit the ground with a solid ordinary thump.

The dark pit reeked of rot and corruption. It took an act of will to convince himself to put his feet on the rungs. Every instant he expected an arrow in his back. His gaze searched the village again, then he took the rungs down two at a time.

He stepped off onto the kiva floor and blinked at the darkness. Ash puffed beneath his feet, and the stench almost gagged him. If someone wished to attack him, now was the time. He held his war club at the ready and fought to keep his breathing even.

When his eyes adjusted, he saw the fire hearth three paces in front of him and the woodpile stacked beside it. A faint crimson gleam lit the hearth's center. Browser went to the woodpile, pulled out a branch, and stirred the ashes until he found red coals. He broke his branch into pieces, placed them on the coals, and bent down to blow on the kindling.

The clawing again.

Desperate, erratic.

"Hello?" he called. "Is anyone in here?"

Something about the urgency of the clawing suggested human hands, someone trying to get to him.

Fighting his own sense of dread, Browser went back to blowing on the coals. A flame licked up. Then a branch popped in the fire, and sparks whirled toward the entry. Light flared.

Browser couldn't move.

The flickering images burned themselves into his souls.

The bodies had no heads.

The feral eyes of wood rats blazed as they scrambled from one bloody scrap of cloth to another. The rats must have gotten in through the kiva's ventilator shaft, a narrow opening in the wall designed to bring fresh air into the kiva.

Most of the bones had been stripped of flesh, then scattered, but a few still had tatters of clothing clinging to arms or legs. He saw an infant's head lying on the floor to his right. It looked as though it had been tossed. Was this a child he'd seen three days ago? One of the happy little boys playing in the plaza when he arrived? He looked to be about four summers old.

Claws. Behind him.

Browser turned and stepped into a pool of blood. "Oh, dear gods."

Walker and Bole slumped against the curving rear wall. They were so recently dead the rats feared to approach them. The little animals raced forward, bit a piece of cloth, and scurried backward, their feet scratching the floor for purchase.

"What happened?" Browser murmured.

The fools must have come down long before his signal. They must have disobeyed . . .

Perhaps they'd been *forced* down.

"Right after Catkin and I left."

Walker's intestines had been pulled out onto the floor and his decapitated head stuffed into the gaping cavity. His wide eyes stared through the slit in his stomach, as though he'd been surprised by his killer.

Bole—he thought it was Bole—leaned against Walker. His face had been mutilated, but the obsidian-studded war club stuffed down his throat had belonged to Bole.

Browser locked his knees. He had seen a great deal of warfare and raiding. This was neither. Raiders killed in haste and stole food and trinkets to take home to their families. Warriors slaughtered their enemies and burned their villages. But this was calm, methodical butchery.

Browser took a shaky step backward and forced himself to count the dead. He had to know if the entire village had been massacred or if some people had escaped before the murderers trapped them.

As he counted, he noticed the layer of soot that coated the ceiling and the black heaps of debris around the fire hearth. Blood covered the new katsinas on the walls, as though someone had filled pots and splashed them with it. All of the babies had been decapitated, but some had not been stripped of flesh. The youngest infants hung from cradle boards. Thick soot furred their chubby arms and legs. The eyes in the babies' severed heads bulged.

"They must have forced the villagers into the kiva, tied them up, then dumped burning wood and bark inside"—he looked up—"and sealed the entryway."

The people had suffocated.

He picked his way across the slaughter ground to the ventilator shaft and looked inside. No wonder they couldn't get air. Someone outside had wedged a newborn in the opening, head-down. A narrow beam of moonlight penetrated around the child's head. The rats' pathway? Had the boy's parents heard him screaming before they died?

Browser forced himself to think. "What happened? They—they—round the villagers up, force them into the kiva and suffocate them, then they come back and take time to strip the bones? That's insane!"

And the heads—where were the people's heads?

He gripped his club and his hand shook. What had they done with the flesh? It wasn't here. He scanned the floor. They must have gathered the piles of meat and taken it outside. Horrifying memories began to flit across his souls. He'd heard Traders talk . . .

Footsteps creaked on the roof.

Browser jerked his leather shirt over his head and tossed it onto the fire to smother the light, then he backed into the black recesses of the kiva.

Is this what had happened to Walker and Bole?

A slender arm passed through the moonlight above the entry, and a copper bell bounced across the kiva floor.

Browser braced his legs. His enemy? Or a survivor?

"Hello?" he called.

Laughter, soft and sensuous. Then a woman whispered, "Who are you, War Chief? Are you one of us, or one of *them*?"

Delicate hands reached for the ladder, and he thought she planned to climb down.

With several quick jerks, the ladder disappeared through the entry, and buffalo hides flopped into place.

"Wait!" he screamed.

For three heartbeats, nothing, then . . .

"Mother?" a little girl called.

They must have been standing right over the hides, probably arranging the ladder to keep them in place.

"Mother, I'm tired. Can we go now?"

Laughter again, almost shrill with delight. "I told you the brightness of the heart flows from bright veins. It was beautiful, wasn't it?"

The child skipped across the roof, and the woman's footsteps followed.

Browser cried, "Wait! Who are you? I'm War Chief Browser from Longtail village. Let me out!"

Silence. But only for a moment.

With the darkness, the rats grew frenzied. They scampered and squealed, fighting over the best nesting materials. The scratching of animal claws on human bone unnerved him.

Browser clenched his fists and shouted: "Catkin? *Catkin!*"

CHAPTER 2

CATKIN KNELT IN the lee of the boulder with her war club across her knees. Wind gusted through the forest, flailing the branches and stroking her flesh with icy fingers. Every muscle in her body cried out for sleep. They had run the canyon rim for three days, stopping only to gobble a bowl of food, or close their eyes for a few hands of time. She needed rest badly.

"Soon," she promised herself.

The mummy swayed and the rope around her middle raked the stone. Catkin reached up to steady her, and her gaze rested on the ridges of scar tissue that crisscrossed the mummy's legs and back. She had been studying the mummy. Several of her toes had been cut off and the bleeding stanched with fire. Hideous burn scars covered her feet.

Catkin whispered, "Who hurt you, Mother? Did you know them, or were they . . . ?"

Feet struggled for purchase on the dirt trail below. Catkin went still.

Browser had a light tread she would recognize a thousand sun cycles from now in the Land of the Dead. Walker or Bole? Young and brash, they both thundered about like bull buffalo in rut. It might be one of them.

Catkin eased to her feet.

Barely audible, a woman's voice rose, deep-throated, anguished.

Catkin had seen warriors drawn into ambushes by women pretending to be injured. She stepped back into the thick shadows cast by the boulder.

A low, wolfish growl eddied on the wind.

Catkin took her club in both hands.

Predators didn't pursue the healthy. The scent of blood and death drew them.

As the terrible growls grew louder, Catkin took deep slow breaths. The fire-hardened wood in her fists felt cool.

Sobs.

Catkin almost stepped out, but forced herself to stay put. The sobs shuddered, as though the woman could find just enough air to give voice to her pain.

The growl became a deep hoarse rumble—the sound made by a wolf that's been chasing wounded prey for days and knows the end is near.

Whatever was going to happen, it would happen soon. The cries and growls closed in.

Catkin searched the trees for hidden warriors. Pines and brush rustled . . . and fingernails clawed at the dirt less than a body length away.

"Halt!" Catkin ordered, and leaped onto the trail with her war club over her head.

The woman lay on her belly. Blood soaked her clothing, and locks of long blood-clotted hair covered her face. Her skin shone like frost, as if she'd lost a good deal of blood—or perhaps she had rubbed her hands with a mixture of corn flour and ground evening primrose in honor of White Shell Woman, the grandmother of Father Sun. But only worshipers did that for rituals. Had the people of Aspen village been engaged in a ceremony when the attack came?

Catkin scanned the trail and the forest behind her, then knelt at the woman's side. "What happened? Tell me quickly."

The woman's head wobbled as she lifted it, and a large black pendant fell from her dress. The jet had been beautifully carved to show a snake coiled in the center of a broken eggshell. Catkin's fingers dug into her war club. She had seen a pendant like that before—*around the throat of a friend who would soon be dead.* Through the thick tangle of bloody hair, one of the woman's black eyes gleamed, as though she sensed Catkin recognized it.

"The War Chief," the woman whispered. "He—he's in the kiva. Hurry."

A shot of fiery blood flushed Catkin's veins. "Were you attacked by Fire Dogs? Flute Player Believers?"

The woman's lips moved. Catkin had to lean down to hear the murmur: "They are coming back. You must go. Now."

"Who's coming back?"

The woman collapsed to the dirt, panting, and moaned, "Don't you understand? They will kill him! As they did the others! They are c-come . . ." Her eyes rolled back into her head and she went limp.

Catkin leaped from the woman and ran with all her might.

THE RATS STOPPED tearing at the cloth when they heard the footsteps on the roof and began anxiously tapping their feet to signal each other of the approaching danger.

Browser stood alone in the darkness, breathing hard.

A sliver of light appeared, and rat eyes sparkled all around him.

He waited, his sweaty palms on his war club.

The hides moved away enough for the person on the roof to smell the blood and corruption, but not enough to expose himself to an arrow from below.

A whisper of wind flowed over Browser's face and he tingled as if he could already feel the sting of the knife as it carved the flesh from his bones.

"Browser?"

"Oh gods, Catkin!" Relief coursed through him, leaving him lightheaded. "Lower the ladder!"

The hides flipped off, and the ladder came down with a thump. Ash glimmered in the sudden flood of moonlight. Catkin started to step onto the top rung, and he shouted, "No! Don't come down! I'm coming up."

He ran for the ladder and climbed.

Catkin extended a hand to him and pulled him off the ladder onto the roof. He saw in her eyes how he must look, his round face streaked with soot, his moccasins dripping blood.

"I am uninjured," he said.

"What of Bole and Walker?"

"In the kiva. Dead."

Her face slackened and he longed to touch her, like a man drawing strength from a Power bundle or finely carved fetish, but her voice stopped him:

"We have to get back up the trail, Browser. *Now.* I found a badly wounded woman. She's the one who told me you were in the kiva. I pray she lives long enough to tell us what happened here." She turned to go.

He gripped her arm. "What woman? The woman with the little girl?"

"What are you talking about?"

"There—there was a woman with a girl on the roof of the kiva. She—"

"Tell me on the way," Catkin said, and hurried across the plaza.

Browser followed her into the dappled moonlight of the trail, but as they started to climb, he stopped suddenly and spun back around. "Catkin? Did you pick up the bells?"

"Bells?" she said, confused. "You mean the one in the dead woman's belly? You took it."

His skin crawled. "Never mind. I'll explain later."

As they neared the top of the trail, Catkin slowed briefly, then broke into a run.

"What's wrong?" he called as he sprinted after her.

Catkin stopped near the painted boulder and stared at the ground. She leaned over, touched something, and rubbed her fingers together.

Browser kept his eyes on the trees. "What's the matter? Where's the woman?"

"She was here when I left." Catkin held up her hand and Browser saw the blood shining blackly on her fingers. "But, then, the mummy was here, too."

Browser jerked around. White paint splashed the boulder, as it had before, but now it shone, radiant in the moonlight. In the mummy's place two figures had been painted, a man and a woman. Both wore the long capes of the Katsinas' People. From the woman's feet, a black line extended, then coiled, getting smaller and smaller, the rings tighter, until the spiral became a dark abyss.

"What is that?" Browser asked.

Catkin stood up and scrutinized the painting. "Us, maybe. Perhaps she thinks we are walking a path into darkness."

"She?" Browser's gaze pinioned Catkin.

"Yes. The woman I thought was injured. Even with the bad light you can see she wasn't dragged or carried from this spot. If someone had pulled her to her feet, there would be long bloody scrapes in the dirt. If they'd carried her, we'd find a blood trail. Unless she wasn't bleeding as badly as it appeared. I think she got up and walked away."

Browser's jaw clamped; he didn't answer for a time. "Perhaps she's trying to tell us that we're doomed to end up like the others down there."

Cold wind teased Catkin's hair around her face. She shivered and started backing away, heading for the trail that led away from the canyon rim. "Let's go, Browser. Whoever painted this is close by. I can *feel* her out there. And I don't believe her only companion is a little girl."

CHAPTER 3

Santa Fe, New Mexico, October 2001

"MY GOD, YOU are beautiful."

William "Dusty" Stewart lifted his magnifying lens and studied the intricacies of the artifact. A master stoneworker had carved the image of a serpent coiled inside a broken eggshell into this flawless piece of anthracite, or jet. It stared up at Dusty with one glistening red coral eye.

Dusty backed the lens away and caught his own reflection in the glass. His freshly washed blond hair and beard shone, but his blue eyes had a worried gleam. A woman he'd rather forget had once told him he'd be drop-dead good-looking if it weren't for the weathered look of his tanned skin. At the age of thirty-seven, lines already etched his forehead and cut crow's-feet at the corners of his eyes. He brushed at the dirt that had fallen from the artifact onto his holey gray T-shirt and faded blue jeans, but it didn't improve his appearance any.

Dusty turned the artifact in his left hand. He had to draw it perfectly for the museum records. As he dipped his crow quill into the ink bottle, a gust of wind rattled the cottonwoods and whistled up the canyon from Santa Fe. The tin walls of his trailer shivered.

That old Keres medicine woman, Hail Walking Hawk, wanted this artifact buried forever. She said it was a witch's amulet.

The thought stuck in Dusty's mind as he cross-hatched the serpent's outline on the paper, then carefully sketched it to represent the original. He remembered the day he'd unearthed *el basilisco,* also called a "basilisk." It had been resting on a dead woman's sternum. Elder Hail Walking Hawk, and her young niece, Magpie, had been horrified and ordered it reburied immediately. Dusty, naturally, had collected it, as he would have any other artifact from the 10K3 site in Chaco Canyon.

In the end, scientific responsibility had won out over his respect for Native religious traditions, and he'd bagged the artifact, catalogued it, and now recorded it for the final report that would be turned in to the Park Service, the NOAA, and the University of New Mexico, where the artifacts and skeletal material would be curated.

Dusty turned the *basilisco* in his hand and watched the polished black artifact flash in the light. His greatest fear was that all such priceless bits of the past would be lost to human greed and ignorance, and with them any chance he had of understanding who the prehistoric peoples were and what had happened to them. He truly believed that modern people had a great deal to learn from the past. Especially from the Anasazi, or Ancestral Puebloans.

During the thirteenth century, the Four Corners region had seen a mass exodus. The Anasazi had abandoned their magnificent multistoried towns and fled to other larger pueblos. No one knew why exactly, but Dusty had excavated enough burned pueblos and skulls with club wounds to put warfare at the top of his list. While he didn't have any solid proof, he suspected it was the nastiest kind of war: holy war. The earliest images of the katchinas dated to the 1200s. The word was spelled many different ways: kachina, thlatsina, ka'atsina. They were often called "ancestor spirits," but the katchinas were a great deal more than that. The invisible forces of the universe manifested themselves in the spirits of the clouds, lightning, animals, trees, the Hero Twins, and the dead. The essence of the universe, the breath of life—that was katchina.

Dusty set the *basilisco* on the table. He had finished everything else, even the bibliography, which he really hated, before turning to documenting the *basilisco*.

"A serpent born of a cock's egg." Incarnate evil, according to the Native peoples of the Southwest.

The 10K3 site had been steeped in witchery, murder, and evil. At least eleven women had been killed and had rocks dropped over their heads to trap their souls in the earth for eternity. Despite the seven hundred and fifty years that had separated Dusty from the murderer, he'd felt the evil, too. It had stalked their camp every night. He still felt it when he held the *basilisco*.

Even the National Oceanic and Atmospheric Administration, which had wanted to place a microwave tower there, had given up on the project and relocated to the rim rock above the canyon, outside the national monument boundaries.

Dusty studied his drawing and made one final inspection of the *basilisco* to make sure he'd gotten it right. Its baleful red eye gleamed.

"Yeah, I see you glaring at me."

Dusty set his quill into the ink bottle, unscrewed the top on a bottle of liquid paper, and smeared a white streak down the smooth curve of the *basilisco*. He held it above the heat of the lamp for a few seconds to dry it, then retrieved his quill and inscribed the catalogue number that would allow other researchers to find it in the museum collections. In a final act of superiority, he unscrewed the cap on a bottle of clear nail polish and sealed the number.

"Science triumphs over evil again." Dusty dropped the polished stone into its Ziploc bag, filled out a catalogue card, and tucked it into the sack with the other 10K3 artifacts. He'd deliver them to UNM tomorrow.

The wind rocked his trailer, and the windows trembled on the worn-out screws that opened and closed them. A car whooshed by on the road outside.

The night had suddenly turned darker, more lonely.

Dusty slipped the drawing into the draft report manuscript, closed the ink bottle, and rose from the threadbare brown couch. As he stepped into the kitchen, the linoleum floor sagged under his weight. He turned on the tap and cleaned the crow quill before dropping it in his drawer. For years he had illustrated archaeological reports, doing pen-and-ink drawings of the artifacts that he and Dr. Dale Emerson Robertson, his father for all practical purposes, recovered from the field.

A crawling sensation ran up the nape of his neck. He glanced at the brown paper sack bulging with potsherds, stone tools, and bone artifacts. He could feel the *basilisco* watching him, as if the layers of plastic and brown paper weren't there.

"I'm losing my mind," Dusty whispered to himself. He grabbed the sack and stepped out into the cool night.

The pinyons and junipers around the trailer roared as another gust of wind came up the canyon. The fragrant scent of pine needles filled the air.

Dusty felt his way along the railing, wishing he'd replaced the burned-out sixty-watt bulb that lit the small plywood deck. When he reached the rickety two-by-four steps, he trotted down them and opened the passenger door on his Bronco. He set the artifact bag on the passenger seat floor amidst the empty soda, juice, and beer bottles. Then he slammed the door hard and looked around at the night.

A white Range Rover slipped past the gaps in the trees. He could see the yellow gleam of lights on the million-dollar houses that hulked on either side of his three point two-five acres.

They hated him and his 1956 turquoise-and-white aluminum trailer. But this was the one thing his father, Samuel Stewart, had left him. Back in 1957, when Sam had bought the place, Canyon Road was just that, a winding road climbing out of the city of Santa Fe. That was before the boom, before the godzillionaires came to buy Navajo rugs, Maria-style pottery from San Idelfonso, and to build palatial adobes with sparkling Saltillo tile floors, thick viga pine logs, and latilla pine pole ceilings.

Stars twinkled in the ebony sky high above him. His father had been a great archaeologist, but he'd committed suicide when Dusty was twelve. Dusty had had over twenty-five years to get over it—and hadn't. Strange, that. You'd think the pain and shock would dim, but somewhere deep inside him, he still felt half-dead and half-alive, like a lonely ghost condemned to walk the earth forever. Dusty had immersed himself in archaeology for a number of reasons, but the most important one was that his boyhood mind had truly believed if he could understand why his father had been so obsessed with studying the dead, maybe he could understand why his father had wanted to join them. It hadn't worked out that way, though. Dusty still did not understand what had driven his father to that final act of desperation.

He rubbed his arms. He swore he could hear the *basilisco* laughing in a hoarse inhuman voice.

"It's the goddamned wind rattling the trees, you idiot."

Dusty glowered at the passenger side of the Bronco, then walked back up the stairs and into his trailer.

He looked askance at his refrigerator for several seconds before saying, "What the hell."

He crossed to the refrigerator, pulled out an egg, and rubbed it over his hands, his arms, around his chest, over his genitals, and down the insides of his thighs. In little more than a minute, he had stroked it along every part of his body.

It was an old ritual, still used in the Southwest. Hail Walking Hawk had cleansed him like this over a year and a half ago. She'd said that the egg absorbed the evil that lived inside a human body. Once the egg was destroyed, the evil was gone.

He opened his squeaky trailer door and used his best pitcher's windup to splatter the egg in his rusty barbecue pit.

"I don't believe any of this shit, of course," he said aloud as he grabbed the Coleman can and dumped white gas over the barbecue pit. He tossed a lit match on top and leaped backward as flames roared to the night sky.

Dusty fumbled around the step for his hatchet, then walked to the gnarled pinyon across the drive. He whacked off one of the lower branches, and the pungent odor of the sap filled the night.

"Forgive me, grandfather," he said as he gently petted the bark, "but I need this branch."

He carried it back, dropped it onto the flames, and watched the white smoke billow up. The Puebloan tribes believed that smoke was the cousin of the Cloud People. Not only would it drive out any evil that might have secreted itself in his flesh, it would carry his prayers to the gods.

"Ah, if the guys at the university could only see me now."

He pulled off his gray T-shirt and blue jeans and tossed them into a pile, then he cupped the smoke with his hands and pulled it over his naked body. As he rubbed it into his goosepimpled flesh, Maureen Cole's image formed in his mind, her perfect oval face framed by long black hair, her black eyes glinting. Over the years, he'd developed a love-hate relationship with the world-renowned Canadian physical anthropologist. Being male, he couldn't help but respond to a beautiful woman, and they shared a great deal: they'd both been raised with the Native peoples, she with the Seneca, and Dusty with the Hopi, Zuni, and Arapaho. They'd both been steeped in the ancient traditions. The difference was, he believed the teachings; she didn't. Maureen Cole had gone into the "hard" science of physical anthropology. Where Dusty would bend over backward to accommodate someone else's beliefs, Maureen discarded them out of hand as groundless superstitions. They'd frequently stood toe-to-toe shouting at each other over how to deal with Native religious fundamentalism.

He hadn't seen her since the 10K3 project, but she stared at him from his memory this instant, silently chastising him for behaving like a fool.

He rubbed the smoke over his entire body, ruffled his blond hair in it, and picked up his clothes. As he tossed them onto the barbecue, he glanced at the passenger side of his Bronco where the *basilisco* rested and called, "Thought you could get me, eh? Take that, you little bastard!"

It took another cup of Coleman fuel to completely incinerate his clothing, then he ran for the trailer.

Maybe Hail Walking Hawk had been right. He should have left the *basilisco* buried in the desert.

Closing the flimsy door behind him, he shivered and found clean clothes.

He felt better. But not much.

He pulled a cold bottle of Guinness from the fridge to help finish the healing process. Popping the top, he flopped onto his battered old couch and stared at the peeling wooden walls. They didn't make wood like that anymore. Some people would say "hallelujah," but he thought it gave the trailer character.

He had just reached for the TV remote when the phone rang. He picked it up. "Hello, but I'm not buying anything tonight, got it?"

"I take it you've had too many telemarketers lately," the gruff old voice said. *"Well, good, William. How's the 10K3 report coming along?"*

"Hi, Dale. As of fifteen minutes ago, it's finished. At least my draft is. You want me to drop it by tomorrow after I leave the artifacts at the university?"

"Yes, that will be fine." Dale Emerson Robertson cleared his throat. Dale was the grand old man of southwestern archaeology. He'd dug some of the most important sites in the world. He was also Dusty's best friend and adopted father. *"Your timing couldn't be better."*

"Why? What's up?"

"I've just got off the phone with some real estate developers."

Dusty winced. "Let me guess. The developers bulldozed a site to avoid the 'archaeology problems' and want to know if the state can still come after them?"

"Actually, no. It seems they bought land specifically because of the archaeology. They want us to come and see if they have anything 'really spiffy.' I believe that was the term they used."

Dusty frowned. "What do they want us to do? Dig the thing so they can sell the artifacts? Turn the kiva into their living room? What's the catch?"

"Quite the contrary, they want to preserve the whole thing. And, if I understand them correctly, they want to make it a community attraction, like a park."

Dusty scratched his beard. "I'm not sure I like this. It sounds too goody-goody to be real."

"Let's at least hear what they have to say, William. From my first conversation, they seem to want to find ways to increase public awareness of archaeological resources and use commercial ventures to preserve them."

"Yeah. Right. I may start believing in Santa Claus again, too. But it's your project, Dale."

"Good. I'll see you tomorrow. Say, around noon?"

"Okay. Then we'll have to start finding crew. It's the middle of the fall semester. Diggers are going to be hard to come by."

"I got a letter from Maureen," Dale said mildly, and Dusty's stomach muscles clenched. *"If we find any human skeletal material, it will have to be analyzed by a specialist. I was thinking—"*

"We aren't going to find any, Dale. I'll make sure I throw every skull out with the back dirt. See you tomorrow."

Dusty hung up and stared at the old black rotary telephone. A site on private land? And the developers wanted to pay for archaeological excavation? Now, that was a new twist on an old knot. He knew all too well that in most cases avarice, not altruism, was at the heart of such requests.

He sipped his beer, and Maureen's face glared from his memory.

Hell, even if they found something, it would most likely be an ordinary Anasazi primary burial with a few grave goods. Maureen wouldn't want to leave her classes for that kind of thing.

"No," he said to himself. "This is going to be an open and shut test excavation. A couple of square holes to determine if these rich liberal developers have a 'spiffy' site, and then Dale and I will backfill and leave."

He gulped the last of his Guinness and listened to the wind ripping through the trees.

It was the wind, wasn't it?

Why in God's name did it sound like laughter?

He reached for the .41 Magnum Smith & Wesson on the table. The cool wooden grips reassured him.

He closed his eyes and rested the pistol on his stomach. He could imagine the disdain in Maureen Cole's eyes. She was Canadian, didn't believe in guns, ghosts, *basiliscos*, or any of the things that scared the hell out of Dusty.

"Maybe"—he yawned—"being a cold-blooded scientist isn't such a bad thing after all."

He had just started to doze off when the laughter brought him bolt upright. He looked around the trailer and rubbed a hand over his face.

"Good Lord, what is that?"

Like a magnet, his eyes were drawn to the trailer window and the Bronco sitting outside in the faint golden gleam.

Dusty whispered, "Tomorrow I'll be rid of you for once and for all, you little son of a bitch, thank God."

CHAPTER 4

"DO YOU SEE them?" Catkin breathed in Browser's ear.

Browser lifted himself to gaze over the tangled pile of deadfall where they'd taken cover when movement caught his eye. The scent of decaying wood filled his nostrils.

Twenty paces ahead, on the ground between the aspens, things moved. The windblown piles of fallen leaves twitched and then sighed and moaned.

"What are they?" he whispered. "Animals? People hiding in the leaves?"

Catkin shook her head. Sweat beaded her turned-up nose and shone across her wide cheekbones. She was almost too beautiful to be flesh and blood. Her long black braid hung down her back like a shiny serpent. "They don't move like living creatures, Browser. Perhaps it's just Wind Baby toying with the leaves."

"Maybe, but—"

A tiny explosion of leaves whirled into the moonlight and pirouetted away in the wind.

Browser watched them curiously, trying to decide. A leaden cape of exhaustion weighted his shoulders. His thoughts didn't want to coalesce. All he wanted was to get home to Longtail village. "It is likely just mice scurrying beneath the leaves."

He started to rise, and she put a hand on his arm to stop him. He glanced down at her slender fingers. Like a war club in his fist, her touch comforted him, made him feel safe. He let out a pent-up breath, and asked, "What do you wish to do?"

Catkin said, "Wait. A few more moments of inspection will not harm anyone."

Browser eased to the ground again and stared out through the filigree of dark branches. The aspen leaves trembled and winked in the moonlight, their white-barked trunks shining.

Browser frowned at the exposed roots that laddered the ground on the far right of the grove. He leaned closer to Catkin. "Is that a hand?"

The "hand" resembled a bloated white slug against the black roots.

Catkin's fingers dug into the fallen tree as she pulled herself up for a closer look.

"It might be. I—"

From beneath, the leaves stirred and panted as though a dozen bodies exhaled at once.

Browser shot Catkin a glance and saw her eyes tighten.

"Survivors?" she asked.

Browser shook his head. "I doubt it."

The Flute Player Believers did not leave survivors wandering the woods. They hunted down every man, woman, and child. Some they enslaved. Others, the sick, the elderly, or those too young to be of use, were slaughtered immediately. Frequently they toyed with captives, forcing a girl to couple with her brother, or a boy to cut out his mother's living heart. In the name of the Blessed Flute Player, creator of their world, they committed every kind of atrocity.

Browser said, "I'm going closer."

Catkin's head jerked around. She examined his face. "You are sure?"

"Can you leave here without finding out what that is?"

She hesitated. "All right. But go slowly."

Browser eased over the deadfall into the aspen grove. Wind cooled his face as he slid forward on his belly through the frost-encrusted old leaves toward the tiny explosions.

To his right, across the canyon gorge, moonlight painted the meadows and washed the sky like a fine paint made of ground azure and quartz crystals. A glowing wall of Cloud People marched up from the south. He lifted his nose and scented the wind. He could smell snow on Wind Baby's breath; it gave him a bellyache. By morning, they'd be out in the flats and wading through ankle-deep mud, soaked to the bone.

Browser saw movement to his left and caught sight of Catkin, a flickering ghost slipping between the trees toward the "hand."

A whistle piped, then the leaves rustled and a low growl rolled through the darkness.

Browser got on his hands and knees and crawled toward the sound. Leaves crunched beneath his palms.

". . . gods."

He tensed at the word and searched for Catkin in the trees. He didn't see her.

He murmured, "What is it?"

Catkin's voice resembled mist rising from warm trees on a cold morning, soft, barely there. *"Don't . . . see it?"*

Browser dropped to his belly and looked around. Her tone told him that what she saw horrified her, and he'd better prepare himself for the worst.

Which means there's an enemy war party out there.

But if that were the case, Catkin wouldn't be speaking at all, would she? He'd fought many battles at her side. In the past, she'd always grown unnaturally silent when she sensed danger.

He saw her. Ahead to his left. Her face flashed as she dodged between two trees.

Browser pulled his war club from his belt and slid forward on his belly.

"Browser . . . see . . . ?"

"No. Where?" he whispered, frantic to know what she saw.

". . . must see it! Right there in front . . ."

Browser's fist tightened on his club. His throat had gone tight; he could barely swallow. *Right there in front of me? Where? Why can't I see it?*

And why would Catkin risk herself to tell him about it? She knew that every time she spoke, she might be giving away her position to the enemy. A sudden wave of fear flooded him. Gods, if anything happened to her, especially if she died trying to warn him . . .

He lifted his head.

Faces stared back at him.

They couldn't be more than ten paces ahead. He hadn't seen them because, in the moonlight, they shone with the same iridescence as the frosty leaves. Thirty, maybe even forty.

The moans returned, this time more like the squeals of wet leather being wrung out.

Leaves fluttered down over the faces, and he wondered how many bodies lay beneath the glittering autumn blanket. Though the nights had been cold, the days had been warm. Sunshine melted flesh. In the summer, he had seen a man killed at noon swell to twice his size by sunset.

That's what the explosions were. Fetid air escaping from rotted muscles and hideously bloated bellies.

Browser longed to slam his club into something.

He got to his feet and walked forward through the moonlit shadows to the killing ground.

He veered wide around the piles of leaves and went directly to the "hand." It turned out to be someone's windpipe. The white corrugated tube looked stark against the black roots.

Browser's nostrils flared. Urine. Human. But not from the dead. The pungent aroma came from the tree trunks. That's why the bodies had not been torn apart by animals. The enemy warriors had urinated around the killing ground. Wolves did the same thing, marking their territory, warning off scavengers. In a few more days the scent would weaken, and predators would fearlessly trot into the circle to savage the corpses. That meant the bodies had only been here a few days at the most.

Browser turned to the line of decapitated heads. They'd been arranged in four concentric circles. A thin layer of frozen leaves filled the center of the smallest circle. Frozen because someone had sat there for a long time, the heat from his body wetting the leaves, mashing them down. The moisture had frozen solid when the person rose.

He recognized the head at the top of the inner circle. Running Elk, War Chief of Aspen village. It took little effort to identify the elderly man. His long, gray-streaked black hair had been feathered into a halo around his wrinkled face. Browser suspected that the four heads around Running Elk belonged to the other members of his war party. They'd been killed days ago, probably right after they'd left the village.

Browser counted thirty-three heads, but there might be more beneath the piled leaves. Below the heads, five headless bodies lay. Distended hands reached out to the shining night. Legs sprawled hideously.

"Gods, maybe I should believe in Poor Singer's prophecy."

Poor Singer had been a great prophet. He'd said that if the Katsinas' People could not find the First People's kiva and return to the underworlds to speak with the ancestors, they would destroy themselves in a terrible war that would last more than two hundred sun cycles.

"Catkin?" he called softly. "You may come out. They're all dead."

After a time, he looked up, wondering why she hadn't answered. Perhaps she'd gone further into the forest to scout the area.

He'd taken four steps toward the bodies when a whisper warned him: *"Don't move. Get down."*

Browser's eyes widened. He dropped and covered himself with leaves.

Catkin's voice had come from somewhere close, but higher than his position. Had she climbed a tree to get a better view?

He forced his breathing to slow and listened intently to the sounds of the forest. Through the thin scatter of leaves he could see branches rocking in the breeze. On the far right of his vision, the glistening wall of Cloud People pushed closer, almost over them now. Leaves twitched and the ground seemed to crawl around him. The scent of rot almost gagged him. Lying here amid the dead might shield him; it might also cost him his life. Decaying bodies spawned evil Spirits. They could sneak into a man and consume his flesh in less than a moon. First the slaughtered in the kiva, now this. When he got home, he would have to undergo a ritual cleansing or . . .

"People," Catkin whispered, and Browser saw her.

A human-shaped shadow moved in the branches almost over his head. As she stretched out, her body blended with the limb where she lay.

"How many?" he asked.

"They're just dark shapes on the trail. Coming toward us."

Browser took the opportunity to scoop more leaves over his legs and face, and Catkin hissed, *"Be still!"*

He went limp.

For twenty heartbeats the leaves sighed and jumped into the air, even more frightening now than earlier. If these were not the warriors who had killed the villagers, the sounds and movement would draw them to look, as they had Catkin and Browser.

A single leaf twirled above Browser, then spun down and landed on his chest, as if to point him out to his enemies.

"If you haven't already loosed your club, do it now," she hissed. *"They're looking into the canyon."*

He clutched his club over his belly and willed his heartbeat to slow. He could feel their approach, their steps like snowflakes landing on leaves.

As they entered the aspen grove, Thunderbirds flashed down from the clouds and seared their images onto Browser's souls. Ten warriors stood silhouetted against a brilliant white web. They wore white ritual capes and knee-high white moccasins. Strange clothing. They couldn't be warriors, could they? Would any warrior be foolish enough to wear white on a moonlit night?

The leader, a tall, heavily muscled man, looked around as though surprised, as if he expected to see someone here. The chert studs on his war club glinted as he cautiously stepped forward to survey the murmuring piles of leaves. He seemed to have no face. Only his eyes gleamed. Which meant that either he wore a mask, or he'd blacked his face with soot.

Browser looked up at Catkin. He couldn't see her, but knew she would have an arrow nocked in her bow and aimed down at the lead man. If they discovered Browser, she would shoot. In the ensuing chaos, when men dove for cover, Browser would have a chance to run. Catkin would cover him, raining arrows down upon their enemies until her quiver lay empty. He might escape. Then they would climb up and drag Catkin down.

Gods, don't move. Don't even breathe!

Lightning flickered and a roar of thunder trembled the world.

Browser raised wild eyes to the sky. As the Cloud People sailed closer, a rumpled black blanket blotted out Sister Moon and the Evening People. If he could just hide until darkness swallowed the light, he might be able to crawl away through the leaves without them hearing or seeing him.

And Father Sun will shine through the night tomorrow, too.

He glanced to his right. The leader of the war party gave a slashed-throat signal, then pointed to the north. Four men split off from the group and headed toward the path Catkin had taken earlier. There must be a deer trail there because they never stumbled, and no twigs cracked beneath their feet. They turned into a line of flashing eyes and teeth.

More warriors stirred the leaves on the southern edge of the grove, three or four paces away. Browser concentrated on their footsteps.

The warriors moved around the circles of decapitated heads, then waded through the piles of leaves toward the dead bodies where Browser hid. He could see them more clearly now, and the sight stunned him. Each wore a wolf mask, exquisitely carved and painted, and black spirals covered their ankle-length white capes.

They walked out of the grove without a word, coalesced into a group again, and headed down the trail that led to Aspen village.

Browser sank back into the leaves and sucked in a deep breath. The relief was like coupling with a woman. A fiery tingle ran through his body.

On the branch above him, Catkin stirred, her slender body hunching like a cat's.

"There's one missing," she said.

Browser tensed. She must have counted nine on the trail.

"Shh. Two coming."

Two?

Browser gripped his club again. Perhaps she'd miscounted. Didn't matter, they could take two. He would leap up and club the first man in the head, while Catkin's arrow lanced the second, but if one of their victims managed to scream before he died, the entire war party would be on them in less than thirty heartbeats. He would move only as a last resort.

Lightning danced in the sky above Browser and lit the aspen grove. Between the flashes, he saw the two people.

A man shoved an old woman before him. The woman stumbled and weaved on her feet as though injured.

Blessed Ancestors, a survivor.

The woman staggered through the deep leaves, clutching the back of her head, as though to block another blow from her captor's club.

Then Browser saw the truth. Her captor's eyes gleamed. Her eyes did not. Black gaping pits stared at the ground. Someone had gouged out her eyes. She couldn't see. The woman reached out to beseech her captor, but her voice came out thick, the words slurred, meaningless. They must have cut out her tongue, as well.

Hatred welled in Browser's gut.

The warrior bent down and said, "You are the last. You know why? Our sacred leader used your eyes to see where your people had fled. We found them all. Now we are done."

He grunted as he clubbed the woman. She sprawled face-first into the leaves near the other bodies. The murderer stood over her for a time, smiling, triumphant.

At the edge of his endurance, Browser had to strain against his rage. His club hand shook with the need to kill.

Apparently sated, the warrior turned and trotted after his companions.

It took an eternity before Browser heard Catkin's familiar steps and reared up from his bed of leaves.

Catkin sat down, pulled the woman's body into her lap, and smoothed hair away from her sightless eyes.

Browser rose to his feet and brushed himself off. "Is she alive?"

"Yes."

"Who is it? Do you know her?"

Catkin said something soft, but he didn't hear.

He went to Catkin's side and knelt, and he no longer needed a name. Despite her mutilation, he recognized Matron Eagle Hunter. Shallow breaths moved her old chest, but the back of her skull had been crushed.

Catkin clutched the dying Matron and rocked her back and forth, whispering, "It's all right, Matron. It's Catkin and War Chief Browser. You are safe now. We're here."

Browser stared at Catkin. He doubted the Matron could hear, but it was very much like Catkin to offer this small comfort just in case.

As he rose, he placed a hand on Catkin's shoulder to thank her, then walked to the trail the warriors had taken. He looked both ways, praying he would see no one. Cloud People had filled the sky and the darkness seemed to ripple with each punch of his heart. The trail more than a few paces away appeared warped and dreamlike.

He cocked his head and listened.

The aspens rustled. The explosions of leaves continued like far-off cries. Catkin whispered.

Then . . . a rush of air.

Catkin gently rested the Matron on the ground. The sound must have been Eagle Hunter's afterlife soul escaping with her last breath.

Browser bowed his head and silently prayed for the ancestors to come and find her soul, to guide it to the sacred lake and the opening that led to the underworlds and the Land of the Dead. He and Catkin could not afford to bury her properly.

"Let's go," he called.

Catkin stood, a slender pillar of gray in the blackness. "I'm ready."

CHAPTER 5

"HE'S A PYGMY," Sylvia Rhone said as Dusty pulled up at the end of a faint two-track, set the brake, and turned off the Bronco's ignition.

"Mr. Wirth is short," Dusty corrected. "I met him in Dale's office yesterday. He seemed okay."

Sylvia tucked a lock of shoulder-length brown hair behind her ear and her thin, freckled face went pensive. She wore a green sweatshirt and blue jeans, with heavy hiking boots. "Yeah, well, if you say so, but check out his hair. It takes a lot of skill to get that much hair spray in one spot. I mean, we're talking years of spray-paint practice. He probably spent his entire youth on overpasses."

"Give the guy a chance, will you?"

"I always give men *a* chance."

"Oh, I feel better. Thanks."

With practiced eyes, she looked out at the site. "So. They've decided to call it Pueblo Animas, eh? Nice touch. Sounds scary."

" 'Town of Souls' is a clever bilingual pun, since it's an Anasazi site on the terrace above the Animas River."

The site didn't look like much, just a mound of rubble spotted with occasional sagebrush, rabbitbrush with its autumn browned tufts, and tawny patches of bunchgrass. Here and there, craters pocked the surface where eighty years of pot-hunting had taken its toll. Finding an intact ruin anywhere in the Southwest was akin to finding a true virgin in a Juarez brothel.

Sylvia's eyes narrowed at the man leaning against the dark blue Mercedes. "What does he do for a living?"

Dusty gave her a sidelong glance. Her tone suggested that Mr. Wirth might be a drug lord, or worse, a politician. Dusty said, "He's an investment banker from New York. Be polite, no matter what he says."

Sylvia's freckled face froze. "Why, is he going to say something to set me off?"

Dusty reached for the door handle. "I think he's used to giving orders, that's all."

"Oh, God," she groaned.

They both stepped out of the Bronco and walked to meet Peter Wirth. Sunlight shot gold and yellow from the cottonwoods that flanked the riverbank east of the site. According to the latest culturally sensitive perspective, they weren't supposed to call these "ruins" anymore, that being pejorative to some ears. The same with the term "Anasazi," though Dusty hadn't heard any of those selfsame politically correct people disparaging the use of "Anglo" when it came to people like him—no matter how offensive it might have been to his Scottish, Irish, and French ancestors.

"Good morning," Peter Wirth called and thrust his thumbs into the back pockets of his twill slacks. The wind didn't even move his white hair, but it tugged at the corners of his tweed jacket.

"Hello. Thanks for meeting us out here." Dusty extended his hand. Wirth shook, and Dusty added, "This is my assistant, Sylvia Rhone."

Sylvia stepped forward and shook, but she eyed Wirth suspiciously. "Hey, great site."

"Glad you like it," Wirth replied. "We want you to get this excavated immediately."

"Immediately?" Sylvia pushed up the sleeves of her green sweatshirt. She had an amused look on her face. "You mean, like, next year?"

Wirth's face went stony. He looked at Sylvia as though she must be joking. He said, "I mean like now."

"Uh, yeah, well," Dusty said, and folded his arms as if in defense. "We will certainly get started immediately, but please keep in mind that archaeology isn't exactly an 'immediate' sort of science."

Wirth's bushy white brows plunged down over his blunt nose. "What does that mean?"

A flock of rosy finches swooped over their heads, chirping and twittering as they soared into a cottonwood tree down by the river.

"It means—" Sylvia said with an evil tone.

Dusty broke in, "It means that archaeology takes time, Mr. Wirth. We—"

"I mean, wow," Sylvia added, missing Dusty's cue to keep quiet, "if we had one hundred people and about ten years, we *might* be able to dig half this site—"

Wirth's eyes narrowed, and Dusty said, "Please, let me explain, sir. This looks like a Chacoan great house, Mr. Wirth. I suspect you have a two-story pueblo with around two hundred rooms in it. I don't think you understand how expensive archaeology can be."

Wirth's mouth smiled, but it didn't reach his eyes. "Let me point out the property boundaries so you don't get lost. My wife and I bought a twelve-hundred-acre parcel that runs from the pinyon-juniper uplands over there, to the irrigated riverfront where you see those cottonwoods and willows. This ruin is the property's crown jewel and our best hope for a payoff on our investment."

"Yes, sir, I understand that, but—"

Wirth interrupted, "Well, let's just start with one portion, something we can show to demonstrate the property's grand past. Maybe a kiva. There should be a kiva here, right?"

Dusty pointed, and his black-and-gray plaid sleeve waffled in the breeze. "You see that big round depression in the middle of the rubble mound?"

"Yes."

"That's it."

"Great." Wirth nodded. "Start there." He slapped Dusty on the shoulder and strode to the driver's side of his Mercedes. Over the roof, he called, "I have to get back to New York. Let me know what you find."

Dusty smiled and waved. "Will do."

They watched him drive away in a cloud of dust.

"Wow," Sylvia said in admiration. Brown hair blew around her face in the wind. "I bet he can handle anything—Heimlich maneuvers, CPR, pulling the switch at the local prison."

"Well," Dusty sighed. "At least it's pretty country."

To his left, the northwest, the land undulated, rising and falling in tan-and-green swells. To the south, an eroded mesa etched a line against the crystal blue October sky.

Sylvia propped her hands on her hips. "How much money do we have? A lot, I gather."

"I don't think he'd approve a request to do remote sensing from the space shuttle."

"Bummer. But we can run all the C-14 dates and palynology samples we want to?"

"I think so."

Dusty started toward the pueblo, his boots grating in the sand as he climbed the slope. "Let's face it, no matter what we have to put up with, this is an archaeologist's dream. We've got an untouched Chaco outlier. Think about it. Aztec Ruins is about fifteen miles south of us, and Salmon Ruins another eight miles straight south of that. We're the first archaeologists to sink a shovel into this thing." He waved his arms in growing excitement. "It's been thirty years since anyone has opened a great house. And we're not on a skinny budget."

"Yeah," Sylvia said, trudging along at his side, "almost too good to be true. I wonder what the catch is?"

"Catch?"

"Oh, come on," Sylvia groaned as though Dusty were stupid. "You don't really think this guy is interested in archacology, do you?"

"I don't have any evidence to the contrary, and I try very hard to live my life as an optimist."

"Yeah, I know," she answered blandly. "I've seen the stash of Trojans in your glove compartment."

Dusty glared at her, but didn't miss a step. Maybe he ought to put them in a paper bag? "Think of it this way, normally at this time of year we're walking some pipeline right-of-way out in the saltbush flats around Aneth. This is a vast improvement."

Sylvia hung her head. "Yeah. Okay. You're right."

He walked to the highest point in the rubble and looked around. Sagebrush and rabbitbrush covered everything. The place looked like a rock outcrop. Now he knew how Earl Morris or A. V. Kidder felt when they first set foot on a huge pile of rubble; and Pueblo Animas was only a small Chacoan outlier.

"You know," Dusty said, as he watched a whirlwind of leaves careen over the ruin, "for the first time I understand why the old guys back in the twenties dug like they did. I mean, we're so used to small sites, collapsed pueblos with a couple of rooms, that we lose the enormity of what it means to excavate a city from scratch."

Sylvia propped herself on the canted chunks of sandstone and looked around. Wind ruffled her straight brown hair. "So, what next?"

"Datum."

"Right, where do you want it?"

The datum was a length of rebar, a metal rod, that they would hammer into the ground. All of their measurements would be tied to that point.

"There." Dusty pointed to the northern edge of the kiva depression. "We need to shoot it in from the section corners." Which meant they needed to survey in the exact location.

Sylvia gave him a sour look. "That's a hard day of packing around the rod. When is Steve going to be here?"

"Tomorrow. But we need this done *pronto*. Life is full of little disappointments."

"I just want you to know—"

Dusty held up his hand and cocked his head to the wind.

Sylvia jerked around wide-eyed, staring straight at the brush-filled kiva. "Did you hear that?"

He didn't respond for a second. "What?"

"Well, I—I don't know. It sounded like children screaming." Sylvia had started breathing hard, and her face had flushed.

Dusty lowered his hand and scowled at her. "I thought it sounded like a far-off engine."

Sylvia just stared at him, her green eyes wide. "What can I say? Ten minutes with an investment banker, and I think it's the Apocalypse."

Dusty looked at her over the rims of his sunglasses. "You're not going to start saying 'Praise the Lord' every other sentence, are you?"

"Not unless I see some guy ride down from the sky on a white horse."

Dusty glanced up at the clouds, then nodded. "Good, you had me worried. I'll get the rod and transit, if you'll pick the datum location in the kiva."

She trotted toward the circular depression in the middle of the rubble mound. "I'm on it."

CHAPTER 6

THUNDER ROLLED ACROSS the low hills.

Catkin pulled her red-and-black striped blanket over her head and hunched forward against the bone-piercing morning cold. Rain dripped from the juniper branches onto her shoulders in a steady *plop-plop.* A faint gray haze brightened the eastern horizon, telling her that dawn had arrived, but Father Sun remained hidden in the bellies of the Cloud People.

Two paces away, Browser knelt beside the fire with the collar of his elkhide coat turned up. Rain ran from his flat nose and sleeked his chin-length black hair against his head. His soft brown eyes stared at nothing, as if he wasn't quite here in this world with her, but far away, running trails she could not see. From the bruised crescents beneath his eyes, his exhaustion matched her own.

They'd run away from the slaughter ground in silence, afraid every step of the way. Four hands of time ago, they'd stumbled to a stop, unable to go any farther. Catkin had stood watch for two hands of time while Browser slept, then he'd stood watch while she tried to sleep. Catkin had lain awake most of her rest period, listening to the howling wind, watching the Thunderbirds soar and flash as they brought the storm.

She'd awakened half a hand of time ago, but Browser had barely spoken to her, and when he had, his voice had come out gruff and strained. He'd been tramping around camp, kicking rocks and dead limbs, as though punishing Our Grandmother Earth for the rain. Catkin had seen it before. He wore guilt like a mantle.

A branch cracked in the fire, and Browser leaped to his feet with his war club over his head.

Catkin said, "You are acting like Vole when he hears Coyote's footsteps in the snow."

"You aren't helping." He gave her a sour look.

She nodded. "I know."

Since she'd awakened, she'd jumped at every peal of thunder or distant flash of lightning. She kept glancing over her shoulder, as though she expected to be grabbed from behind. She'd ripped her club from her belt so often that she decided to just lay it across her lap. It saved time.

Catkin sighed. "We are hungry and tired, Browser. Perhaps if we take care of those things, our nerves will stop tingling."

"Maybe yours will."

He knelt again, and tossed another branch on the fire. White smoke rose from the wet wood. "We'll get a hot cup of tea yet."

Browser blew on the fire until flames leaped and crackled, then began adding more wood.

Catkin pulled a piece of venison jerky from her belt pouch and tore off a hunk with her teeth. It tasted rich and smoky.

Her gaze roved the hills, landing on branches that seemed to sway too much, or patches of grass with unusual colors. Any shape that did not seem to match its surroundings sent blood surging through her veins.

There's nothing there. Stop this.

She had been living with fear for two sun cycles, since the day she'd run away from home to join the Katsinas' People. One would think she would have grown used to it.

"Browser, we haven't spoken about last night, and we must."

"Yes, we must," he answered gruffly, but didn't offer any information.

Catkin eyed the tendons sticking out on his neck. "Were Walker and Bole dead when you arrived?"

After a few heartbeats, he nodded. "Yes. They had been dead for some time."

Catkin blinked, recalling the timing of last night's events. "How is that possible? You signaled them just before you left me."

Browser shook his head and water fell from his black hair onto his coat. "By the time I signaled, Catkin, they were already dead. I think someone captured them right after we walked away and forced them down into the kiva."

Guilt thickened his voice. They had spent a good deal of time examining the mummy. He must be thinking that if they hadn't stopped to look, Walker and Bole would be alive.

"Do you think that's why they hung the mummy at the top of the trail? To give the killers more time?"

Browser blinked thoughtfully. "I believe the mummy had another purpose. She was supposed to tell us something, Catkin. We are just too dim-witted to understand."

Catkin remembered the scars on the elderly woman's back and feet and the skeletal hand twined in the magnificent collar. A highly prized slave who had choked herself to death to end the pain—or perhaps her torturer's pleasure.

"You were right. I should have listened to you." Browser angrily jerked a stick from the woodpile and stabbed at the flames. Sparks crackled and whirled into the rainy sky. "It wasn't wise to separate last night. We should have stayed together."

"I was not right," Catkin replied. "If we'd done that, we'd all be dead. I suspect Walker and Bole held their attention long enough that we—"

"No." Browser pointed at her with the stick, and his brown eyes bored into hers. "We are alive because they let us go, Catkin. That is the only answer. A slaughter is no good unless someone is left alive to tell the story." He shook the stick. "That's us."

Catkin ripped off another hunk of jerky. She could feel strength stealing back into her tired limbs. It always amazed her that a scant morsel of food could rejuvenate the body. "If that is true, what role did the wounded woman play?"

"Maybe the woman was supposed to create a diversion so that the rest of her war party could make their way up the western trail and out into the forest without being seen."

"The warriors could have solved that problem by killing me, Browser. You would have been alive to tell the story. I think there is more to this. What else did you see in the kiva?"

Browser put his stick aside and pulled the tripod with the teapot over the flames. The soot-coated pot swung. "I counted forty-two dead, including Walker and Bole."

Catkin's mouth opened, but she couldn't find words. She stammered, "Are—are you sure?"

"There may have been a few more or a few less. At any rate, they were headless." He looked at her from under his heavy brows as though she should know what that meant.

"Those are the heads we found . . ."

"I'm sure of it."

The wind shifted, and smoke billowed up, filling the air between them. Catkin could barely make out his face in the gray haze.

"But if the Matron survived, there may have been others—"

"She didn't 'survive.' Don't you understand what we witnessed last night?"

Catkin paused. "Why don't you tell me."

Wind Baby gusted through the juniper grove, slapping the branches and flinging rain in every direction. Catkin pulled her blanket closed at her throat.

"They blinded the Matron, cut out her tongue, and arranged the heads of her loved ones around her. She sat in the midst of the heads for a while, then she must have wandered away into the forest. That's why the leader seemed surprised when they came into the aspen grove. That's why he made the slashed-throat sign and split up his war party. He was ordering them to hunt her down and kill her."

Catkin watched the raindrops splash into the pool at her feet. "Why? Why would they do that?"

He threw up his hands. "I don't know!"

"Do you know who they were? What clan? I noticed their strange clothing."

He shook his head. "No. If I did, I would hunt them down."

Catkin chewed another bite of jerky before asking, "Tell me more about the headless bodies in the kiva."

He waved a hand, as though uncertain how to proceed. "Last summer Old Pigeontail told me stories I didn't believe. He said that it was common for the Flute Player Believers to kill Katsinas' People, strip their bodies of flesh, and force the survivors to carry the butchered remains of their loved ones to a place where the meat could be prepared. Pigeontail said that once the flesh had been smoked and dried, people couldn't tell it from antelope or deer. He claimed it had become a valuable Trade item."

It took a few moments for Catkin to understand.

"Blessed gods, are you telling me that the people in the kiva had been butchered?"

"Yes," he said in a hoarse voice. "Even some of the infants."

Rain beaded Catkin's long lashes, creating a rainbow shimmer at the edges of her vision. Horrifying memories flashed across the canvas of her souls . . . *Straight Path Canyon nine moons ago . . . the masked Wolf Katsina cutting the flesh from their friend Hophorn's body . . . Browser shooting the katsina, watching it reel, and run, then the terrible instant when he tore the mask from the dying murderer's face . . .*

"Browser, who could have done such a thing? The white-caped men we saw—"

"Perhaps they did it. I don't know. Surely it was someone who hated the katsinas."

"Why do you say that?"

Browser toyed with a stick in the woodpile. He pulled it out and tossed it into the fire. "The attackers painted katsinas across the front of the village, then ritually killed them. Each katsina had a huge gaping hole in the middle of its chest."

Catkin pulled her wet blanket over her head and studied the glowing center of the fire. Just concentrating on it seemed to make her feel warmer. "Browser, why would our enemies waste time killing gods they don't believe in?"

Browser shrugged. "I do not know."

Catkin continued in a soft voice, "If I hated the katsinas, I wouldn't paint them at all. I would paint the Flute Player on my enemy's village instead. Or better yet, I would paint the Flute Player *over* the katsinas. If someone obliterated my gods and replaced them with their own, it would infuriate me."

He drew up a knee and propped his elbow on it. "Perhaps the attackers believed in different katsinas than we do. I have heard of such things. Ant Woman, the Matron of Dry Creek village, told me that the special Spirit Helpers far to the west are the Mouse Katsina and the Butterfly Katsina. Gods that are foreign to us."

Browser didn't take his gaze from her for a long while, then he bent over the teapot. "This is warm. Toss me your cup. We should drink and be on our way."

Catkin dug around in her belt pouch and threw him her wooden cup.

Browser dipped it full, handed it back, and filled a cup for himself.

As he sipped, his rain-shiny brow furrowed. "There were other things, too, Catkin. In the plaza last night, I found five copper bells like the one you discovered in the mummy's belly."

"In the plaza? Just lying on the ground?"

"Yes. They had been polished to make them shine in the moonlight, then placed in a line leading from the eastern trail to the kiva."

Catkin's hands tightened on her cup. *"Bait?"*

"Probably, yes."

"And you climbed into the kiva anyway?" she almost shouted.

He lifted a hand to halt her tirade. "No, not at first. I went from room to room in the village, and climbed halfway up the western trail before I turned back. I had to look in the kiva, Catkin."

"You, who are like Packrat and always need an escape hole? Great gods, Browser, why aren't you dead?"

He looked up and rain beaded his eyelashes. "I've been asking myself that same question. I should be. I heard them coming. The woman threw a copper bell down into the kiva before she pulled out the ladder."

"Taunting you?"

Browser swirled his tea in his cup. "I can't be sure, of course, but I had the feeling it was payment."

"Payment? For what?"

He shrugged. "It's just a feeling. I think she wanted a witness."

Her mouth quirked. "Most killers murder witnesses. They don't pay them, Browser."

"I know I must sound crazy, Catkin, but I am trying to think of different reasons for what I saw last night. None of this may be correct."

Catkin released her hold on her blanket, and it slipped back from her head and onto her shoulders. Rain misted her face. She was good at figuring things out; it was one of her few talents. She had never learned the skills most women cherished, what to plant and when, cooking, making beautiful pottery. But she had an uncanny ability to slip into her opponent's souls and view the world through his eyes.

"Tell me everything, Browser. You climbed down into the kiva and the woman walked up, pulled out the ladder, and left you."

He gestured with his teacup. "There is one other important thing. Remember I told you about the girl? While the woman was arranging the hides and weighting them down with the ladder, I heard the little girl's voice."

"What did she say?"

"She called the woman 'Mother.' "

"You mean you think there were two women last night? Working together? One trapped you while the other occupied my attention?"

He ran a hand through his hair, squeezing out the water. It cascaded down the collar of his elkhide coat. "It could have been one woman, I suppose, but that means she would have had to hide her daughter somewhere while she distracted you."

"Maybe she sent the girl up the western trail with instructions to hide in the forest. After I left, the woman could have gone to find the child and run away."

Browser finished his tea, set the cup down, and pulled a strip of jerky from his pouch. As he ate, his eyes searched the rain-drenched forest. Juniper branches trembled in the wind, rattling like old bones, and the rich pungent fragrance of wet cedar enveloped them. His gaze roamed the tufts of cloud on the distant hilltops.

"I think I've told you everything important," he said, and looked back at her. "Now. What of your night? The wounded woman crawled up and told you I was in the kiva. What else did you see?"

Pale blue flames danced at the base of the largest log. Catkin focused on them, remembering: "I spent a good deal of time examining the mummy. I think they forced her to walk through fire, Browser. She had burn scars on her feet and legs, and her toes were gone. At first, I assumed someone had cut them off, then stanched the blood with fire. But"—she shook her head—"it would have taken more than that to cause such hideous scars. I think they made her walk through fire until it burned off her toes and roasted her legs."

Irritated, he said, "What does that have to do with Aspen village?"

She shrugged.

He propped his sandal on one of the warm hearthstones and gestured with his jerky. "Remember everything you can. Matron Flame Carrier will wish to hear the details when we return."

Lightning flashed right over their heads and they both hit the ground on their bellies, their clubs in hard fists, ready to strike the first thing that moved. Rain dripped into Catkin's eyes.

When the Thunderbirds flew away, Browser got to his knees and gave Catkin a disgruntled look. Mud coated his chin and the front of his coat. He said, "We should leave before we kill each other by mistake."

She pulled herself up and brushed at the mud on her cape. "If we run straight through, we might make it home before dawn tomorrow. Perhaps

Matron Flame Carrier and the other elders will understand these things better than we do."

Determination lit Browser's eyes. "On my souls, Catkin, I will gather the village elders as quickly as possible to ask them. I *will* find the answers."

CHAPTER 7

THE HOT WIND was unusual for the middle of October, bearing with it the smells of sage, dry earth, and the tang of coal dust from the Four Corners power plants. Showers of yellow leaves blew from the cottonwoods and spiraled away in the murky river current.

Dusty stood chest-deep in the kiva, balancing precariously on the uneven footing. Beside him, Steve Sanders stopped and wiped sweat from his ebony face. He had doffed his shirt a little before ten; now, at two-thirty, the temperature had reached the high eighties. Mud mottled Sander's dark skin and accented the rippling muscles in his back and shoulders.

"Gimme a hand, boss," Steve called, bending down to grasp a protruding rock.

Dusty found a grip and levered the big square chunk of sandstone from the ground. Together, he and Steve tossed it up into the wheelbarrow four feet above their heads; it landed with a hollow clunk.

"Charcoal," Dusty said, squinting down into the hole left by the rock. He looked around the curving walls that hemmed them. "About time."

"Got that right, massa."

Dusty's mouth pursed distastefully. "Did I ever tell you how much I hate that?"

"Don' worry, boss. If'n I find myself offensive, I'll report myself to the NAACP." Steve grinned.

Dusty said, "You know, a man with an IQ of one hundred and seventy-six, a GPA of four point three, who's finishing his Ph.D. dissertation on an analysis of Chacoan religious philosophy within a Jungian context shouldn't talk like Uncle Remus all the time."

"I'll keep dat in mind." Steve bent down and frowned at the ground. "Is that what I think it is?"

"Roof beam, I'd say." They were finally coming down on the bottom. Excavating kiva fill was one of the least favorite things in archaeological excavation. The only thing he anticipated with more dread was backfilling.

Kivas, as a matter of course, were large holes in the ground. Gravity had a thing about holes; it spent all of its time filling them back up again. In this case, collapsed walls, wind-borne dust and sand, bits of twigs and seeds, and anything that seven hundred and fifty years of rain could wash in had collected over the collapsed roof, and the cultural level on the original kiva floor.

Dusty surveyed the rock-stippled brown earth and the one broken section of charred beam. "I think this is going to be a son of a gun."

Steve nodded. "In the old days, they would have just chunked that stuff out."

"Yeah, well." Dusty looked up at the shiny steel datum stake they'd driven into the ground. "We'd better get an elevation on that charred beam. If we do this right, we can have the rest of the fill out of here by quitting time."

Instead, it took until noon the next day before Dusty and Steve had removed the last of the wall rubble. Dusty crouched on one of the pilasters overlooking the floor and updated his notes while Steve used a flat shovel to begin scraping through the silty sand that had trickled down over the collapsed roof. Because they'd been burned, the heavy beams had been preserved, and the actual shape of the roof could be determined.

"Whoa!" Steve laid his shovel aside and reached into his back pocket for his trowel. "I've got bone here, Dusty."

Dusty arched an eyebrow as he put the finishing touches on a sketch map of the kiva floor. A slight red discoloration of the soil was the only discernible feature beyond the scattered charcoal and root casts from long dead plants. "What kind?"

Steve dropped to his hands and knees, his trowel ringing as he scraped away the surrounding soil. "Better come look; this is weird."

Dusty lowered himself from the pilaster and crowded next to Steve. Where the shovel edge had cut the bone surface, it gleamed oddly yellow against the dark, ash-filled soil.

Dusty took a brush from his back pocket and whisked the dirt away. The bone had a mottled look. "Burned. Probably the same time the kiva went up. Small, though. Maybe a deer or antelope?"

"I don't think so." Steve shifted to allow the slanting sunlight to shine on the bone. "Cortex isn't thick enough for deer."

"Well, it's not an adult." Dusty had worked on burials not so long ago. He could imagine Maureen's black eyes narrowing as she examined the bone, knowing with certainty what it was.

Steve said, "I'm guessing this is a humerus, an arm bone. But it's missing the condyle. Epiphyseal line hasn't ossified."

"Right." Dusty gave Steve a disgusted glance. "Sounds Greek to me."

"Very good, Mr. Principal Investigator, sir." Steve turned it over in his hand. "But I can't even guess as to age, sex, or any of that other stuff."

"It's one bone," Dusty said, straightening and clapping the dust from his hands. "Shoot it in, photograph it, record it, and let's get on with life."

"Yassuh, massa."

"Quit that."

Steve saluted.

Dusty climbed back up, balanced on the ladder that allowed them access in and out of the kiva, and levered his butt onto the pilaster, where he reopened his notebook to the level form and began a notation of the burned fragment of humerus.

Steve yelled, "Whoa! Dusty, you'd better get back down here."

"Why?" Dusty scrambled down and stood over Steve as he carefully scooped back the moist black dirt from yet another bit of bone, this one irregular, also mottled. The thing looked like a big flat cashew nut that a giant's foot had squashed. "Innominate," Dusty said.

"Illium," Steve agreed. "A child's hip. I'd guess a kid about six or seven." He used the tip of the trowel to pull back the soil below the end of the bone. "Yep, here's the swell of the ischial tuberosity." He tapped the soil. "Pubis bone ought to be right under here." He scraped away more dirt. "Right there. Damn, I'm good."

Dusty dropped to his knees and pulled his own trowel from his back pocket. "Let's peel this back. If we've got more than just a single kid, I want to know about it sooner rather than later."

The trowel cut thin shavings of rich dark soil. Bits of root snapped and popped, while gravel and spalled sandstone rang against the tempered steel. In three passes, the rounded curve of a skull lay exposed. Dusty grunted and worked faster, freeing the brow ridge from the layer of earth. Two eye sockets stared at him from plugs of black earth. "Adult. A woman—"

"I don't believe it!" Steve breathed. "Look at this. It looks like I've got another skull. Younger, though, a little girl, I think. Bone is coming up all over!"

Dusty shoved his hat back on his head and expelled a breath. "Contrary to what I told Dale, I don't think I can throw all of this out with the back dirt."

Tentatively, Steve said, "Looks like we need a physical anthropologist. Talked to Dr. Cole lately?"

"God forbid," Dusty said, and grimaced at the thought. "But my future isn't looking as bright."

CHAPTER 8

MATRON FLAME CARRIER rolled onto her side, and long gray hair streamed across her red blanket. Wind Baby fluttered the prayer feathers that framed her door, then swept into her chamber, sniffed at the pots and baskets along the white plastered walls, and rattled the dried corn hanging from the ceiling rafters. The brittle scent of autumn filled the air.

She rubbed her tired eyes.

"Great Ancestors, I haven't slept well in nine moons."

Not since she'd led the Katsinas' People away from the horrors in Straight Path Canyon.

Where were Browser and Catkin tonight? Still protecting Aspen village, or on their way home? She prayed the latter. Twice in the past seven days they'd seen warriors approaching, grabbed their bows, and taken refuge in the village. The warriors had turned out to be refugees looking for food, but some day soon they would be enemy raiders, and she would need to muster every person in their small village who could shoot a bow or swing a war club.

Flame Carrier took a deep breath and let it out slowly. It had to be five or six hands of time before dawn. Around the swaying door curtain she could see the Evening People glittering.

"You're not sleeping," she whispered gruffly to herself. "You may as well rise."

She sat up and frowned at her reflection in the polished pyrite mirror on the wall to her left. A few kinky gray hairs curled over her small, narrow eyes. They didn't much look like eyebrows anymore, and her bulbous nose resembled a brown plum stuck in a nest of deep wrinkles.

The fire pit had burned down to coals and cast a crimson gleam over the Blessed Katsinas painted on the walls. Her heart swelled at the sight. Larger than life, the gods wore dark, feathered masks and carried lances in their hands. White dots of stars covered their black arms and legs, and red streaks of rain adorned their tan kirtles. Each god had a foot lifted, preparing to step off the wall and into her world. Many times in the past moons, when Flame Carrier had been fasting and praying for guidance, the katsinas had done that. They had walked right out of the walls and crowded around her, whispering and advising, their tall bodies scented with rain.

"I wish you would speak with me tonight. I'd like to know what's happening in Aspen village."

They peered at her through glistening eyes, but remained silent.

The entire country was on fire. Refugees flooded the roads heading south and east. Every evening she hobbled to the highest point behind Longtail village and counted the lines of fleeing people.

The number of refugees grew steadily. Soon, there would no one left to fight for the katsinas.

The Flute Player Believers would never let them rest. They struck like locusts, cleaned out food stores, took women and children as slaves, and burned the villages before they disappeared into the hills.

Starving war victims kept straggling in, begging for food and shelter. Flame Carrier would take in anyone. Mothers and fathers often brought their children to her to guard while they went off to fight. Most never returned. The orphans took a toll on their scant resources, but what else could she do? In the past four moons, they'd adopted twenty-four children. That meant they had a total of seventy children in the village, fifty under the age of six summers.

Flame Carrier had formed the Katsinas' People four sun cycles ago, after the death of her mother, Spider Silk. Spider Silk, the daughter of Born-of-Water and Golden Fawn, had been raised with two of the greatest holy people in history, the Blessed Cornsilk and the Blessed Poor Singer. Just before Spider Silk died, Poor Singer had come to her in a Dream and told her that she must find the legendary white palaces of the First People. Poor Singer had proclaimed that if Spider Silk could find the First People's original kiva, the hole where they had actually emerged from the underworlds—and she could restore and resanctify it—the wars would end, and the evil Spirits who roamed the land would disappear. Spider Silk had said that the restoration would open the sacred doorway to the underworlds again and allow ordinary humans to descend and seek the advice of the ancestors in the Land of the Dead.

Spider Silk had related the story to Flame Carrier only moments before her death, and Flame Carrier had known immediately what she had to do.

Since that time the Katsinas' People had restored several dilapidated kivas, but no doorway had opened. It tore Flame Carrier's heart. She *believed* the prophecy. Why couldn't they find the right kiva?

Flame Carrier slipped her moccasins onto her socked feet and hobbled across the floor to where her brown-and-white turkey feather cape hung on the peg by the door.

Her slave, Redcrop, slept in the next room. Usually, Flame Carrier would have asked the girl to accompany her on her walk, but she didn't wish to wake her. The Falling River Moon was one of the hardest times for her people. Redcrop had been working from dawn until well after dusk, picking the last of the corn and reverently carrying it back to the village where it would be dried. Each evening Redcrop helped husk the corn, selected and set aside the best ears for spring seed, and finally, well after dark, Redcrop and the other children spread the remainder of the day's crop out on the roofs to dry. By the time Redcrop came home for supper, she resembled a bedraggled wraith.

The girl needed her rest far more than Flame Carrier needed company.

She swung her turkey feather cape around her bony old shoulders, then grabbed her walking stick and ducked beneath the twisting prayer feathers and out into the darkness.

The night mesmerized her. A red hue of reflected firelight tinted the smoke that hung over Longtail village. Two stories tall, the village spread around Flame Carrier in a gigantic "E." Her chamber sat in the eastern half of the village. To her right, the tower kiva, a circular ceremonial chamber, made up the center part of the E. The kiva's roof stood taller than any other part of the village. Flame Carrier could see the guard standing on the roof. A woman stood next to him. *Probably Water Snake and Obsidian.*

Flame Carrier's eyes narrowed. She shook her head. In the past few days, she had learned things about Obsidian that left her feeling anxious and angry. The young woman flaunted a status that no longer existed in this world, and for that, Flame Carrier could not forgive her. Such foolishness could endanger them all.

Laughter drifted from the kiva's roof, but Flame Carrier refused to look.

She had heard nothing from Browser or Catkin in the past eight days and feared they might be dead. Gods, what a blow that would be.

When Flame Carrier's people had first approached this village, the Longtail Clan Matron, Crossbill, had run out to meet them and begged them to stay. Less than a moon before their arrival, the healthy men over the age of thirteen summers had gone out to meet an enemy war party. All had been lost. Longtail village had needed warriors, and especially an experienced War Chief, as badly as Flame Carrier and the Katsinas' People had needed a new home.

Flame Carrier walked out into the starlit plaza. From her left came the sound of gobbles and ruffling feathers. They kept thirty turkeys penned in the long rectangular room on the southeastern corner of the village. Dust wafted through the rooftop entry and glittered in the soft evening glow. Somewhere in the distance, an owl *hoo-hooed.*

She followed the sound.

Flame Carrier stopped near the great kiva, which sank into the southwestern corner of the plaza. The subterranean ceremonial chamber stretched seven body lengths across. They had re-roofed the kiva three moons ago. The entrance was on the north side, to Flame Carrier's right. The circular roof groaned beneath stacks of yellow, red, black, and blue corn ears. In the daylight the kernels glittered like a wealth of jewels, but night had drained their colors away, leaving only a shimmering sea of black and white.

Her feathered cape waffled around her legs as she stepped onto the trail that led down to the Prancing Spirit River. A black tracery of shadows enveloped her, and Flame Carrier's feet *shish-shished* in fallen leaves. She used her walking stick to brace herself as she waded through them. The pungent scent of the river, of wet earth and soaked wood, filled her nostrils. Starlight illuminated the trembling leaves of the cottonwoods.

It felt good to walk alone. She could think, and she didn't have to worry about how someone else felt. If Redcrop had been here, the girl would have insisted on supporting Flame Carrier's elbow and speaking to her in soft soothing tones. Flame Carrier loved Redcrop with all her heart, but she needed to do things by herself now and then.

The trail angled down toward the river bottom.

Flame Carrier planted her walking stick and carefully made her way to the sandy shore. Every fallen leaf and grain of sand glimmered. Light twinkled where the water swirled over rocks and pieces of driftwood.

If only she could remain in this tranquil place forever. If only the wars would end. If only . . .

Too much longing strangled the heart. Poor Singer had said those words more than a hundred sun cycles ago. But Flame Carrier had been filled with longing all of her life. She couldn't stop now. Not when everywhere she looked she saw suffering.

The traditionalists among the Straight Path Nation, including the group who called themselves the Flute Player Believers, hated the new Katsina religion. They considered it evil, and killed every member of the faith they could. As more and more villages converted, more were destroyed, and the sizes of the few remaining villages increased dramatically. Clan matrons willingly took in refugees. It made sense. The more warriors a village possessed, the greater the likelihood it would survive; but as different clans were thrown together, people began to feel like strips of rawhide stretched over a drum. The strain frayed nerves.

Just last moon Obsidian had gotten into a fistfight with an exhausted young woman who had dragged into Longtail village asking for food. Obsidian had shouted, "If we give away any more food we won't have enough to feed our own children! Go beg somewhere else!" The dispute had grown ugly. War Chief Browser had broken it up, but the sight had wounded Flame Carrier. She'd taken the weeping young woman aside, given her bags of cornmeal, beans, and giant wild rye seeds, and pleaded with her to stay with them where she'd be safe. The woman had taken one look at Obsidian's hateful face, thanked Flame Carrier, and left.

Wind Baby frolicked along the river bottom, slapping at the brush, and whipping the autumn leaves into tiny tornadoes. Flame Carrier watched them careen down the shore, then kicked at a pile of leaves.

"If you'd had the wits of a mosquito, you'd have ordered your people to pack and gone with her, you old fool."

They couldn't fight the Traditionalists. She knew it, but leaving would mean giving up the prophecy. The kivas of the First People were here, in this land, not far to the south. If the Katsinas' People left . . .

"Grandmother?"

Flame Carrier turned.

The whisper seemed to come from everywhere at once—the sky, the water, the swaying trees.

"Redcrop? Is that you?"

The brush across the river rustled, and Flame Carrier took a tentative step toward it. "Who's there?"

An odd shadow hunched at the edge of the brush, but it didn't move.

Flame Carrier looked behind her at the leaf-covered trail and trees.

Whimpers seeped from the brush, soft and pathetic. Flame Carrier turned back. It sounded like a hurt little girl. Another orphan?

"Child?" Flame Carrier called. "Let me see you? I won't hurt you."

The black shape moved, wavering as if winged and preparing to take flight.

"Don't be afraid. Please, come out." Flame Carrier kept her voice soft and soothing. "You are welcome here."

The shadow blossomed into something tall and dark.

Flame Carrier stopped breathing. She could see a woman's fringed buckskin dress, but long ears and gray fur gleamed in the starlight. The figure wore the mask of the Wolf Katsina. Among their people, only Cloudblower, the sacred Man-Woman, had the right to don that mask. Wolf had led the First People up from the underworlds. He had taught them to make fire, and to hunt. The mask of the Wolf Katsina was the most powerful mask of all. Usually the katsina's soul slept in the mask, but when someone put it on, the soul awoke and stalked the night.

"Cloudblower?" she called. "Is that you? Why are you masked?"

The figure tiptoed toward Flame Carrier. *"I am not Cloudblower. I am the Summoning God. You have been summoned, Grandmother."*

A woman. Her soft voice strained against tears.

Flame Carrier's heart pounded. "What do you want? Who are you?"

"Don't you remember me?"

The katsina tiptoed into the river and waded toward Flame Carrier. Shadows filled the hollows of her eyes, turning them into huge black abysses. In a sobbing voice, the woman mewed, *"Grandmother, I loved you. Why did you hurt me?"*

A haunted sensation tingled through Flame Carrier's body. "Tell me your name, child!"

"You do not remember me?" the woman murmured in a choking voice.

"I remember everything about you. I remember your touch and the sound of your voice when you told me stories at night."

The woman continued wading the river. Flame Carrier had put many children to bed with her stories. Which one might this be?

"Are you one of the Katsinas' People, child? Or—or a member of my old clan? Are you Ant Clan?"

The katsina stepped out of the water with her furred head bowed. The fringed hem of her dress dripped onto the river cobbles, and her soft cries rode the breeze. Like a warrior preparing for one final battle, the woman slowly untied a hafted chert knife from her belt, kissed the glinting blade, then gripped it in a shaking fist.

"What do you want?" Flame Carrier cried, and hurried up the trail as fast as her legs would carry her.

The katsina called, "You do know me! I knew it!"

"I don't know you!" Flame Carrier shouted.

Feet pounded the trail behind Flame Carrier.

As the katsina closed in, Flame Carrier whirled around with her walking stick up to defend herself. "Stop! I don't wish to hurt you, child! Leave me alone!"

Tears glistened in the eye sockets of the mask.

"Oh, Grandmother," she whispered. "I tried not to come here. Father made me. He said you would remember me."

Flame Carrier shook her head, uncertain. The voice did sound familiar, but she couldn't place where she'd heard it. "I do *not* know you!"

The katsina cocked her head one way, then another, as if trying to see Flame Carrier better through the mask's eye holes. She lowered her head like a wolf on a blood trail and a low growl issued from her mouth.

Flame Carrier shouted, *"Water Snake? Obsidian? Anyone! Can anyone hear me? I need help!"*

The katsina came forward, each step placed with care, rustling in the fallen leaves. Her jaw dropped open and sharp teeth shone in the muzzle.

Flame Carrier let out a hoarse cry, and ran, screaming, "Help! Help me!"

She made it to the top of the trail and gathered her strength for the run into the plaza . . .

The katsina leaped on her back and knocked her face-first into the damp autumn leaves. The woman gripped a handful of Flame Carrier's gray hair and twisted her head around to meet her eyes.

"I am Copper Bell, Grandmother," she said, weeping. Slowly, reverently, she pulled a magnificent turquoise pendant from the front of her dress. The wolf dangled before Flame Carrier's eyes, shimmering pale gray in the moonlight. "Please, *please,* remember me, Grandmother!"

Flame Carrier's gaze clung to the wolf, and a sick sensation rushed through her. "Oh, gods, no. You can't be—"

"Yes, you know now, don't you?" the katsina whispered. "You know why you've been summoned."

Flame Carrier wrenched her head free... and screamed.

THE HOARSE SCREAM brought Sylvia bolt upright, gasping and lunging for her aluminum baseball bat. She clutched it to her chest as her foggy brain replayed other screams in other places... and then she placed herself. New Mexico. Pueblo Animas. Field Camp.

"Jesus Christ!" she heard Steve yell. "What was that?"

Sylvia had to swallow her heart before she could find the voice to answer, "If it wasn't you or me..."

She turned her head to the right, toward the camp trailer where Dusty slept, and called, "Yo, Dusty! You all right?"

Silence.

Sylvia blinked in the darkness. One by one she catalogued the night sounds: the whisper of a breeze in the sage; the late season cry of the nightjar; a rustle of leaves behind the camp; and... Something scratched the nylon of her tent, and the hollow sound of gnawing came from the rear pole.

"Stop that !" she hissed, and jabbed her baseball bat into the fiberglass pole. The panicked packrat shinnied down the side of her tent and thrashed away through the grass outside.

Dusty whimpered.

Sylvia leaned forward and unzipped the door to her tent. She cocked her head and heard muffled sounds coming from the camp trailer. Noises like that had two causes. Since Dusty didn't have a woman in there with him, it had to be the second.

"Dusty?" Sylvia's breath frosted in the cold night air. Over her head a thousand stars twinkled. "Wake up! You're having a bad dream!"

Dusty often woke up field camps with his nightmares—but so did she. It was one of the joys they forced other people to share.

Dusty moaned and the camp trailer rocked as he flailed in his sleep.

"Dusty!"

She thought about slinging the baseball bat in his direction, but it would be just her luck to chuck it through the window. Instead, she grabbed up a handful of gravel and pitched it at the aluminum siding.

"Wake up!" she ordered.

She heard him mumble, then he said, *"Shut up, you little son of a bitch."*

Sylvia reconsidered throwing her bat. "Who's a son of a bitch?"

As though not really awake, he said something she couldn't hear, then the trailer squeaked as he turned over, and she caught the words "witch" and *"basilisco."*

In less than ten seconds, he was snoring.

Sylvia rezipped her tent, and pulled her sleeping bag up to her chin.

Out of the darkness, Steve whispered, "Boy, that thing has really got a grip on his subconscious. How many does that make this week?"

For a long time, Sylvia just lay there. Then she said, "Too many. He's starting to worry me."

CHAPTER 9

I STRETCH MY arms to the cold crystalline night, and the gentle breeze that sweeps the desert flaps the brown-and-white turkey feather cape around my naked body.

"I remember everything about you, Grandmother," I say softly. "When I had seen five summers, you told me I would be all right, that I was not alone, because a thousand ancestors slept inside my bones, watching and whispering to me."

The brilliant lavender gleam of dawn enamels the eastern horizon, but straight over my head the strongest of the Evening People continue to sparkle, their bodies pure white against the deep blue sky.

"You told me that I would only be lonely until I learned to crawl inside my own bones and speak with the ancient voices that lived there."

I lower my arms, and expel a breath; it puffs whitely before drifting away on the wind. As I look down, an odd sensation spreads through me.

"Oh, Grandmother, I remember so much."

I grip the old woman's ankles and drag her through the brush toward the river below. Blood-soaked gray hair streams out over her head. Her toothless mouth gapes, and a moan seeps from her lips.

"Shh," I whisper. "We do not wish the others to hear us. The village is less than a half a hand of time away."

To my right, blue smoke rises into the sky. Soon, someone will notice that she is missing. They will mount a search party.

Cottonwoods line the river, their limbs arching over the water like dark twisted arms. Yellow leaves cling to the branches, and I can smell their delicate autumn scent. It is a fragrance I know from my childhood thirty sun cycles ago.

Tears constrict my throat. "I never wished to return here, Grandmother. I tried to stay away. I tried very hard."

The breeze changes, and the stench of her fear fills the predawn morning, smothering the cottonwoods' perfume. I fill my lungs and hold the stench inside me for as long as I can. My heart burns as if it might explode in a shower of bright hot splinters.

The night was long and cold. For both of us.

I gaze at her. A thin veneer of translucent skin clings to her bones. Her chest rises and falls. She is more like an old skeleton than a woman. Her ribs are bars, her hip bones as sharp as knives. Her breasts resemble withered flaps of loose hide. Her face is gone.

I pull her through piles of golden leaves toward the glistening pool at the base of the hill. Three body lengths across, the pool fills a washed-out niche in the riverbank. Purple light twinkles across the pond's surface.

I stop at the edge and gaze down at my watery reflection. The gray fur of my wolf mask shimmers. The ears are pricked as if listening to the soft sounds of daybreak: birds chirping, leaves rustling, water flowing over rocks. I try to see my eyes through the mask's holes, but only black, bottomless darkness looks back at me. Tall and slender, I have seen the passing of thirty-five summers.

As I remove her cape and drop it to the sand, wind chills my naked body. Cold pimples rise on my skin.

The cottonwoods were not here thirty sun cycles ago. There were no trees for a day's walk up or down the Prancing Spirit River. We cut them all down to heat our chambers, cook our food, and fire our pottery. Only when my people moved on did the trees dare to grow again.

My people moved on.

I did not. They left me behind, hoping I would die. I had seen five summers.

I clasp my grandmother's ankles and drag her over the rocks that ring the pool. Her head thumps the stones, producing a dense meaty sound.

"Yes, I remember, Grandmother. I remember being terrified, starving, running from place to place searching for a scrap of food, stealing what I could. Anyone who saw me chased me away. I remember crying until I couldn't breathe."

I step into the pool and pull the old woman in behind me. Icy green water rises to my waist. She floats for several instants as the river swirls and eddies, then it swallows her ruined face.

I let go of her ankles and step back.

Bubbles escape her mouth and perch on the water's surface like glistening eyeballs. Does she feel the cold liquid filling her lungs? For just a moment, I fear she might suddenly awaken and begin to struggle.

I tremble, both from weariness and from seeing her like this. In the newborn light her gray hair swims as if alive.

"I learned to hear the voices, Grandmother. Just as you told me I must. I learned to live inside my bones with them. That's how I survived until he *came for me."*

Father Sun peers over the eastern horizon, and golden light touches the pond. One by one, the bubbles burst, and in their places bloody red flowers bloom.

My eyes widen as I watch each petal unfurl in a single moment of glory before it fades and blends with the water.

I bend over until my eyes almost touch the bloody surface and whisper, "Hello? Are you down there? Can you see me? Let me in."

. . . behind me.

Sandals on dirt.

The footsteps are soft, whispers barely heard. He is the blackness, the animal that has haunted me since my first memories. Like dark wings, he flaps through my nights, his touch feathery, caressing, melting the world. His long white cape sways as he kneels.

The water stirs and flickers.

I wait anxiously for a door to open, for faces to appear beneath the green surface.

I feel the other me *receding, draining away into the dark hole where she lives, and I sink against the bank and wonder where the night went. The sounds of the morning are loud in my ears.*

I blink at the old woman's wide, toothless mouth gaping beneath the water. A sudden rush of bubbles explodes and she flails her arms.

"She's alive!" *I blurt.*

I stare as he removes his sandals and carefully walks barefoot on the stones around the pool. He pulls his deer-bone stiletto from his belt, grabs her hair, and wades into the pool. He tows her to the middle and stabs her over and over. He stabs her so many times that I think it will never end. Five, ten times . . . more. Then he stops, breathing hard, and shoves her away. Before he wades out, he thoroughly washes himself off.

I tilt my head, studying her through the eyeholes of the mask. "I—I thought I knew her, Father. I thought she was the one who cast me out of my mother's clan."

His laughter is velvet on a spiderweb.

"Is she the one, Father?"

My souls seem to be floating above my body. I am shaking from memories that I do not actually remember, but my flesh does. I fear that if I try to move my arms and legs, they will crack and shatter into a thousand pieces. I peer intently at the corpse. "She is, isn't she? I know her. I do. I remember her.*"*

He strokes the locks of long black hair that have escaped my wolf mask and fall down my naked back. I shudder and lean into his touch. The black serpent pendant he carved for me rests warmly between my breasts, cradled in the soft warmth beside the turquoise wolf, both so close to my heart.

"I wish you hadn't brought us back here, Father. You know I hate this place. Since we arrived, I've heard her hissing at me every moment."

He lightly draws his fingers down my throat.

I stand for a long while staring down at the water, watching the twinkles of morning that reflect in the dead woman's eyes. They are very beautiful.

"I'm sure she's the one, Father. Why won't you answer me?"

I hear him rise. He takes his hand away.

"I'm sorry," I whisper. "I know we should go before they come. I left your soul pot on the bank above. It's your favorite, the one with the Flute Player painted in the bottom. Let me get it."

I wade out of the pond and reach for her cape where it rests on the rocks. The turkey feathers are soft against my skin, and fragrant, as though she kept her cape near her herb pots.

I walk up the hill in a sun-drenched dream.

CHAPTER 10

EVENING FELL OVER the desert in soft lavender veils and drained the golden hues from the broken hills. The square-topped buttes turned the color of a mourning dove's wings. Scatters of yellow fell from the cottonwoods that lined the Animas River. In the distance, cattle lowed.

Sitting atop the rubble overlooking the partially excavated tower kiva, Dusty propped his elbows on his knees and watched as sunset streaked the clouds. He wore mud-encrusted cowboy boots and a battered brown cowboy hat. In his hands he cradled a toothless human skull, the bone stained a light shade of umber after centuries in the earth. The wind had cooled, the temperature down into the sixties. He flipped up the collar of his canvas coat.

Beyond the borders of the ruin, his archaeological field crew sat around the nightly campfire. Steve Sanders said something Dusty couldn't hear, and Sylvia Rhone laughed. Steve's rich black skin gleamed in the firelight, contrasting sharply with Sylvia's freckled face. Steve was up from the University of Arizona on the pretext that he was adding to his dissertation research. In reality, he'd caved in to Dale's abject pleading. He had aced his comps last June and just had his dissertation to finish before being awarded his Ph.D.

They'd set up their four green tents in a semicircle around a central fire pit with Dale's old Holiday Rambler camp trailer parked to the west. Along with the small grove of juniper trees behind the camp, it created a decent windbreak. Sunset gleamed off the windshields on the crew vehicles parked in a line behind the tents.

The collapsed walls of the ancient pueblo seemed to glow an unearthly blue in the twilight. Two-by-two-meter excavation units created black squares in the tower kiva. When they'd quit work at sunset, they'd covered the units with black plastic and lined the edges with every heavy object within reach: shovels, picks, screens, rocks. The idea was to keep the bone from drying and splitting.

The bone. God, they had bone everywhere. It covered the kiva bottom in a layer twenty centimeters deep, not a surface scatter like he'd first thought. Their finds today had included the elaborately etched skull in his lap, the skull of a girl, and a handful of what appeared to be ceremonial Mesa Verde black-on-white potsherds.

He looked down at the skull. The delicacy of the brow probably meant it had belonged to a woman, though he couldn't be certain. He was an archaeologist, not a physical anthropologist. He didn't see as much in bones as other people did. Artifacts told him a whole lot more about a people's behavior than skeletons.

He tipped the skull to study the quarter-sized hole that gaped in the middle of the left coronal suture. Someone had drilled seven small holes, etched the spaces between them with a stone tool, then lifted out the circlet of skull. A surgical incision, clean, precise. Four lightning bolts zigzagged out from the hole. In modern-day Puebloan mythology, lightning bolts signified spiritual power.

Metal clanked and Dusty saw Steve empty a can of something into the big stew pot hanging on the tripod at the edge of the flames. When the wind gusted just right, he could smell coffee perking.

For the tenth time, he stared at the address he'd written on the front of the envelope, and his gut squirmed: *Dr. Maureen Cole, Department of Anthropology, McMaster University, Hamilton, Ontario, Canada.* Her face drifted through his mind, straight nose, glinting black eyes, full lips, long black hair.

Dusty folded his arms across his chest like a shield.

Sending a letter was the coward's way out.

Dale stepped out of the camp trailer and walked carefully down the trail that led to the ruin. He wore a tattered gray canvas coat that Dusty had seen on a hundred excavations. It had to be thirty years old. White insulation peeked through the holes in the elbows, and there were numerous rips around the cuffs. Dale picked his way, step by step, over the irregular rock, and paused two paces from Dusty to stare down into the excavation. A thatch of wiry gray hair stuck out beneath the brim of his fedora.

In his seventies, Dale was still fit. He had worked with the best, Neil Judd, Paul S. Martin, Harold Colton, Emil Haury, and the other giants in the discipline. Though a professor emeritus, he just couldn't stay away from the field. His love had always been dirt archaeology. Dusty supposed he would eventually die on a site somewhere.

"I've just been on the phone to the Wirths. They want some photographs of the kiva bone bed. Apparently, they're going to start planning their subdivision."

Dusty looked up. "Oh, great. What do you think of all this? An archaeology subdivision?"

It sounded like Dusty's worst nightmare. He could just see the owners out with their shovels, destroying every subtle bit of data the site contained to get to the best artifacts—which they would probably sell on the open market to people who could care less who the Anasazi were or what had happened to them.

Dale tipped his fedora back on his head. "To tell you the truth, William, if it saves one archaeological site from destruction, more power to them."

"You think this will *save* sites? And Sylvia calls me an optimist."

Dale paused. "William, the political entanglements of archaeology in this country today are forcing more and more landowners to bulldoze sites. Perhaps subdivisions like this will help to educate people. I think it's worth a try."

"Yeah, I suppose," Dusty answered. "But what about us? I mean, if it comes down to a choice between professional ethics and the Wirths' financial interest, what do we do?"

"We do what's right for the archaeology, William." Dale's bushy eyebrows arched. "But I think the Wirths are genuinely interested in making archaeology an integral part of their subdivision here."

"Right." Dusty looked down at the skull in his hands. He tried to imagine the old woman's response to the knowledge that people in the future were going to try and make money off the ruins of her culture. Could she even have conceived such desecration?

"What have you got there?" Dale indicated the skull.

"I think she's an old woman."

"And that?" He pointed to the hole. "Trephination?"

"Maybe. I can't tell if it was done when she alive, or after she died."

Dale glanced from the skull to Dusty. "I know someone who could tell." He paused, trying to read Dusty's expression. "You could call her, William."

Dusty gut tightened. "She's in the middle of her semester, Dale. She has classes, students, all that academic bull that lab rats insist on. But I thought maybe I'd write her."

"She's tenured," Dale said mildly. "You can bet that if Maureen Cole, one of the world's foremost physical anthropologists, walks into the dean's office and says she needs to leave for a couple of weeks to conduct research, he'll grant it."

"Just like that?"

"He's no fool. Maureen could have a position at any university in North America."

"So, why does she stay at McMaster? There are bigger, more prestigious places."

Dale sighed and kicked halfheartedly at a square piece of sandstone. "Firstly, McMaster is an excellent school; but more important, her house is there. John is there . . . if only in her memories and dreams."

Dusty looked out at the river, dusky now, the yellowing leaves white in the growing darkness. "Must have been quite a guy."

"John was brilliant. As the old saying goes, they broke the mold when they made him. You would have liked him. He was different from you, quieter, reserved, but he had a special quality that made him stand out in a crowd." Dale handed him a cell phone from his back pocket. "I'd imagine she's home about now. I used my Sharpie pen to write her number on the top of the phone."

Dusty stared at it. "What should I tell her?"

"Tell her about the skeletal material in the kiva, William. Tell her what you think happened here. Just dial and press the send button."

Dusty shied away from the phone. "It would be a lot more effective if the legendary Dale Emerson Robertson called. You have pull. I'm just a lowly field archaeologist."

Dale's brows lowered, and Dusty wished he could take the words back. They'd sounded cowardly, and Dale's expression let him know it.

"As I've told you before, William, not every woman anthropologist is your mother. You *can* trust a few of them." Dale jammed the phone into Dusty's hand before he walked off for camp.

"And as I've told you before," Dusty called after him, "my mother has nothing to do with this!"

Dusty's mother, the great Dr. Ruth Ann Sullivan, was a cultural anthropologist at Harvard. She'd abandoned the family when Dusty was six years old. His father, Samuel Stewart, had fallen to pieces. He'd tried to commit suicide three times that first year, and Dusty had been there watching each time, screaming and crying, trying to jerk the gun, or knife, or bottle of pills, from his father's hand.

Dale had been the one to take action. It had broken Dale's heart, but he'd committed his best friend to an asylum. Dale went through all the family he could find, but no one wanted Dusty, so he'd raised Dusty himself. Thank God. Dusty had spent most of his life in archaeological field camps, digging during the day, and at night listening to the best archaeologists in the world argue about ancient cultures. He'd been a very lucky kid, despite a tough start in life.

Dusty slipped the phone into his coat pocket and lifted the skull to gaze into the woman's empty eye sockets. The bone gleamed softly. "Well, one thing for sure, Maureen would be able to look at you and tell exactly who you were and probably even why someone drilled that hole in your head."

Sylvia stepped away from the campfire and cupped a hand to her mouth. *"Hey, Dusty! Dinner's hot!"*

He waved to let her know he'd heard.

"Be honest," he whispered to himself. "You need her here, you know you do."

More interesting, perhaps, was that he actually wanted her here.

Which scared the holy hell out of him. Every time he got close to a woman, he turned into a man he didn't know. He said and did outrageous things he didn't mean and generally made an ass of himself. A normal man liked it when a woman looked up at him with unabashed adoration in her eyes. Those looks opened frightening doors in Dusty's mind. As the spooks drifted up to stare him in the eyes, Jack the Ripper's story started sounding sympathetic.

Dusty angrily clutched the skull to his chest and walked down the hill. The spindly arms of sagebrush and greasewood scraped against his faded blue jeans.

He walked into the orange halo of the firelight and said, *"Hola, amigos."* His bearded face tingled from the sudden warmth.

Sylvia looked up with bright green eyes. The wind had worked brown strands loose from beneath her gray wool cap, and fluttered them around her freckled face. The cuffs of her faded denim coat had frayed. She gestured to the skull. "What did Yoric reveal to you about his life?"

"I think he's a she."

"Okay, what did Yoricelle tell you about her life?"

"She told me she's hungry. What's for dinner?"

Sylvia looked at him from one narrowed eye. She always evaluated his moods before she laid things on him, probably because they shared similar wounds; they'd both suffered through difficult childhoods, though Sylvia's had been much worse than Dusty's.

Sylvia said, "I wagered you'd eat crow and invite Maureen to come. Steve said you'd rather starve to death. I've got ten bucks bet. Spit it out. Which is it?"

Dusty gently placed the skull into the wooden box on the examination table beside Dale's trailer, picked up the lawn chair, and set it in front of the fire. A loaf of rye bread nestled on the hearthstones, warming. He leaned over the pot and sniffed.

"Good God, not Dinty Moore's beef stew again. Doesn't anybody in this camp know how to make burritos?"

"Sure," Sylvia said, "but me and Steve have to work in the same pit tomorrow. We decided to spare each other the consequences."

Dusty swiveled around in his chair, opened the white lid on the red ice chest, and searched around until he found a cold bottle of Guinness stout. The opener hung from the chest by a string. Dusty flipped off the cap and clamped his mouth over the top of the bottle. Rich brown foam bubbled up. It tasted heavenly.

"Thank God for the Irish."

Sylvia turned to Steve and gave him a knowing look. "He's stalling."

Steve sipped from his steaming coffee cup. His ebony face gleamed. "I noticed." He looked like a young Denzel Washington, his black hair closely clipped, his eyes the color of antique mahogany. He'd buttoned the collar of his tan coat around his throat. "It's not going to get any easier," Steve reminded. "If I were you, I'd just make the decision and leave the rest to the gods."

"The gods?" Dusty answered incredulously. "You can't trust them."

Dusty took a long drink of his Guinness and fixed Sylvia with a curious look. "She wrote you a couple of weeks ago, didn't she? What did she say?"

Firelight glimmered from Sylvia's freckles. "Not much. It was like she was testing the water: 'How's Dusty?' 'What are you working on?' 'Seen any flying saucers lately?' You know, chitchat kind of stuff."

"Wonder why she never writes me."

Sylvia squinted. "Do you ever write her? Figure it out, Einstein."

Dusty turned his bottle in his hands. "Okay. Guilty as charged."

His gaze drifted around the camp, landing on the Coleman lantern on the opposite side of the fire, the wooden box marked TRASH, and the array of ice chests, foot lockers, and green ammo boxes stacked in front of the tents. He could hear Dale rattling dishes in the camp trailer to his left.

"Did you ask her to come out?" Sylvia asked.

"I haven't decided. We're not exactly best buddies."

Sylvia picked up a bag of those awful little cheezy fishes. Her favorites. Around a crunchy mouthful, she said, "If she wants to come, we could use her."

Dusty tucked his Guinness between his knees and pulled the cellular phone from his coat pocket. Sylvia and Steve watched him with curious eyes.

Steve said, "What's the verdict?"

Dusty tossed the phone to Sylvia. "I'll tear up my letter, if you'll call her and ask."

"Wow," Sylvia said in awe. "Another example of Dusty the Lionhearted." She tossed it back. "How about if I tear up your letter, while you call?"

Dusty caught the phone and scowled at it.

Sylvia tipped her head and said, "If she can come, ask her to meet us at the bar at the Durango Doubletree Hotel. It's nice."

Dusty's stomach muscles knotted. He stared at the number scrawled across the top of the phone, then punched in the numbers with one eye closed.

Sylvia whooped and stuck out her hand. Steve groaned, pulled his wallet from his back pocket, and stuffed a ten-dollar bill into Sylvia's hand. She grinned.

While the phone rang, Dusty waved a finger at the bowls. "Let's eat. My upset stomach can use something else to chew on."

CHAPTER 11

"GRANDMOTHER?"

Even before the sound of her voice died away, Redcrop knew something was wrong.

She and the Matron lived in three interconnected chambers on the east side of Longtail village. The rooms, eerily quiet and cold, had an ominous stillness.

Flame Carrier always awoke long before dawn and by now had a fire going and food cooking.

Redcrop pulled on her moccasins and slipped a doehide cape over her blue sleep shirt. Long black hair tumbled down her back.

She ducked through the doorway into the large chamber where Flame Carrier slept. The coals in the fire pit had burned down to gray ash. Morning light filtered around the door curtain and striped the room.

She bent to feel Flame Carrier's blankets. Icy cold.

As she straightened, Redcrop caught her reflection in the pyrite mirror on the wall. Her large black eyes shone like polished stones. She brushed at her hair, smoothing the worst tangles. She had seen fourteen summers, most of them as Flame Carrier's slave. She and her mother had been captured in a raid when she was less than a sun cycle old, but she had never felt like a slave. Flame Carrier treated her as a granddaughter, caring for her when she fell ill, giving her beautiful clothing and jewelry, loving her. Flame Carrier was the only mother Redcrop had really known.

"Matron?"

She shoved the hide door curtain aside and stepped out into the village plaza.

She couldn't see Father Sun, but she knew that beyond the distant bluff he'd crested the horizon. The sky glowed a pale luminous gold. Shadows filled every undulation, turning the rolling hills around the village into a patchwork of light and dark.

People had just begun to rise. Two women hunched over the plaza fire pit, arranging kindling. In the distance, three boys trotted along the shore of the river. Probably Little Calf, eight summers old, and his younger brothers. Their soft laughter carried on the morning wind.

Redcrop scanned the plaza for Flame Carrier. Longtail village spread around her. Two stories tall, it contained two hundred and ninety rooms and stretched seventy-five body lengths long and about thirty wide. An old place, half the chambers had collapsed and brimmed with fallen roof poles and weeds. They could not be entered. The Katsinas' People had been working tirelessly, cleaning, replastering, and repainting the rooms where they lived.

Redcrop shielded her eyes against the slanting morning light and turned to look at the tower kiva, which formed the central portion of the E. The stocky warrior, Hummingbird, crouched on the flat roof. He stood guard every night. Short and built like a tree stump, he had an oval face with amused brown eyes. Instead of the usual bun most warriors wore at the base of the skull, a waist-length black braid draped the front of his painted buckskin cape.

Redcrop cupped a hand to her mouth and called, "Good day to you, Hummingbird! Have you seen the Matron?"

The warrior shook his head. "No, why?"

"She was gone when I woke."

Hummingbird propped his war club on his muscular shoulder. "I saw no one leave your chamber, Redcrop. Do you wish me to help you search for her?"

They'd been raided less than half a moon ago. She did not wish to take any of the guards from their positions until it became necessary.

"Not yet, but I thank you. I will look for her for a time first."

Hummingbird lifted a hand and nodded.

Redcrop walked across the plaza toward the two women standing before the fire. Flames crackled and leaped, sending up a haze of sparks. The rich scent of burning cedar filled the cold morning air.

"Good day, Obsidian." She bowed to the cloaked woman on her left, then to the skinny, white-haired elder on the right. "And to you, Matron Crossbill. Have you seen Matron Flame Carrier?"

Crossbill tossed another juniper log onto the flames and brushed the duff from her knobby hands onto the red blanket tied around her shoulders. She had a deeply wrinkled face. "No, child, but I haven't been up long. When did she leave?"

"I don't know, Elder. Some time in the night."

Obsidian turned, and her dark blue hood rippled around her exotic slanting eyes. A triangular face was the mark of great beauty among their people. Her wide cheekbones narrowed to a pointed chin. The rich spicy fragrance of blazing star petals scented her body and clothing. Crossbill's clan, the Longtail Clan, whispered that Obsidian had flown down from the skyworld as a meteorite. They said her mother had caught the meteorite, and when she'd opened her hands, a baby girl lay there. Redcrop believed it. Only one of the gods could be that stunningly beautiful.

"I haven't seen her this morning." Obsidian leaned forward to pull a long branch from the woodpile. Wind flapped her cloak, revealing the precious stones that sparkled on her wrists and ankles, even in her hair. "Have you looked behind the village for the Matron? The War Chief shot a deer this morning. Flame Carrier may be Singing the animal's soul to the afterlife."

"Oh, I didn't know the War Chief had returned. Thank you."

Redcrop trotted toward the southeastern corner of the village, passed the turkey pen, and headed north along the towering eastern wall of the village. When she rounded the northeastern corner, she looked westward, down the long rear wall. Five body lengths away, Straighthorn and War Chief Browser knelt over a young doe.

"A pleasant morning to you, War Chief," Redcrop said. "When did you arrive home?"

Browser smiled, but he looked tired. Crescents darkened the skin beneath his soft brown eyes, and his chin-length black hair hung limply, as though it needed washing. He had a round face, with thick black brows and a flat nose. The War Chief had endured much pain in his life, and she could see it in the deep lines around his eyes and mouth. Blood stained his elkhide jacket. Dried blood. Had there been a fight at Aspen village?

He said, "Catkin and I returned just after midnight. But I couldn't sleep. I was up early this morning. Would you like to help us with the deer?"

As a slave she could not refuse, no matter how much she longed to find Flame Carrier. She trotted forward and knelt across the deer from Straighthorn. "What do you need me to do?"

Straighthorn smiled at her and Redcrop smiled back. He had a thin face, with a hooked nose, and brown eyes much too old and wise for the sixteen summers he had seen. He wore a threadbare red cape. A braided leather headband held his long black hair in place. They'd become best friends and often stayed up late at night talking of their dreams and fears.

He had been deathly ill when the men of Longtail village left and never returned. He'd lost his father and brother. His wife, Siskin, had died a few days after Straighthorn had recovered from the fever. He now grieved alone in a small room near the tower kiva.

Straighthorn stroked the deer's coat and whispered, "Thank you for your life, mother. We will use it wisely, I promise." He tipped his face to the morning sky, and Sang:

"Come Deer Above,
Come for your daughter's soul,
Take her running beneath the waters of the sacred lake,
And along the starry trail to the Land of the Dead.
Come Deer Above,
Guide your precious daughter's soul home."

Redcrop lifted her voice to join Straighthorn's,

"Come Deer Above, come for your daughter's soul . . ."

War Chief Browser held a white clay pipe to his mouth, inhaled tobacco smoke, and blew it over the deer's hair, preparing and sanctifying her for the long journey to the afterlife. Browser handed the pipe to Straighthorn, then untied a small buckskin pouch from his belt.

"Here," he said, and gave the pouch to Redcrop. "I've already dug a burial pit for the doe's organs."

Browser lifted the bloody lungs and bladder and carried them to a small hole about thirty hands away. As he gently lowered the organs into the grave, he said, "Please sprinkle them with the strong cornmeal while I gather the rest of her organs."

"Yes, War Chief."

Redcrop tugged the laces open. Strong cornmeal was a powerful offering to Our Grandmother Earth. It contained the most cherished things in the Straight Path Nation: cornmeal, ground turquoise, and powdered white shell from the great ocean in the west.

Redcrop reverently sprinkled the organs with the meal, then used her right hand to push the dirt back into the grave.

Browser returned with the stomach and intestines. He placed them on top of the grave, and said, "For our relatives, the Raw Persons, mountain lion, coyote, bobcat, and wolf, so they will know we have not forgotten them."

Redcrop petted the organs, and whispered. "We have not forgotten you, Raw People."

"Thank you, Redcrop." He rose to his feet and smiled down at her. "If you will come back with me, I will slice off a thick steak for you and Matron Flame Carrier."

As he started back for the deer, he drew a long black chert knife from his belt.

Redcrop trotted at his heels. "War Chief? Have you seen the Matron? I'm looking for her."

He stopped. "Is she missing?"

Straighthorn looked up suddenly. "What's wrong?"

"Well, I—I don't know," Redcrop said self-consciously. She was a slave;

she should not be bothering anyone until she knew for certain the Matron was in trouble. "When I awoke, she was gone. It may be nothing."

Browser's thick black brows drew together. He stood quietly, but his gaze moved over the landscape as if searching for a hidden enemy.

"She may have just gone down to the river to fill a pitcher with water," Straighthorn said. He inhaled smoke from the pipe and blew it into the deer's nostrils, purifying the breath-path for her soul to leave her body. "Or perhaps she decided to offer her morning prayers from one of the high points around the village."

"Possibly," Browser said. He knelt and skinned the hide back from the deer's left hindquarter, then sawed off a thick steak. As he handed it to Redcrop, he stared into her eyes and she could feel his fear. It left a queasy feeling in the pit of her stomach. Browser said, "I will be a few moments longer, then I will help you search for her."

"Thank you, War Chief."

Redcrop couldn't take her eyes from his. Over the past few moons, Flame Carrier had been speaking more and more of what would happen to the Katsinas' People when she was gone, of who would take over and become the new Matron, of which villages they would seek out after they'd finished repairing this one—as if she knew she were dying and wanted to prepare them for the inevitable.

Is that what she'd done? Gone off by herself to die?

Tears blurred Redcrop's eyes. The warm steak in her hands shook.

Browser stood up and tenderly touched her hair. "Don't worry. There may have been a village crisis that none of us knows about, a child who sickened in the night or a difficult birthing that required her presence. Why don't you return to the plaza to wait for me. You will probably see her before I get back, but if not we will find her."

"Yes, War Chief." Redcrop held tight to the sweet-smelling steak. "Thank you, and thank you, Straighthorn."

"The joy is mine," he said, and smiled. He'd tied his leather headband on the side, and the ends flapped in the breeze.

As she headed back to the plaza, Redcrop's heart started to pound. She broke into a run.

BROWSER BENT DOWN to clean his knife in the sand, but caught the look of yearning Straighthorn cast after Redcrop.

Straighthorn whispered, "Sometimes I think I will die before she becomes a woman."

"It won't be long now, Straighthorn."

Straighthorn shook his head. "It's strange. I don't recall suffering this terrible longing before my first marriage. Did you suffer this way before yours?"

Images of Hophorn's beautiful face formed behind Browser's eyes, but she had been his lover, not his wife. His stomach knotted. "No. I had another friend before my marriage. She kept me company."

His mother had forced him to join with Ash Girl, though she knew he loved Hophorn. At the end, he and Ash Girl had hated each other.

Straighthorn said, "I pray nothing has happened to the Matron. It would be like a lance in Redcrop's heart."

Grateful for the change of subject, Browser answered, "In all our hearts."

Browser had never seen a warrior with such keen abilities to sense other people's emotions. The Longtail elders often teased Straighthorn for stepping between angry people and trying to soothe their hurt feelings. He'd become known as a peacemaker—though the term wasn't always meant fondly. Many of the warriors considered him fainthearted. Even Browser had to admit that Straighthorn's timidity often annoyed him.

Browser stroked the deer's side. "It may be nothing, Straighthorn, though it is unusual. Flame Carrier almost never varies her daily routine. She rises, cooks breakfast for herself and Redcrop, then joins the people in the plaza to help plan the day's chores. If she was not there when Redcrop wakened, she left very early, and that is curious."

"Perhaps bodily needs?" Straighthorn gestured awkwardly.

"Probably." Browser slipped his knife back into his leather belt sheath. "Let me help you lift the doe. We'll carry her into the plaza, and then I'll accompany Redcrop on her search."

"Perhaps we should organize a search party?"

"If Redcrop and I do not find her in the next half a hand of time, that is exactly what I will do, but let's not worry anyone else until that time comes."

"Yes, War Chief."

Browser knelt and picked the deer up by the two front legs. Straighthorn lifted her back legs. They carried the doe around the northeastern corner of the village onto the trail that led to the plaza.

Sunlight glittered through the yellow cottonwood leaves, scattering their path with wavering diamonds. Someone had started breakfast. Roasting corn cakes flavored with peppery beeweed scented the air.

Straighthorn said, "How was Aspen village? Since you are home, I assume it was just a scare."

Browser answered, "Once I've spoken with the elders, I'll ask that they call a village council meeting. That way everyone can hear at once."

"Oh, yes, of course. Forgive me."

Browser scanned the high points around the village, then traced the shadowed drainages that cut the tan-and-gray hillsides. He saw nothing out of the ordinary, but there could still be someone out there, watching them. The last attack, half a moon ago, had been swift and brutal. The warriors had come up the river drainage during the night. When they'd launched their attack just before dawn, there had been only a few people up to kill, four guards and three old women. They'd hit the food storage rooms that lined the plaza, grabbed several baskets of corn, bags of dried beans, and rice grass seeds, then raced away before Browser, half-asleep, had even made it into the plaza. He'd mounted a war party and pursued the invaders, but lost them in the rocks a day's walk to the south.

Eight people stood near the plaza fire, including three of the most respected village elders: the Longtail Clan Matron, Crossbill; Cloudblower, the sacred Man-Woman; and old Springbank. Springbank had seen sixty-five summers. He had a long, age-spotted nose and wrinkled lips that sunk in over his toothless gums. A few white hairs dotted his freckled scalp. Springbank smiled, elbowed the two young warriors standing next to him, Skink and Water Snake, and pointed to the deer. People turned to look.

Browser's steps faltered when he noticed that Obsidian also stood in the crowd. Straighthorn gave Browser an uncomfortable glance, and Browser continued on.

A smile turned Obsidian's lips when she saw him. He lowered his gaze and watched his feet. Something about her disturbed him. From the first instant he'd met her, he'd had a feeling that he'd known her long ago, but couldn't place where or when.

They carried the deer to the edge of the fire and eased her to the ground. People encircled them, smiling, waiting for a thick slice of venison.

Browser said, "Do you need my help skinning her, Straighthorn?"

"No, War Chief, thank you." He pulled a stone knife from his belt. "You have more important duties. Besides, I'm sure I can find all the help I need."

"I will help you," Springbank said, and hobbled forward with his toothless mouth open in a grin. "Perhaps you will grant me a piece of the tenderloin."

"Gladly, Elder." Straighthorn smiled.

Browser searched the gathering for Redcrop. She stood almost hidden behind Obsidian. He glimpsed her long tangled black hair hanging down her back and strode forward.

"War Chief?" Cloudblower excused herself from the discussion and caught up with Browser. "A moment?"

"Of course, Elder."

"I just heard that Flame Carrier is missing."

"As did I."

Forty summers old, Cloudblower had long, gray-streaked black hair, graceful brows, and a sharply pointed nose. Though Cloudblower had a male body, she had fémale souls, and dressed as such. Long fringes dangled from the sleeves and hem of her finely tanned doehide dress. She had knotted a yellow-and-brown blanket around her shoulders.

Cloudblower whispered, "Do you fear something's wrong?"

"No. For now I am just curious as to her whereabouts."

Browser continued toward Redcrop with Cloudblower at his side.

Cloudblower looked at him with worried brown eyes. She said, "How is Aspen village?"

"I haven't reported to the Matron yet, Elder. After I have spoken with her, I will be glad to answer all of your questions."

Cloudblower must have heard something in his voice. She gripped Browser's shoulder and panic lit her eyes. "Is Eagle Hunter alive?"

Browser hesitated. He saw Obsidian watching him and made a point of scanning the faces of the people around her. "I vow that I will speak with you about this *later*, Elder."

Cloudblower held his gaze for a time, obviously longing to ask more, but said, "I will be waiting for you after you have informed the Matron."

"I will come directly to you."

Redcrop stepped away from Obsidian and called, "Are you ready, War Chief?"

Browser nodded. "Yes. I thought we would search down by the—"

"I'm going with you," Cloudblower said, and began tying the laces on the front of her cape.

"Please remain here, Cloudblower. I do not wish to alarm people. If we both rush off, it might cause speculation. Redcrop and I will search. If we do not find her, we will return and seek the help of others. It would help if you would search the village while Redcrop and I search the sacred places, the hilltops, and shrines."

Cloudblower shook her head as though it pained her, but she said, "I will, of course, work where you need me."

"I'm grateful, Elder."

Cloudblower bowed to him and hurried for the ladder that led up to the second story near the tower kiva.

Redcrop tugged at Browser's sleeve. "War Chief? Please, I—"

Obsidian stepped toward them, filling the space Cloudblower had left open, and Browser stiffened.

To say that her enormous eyes were brown would have been like describing the inside of a seashell as white. In the gleaming rays of dawn, her eyes shone with a pearlescent golden fire. She had a slender, shapely nose, a pointed chin, and lips that seemed to beckon.

"Did you wish to speak with me, Obsidian?"

She pulled her dark blue hood back, and a thick wealth of black hair tumbled out. Long loops of jet beads flashed from her ears. Browser's gaze instinctively dropped to the sun-bronzed tops of her breasts and the large turquoise bird pendant that rested there. He had to force his gaze back to her eyes, but he did not know which threatened him more.

"I saw the Matron last night," Obsidian whispered.

Redcrop's mouth gaped. "Why didn't you tell me earlier when I first asked?"

Obsidian didn't even look at the slave girl. Her eyes remained locked with Browser's.

He said, "At what time?"

"About midnight. She left her chamber and walked straight down to the river." Wind fluttered hair around her face, tangling it with her eyelashes. She brushed it away with a bejeweled brown hand.

"Did you speak with her?"

"No. I was standing high up on the tower kiva. I just saw her leave."

Browser cocked his head. "What were you doing up at midnight, Obsidian?"

"Water Snake was standing guard. He valued my company."

The way she said "company" told Browser more than he wished to know. Redcrop ducked her head as if embarrassed.

Browser said, "If you saw our Matron go to the river, did you see her return?"

"No, but I was only out for a hand of time. I left when Hummingbird came to relieve Water Snake. Perhaps you should ask him—"

"I asked already," Redcrop broke in, "when I first got up. Hummingbird told me he had not seen the Matron."

The soft warmth in Obsidian's eyes struck Browser like a physical blow. He folded his arms over his heart to protect himself. Nine moons ago, he'd lost everyone and everything he loved—his son, his wife, his beautiful Hophorn. Loneliness stalked him like a lion. It made it more difficult that Obsidian seemed to know and used it against him.

In a soft, intimate voice, Obsidian said, "I hope you find the Matron soon, War Chief."

"We will, Obsidian."

Browser turned to Redcrop. "Perhaps we should search the river, Redcrop. That's where the Matron was last seen heading."

"Yes, please, let's hurry."

She marched forward very quickly, and Browser had to trot to catch up.

"Allow me to lead the way," he said, and smiled as he walked out in front of her. "I think my eyes may be a little sharper than yours when it comes to spotting enemy warriors hidden in the brush."

"Oh, I'm sorry." She fell in line behind him. "I did not think of that."

He looked back at her. Redcrop walked with her head down and her fists knotted. "And stay close to me."

"Yes. I—I will, War Chief."

CHAPTER 12

DR. MAUREEN COLE sat on the edge of the table beside the lectern and straightened her tan wool sweater over her crisp brown slacks. She'd clipped her long black hair up in back. As she pressed the button that projected a slide onto the screen, she peered out at the bright eyes of the students in her Introductory Physical Anthropology class. Well, mostly bright eyes. On her far left, Stephen Willson slumped in his chair, sound asleep. He'd been snoring off and on for the past forty-five minutes.

Maureen picked up her laser pointer and shone the red dot on the slide of the bones. "What you see here is an adult female, age twenty-two. She was recovered in an excavation in New Mexico last year. Her bones tell us a very interesting story. The scarring on her pubis indicates that she had at least one child. She stood one meter forty-eight. She broke her right wrist when she was a child. I can tell you for a fact that her diet consisted almost entirely of corn. She was anemic when she died, suffering from extrapulmonary tuberculosis, and, even more interesting, she was murdered."

Even Willson woke up at that. He stared wide-eyed at the skull. Maureen moved her pointer to the dent on the side of the woman's skull. "That is the blow that killed her. Probably delivered by a right-handed individual with a stone-headed war club. So, you see, just a cursory inspection of the woman's skeleton tells us a great deal about her, even though she lived almost eight hundred years ago."

"But . . ." Karen Jones sat up in her chair and brushed blond hair behind her ear. She wore a black turtleneck sweater. "There are a number of other dents in her head, Dr. Cole. What does that mean?"

Maureen looked up at the cranial depression fractures that covered the woman's skull. "What do you think it means, Karen?"

Karen tilted her head thoughtfully. "If you ask me, it looks like she was a battered woman."

Maureen smiled. "Very good."

Her students shifted when the door at the rear of the room opened, and the department secretary, Nora Lander, walked in and checked the clock on the back wall. The students checked it, too. Three minutes left.

Maureen said, "Okay. On the final exam, I will expect you to speculate about why this woman was murdered. Who hit her? What was her probable station in life? Why did they strike her? I'll also expect you to describe in detail the test I ran that allowed me to prove her diet consisted almost entirely of corn. Any questions?"

Somebody called, "Her diet was corn because she didn't have a Tim Horton's close!"

The bell rang and notebooks closed in a flurry of pages. Students stood up and gathered their coats, backpacks, purses, and other belongings. As they shuffled toward the door, conversations broke out.

Maureen walked around behind the table for her buffalo-hide purse and black down coat.

Through the narrow aluminum-framed windows to her right, she could see snow falling over the McMaster campus. Steam curled from the silver vents on the building rooftops. When she'd arrived at the university this morning, the temperature had been four degrees below zero Centigrade. It was supposed to hit ten below by the time she left the physical anthropology lab tonight.

Nora waited until the flood of students passed, then came forward with a letter in her hand. An attractive woman in her mid-twenties, she had short brown hair and a pointed nose.

"How is everything going, Nora?" Maureen asked as she hitched her purse onto her shoulder.

"Oh, I'm fine. My biggest worry is getting my ex to pay half the cost of fixing the furnace. Yours, it would seem, is getting packed. The dean's approved your leave and this came in on the fax." She handed a letter to Maureen. "I have to admit, when Dale Emerson Robertson makes a request, things happen."

Maureen took the letter.

"Thanks, Nora."

"Great! Have a nice trip, Dr. Cole."

Maureen nodded and watched Nora walk toward the exit.

She opened the envelope and pulled out the fax. Quick and to the point, it explained that her flights had been booked, and all she needed to do was pick up an E ticket at the United counter in Toronto. An additional note had been scrawled across the bottom of the page. She had to tip it sideways to read it: *"I'll meet you at the Doubletree Hotel bar at 9:00 P.M. on the 20th. Bring your own tent."*

For Stewart, that was an epic. She refolded the letter and started for the door. Her brown boots clacked hollowly on the floor.

"I don't know about this, Stewart," she whispered to herself. "I hope we don't kill each other."

Maureen walked out of the room and strode down the long white corridor that led to the P.A. laboratory. Students rushed past, moving from one class to another.

At the last site she'd worked on in New Mexico, she and Stewart had almost come to blows over a mass grave of women and children. The victims had been clubbed in the head repeatedly, but all of the cranial depression fractures had healed, barring the last one, which had killed them. After extensive excavation and analysis, she'd discovered a pattern to the burials. It wasn't an ordinary mass grave where the women and children had been struck in the heads haphazardly, as slaves, or other second-class citizens would have been. No, this was something far more sinister—the work of an ancient serial murderer, a madman who had used a club to systematically test brain function. They'd excavated eleven women and children, but she'd felt almost certain there had been more bodies buried in that mass grave. They'd barely scratched the surface of the site when Indian religious fundamentalism had shut down their work. The American government had actually passed a law saying it was sacrilegious to do scientific work when any person of Indian descent considered it against his or her religious beliefs—something the U.S. government would never do for a Christian or Muslim fundamentalist. It was a federally approved form of cultural genocide. If scientists couldn't determine who and what the ancient peoples had been, that legacy would be lost forever. Apparently, that was what the U.S. government wanted. It was just another way of killing Indian culture by taking away their ability to know their own past. It made it very difficult for a physical anthropologist from anywhere else in the world to want to work in America. Especially a Seneca physical anthropologist.

Though Maureen's father had been White, her mother had been a full-blooded Seneca. She'd raised Maureen as a devout Catholic, but insisted she learn about her own Iroquois heritage as well. By the time Maureen was thirteen, she was skilled at pottery making, porcupine quillwork, beadwork, basketry, even bow hunting, skinning and tanning the hides she harvested. She'd gone off into the forest alone for days at a time to listen to the animals, to study their habits. That curiosity and independence had served her well when she'd entered college at McGill University in Montreal. She'd excelled in the sciences of physiology, chemistry, and anatomy. She'd also been a radical student, a hothead who had worked hard to get the government to establish an aboriginal people's homeland in Canada. If Quebec deserved a separate identity because they had a unique culture, didn't the Native peoples?

"Good morning, Maureen."

She looked up into the eyes of Dr. Philip Morgan. "Hello, Phil. How are you?"

"Smashing, thank you." Six feet three inches tall, with dark brown hair and an olive complexion, he looked Italian, though he'd been born in England. In an insecure gesture, he loosened the black tie at the throat of his gray shirt, and smiled—the smile of a rich fop, a man untroubled by anything except his hairdresser's latest recommendations on style. What else could you expect from an archaeologist who specialized in statistical seriation, whatever that meant.

"I just heard you're leaving town, heading off to the Wild West."

"News travels fast. I just heard myself." Since her husband's death four years ago, Phil had driven her crazy, practically begging her for a date. She added, "I don't expect to be back from New Mexico until next term."

"New Mexico. Really? Those people use AK-47s for home defense, you know?"

She started down the hall again. "Don't worry. I plan on buying my own just to even the odds."

It surprised both of them that she'd said that, especially since she considered weapons to be the spawn of Satan.

"Uh. Right." Phil forced a laugh. "I heard that Dr. Robertson pulled some strings. You're not planning on working with that Stewart fellow again, are you? The Madman of New Mexico? From what I've heard, he's a womanizer, a thug, a thief, and may not even be a member of the human species. More like a gorilla with a trowel."

"Gorillas are highly intelligent, Phil. You might try reading Schaller, Fossey, or some of Penny Patterson's work before you—"

"Before I insult them by comparing them to Stewart?"

She threw him a disgusted look. "He really dislikes being called the Madman of New Mexico, Phil."

"I've heard that he earned that nickname the hard way. By deserving it."

Maureen checked her watch. "I have to go, Phil. Sorry. I've got a graduate seminar scheduled in the lab. It starts in one minute." She broke into a brisk walk.

"Maureen, are you sure about this project?" he asked, matching her stride again.

"Why do you care, Phil?"

"Well, I've heard some things. About Stewart's mother, Ruth Ann Sullivan—you know, the cultural anthropologist from Harvard. Did you know she abandoned the family when Dusty was six years old. Apparently, he wasn't even normal as a child."

"Are you trying to make a point, Phil? That was over thirty years ago."

"Yes, but that's just the beginning of the story. Did you know that after Robertson committed Sam Stewart to a mental institution, he went through all the family he could find, but no one wanted the kid? That should tell you something. No wonder he can't carry on a decent conversation—"

"That's not true, Phil. I've heard Stewart carry on fascinating conversations about archaeology."

His mouth twisted with contempt. "Be serious. The guy's an American *field* archaeologist. If you can name every beer in the world, they'll sacrifice a human child in your honor. Stewart—"

Maureen stopped dead in her tracks and turned to face Phil. "Have you been researching Dusty Stewart, Phil?"

He tried to make light of it. "Given your interest in the Southwest, I thought it prudent to find out more about this madman—"

"For your information, Dusty's nickname is based on his unorthodox field methods, not his father's illness."

She headed for her classroom again, remembering the time she had made the mistake of telling Dusty he was as nutty as his father. The mixture of hurt and fury on Dusty's face had made her want to slither back into the hole she'd crawled out of.

Phil caught up with Maureen. "Aren't you having lunch? I was hoping—"

"Do all archaeologists suffer from attention deficit disorder, Phil? I have a seminar."

He spread his hands in a pleading gesture. "Listen, Maureen, all of this work in the States is interesting, of course, but wouldn't you rather try an exotic location with more complex physical specimens? I know the director of The National Museums of Kenya. He's been begging me to come for years. I'm sure I can arrange for us to spend—"

"Thank you, no."

"But—"

"Phil, give it a break!"

Maureen opened the door to the P.A. lab and ducked inside. Her five graduate students, three women and two men, looked up with quizzical expressions. On the tables in front of them a variety of skulls and bones lay in neat rows.

"Sorry I'm late," Maureen said, as she tossed her coat and purse on the desk by the door and headed for the examination tables. "I was ambushed by a microbrained protosimian."

She'd just placed Phil on the evolutionary ladder at about fifteen million years ago—long before anything remotely human.

They laughed.

"Okay. Let's get started. Max, you've been studying Laetoli. Three point seven million years ago three hominids, your distant relatives, walked through a layer of fresh volcanic ash, and they were walking upright, side by side. What was happening almost four million years ago that caused your human ancestors to start walking upright?"

Maxwell Conners, a short young man with wide blue eyes and sandy hair, sat up straighter. "Well, first of all, natural selection doesn't create new traits. It works with genes we already have inside us, which means that sometimes it isn't successful. If the environment changes too fast, or the change is too severe, a species may not be able to adapt quickly enough to survive, à la *T. rex*."

"Right. Go on."

The sudden scent of the desert filled Maureen's nostrils, and her mind filled with images of spectacular wind-carved buttes and lofty blue mountains. She felt happy, light-headed. She could hear Maxwell's voice coming from somewhere far away... but her soul had already flown to the rugged deserts of New Mexico.

CHAPTER 13

BROWSER PASSED THE great kiva at the southern edge of the plaza. Four hands of the kiva roof stuck up above the plaza floor. Nearly twice the size of the tower kiva, it resembled a gigantic circular pot ring covered with brightly colored ears of corn; the kernels created a shimmering blanket of red, blue, yellow, and white.

Redcrop walked anxiously beside Browser, her face down, hands tucked beneath her cape.

Cottonwood and juniper trees lined the bank, forcing them to walk through a well of cold shadows and piles of fallen leaves. Browser studied the brush. They'd hacked at it and cut it out to use as firewood or split-twig mats, but the tangled briar still stood the height of a man in places.

"Did you hear anything last night, Redcrop? Her steps when she rose? Her blankets being thrown back?"

"No, and I don't know why. Usually I hear her every time she turns over."

"Well, perhaps she was trying not to wake you. You've been working very hard on the harvest."

Beyond the brush, a faint sound erupted. Browser cocked his ear, and his hand went to his war club. *Probably a deer in the water . . .*

Redcrop said, "But she always wakes me, War Chief. If there is a village emergency, the Matron asks me to help. You know, to carry water, or gather wood for a fire. She has never..."

The thrashing turned to panting. Feet kicked dead leaves.

Browser gripped Redcrop's arm and tugged her backward with one hand, while his other hand raised his club.

Her dark eyes widened. "Wha—"

"Shh."

Redcrop went as still as Mouse beneath Hawk's shadow.

The sound grew louder: several people panted as though running.

Browser flared his nostrils, instinctively sucking in more air, preparing...

Three boys came bobbing out of the brush.

"Little Calf!" Browser said. "Why are you running?"

Little Calf had a broad flat face with front teeth like a beaver's. His dark eyes went huge when he saw Browser. "War Chief, come quickly! We found a dead woman in the bathing pond!"

"A dead woman?" he called. "Who is it?"

"I don't know, War Chief! They skinned her face! She has gray hair. I thought it might be one of our elders."

Redcrop let out a small wretched cry, lurched from behind Browser, and raced down the path.

"Redcrop, wait!"

She disappeared into the brush.

Little Calf started to run by, and Browser caught him by the wrist. The boy looked up in terror. Browser sternly said, "When you get back to the village, tell Catkin what's happened. She'll know what to do. Do you understand? Go straight to Catkin."

"Yes, War Chief!" Little Calf dashed for the village with the other boys on his heels.

Browser sprinted after Redcrop. As he cleared the brush, he saw her charging down the hill in front of him, her long hair flying out behind her.

"Redcrop!" he shouted. "Please, stop! There may be danger! We don't know what happened. She may have been attacked by raiders!"

Redcrop leaped a log that lay across the trail and half-stumbled down the hill before catching her balance and sprinting on.

Browser's legs pumped, trying to catch her. "Redcrop!"

The girl splashed through the shallow river, crossed to the trail on the other bank, then ran flat out.

Browser scanned the trees and brush as he splashed through after her. Tracks dimpled the wet sand: Redcrop's, the boys', and the tracks of one adult. They probably belonged to the dead woman, but they might be the killer's tracks. Browser couldn't afford to study them now. The bathing pool lay just around the bend in the trail ahead.

Redcrop battered her way through a thicket of brush that clotted the trail. Browser caught up with her, grabbed a handful of her buckskin cape, and jerked her backward. "Wait!"

"Let me go! I have to go to her!" Redcrop cried.

Browser grabbed her by the shoulders and spun her around. Her face had contorted with terror. "Listen! I have seen many ambushes that begin like this, Redcrop. People rush down to see who's been killed, then enemy warriors emerge from the surrounding hills and kill them all. It's my duty as War Chief to see that no one else dies today. You will stay here in the brush. Let me go down and make certain this isn't a trap. If it's safe, I will call to you."

She looked up at him through brimming eyes and choked out, "Soon? You will call me soon?"

"Yes. I promise."

She nodded and Browser released her.

Finches and siskins flitted through the autumn trees. They didn't seem to be watching anything. The air rang with their songs. A flock of pinyon jays circled overhead. Smart birds, they examined him as they flew over, but did not pay undue attention to anything else along the river. They landed in a cottonwood fifty paces away and began socializing, calling *rack! rack! rack!* and trilling in beautiful voices.

Browser cautiously worked his way through the thicket. Ten hands below, the bathing pool sparkled in the sunlight. The woman's body floated at the water's edge. The deep stab wounds in her chest were clearly visible, and she'd been savagely beaten. Her face resembled a pink mask with bugged-out eyes. Browser clutched the bone handle of his knife and took the path down. As he made his way across the rocks that ringed the pool, his gaze noted every place a killer might hide.

Browser tucked his knife into his belt sheath and grasped the woman's arms. Her flesh chilled his fingers, feeling rubbery in his grip. He dragged her from the pool onto the rocks. Blood began to pound in Browser's ears, the rhythm slow, sickening. He saw the large freckle that darkened the side of her throat.

Gods, the Katsinas' People will go mad. She was our heart, the one person we looked to for solace and hope. Flame Carrier kept the Dream alive.

Browser glanced up. Redcrop stood in the brush watching him.

He vented a breath, and called, "Redcrop, you may come down."

"Is it . . . ?"

For the next four days, no one would speak the Matron's name aloud, and they would try not to dream of her, for fear that they might pull her afterlife soul back from its sacred journey to the Land of the Dead.

"Yes."

Redcrop stood woodenly for a moment, as though too stunned to move, then she raced down the path, crying, "No, no, it can't be!"

The breeze picked up, rocking the trees and blowing long black hair around Redcrop's pretty face as she hurried across the rocks. "H-how do you know it's her?"

Browser gave her a short while to take in what she saw, before he turned Flame Carrier's head to show her the freckle.

Redcrop did not make a sound, but she started shaking badly.

Gently, he said, "Please, Redcrop, sit down."

"No," she sobbed, and stepped backward. Tears dripped from Redcrop's chin and beaded the curtain of her black hair.

Browser waited.

After several moments, she came forward again, dropped to her knees, and whispered, "Are you certain it's her?"

Patiently, he said, "Yes, Redcrop."

Redcrop studied Flame Carrier's bloody face with widening eyes, then gasped, "Oh, gods, no." She threw herself over Flame Carrier's body and sobbed, "Grandmother! Grandmother!"

Browser touched her hair. "I'm sorry. I know how much you loved her."

Her cries turned shrill.

As his gaze scanned the trees, Browser said, "You are not alone. I hope you're not thinking that. You are a member of the Katsinas' People, and we all love you." She was also free now, no longer a slave. She could leave them if she wanted to. "I pray that you will stay with us, Redcrop, to help us in our quest to find the First People's kiva and fulfill the Blessed Poor Singer's prophecy. I know that the Matron would wish . . ." The words died in his throat.

Movement—in the trees above the river . . .

Browser touched a finger to Redcrop's lips. She understood immediately. Her gaze riveted on the trees.

Browser drew his war club from his belt and slowly got to his feet. He whispered, *"Stand up. Be ready to run."*

Redcrop rose on shaking legs.

Browser backed toward the river, but his eyes never left the bank in front of them.

Twigs cracked straight ahead.

A familiar piercing cry wafted on the wind, *keee-ar, keee-ar.* The song of the flicker . . .

"Why didn't you signal me earlier?" Browser called, and lowered his war club.

Catkin emerged from the brush with her bow in her hands. She wore a knee-length red war shirt painted with the white images of wolf and coyote. Despite the cold, sweat glistened on her turned-up nose and across her cheekbones. "I thought you might be surrounded by enemy warriors, and I believed it wiser to sneak up behind them so they wouldn't just shoot you and run."

From every direction, warriors began to appear, sneaking out of the brush, rising from the river.

Catkin walked down the trail toward him. "But forgive me for the delay. I ordered our warriors to scout the area first." She slung her bow over her right shoulder and slipped a slender arrow back into the quiver that draped her left shoulder. She looked at the corpse lying beside the pool.

Redcrop knelt at Flame Carrier's side, drew the Matron's hand into her lap, and clutched the cold fingers as though she would never let them go.

Catkin stopped in front of Browser. "You are sure—"

"I'm sure."

Grief tightened her eyes. She glared at the rocks for a long moment. "By the time the boys ran into the village, your great-uncle Stone Ghost had risen. He wished to come with us. I wouldn't allow it, of course."

Browser sighed. "Thank you. I think sometimes that he does not realize his age. He—"

"He said something that worried me, Browser." She fixed him with penetrating eyes.

He cocked his head. "What?"

"He said, 'It would seem The Two have finally come home.' "

After several moments, Browser whispered, "The Two? But I thought—I mean, after my wife's death—Isn't there only one? The witch named Two Hearts?"

Catkin just stared at him.

The legendary witch, Two Hearts, preyed upon women and girls. He lured them from their blankets, killed them, and then dragged their bodies through the village plaza, as if to mock their relatives, before finally burying them in the shallow mass graves.

Browser whispered, "I must speak with him."

"He's waiting for you in the plaza."

CATKIN WATCHED BROWSER, Redcrop, and three warriors carry the litter with Flame Carrier's body along the brush-choked trail that led back to Longtail village. Redcrop trotted beside Flame Carrier, holding the dead Matron's limp hand. The sight wrenched Catkin's heart.

Straighthorn and Jackrabbit stood beside Catkin. Barely fifteen summers old, lines already incised Jackrabbit's forehead. He had a pug nose and wide mouth. "I pray that Redcrop has the strength to stand it," he said. "The Matron meant everything to her."

"She has the strength," Straighthorn answered softly. "She just doesn't know it yet."

Straighthorn frowned at the blood-streaked rocks at his feet. Long black hair fluttered around his braided leather headband and stuck to the sweat that beaded his long hooked nose. "Catkin? Forgive me, but I heard you say something to the War Chief that I did not understand."

"What was that, warrior?"

"The Two. Who are they?"

Jackrabbit clenched his fists. Straighthorn noticed, and tensed.

Catkin considered not answering out of fear that he might panic, but he would hear the story soon enough. Better that it come from her than someone who might embellish for effect. "Nine moons ago in Talon Town a woman named Hophorn was struck in the head and then one of our warriors, Whiproot, was murdered. We think they were killed by the witch, Two Hearts."

"I remember as if it were yesterday," Jackrabbit said and kicked at a rock.

Straighthorn glanced between them. "But you said there were two of them."

"Yes."

Catkin studied the footprints. A man and a woman had walked around the pool, their feet slipping off the dew-slick river cobbles and into the sand. She put her hand over them, measuring their sizes. "A woman helped Two Hearts with the murders. Hophorn saw them, but the blows to her head had damaged her ability to speak. All she could say was that 'The Two' had done it. Then, when old Stone Ghost examined Whiproot's body, he found evidence that one person had held Whiproot while another stabbed him."

Straighthorn wet his lips. "Stone Ghost thinks those same people are here? That they killed your Matron?"

"It would seem so."

Catkin moved around the pool, separating Browser's and Redcrop's tracks from those of the killers. She glimpsed her reflection in the water. Faint lines zigzagged across her forehead and etched the corners of her eyes. A slash of dirt smudged her turned-up nose. She had seen twenty-seven summers. Most of them had been happy. She had been married once to a man she'd loved deeply. She'd lost him to the coughing sickness over two sun cycles ago. Since that time, she'd only loved one man. Her eyes lifted to the burial party on the trail in the distance. Shadows dappled Browser's tall body. He had barely looked at a woman since the death of his wife, though she had let him know she was there if he needed her.

Jackrabbit followed Catkin as she searched the pool area, his steps calculated to stay on the rocks so he didn't disturb any of the sign. "When Stone Ghost said The Two had finally come home, did he mean Longtail village was their home?"

"Apparently."

Straighthorn clutched his club. "I do not recall any murderers living in our village. I think we would have known."

"It may have been long ago, Straighthorn. People have lived in this village off and on since the First People built it over a hundred sun cycles ago, but not always the same people. When did your clan come here?"

"Ten sun cycles ago. We were driven from our home in the south by the Starburst warriors."

"The Two may have lived here long before you arrived."

Straighthorn seemed to be thinking about that. "Did Stone Ghost say why they would wish to kill your Matron? She was a good woman. I never heard anyone speak ill of her, Catkin. She tried very hard not to hurt others."

"He didn't say." She stretched her back. Though she'd slept six hands of time last night, she still felt numb, and exhausted. "But I can tell you that killers often have reasons that ordinary people cannot understand. I remember one old man who murdered little girls because he said their voices gave him headaches."

She knelt to examine what appeared to be drag marks. The killer had hauled Flame Carrier by the feet; the Matron's limp arms had scraped the sand. Here and there, gray hairs clung to rocks.

"The woman was alone when she dragged the Matron down. The man came later."

Jackrabbit crouched beside her. "How can you tell?"

Catkin pointed to the sandal's intricate weave recorded in the blood. "The Matron's blood had dried enough on the stones that they took his large sandal prints clearly. He didn't slip in the blood; his feet stuck." She cocked her head and memorized the distinctive sandal pattern: one over, three under.

Jackrabbit bent forward to look more closely. "Catkin, why would two killers pursue us here? I can't make sense of that."

"I cannot say." But she had to fight against the shiver that climbed her spine.

Straight Path Canyon. Everything returned to that. Like watching Father Sun rise in the morning. Nine moons ago, she and Browser had been searching the area around the fire pit where Hophorn had been attacked when he'd found a small wolf sculpture, exquisitely carved from turquoise.

"Blessed Spirits," Catkin had whispered in astonishment. *"Do you know what someone would do to possess that wolf?"*

Steal, kill, wage war.

For uncounted hundreds of sun cycles, the First People had given turquoise wolves as gifts. But only to a few.

As they bravely climbed through the underworlds to get to this world of light, the First People had gained secret knowledge about those worlds. They had whispered that the paths were tangled and haunted by monsters. They'd told of traps and snares that lined the way, and the false paths leading to eternal torment. Their stories had terrified the Made People. Every soul had to travel through the underworlds to get to the Land of the Dead. How would they know which path to take unless the First People told them? Made People had once paid huge sums for the barest details of the journey. The First People, however, never told anyone the whole truth. They always kept critical details hidden. They often forgot to mention a fork in the trail, or a landmark.

On very rare occasions the First People rewarded a special Made Person by giving him a magical Spirit Helper, a turquoise wolf in the form of a pendant to personally guide him through the maze to the Land of the Dead. A person didn't need their secret knowledge if he had a Spirit Helper who knew the way.

Glorious stories surrounded these magical turquoise wolves, but until nine moons ago she had never known anyone who'd seen one, let alone held one of the wolves in her hand.

The killer must be desperate to get it back.

Catkin rose to her feet and started up the slope, following the drag marks.

"Catkin?" a warrior on the bank above called. "You will wish to see this!"

"What is it?" She trudged up the trail with Jackrabbit and Straighthorn close behind.

When she crested the bank, she gazed out through the sun-mottled cottonwoods and saw Skink and Water Snake kneeling over what appeared to be a fallen branch. Skink stood twelve hands tall and had a face like a bobcat, flat, with heavily lashed eyes and chin-length hair. He wore a plain doehide cape that hung to his knees. Water Snake stood a hand shorter than Skink and had the lean, feral face of a weasel. He'd twisted his black hair into a bun at the base of his head.

As she approached, they rose and gazed at her with their hands clenched at their sides.

"Well?" she said.

Water Snake just pointed to the ground.

Catkin's gaze took in the knotted cloth, the yucca cords, the bloody pieces of wood.

Straighthorn worked into the circle and swallowed as if his mouth had suddenly gone dry.

The sand told the story. Four holes marked the places where Flame Carrier's hands and feet had been staked down. Her killer had probably used the bloody cords to tie her wrists and ankles to the stakes, then she'd shoved the blood-soaked cloth into Flame Carrier's toothless old mouth and taken her time beating Flame Carrier with a variety of makeshift clubs, branches broken from trees, driftwood collected from the river. Finally, the murderer had skinned Flame Carrier's face.

What kind of a person would brutalize an old woman?

An unpleasant stinging sensation filtered through Catkin's body. She slowly walked around the torture site. Two sets of prints marked the ground, Flame Carrier's and the woman's. The man hadn't been present for the torture.

If these were the same two who had terrorized the people in Straight Path Canyon, then Catkin knew him. *He* had captured her on the cliff above Talon Town and turned Catkin over to his daughter to kill. Catkin never saw him, but she knew his voice. He'd sounded so much like Browser that she'd been distracted long enough for someone to club her from behind.

The next morning while she lay tied on the ground, her vision blurry, her head throbbing, Browser had sneaked into the snowy camp and shot an arrow through her masked assailant's chest. He'd saved Catkin's life—and killed his own wife: Two Heart's daughter.

Catkin looked up into Skink's eyes. "Where did she come from? Did you follow her tracks out of the trees?"

"We followed the Matron's tracks down to the river from Longtail village. Her murderer met her just over there"—he pointed to a place across the river in the thickest cottonwoods—"but the murderer came from nowhere, Catkin. Her steps disappear about fifty body lengths up the river. It is as if she flew down from the trees, and flew up again."

Murmurs filtered among the warriors. They shifted from foot to foot, casting nervous glances at each other. Witches often disguised themselves as birds and flew about doing mischief, spying on people, killing those they hated.

She said: "These are humans we hunt. Humans who murdered our clan Matron and skinned her face!"

Straighthorn glanced up at Catkin from beneath long lashes, then quickly looked away.

Skink refused to meet her eyes.

They didn't believe her.

Catkin said, "I must return to tell the War Chief what we've found, but in my absence Skink will lead the search party."

He looked up. "Me? But, Catkin, I—"

"Split your warriors into two groups. I wish them to search both sides of the river until there's no longer enough light to see. Run as far as you can before darkness. The murderers left tracks somewhere. *Find them.*"

"Yes, Catkin." He backed away and trotted for his warriors.

Catkin turned. "Straighthorn, you are the best tracker in the village. You will lead one of the groups."

His brows lifted as if in warning. He whispered, "Skink will not like this, Catkin. I am much younger than he, and, well, he imagines himself to be the best tracker."

Catkin sought out Skink where he stood with his warriors in the cottonwoods. "Skink?" His cape whirled as he turned. "I wish Straighthorn to lead one of the search parties and you to lead the other. You understand?"

Skink glanced distastefully at Straighthorn, but nodded. "Yes, Catkin. It will be done."

"Good. If I am asleep when you return, wake me. I will wish to know of your discoveries immediately."

"I understand." He returned to his conversation.

Straighthorn said, "Catkin, when you get back to the village, could you tell Redcrop that I will be away until late tonight, but that I will come to see her when I return?"

Catkin nodded. "I will, but remember that you can help her most by finding the people who killed our Matron."

A swallow went down his throat. "I will work very hard to do that, Catkin."

"I know you will. Now go. Darkness will come sooner than you realize."

He trotted toward Skink. Jackrabbit followed.

Catkin started back up the trail toward Longtail village.

MY WHITE BUCKSKIN cape flaps in the wind as I gracefully kneel behind the tan boulder on the hilltop.

Father lies in the currants and willows along the river's edge, a bow shot below. The warriors do not see him.

He sees nothing but them.

I breathe in the damp earthy scent of the morning and wonder.

I have stood in awe watching death's languid red rivers flow over my hands and understand the need to watch, to feel the warmth and taste the metallic tang on my tongue. But I do not grasp his need to watch them come. He must see the search, hear the shouts and cries.

He keeps the death alive by watching.

He once told me, "We sit together, death and I, until only death remains."

The warriors below close in around Father, moving, thrashing the willows, calling to each other.

I creep forward for a better look . . .

"Hungwy," a voice whispers from behind me. "Where's camp, Mother?"

Tiny fingers slip into mine.

"Hungwy, Mother."

Piper's Song has seen eight summers. She has my beautiful mouth and nose, but deep black eyes. His eyes.

I pull her down to the dirt and hiss, "Look. Listen."

In the desert I have often seen things very clearly that were not there. Someday, she will, too. Disembodied mountains floating in the sky with the Cloud People, cottonwoods singing in voices very pure and sweet.

Once, when I stood on a high mountain during a storm, brilliant threads of light flowed across the face of Our Grandmother Earth, connecting all living things in a single moment of blinding darkness.

That is what this child is.

A moment of darkness.

Another voice to torment Father.

CHAPTER 14

THE FLIGHT ACROSS the Rocky Mountains had been spectacular, the little blue-and-gray prop plane droning its way over jagged peaks capped with brilliant new snow. The turbulence, however, hadn't been so pleasant. Every nerve in Maureen Cole's body tingled, her white fingers gripping the new Norman Zollinger novel she'd picked up at the Benjamin Books in the Denver airport.

The little plane dipped and banked over wrinkled uplands carpeted with pines and junipers. She could see isolated roads, houses, and power lines. Here and there, bands of sandstone and shale stuck out of broken ridges. The plane dove down into the irregular valley and Maureen saw the airport. On approach, the plane hung for an eternal instant, then dropped like a rock, bumping and vibrating down the runway. The props roared as the pilot reversed them and deceleration threw Maureen forward. Buildings, construction equipment, and fences flashed past the shivering plane as it wheeled for the terminal.

After Maureen had claimed her baggage, she caught the shuttle bus, and within fifteen minutes, found herself standing at the registration desk in the Durango Doubletree Hotel. She wasn't sure what she'd expected. With Stewart, a roof, bed, and walls might have been the only criteria for comfort. What she found was a modern, airy hotel, with floral carpet patterns, oak wainscotting, lots of glass, polished brass, and gleaming chandeliers that cast light through white glass globes.

"Thank you, Dr. Cole. Enjoy your stay with us."

Maureen took the plastic card key from the young dark haired woman who stood behind the check-in counter. "Which way is my room?"

"Just walk to your right, take the first left, then the next right, and continue down the hall. You can't miss it. Oh, wait! I almost forgot your cookie!"

The young woman walked a short distance away and reached beneath the counter.

"Cookie?" Maureen asked as she picked up her suitcase and hefted the strap of her field kit onto her shoulder.

"You betcha. It's our trademark. We make the most delicious chocolate-chip cookies on earth." She handed Maureen a brown paper bag. "Have a pleasant evening, Dr. Cole."

"Thank you."

Maureen strode down the length of the check-in counter, passed the telephones, turned left, went ten paces, and turned right. A middle-aged couple holding hands passed her heading in the opposite direction. She caught herself thinking about John, about all the things they'd planned to do when they were old and gray, and she suddenly missed him desperately. God, she was tired of being alone.

Maureen found her room, inserted the key, and opened the door. Nice. A king-sized bed sat against the wall to her right, and a table and chairs nestled in front of the large window in the rear. The view was gorgeous. A mixture of bare trees and red and gold aspens covered the mountainside behind the hotel.

She dropped her suitcase outside the bathroom, set the field kit on the floor, and tossed her purse onto the bed. Less than twenty meters from her window, a beautiful tree-lined river rushed over rocks. In the light from the hotel windows, the water looked golden.

She took a deep breath and let it out slowly. She'd entered a different world, somehow wilder and more exotic than her own. The shuttle from the airport had passed classic Old West–style buildings with high Victorian false fronts and lots of delicate gingerbread architecture. Indians from a variety of southwestern tribes had walked the streets, smiling as they gazed into the store windows.

Maureen opened her brown paper bag and the entire room smelled like warm chocolate-chip cookies. She pulled the cookie out and took a bite as she walked toward the window.

"Um," she said. "This *is* delicious."

Her gaze drifted from the river to the trees, now mostly bare of leaves. In the short time since she'd landed, night had fallen.

Maureen took another bite of the warm, gooey cookie. On the plane three hours ago, she'd had a meal fit for a leprechaun: a piece of fish as big as her thumb, and a salad consisting of what looked like pre-chewed bits of lettuce. Perhaps more remarkably, the magicians they hired as airline chefs had managed to make them taste exactly the same.

As she flipped the switch by the door, fluorescent light filled the room. Maureen gazed at herself in the big mirror. Her straight nose and full lips shone. Though she'd slept on the flight from Toronto, her large black eyes looked tired. Her braid draped her left shoulder, falling to her waist. She straightened her cream-colored turtleneck sweater and scrutinized her wrinkled black Levi's. She didn't feel like changing. Besides, Dusty Stewart wouldn't notice anyway.

Maureen washed her hands and walked back into the room for her purse.

As she closed her door and headed down the hallway, she felt an odd sort of freedom. Her steps seemed lighter, her heart happier. In all her years of teaching, she had never taken a sabbatical, or even a vacation for that matter. When John had been alive, she'd never needed one. They'd spent each summer sitting on the porch of their home in Niagara-on-the-Lake, laughing and talking, discussing human evolution and the destiny of the species, planning their future together. All she'd had to do was look into John's eyes and she was on holiday.

Maureen walked past the registration desk with its wooden pigeonholes, took a right past the French windows of the gift shop, and followed the signs to the Edgewater Lounge.

A tall, brown-haired man passed her, did a double take, and smiled. She made a point of not smiling back. There was no sense in giving him an excuse to try and keep her company. She'd been fighting off men her entire life. Most of them saw only her beauty; they didn't care about anything else. In Maureen's mind, the worst insult was to be thought of as a pretty face. And, good Lord, she was almost forty. Wouldn't it ever end? That was one of the things that had drawn her to John. His eyes had looked straight through her exterior and into her soul.

Besides, she expected Stewart to be late. Archaeologists didn't work on normal schedules. He might have unearthed something spectacular two seconds before he was supposed to leave the site and spent the next two hours digging by lantern light.

Maureen found the Edgewater Lounge and walked through the hallway with its artistic wooden relief, some of it carved, some sandblasted. She checked herself one last time in the mirror and entered. Three men sat on stools at the bar. Round acrylic-topped tables lined the walls. The bartender gave her a welcoming nod. Short and stocky, his salt-and-pepper hair was held back in a ponytail. A white scar slashed his forehead. He wore granny glasses, and his name tag read BRUCE. She guessed he was about her age.

"Good evening," he said.

"Good evening," Maureen answered, pausing. "I'm just going to have coffee, please."

"Anything in that?" Bruce asked. "A little whiskey? Maybe some dark rum to warm you up on this cold night?"

"The only thing I'd like in it is plenty of coffee. Strong, please."

Americans tended to make coffee weak enough to be mistaken for water unless the light was just right.

"Yes, ma'am," Bruce said. "Coming right up."

Maureen walked to the rear and took a seat at a table. She checked her watch. Dusty was due in another twenty minutes.

Two of the three men at the bar turned in unison to look at her, then whispered something to each other and smiled.

Maureen stared at them as if she'd seen more appealing things under the rim of the toilet bowl. Their smiles faded; they turned back to their drinks.

Bruce edged from behind the bar, carrying a tray. As he set the steaming cup of coffee down before her, he said, "I brought sugar and cream in case you needed them."

"Thanks. I drink it black, though."

"Okeydokey. I'll take the accessories back. Did you want to charge that to your room?"

Maureen looked up into his green eyes. The thick granny glasses made them look huge. She handed him a credit card. "Could I run a tab? I'm waiting for a friend."

"Sure. No problem. Just give me a holler if you need anything else."

"I will. Thank you."

He walked back to the bar.

Maureen picked up her cup and watched the steam rise in curlicues before she took a sip. She always felt odd sitting in a bar drinking coffee, but seeing the elderly couple in the hall had made it worse. Loneliness always intensified her desire for a drink.

It had been four years since she'd had anything alcoholic, but every day was a struggle. Four years, six months, and seven days ago she'd come home to find smoke billowing from their house, rife with the smell of burning spaghetti sauce. She'd run through the front door like a madwoman, shouting John's name. When she'd stumbled through the smoke and into the kitchen, gasping for breath, she'd seen him lying on his side on the floor, his sandy hair drenched in sweat, his mouth ajar. He'd had a surprised look in his wide dead eyes.

The doctors had tried to explain his unusual heart flaw to her, but Maureen had barely heard them. Somewhere deep inside her a small terrified voice had been screaming: *No, no, God, please. I'll do anything.*

She took a long drink of coffee. The day after the funeral, she'd poured herself a Scotch and stood alone at the window looking out at Lake Ontario. Every breath of wind had sounded like John's voice. Every time the old wooden floors had creaked, she'd whirled around, praying to see him.

It had started out as a couple of drinks at night to help her sleep. Then she had needed four or five drinks to barricade her heart against the loneliness. Six months after John's death, she'd found herself emptying the last drop of a freshly opened quart of whiskey into her Saturday morning coffee and heard John's soft, concerned voice say, *"I finally understand what Hell is, Maureen. It's having to stand by and watch someone you love destroy herself. I know you can't hear me, but I wish you'd stop this."*

Maureen had staggered up from the table and spent the rest of the weekend throwing up. She'd never been certain if it had been the alcohol, or the idea that the living created the Hell their dead loved ones had to endure . . .

"Am I disturbing a private conversation between you and you?" a deep, familiar voice asked.

Maureen looked up.

Dusty Stewart stood in front of the table, tall, blond, deeply tanned. He wore a red-and-black checked wool shirt and jeans. His blue eyes went straight for her soul, nervously probing, measuring. In that way, he was much like John had been. He always seemed to be looking past her beauty to something deeper. It was one of the things she liked about him.

Maureen smiled. "Yes, you are, but sit down anyway. How are you, Stewart?"

"Fine, Doctor, thanks." He dropped into a chair and propped his elbows on the table. Sand trickled from his left sleeve onto the green leather upholstery of the chair.

Maureen's brows lifted. "You came in straight from the field, didn't you?"

"I can't imagine how you could tell," he said as he waved at the haze of dust that sifted down around him, sparkling in the dim light. "That's why I'm ten minutes early. How was your flight?"

"Bumpy air between Denver and Durango. The man behind me filled his airsick bag and the aroma started a chain reaction across the plane."

Dusty grimaced, and the lines around his eyes deepened. "Sounds exciting. How about you? Did you get involved in the show?"

"Me? I boil decaying human bodies for a living, Stewart. Nothing makes me sick."

Bruce, the bartender, walked up in the middle of the sentence with an order pad in his hands. He stared at Maureen through squinted eyes. "What kind of work do you do, ma'am?"

Dusty smiled genially. "She's the dinner coordinator for the annual Alfred Packer Day's celebration up at the University of Colorado."

Maureen gave Dusty a questioning look.

Bruce peered at her over the rims of his glasses. "I thought you people used fresh stuff."

"Uh, well," Maureen answered vaguely, "it depends on what the police bring us."

"The police?" Bruce looked perplexed.

Dusty explained, "Authenticity is the key, buddy."

Bruce just stared. "Yeah. Right. Okay. What can I get you?"

"Do you have a bottle of Guinness back there?"

"Absolutely. Anything else?"

"Yeah, how about an order of nachos smothered in fresh jalapeños? I haven't eaten since noon."

"No problem. Might take a few minutes, though. I'll have to check with the kitchen. Last time I was in, they were really backed up."

"I have time. I'm spending the night in town."

"Great. I'll bring your beer right out."

Bruce headed back for the bar, and Dusty turned blue eyes toward Maureen. He leaned back in his chair and folded his hands over his stomach. In the low light, his blond hair and beard shimmered silver.

The silence stretched into an awkward ten seconds, then Stewart said, "You're looking well."

"Thanks. You, too. Where's the crew?"

"Crew?"

"I thought you'd bring Sylvia for protection. You know, to even the numbers?" Maureen held her coffee cup in both hands.

He smiled uneasily at that. "Actually, I dropped them off downtown. By now Steve and Sylvia are knocking back shooters and eating *carne adovado* at Gaspacho."

They'd be doing this for a few days—negotiating the minefield that lay between them, searching for safe footing. "Who's Alfred Packer? Local politician?"

Stewart smothered a grin. "I guess that depends on how you look at it. He ate all of the Democrats in Routt County, Colorado. A century ago, that earned you your own parade."

"My goodness, and people still celebrate his accomplishment?"

"This is Colorado, Doctor. They even named the cafeteria at the university after him." Bruce returned with a bottle of Guinness, an icy mug, and an enormous platter of nachos. As he set them down on the table, he said, "I used my considerable leverage to get your nachos done pronto. What do you think?"

Dusty nodded appreciatively at the enormous pile of chips covered with meat, cheese, and peppers. "I think that will feed four people, which ought to be just about right. *Muchas gracias.*"

Bruce smiled and turned to Maureen. "How's your coffee holding out?"

Maureen checked it. "Half full. I'll be all right for another ten or fifteen minutes."

Bruce started to pour Dusty's Guinness and Dusty grabbed the bottle. "If you don't mind. I've been fine-tuning my pour for thirty-seven years."

"Sure thing. I'll check back in a few minutes."

"Uh," Maureen said, stopping him before he could leave, "I don't want to complain, but is there a way I can get a really strong cup of coffee? I'll pay extra."

Bruce smiled. "I'll see what I can do."

He left, and Dusty tipped his mug sideways and very gently poured the Guinness down the side of the glass. Creamy foam bubbled up. The rich scent made Maureen want to groan.

"Help yourself to the nachos," Dusty said. "I have something I want to show you."

"If it's a sorority pin, I don't want to know about it."

He gave her a disgusted look. "Cute, Doctor."

Maureen pulled out a chip dripping with cheese. As she ate the spicy concoction, Dusty swigged down half of his beer in four swallows and started stuffing nachos into his mouth like a man who hadn't eaten in three days.

"Let me start out by telling you that the site is about a forty-five-minute drive to the south," Dusty said. "You'll be working with me, Dale, and Sylvia, as well as a graduate student named Steve Sanders. He's in the Ph.D. program at the University of Arizona. Very sharp. Conscientious. The Salmon Ruins site lies straight south of us, and Aztec Ruins National Monument is just down—"

"There are Aztec ruins in the States?"

He squinted at her as if appalled by the question. "Don't they teach you anything in Canada? They're Anasazi ruins. Some fool geologist named John Newberry called them that in the 1850s and it stuck."

"Oh, I see. Go on."

Dusty leaned back, reached into his pants pocket, and pulled out a small plastic bag labeled; *Non-diagnostic bone artifact, 2.36N. 4.87E., 35 cm.*

He took a long drink of his stout before wiping his mouth on his sleeve and saying, "We found it today. It's definitely bone, but I don't know if it's human or animal. It sort of fits into a hole in a skull we found in the tower kiva, but it doesn't look quite right."

Maureen took the bag and tipped the artifact to the poor light. The piece was the size of a loonie—a Canadian dollar—cut into a rough circle, the edges smoothed, then a large hole had been drilled into the center. Four etched lightning bolts radiated outward from the hole on the outer table. She flipped it over and looked at the back. She couldn't be certain, but the crude shape etched into the irregular surface of the inner table appeared to be a dog. The creature had its muzzle up and open, as if howling.

Just holding the artifact made her uneasy.

Around a mouthful of nachos, Dusty said, "So, what do you think? Human or animal?"

"Definitely human."

He leaned forward. "Okay. What is it?"

"It's part of a skull. Mostly parietal, I'd say. This is the coronal suture here. I'll have to see the skull you found to know if it actually fits in the hole. Male or female?"

His blond brows lowered, as though assessing the physical anthropology made him uncomfortable. "Female. Maybe. I don't want to risk my neck in front of an expert."

"Elderly woman, then. See the porosity, the foamy appearance of the bone?"

Dusty nodded. "Osteoporosis?"

"Most likely."

She studied it again. "Where did you find it?"

"In a room next to the tower kiva."

She looked at him. "I thought you said it fit into a skull that came from the tower kiva?"

"I think it does."

"But you found it in a different room?"

"Correct, Doctor."

Maureen cocked her head. "That's odd, don't you think?"

"Yes, but I can't explain it yet."

Maureen placed the bag on the table between them and reached for another nacho, this one filled with peppers. She ate it in one bite and washed it down with coffee before it could burn. Coffee didn't seem to help when it came to peppers. "What do you think it is? A pendant?"

He shook his head and his blond hair and beard flashed golden. "Doubtful. The hole is in the wrong place. If you were going to put this on a cord, you'd drill the hole high, not in the center. It's probably a big bead."

Maureen studied the edge of the bone. "The edge doesn't look like it was cut out after death. I'd say the bone was green when they drilled and cut. Maybe it's a keepsake from a trephination?"

He made a face and reached for another nacho. "Wouldn't it be unusual to cut out a chunk of skull because of medical concern and then keep it and turn it into a bead?"

"Yes, it would."

He ate his nacho, and his eyes glinted, as if with secret knowledge.

Maureen drummed her fingers on the table. "Are you going to tell me what you're thinking or not?"

He used his red-and-black sleeve to clean a dribble of dark beer off the table. "Oh, I've heard of some interesting rituals involving trephination that don't have anything to do with relieving pain."

"Really? Go on."

"You sure? It's not hard science."

Maureen exhaled hard. "Nothing you do is hard science, Stewart. Please continue."

Dusty smiled. "Okay. A couple of years ago, an old medicine man told me that his ancestors believed a soul could not reach the Land of the Dead unless it began the journey from the Pueblo Alto, in Chaco Canyon, New Mexico."

Maureen remembered the rugged terrain, the buff-colored canyon walls and magnificent ruins. "And?"

He waved a nacho. "Well, think about. This belief posed a problem. Sometimes people died far away from Chaco Canyon, and it's not always practical to drag your dead relatives back to bury them. Ruff-legged Hawk said that his ancestors solved this problem by capturing their relative's afterlife soul in a soul pot, which they carried to Pueblo Alto on ritual feast days and gave to the priests who lived there. For a fee, the priests ritually broke the pot and released the soul onto the Great North Road which led to the Land of the Dead."

"Hmm. Are there a lot of potsherds at Pueblo Alto to support Ruff-legged Hawk's story?"

"Let me put it this way: we think about twenty-five people were permanent residents at Pueblo Alto, and they lived there for around sixty years. In *one* trash mound we found evidence for over one hundred fifty thousand broken pots. Granted the breakage occurred over a sixty-year period, but that still means they broke about two thousand, five hundred pots per year."

Maureen lifted her coffee cup and steam swirled around her face. "That's a lot of pots. I'm not even that bad in my own kitchen."

"Me neither. Although I suspect I come closer than you do."

Maureen braced her elbows on the table. "How did they 'catch' the soul to bring it back to Pueblo Alto where the priests could release it?"

"Well, that's interesting, too. Ruff-legged Hawk told me that his ancestors usually held a pot over the mouth of a dying loved one and captured the soul that came out with the last breath."

Maureen smiled, delighted by the discussion. Phil would be snorting in derision. "In other words, breaking soul pots amounted to a ceremonial industry in Chaco Canyon?"

"Apparently. Providing that old Ruff-legged Hawk was telling me the truth. You'd be surprised how much pleasure it gives some Native people to jerk an anthropologist's chain. Particularly if his specialty happens to be archaeology."

"No," she said. "I wouldn't be surprised. Remember, I *am* one of those Native peoples."

"That's right," Dusty said, and looked down into his beer mug. "I guess that gives you license to yank my chain on occasion."

"I promise not to do it too often. So, what does a trephined skull have to do with filling a soul pot?"

"Some people apparently didn't want to take the chance that they'd miss it."

"Oh." Maureen winced. "That's grisly."

"Especially for the dying person. Imagine how it felt to have your skull opened and your soul stolen before you were ready to leave your body."

To hide the sudden unease in his eyes, Dusty held his empty mug up to Bruce. Bruce lifted a hand and walked to the cooler behind the bar. Dusty set the mug down and turned back. The way he looked at her made Maureen's eyes narrow.

He didn't say anything for a time, just stared at her with unblinking blue eyes. "I was wondering..."

"What?"

He toyed with his mug, pushing it around the table. "Why are you here?"

Maureen sank back into her seat. "As I remember, you called me. Why are you surprised that I came?"

"Well, for one thing, you've never done anything I asked. And for another, you showed up PDQ. I figured you'd have to think about working with me for a while."

"I did think about it."

He shrugged his broad shoulders. "I was surprised, that's all. I just thought you might have had other reasons. We both know you wouldn't come all this way just to bask in my dazzling presence."

Maureen rearranged her napkin on her lap. "I had a number of reasons, Stewart. Actually, I did want to see you again"—when he looked up and pinned her eyes, she hurriedly continued—"You taught me a lot about archaeology the last time we were together, and I fell in love with the Southwest. I've wanted to come back for long time, but I had obligations, Dusty. Things I had to take care of at the university, and with my family in Toronto. When you called about this site, well, you made it sound very intriguing."

"Okay," he said softly, and shoved his empty mug back and forth between his palms.

Bruce interrupted them by setting an open bottle of Guinness on the table, then he held out a coffeepot to refill Maureen's cup. "Ready?"

"Sure. Smells good," Maureen said as he poured.

"Sorry it took so long. I had to brew a new pot. I put three times as much coffee in the basket as they tell us to. I hope it doesn't keep you up all night." He peered at her over the tops of his granny glasses.

"It won't. I'm used to it."

"Right. Let me know if you need anything else."

"We will."

Bruce walked back to the bar, and Dusty glanced at her speculatively as he filled his mug. He took a few swallows, set the mug down, and pulled another tortilla chip from the dwindling pile. Before he put the chip in his mouth, he said, "Why did you write to Sylvia first? Trying to find out if I wanted you here?"

Maureen's cup stopped halfway to her mouth. "No, Stewart. I wrote her first because I like her better than you."

He chewed his chip, apparently trying to gauge the truth of her words. Stewart was like that. He seemed to be able to sense the deeper emotional currents that ran beneath people's words or expressions, and spent a good deal of time trying to figure them out.

Finally, he said warmly, "I'm glad you came."

Their gazes held.

"Yeah?" she said. "Why?"

He ate the nacho, then replied, "I really need you on this project."

She couldn't keep the surprise from showing. "Why?"

"Well, to begin with, this is a strange site." He gestured to the bag on the table. "The bone bed is fabulous. We need more than a physical anthropologist out there. We need a great physical anthropologist. You."

"So," she said, attempting to make light of the compliment. "Tell me about the site."

Dusty frowned. "Most of the bone fragments are tiny. I can't identity them. There may be fragments of *odocoileus,* deer bone, but I think most of it is human." He fiddled with a nacho, scooping up more cheese and meat than it could hold. "And there's another thing."

She sipped her coffee. "Why do I hear hesitation in your voice?"

He shifted uncomfortably. "Let's say I've got a feeling about this. Down deep in my gut."

She chuckled at that. "Your famous gut is batting fifty-fifty, Stewart. You were right about that Iroquois site in New York. Remember, the one with the achondroplastic dwarf?"

He nodded. "Yeah, and I was wrong at Chaco Canyon. My slaves turned into murder victims." He sobered. "This time, however, well, this one's spooky. You were at 10K3. This one *feels* worse."

His gaze bored into her, and a chill slipped up her spine. She said, "I don't believe in spooks, Stewart. Let's just see where the data take us, all right?"

"It's a deal, Doctor." He held out his callused hand and they shook over the wreckage of the nachos.

The physical contact lasted longer than either of them had intended. Conflicting emotions flashed in his eyes: fear, hesitation, longing.

Maureen pulled her hand away. Her fingers tingled, as though an electrical current had passed from him to her. She took a breath. "Okay, now that we've gotten the lunge and parry part down, tell me more of the site details."

CHAPTER 15

SUNLIGHT STREAMED THROUGH the tower kiva's roof entry and illuminated Browser's buckskin cape. He crouched and added twigs to the newly built fire. The flames warmed his round face and chin-length black hair.

To his right, old Stone Ghost and Cloudblower examined the Matron's naked body. She lay on her back on the plastered bench that ran around the interior of the circular chamber. Every time Browser looked at her, he ached.

The tower kiva stretched about four body lengths across. Life-sized figures of the gods Danced around the tan walls. The *Yamuhakto*, the Great Warriors of East and West, stood on the west wall in front of Browser. They were the sacred Hero Twins of the Katsinas' People, and carried lightning bolts in their uplifted hands. The katsinas surrounded the warriors, their feet raised, arms stretched out. They watched Browser with shining inhuman eyes. When he dared to look back at them, his insides seemed to shrivel.

Eight evenly spaced stone niches had been built above the bench and filled with precious offerings to the gods: polished stones, turquoise and shell beads, small bowls of cornmeal. Over each niche a sacred mask blazed in the firelight, its Spirit sleeping until the next ritual Dance.

"She is already stiffening," Cloudblower said in a low voice. Long, gray-streaked black braids dangled down the front of her red cotton cape. She held one of the Matron's hands as though it were an egg that might be crushed.

Gray hair fanned out around the Matron's mutilated face. She lay with her arms at her sides, her eyes staring, as if shocked by what she saw. Her pupils resembled enormous black holes.

"It is natural," Stone Ghost responded as he hobbled toward Cloudblower. White hair fell to his shoulders. He wiped his beaked nose and sighed. He had bushy white eyebrows and wore a tattered brown-and-white turkey feather cape. "As the body cools, the flesh breaks down. The rigor first affects the muscles of the hands, feet, and face, then it moves to the rest of the body. At the height of the stiffness, a man becomes as rigid as a log."

Browser walked to the body and pointed to the bluish-purple splotches that had begun to appear on Flame Carrier's sides. "What is this, Uncle?"

Stone Ghost's bushy brows lowered. "That is the result of blood draining from the meat and organs. When the heart stops pumping, the blood settles in the lowest places." Gently, Stone Ghost rolled the Matron to her side. "You will notice that it spreads across her back. It takes about two hands of time for the bruising to appear, and about twelve hands before it becomes fixed." He rolled her to her back again and tenderly patted the Matron's arm. "Because blood seeps to the lowest points, you can tell if a body has been moved from its original location."

Browser cocked his head. "I don't understand."

"I mean that if you find a dead person lying on her stomach and these dark purple splotches on both her stomach and her back, you know that she was rolled over between two and twelve hands of time after death. Sometimes people trying to cover up a murder move the body to confuse people like me."

Stone Ghost had solved some of the most grisly murders in the history of the Straight Path Nation, including the murder of his own sister—and Browser's grandmother—Painted Turtle, twenty summers ago.

"Browser?" Cloudblower said.

"Yes, Elder?"

Her sharply pointed nose appeared bladelike in the wavering amber gleam. "Catkin told me about the torture site, about the . . . the stakes and bloody cords. Why would they torture her? What were they trying to find out? I have been searching my souls, but I—"

"They weren't looking for information, Healer," Stone Ghost replied softly. "Your Matron ignored the call. That's why she was killed."

"The call?" Browser asked.

Stone Ghost nodded as he lifted the Matron's hand and squinted at her fingernails. After studying them, he eased the hand back to the bench. "Yes, Nephew. Have you ever stood at a burial and noticed that when one person begins to cry, soon everyone is weeping? Even people who did not know the dead?"

"I have." Browser eyed his uncle curiously, wondering what he was getting at. "Why is that important?"

Stone Ghost slowly worked his way down the bench, inspecting the Matron's body, until he stood over her feet. "I have witnessed the same thing with newborn babies. One begins to mew, then cry, and every baby within hearing range bursts into tears. Their cries do not come from anger or fear, but because they feel the first baby's pain. Just as the strangers at the graveside feel the anguish of the other mourners." He held up a hand when Browser, irritated, started to interrupt. "I mean that our human instincts go far beyond the search for food or warmth, or companionship, Nephew. We respond instinctively to another's pain. We feel it and generally wish to ease it."

After what Browser had witnessed in Aspen village, and at the killing ground, the very idea seemed ludicrous. "You are a Dreamer, Uncle."

Stone Ghost glanced at him with luminous eyes, smiled faintly, and looked away.

Cloudblower shifted and her red cape gleamed in the firelight. "I don't see what that has to do with our Matron's murder, Elder."

Stone Ghost examined the soles of the Matron's bare feet. "Every murder is a cry, Healer. A call for help."

Before Browser realized it, he started clenching and unclenching his fists. Stone Ghost looked at him from beneath bushy white brows.

"You disagree, Nephew?"

"No, Uncle. I was just thinking that it would be my pleasure to ease their pain—with a few blows from my war club."

Cloudblower gave Browser a hurt look and moved closer to Stone Ghost. "Please, Elder, finish what you were saying."

Browser looked down at the dead Matron. She had been ruthlessly beaten in the head, her nose and cheekbones crushed, her toothless mouth turned to blue-black mush, then her face skinned. What sort of person would care if the murderer was in pain?

Stone Ghost said, "Tell me, Nephew, in the heat of battle when you are rolling on the ground, struggling to keep your enemy's knife away from your chest, have you ever found yourself praying to the gods? Praying for strength, or that you will get away. Saying, 'Just let me live and I will do anything you wish.' "

Browser grudgingly answered, "Yes, Uncle." He often found himself praying to gods he did not even believe in. Or maybe, in that instant, he did.

"For the murderer, every moment of the kill is a prayer."

Cloudblower said, "I do not understand."

"Nor do I, Healer," Stone Ghost granted through a long exhalation. "Apparently, the murderer has the ability to send his souls into his victim. When the victim dies, all of the murderer's pain and guilt die, too. For that brief instant, he's free." Stone Ghost looked up. "That's what makes the kill intoxicating. Unfortunately, the murderer's souls always return to his own body. That's why he has to do it over and over again."

Cloudblower sat down on the bench and folded her hands in her lap. "I have heard of clans that send their evil thoughts into an animal, and when they kill the animal, they believe they have cleansed the clan. Perhaps it is similar."

Browser, tired of the discussion, interrupted, "I saw you look at her hands and feet, Uncle. What did you find?"

Stone Ghost paused. "Oh, many things, Nephew. Her fingernails are jaggedly broken and there is skin and blood under them."

"She fought?"

"She fought like a cornered bear."

A huge hand seemed to close around Browser's heart, squeezing. It would have taken little effort to overwhelm her, no matter how hard she'd fought. "And her feet, Uncle?"

"Ah—" Stone Ghost shook a crooked finger. "That is interesting. Did you find her sandals or moccasins this morning?"

"No. Nor did we find the clothing she was wearing."

His ancient brow furrowed. "Her heels and the backs of her legs are cut and scraped, but the bottoms of her feet are neither bruised from the river rocks nor torn from the brush and cactus. The murderer must have knocked her unconscious, stripped her, and dragged her to the torture site."

Browser's gaze drifted over the katsinas painted on the walls while he considered this. Witches often burned their victim's clothing to assure that the dead person's after life soul had not hidden in the folds, waiting for a chance to slip out and sneak inside them to kill them, but they'd found no smoldering hearth, no ash pile.

Stone Ghost walked to the Matron's head and parted her gray hair with his fingers to examine her battered skull. Despite the fact that the Matron had lain in the pool for some time before they'd found her, blood clotted the hair around the wounds. "I thought we might discover—"

Stone Ghost's hands went still. He leaned over the body. In an ominous voice, he said, "Browser, Cloudblower, come here, please."

They both rushed forward.

"What is it, Uncle?"

"What did you find?"

The Matron's stiffening neck would not turn. Stone Ghost had to roll her to her side before they could see what he pointed to.

Cloudblower's mouth trembled. "Blessed gods, the skull was opened."

Stone Ghost nodded. "Yes, and by a hand that had done it many times. Notice how carefully the murderer cut away the bone, then replaced it. Later, she tried to glue the scalp back in place with blood to hide the hole."

Browser's throat went tight. "Why would the murderer try to hide the hole? What difference would it make?"

Stone Ghost took Browser's arm and headed him toward the ladder. "I am finished here, Nephew, and Cloudblower needs to wash and prepare your Matron's body. Let us go and give her the silence she needs."

"But, Elder," Cloudblower said. "I wish to hear more. Please—"

"I promise we will speak again later, Healer. I have things I must do, too."

"Yes, Elder," Cloudblower said, but she looked disappointed.

Stone Ghost climbed the ladder, and Browser gave Cloudblower a helpless look.

Her dark eyes softened. "Your uncle is right. We all have duties."

"I will speak with you later, as well."

"I look forward to it, War Chief."

Browser followed Stone Ghost out into the late morning sunlight. Stone Ghost walked to the edge of the kiva roof and stood quietly watching the children running through the plaza with dogs barking at their heels. In the distance, the yellow trees along the river glistened.

Stone Ghost did not turn when Browser walked up beside him, but he said, "Take me to the place she was killed, Nephew."

"Of course, Uncle, but, first, please tell me why the murderer cut a hole in our Matron's head."

Stone Ghost looked up at him with remarkably gentle eyes. "It is a part of the murderer's ritual, Nephew, and once we understand the ritual, we will understand the murderer."

"Does that mean that you do not know why she opened our Matron's skull?"

Stone Ghost took Browser by the arm, patted his hand, and led him across the rooftop toward the ladder down into the plaza. "I may know," he answered cryptically. "But let us hope I am wrong."

CHAPTER 16

MAUREEN YAWNED AND looked out at the dawn visible through the restaurant windows. The shadowed river tumbled and swirled like a thing alive.

The waitress smiled as she brought Maureen's "Breakfast Burrito," a wonderful concoction of eggs, onions, sausage, cheese, and green chili. The nachos she'd shared with Dusty last night had worn thin.

At least I don't have to fight the battle with my waistline. Air travel had its benefits around the belt. She picked up a fork and stirred the eggs into the chili. As she took her first bite, she studied her reflection in the mirror behind her booth. The restaurant made opulent use of mirrors and glass, all lit by chandeliers with brass and white globes; the effect was a mixture of modern and Victorian themes.

"Hey, lady!" Sylvia called.

"Sylvia!" Maureen stood up to hug her, then held her at arm's length, studying Sylvia's lean face and green eyes. She'd braided her shoulder-length brown hair. Muscle packed her shoulders. "You look great. How are you?"

"Hungover to beat hell," Sylvia said and turned. "Washais, this is Steve Sanders."

The slender black man smiled and offered a hand. "Pleased to meet you, Dr. Cole." His grip was firm, professional. He wore a pale blue denim shirt that accentuated the mahogany tones of his skin.

"I'm Maureen to my friends. Would you care to join me?"

"Sure thing, Washais." Sylvia slid into the booth and moved over to allow room for Steve. "God, I need coffee. Where's the waitress?"

As Sylvia took a deep breath, Maureen said, "It looks like you had a hard night."

"Understatement of the year." Steve groaned. "I suffered a bout of memory loss last night."

"You did?" Sylvia glanced sidelong at him.

"Yeah. I forgot how much I hate tequila."

Sylvia chuckled, and Maureen smiled and took another forkful of burrito. "I hear you're about finished with your degree, Steve."

"About," he said and grinned as he caught the waitress's eye and made a pleading motion with his coffee cup. She immediately brought a pot and filled the cups that Steve and Sylvia cradled as if in worship.

"The burrito," Sylvia ordered, "for both of us. Right, Steve?" He nodded and Sylvia continued, "Heavy on the jalapeños, please." She narrowed an eye. "You do have *fresh* jalapeños, right?"

"Right. Got it." The waitress walked away writing in her book.

"Fresh jalapeños?" Maureen asked.

Sylvia nodded. "You bet. The rule of thumb on Mexican food is that if they have fresh jalapeños, then the food is almost always super. If the peppers come drowned in a can of vinegar, the food will probably gag a maggot."

"Oh, God. Don't mention gagging." Steve gulped his coffee.

Sylvia grinned. "Yeah, we had a great time. I half expected Dusty to drag you along, Maureen."

"Well," Maureen said with a shrug. "A teetotaler isn't much fun to drag along."

Sylvia nodded. "Yeah, I forgot the 'Mary the Hun' thing."

"Mary the Hun?" Steve asked, frowning. His eyes were the color of a buffalo's coat, a deep shining brown, almost black.

"You had to be there," Maureen told him. "It's part of the ongoing battle between Stewart and me."

"Washais doesn't drink," Sylvia translated, and paused to give Maureen a penetrating look. "Speaking of which, Boss Man said he'd catch up with us last night. We never saw him. What happened?"

Maureen gestured with her fork. "Got me. We called it quits at about ten-thirty. I'd been flying all day, and to be honest, I was beat. Stewart said he'd see me for breakfast at seven." She checked her watch. "It is now seven-thirty-two."

Sylvia frowned. "That's odd. Uh, don't take this the wrong way, but he didn't spend the night in your room, did he? I mean, not that it's anybody's business—"

"Good Lord, no!" Maureen blurted, surprised. "What could possibly make you think that Stewart and—"

"Whoa!" Sylvia raised her hands defensively. Steve Sanders was watching with bland amusement. Sylvia gave Maureen a crooked smile. "I asked because the three of us figured we'd share a room here, you know, split the cost three ways for a nice room and shower with all the fixins. But Dusty didn't show up last night. So I just kind of figured—"

"At all?" Maureen said as she cut up her tortilla.

"Nope." Sylvia tried to look mild. "That's why I thought that, well, you know, maybe he crashed on your chair, or something."

"He didn't." Maureen washed the last bite down with coffee. "But, to tell you the truth, he didn't look good when we left the bar. He said he was going for a walk. Maybe he's got friends in town? As I understand it, he knows just about anybody who is anybody in archaeology. Isn't there a college here?"

"Fort Lewis, and yeah, they have a really good anthropology department. There's a lot of archaeologists around, too." She gave Steve a sidelong look. "I just hope it isn't the spook."

"The spook?" Maureen asked.

"Maybe we'd better let Dusty—" Steve began.

"Naw, this is Washais. We've been witched together, and cleansed, and fought evil at 10K3. Washais is cool."

Maureen stiffened in spite of herself. "Just what 'spook' are we talking about?"

Sylvia sipped her coffee before replying. "Dusty was sleeping in the camp trailer. Or, I should say, trying to sleep." Sylvia made a face suddenly, turned slightly green, and placed a hand to her stomach. "Uh-oh." She swallowed hard, took a deep breath, and squinted until her stomach relaxed. "Sorry. Breakfast better get here quick or that waitress is going to have a really nasty morning."

"You were saying about Stewart?" Maureen prodded, hoping to distract Sylvia and buy the waitress, and everyone else in the restaurant, a more pleasant breakfast.

Sylvia sipped cautiously at her coffee. "Yeah, well, I think you as much as anyone can relate to this. Dusty was crying out in his sleep. I mean, wow, this was a really bad nightmare. He was groaning and moaning—"

"Stop it, you're getting me excited," Steve growled. "Just get to the point."

"The point," Sylvia rubbed her stomach, "goes back to the 10K3 site in Chaco Canyon. Do you remember that pit that Mrs. Walking Hawk had us dig?"

"The one outside the impact area?" Maureen remembered. They had uncovered a female skeleton. A young woman in her twenties with a rock on her head and a three-month-old fetus nestled in the arc of her pelvis: the "Haze child" of Elder Walking Hawk's vision. And on the woman's breastbone...

"Dusty was saying, 'Shut up, you little son of a bitch.' He sounded really scared. So I said, 'Who's a son of a bitch?' you know, just smarting off in the darkness. I only caught two words: he said 'witch' and '*basilisco*,' and went silent."

Maureen remembered the gorgeous black fetish, a red-eyed serpent coiled in a broken eggshell.

"I thought Dusty buried the basilisk, as Mrs. Walking Hawk asked."

"Well, Dusty's funny," Sylvia said. When she tilted her head, her shoulder-length brown hair caught the morning light. "I mean, he'll do some pretty unorthodox things, but he's still an archaeologist. He slipped out when no one was looking, dug it up, and bagged it. He curated it with the rest of the 10K3 collection. By now it's on the shelves at UNM."

"Sounds like he should have done as Mrs. Walking Hawk asked," Steve said.

Maureen shook her head. "Sorry. I'm with Dusty on this one. You can't start biasing science to please religious fundamentalists. Spiritual beliefs change with each generation. If you give in to one religion now, somebody in the future is going to hit you for showing a 'preference.' You can't do it, Steve."

Steve ducked, as though dodging a punch. "In this part of the world such a politically incorrect statement can call down lightning strikes, the ACLU, even the Native American Graves Protection and Repatriation Act advisory council, not to mention Indian lawyers in three-piece suits."

"I'm an Indian," Maureen said dryly. "We're not all antiscience."

Fortunately, breakfast arrived. Sylvia's color seemed to return as the waitress set her plate in front of her and she got the first bite down.

Maureen watched Sylvia and Steve eat for a while, then sat back in her chair with her coffee cup and said, "So, the basilisk is disturbing Dusty's dreams?"

Sylvia swallowed a mouthful of food and let out a relieved breath. "I guess. I'd be careful mentioning it to him, though. He's really sensitive about being cowardly. You know, it's a macho thing."

Maureen looked up when Dusty walked around the glass partition and strode toward their table. Across the restaurant, women's heads turned, their eyes following him as he crossed the room.

He did look good in his worn Levi's, khaki shirt, and cowboy hat. The light glinted in his blond hair, and his beard shone. Those broad shoulders and narrow waist would catch any woman's eye. Maureen couldn't help admiring him herself.

He pulled out a chair and sat down, and Maureen saw his red-rimmed eyes. He didn't look like he'd slept well. "Good morning."

Sylvia gave him a sidelong glance before asking, "What happened to you last night?"

He lifted a hand to hail the waitress, and when she waved back, he turned around and answered, "Let's just say that when the devil wants to destroy you, he first makes you pray."

Steve replied, "Really? He makes me horny. How about you, Sylvia? Maureen?"

Sylvia choked on her food, then squinted one eye, as if her stomach had started to rebel again. After a difficult swallow, she said, "Mine makes me yearn for the worm." When everybody shifted to stare at her, she added, "Mescal! You dirty-minded dopes."

Maureen laughed. "I'd forgotten how much fun you westerners can be."

"Us? Fun?" Dusty said.

"Absolutely. Where else could I get this kind of stimulating theological debate over breakfast?"

Dusty laced his fingers on the table. "And you're not even on site yet. Just wait."

CHAPTER 17

BROWSER, FOLLOWED BY Stone Ghost, waded the river with his war club in his hand. Sunlight fell through the cottonwood branches above him and scattered the water like shattered pieces of amber. Where the sun struck floating yellow leaves, they seemed to spark and flame before bobbing away on the current.

"This way, Uncle."

Browser stepped out onto the trail and looked down at the tracks. Stone Ghost continued splashing through the water behind him. The dirt had been churned up by too many feet. Any chance he might have had to find further evidence of the murderer's passage had vanished.

Stone Ghost waded out of the river into a shaft of sunlight, and his white hair glowed. His deep wrinkles cast a thousand crisscrossing shadows over his face. He gestured to the trail and said, "Please, lead the way, Nephew."

"Yes, Uncle."

Browser walked toward the brush thicket and the bend in the trail above the bathing pool. As he shouldered through the brush, the scent of damp earth and wet plants filled the air. Birds sang in the cottonwood branches. The serenity of the place seemed strangely out of kilter with the fact that an old woman had been murdered here only a few hands of time ago. He stepped out of the thicket and used his war club to hold the brush aside for his uncle.

Stone Ghost said, "I thank you, Nephew." He came through, and his gaze went to the bathing pool ten hands below. Sunlight dappled the cool green water.

"Where did you find your Matron?"

Browser pointed. "There, floating at the water's edge. Do you wish to see the place?"

Stone Ghost's sharp old eyes took in everything, the blood on the rocks that ringed the pool, the tracks, the drag marks along the shore. He shook his head. "Perhaps, later. The torture site is more important right now."

"Very well, Uncle."

They walked side by side into the trees. Most of the autumn foliage lay in windblown piles at the bases of the cottonwoods, but a few golden leaves flipped around his feet. Browser had visited the site earlier with Catkin, but as he approached the place where Flame Carrier had been tormented, rage twisted his gut.

"I see it," Stone Ghost said. He stopped a short distance from the torture site and studied the tracks.

Browser stood behind his uncle. "The four holes that you see—"

"Are where she was staked down, yes, that's clear." Patiently, methodically, his uncle's gaze moved from the holes to the bloody cords, the blood-soaked cloth, then lingered on the broken branches and pieces of driftwood the murderer had used as clubs.

"So," Stone Ghost said softly. "The man was not here when she tortured your Matron."

"No, he wasn't."

Stone Ghost turned to look back toward the bathing pool. Wind gusted through the trees and tore a brown-and-white feather loose from his tattered turkey feather cape; it spun away with a whirlwind of yellow leaves. "He met her at the pool?"

"Yes."

"And the woman's tracks, what did you find?"

Browser aimed his war club across the river. "The woman's tracks begin there and proceed down the river about fifty body lengths, where her steps meet our Matron's. They struggled on the ground. The woman must have forced our Matron into the water, then they crossed the river to this place where the murderer staked her down—"

"When she finished, she dragged your Matron into the bathing pool?"

Browser nodded. "Yes."

Stone Ghost exhaled hard as he looked around. "That is curious, don't you think?"

"What is?"

"That she dragged the Matron into the pool."

Browser shook his head in confusion. "Why is that curious? I assume she was still alive and the murderer wished to drown her."

"But she didn't drown her. She stabbed her to kill her."

Stone Ghost's bushy white brows plunged down over his beaked nose. He walked away into the densest trees, and said, "When I was a boy—let me see, that would have been about sixty-five summers ago—that pool was known as the Witches' Water Pocket."

"The Witches' Water Pocket? What did it mean?"

Stone Ghost used the toe of his sandal to move a patch of yellow leaves on the ground. "It was whispered that an army of witches lived beneath the water. To open the doorway to that underworld, a witch had to coat the water with blood. Only through a haze of blood could the witches below see his face, identify him, and decide if he should be allowed to come down."

"How did they get the blood?"

"According to the legends, they summoned people here, then they cut their chests open so that the heart pumped blood straight into the water."

The breeze fluttered black hair over Browser's eyes. He brushed it away. "What are you saying? That a witch killed our Matron? That she dragged her into the pool to coat the water with blood—"

"I'm not saying anything yet, Nephew. At least nothing of consequence." Stone Ghost bent down to examine the small spot he'd cleared of leaves. "I was merely telling you the legend. It is interesting, don't you think?"

Browser stared at the sparse white hair on top of his uncle's head. Stone Ghost never told stories just for the sake of relating legends.

"It's interesting," Browser granted, and continued, "Uncle, this morning Catkin told me you said, 'It would seem The Two have finally come home.' What did you mean by that?"

"Hmm?" Stone Ghost frowned. "What did I mean? Well . . ." He paused and appeared to be considering his answer, then lowered his finger to the ground. "Do you see this, Nephew?"

Browser dropped to one knee. "What is it?"

"Someone placed a pot here. See how the rounded pot bottom smoothed the dirt?"

"Yes."

"And look here." His crooked old finger moved. "This looks like a child's toeprint, but it might be a small woman's. Most of the track has been obliterated by this larger print—a man's, possibly. Do these look like the same tracks you found near the bathing pool?"

Browser's eyes went wide. "The man's tracks, and the woman's tracks! Right here! How did we miss them?"

Stone Ghost put an affectionate hand on Browser's shoulder. "The leaves, Nephew. Wind Baby keeps blowing them around. I suspect they cover much of the sign."

"Great Ancestors, I will have the women come down immediately and sweep—"

"No, Nephew, let us look ourselves. The fewer people who come here over the next few days, the better luck we will have finding evidence of the murderers' activities. Were I you, I would order my villagers not to come here at all until I had finished my examinations."

Browser swallowed hard. He should have already done that. The Matron's murder coming so soon after the Aspen village slaughter had muddled his thinking. What else had he missed? "I will do that the instant we return, Uncle."

Stone Ghost patted his shoulder and lowered his hand to brush at more leaves. The tracks had sunk deeply into the damp earth, but the pot bottom had barely left an impression.

"The pot must have been empty," Browser said.

"Perhaps," Stone Ghost replied. "But things like herbs are almost weightless."

Browser inclined his head. "That's true. Do you think the murderers carry herbs with them? Healing herbs? Herbs used to witch people?"

"I think the murderers carry a small light pot. That's all I see here." He struggled to his feet. "Walk with me, Nephew. Let us see what else we might find beneath the blanket of golden leaves."

Stone Ghost wandered from place to place brushing at leaves, grunting to himself. He surveyed every spot that had been blown clean by the wind and brushed the leaves from many others, particularly close to the torture site. Browser followed along, his gaze on the hills and trees, anywhere a warrior might hide.

"Hmm." Stone Ghost leaned over a white oblong river cobble.

"Looks like chert," Browser said.

"Looks like an old fire pit to me."

Browser bent to examine it. Tiny hackling fractures veined the rock. Someone, many summers before, had thrown the rock into a fire. The heat had cracked it. Browser's people heat-treated chert to make it easier to work into stone tools, but Browser hadn't noticed the fractures until his uncle mentioned them.

"Your eyes are still excellent, Uncle. Better than mine." He peered at his uncle. "But why would an old fire pit matter today?"

"I don't know yet."

Stone Ghost touched the cobble. "Who was standing guard last night?"

"Water Snake."

"Was he alone?"

Distastefully, Browser said, "No. Obsidian was there part of the time."

Stone Ghost turned the cobble in his hands. "Did either of them hear anything?"

"I haven't spoken with Water Snake yet. Right after I found our Matron's body, Water Snake left with the search party. I will question him tonight when he returns."

Stone Ghost placed the cobble back on the ground and took a few moments to fit it into the shallow hole it had come from. "What did Obsidian tell you?"

Browser propped his hands on his hips and filled his lungs. "She says she heard nothing. But she saw our Matron leave and walk down toward the river. That's why Redcrop and I searched the river first. I thought that—"

"Yes, I would have too." Stone Ghost stood and pinned Browser with sharp old eyes. "What did you find in Aspen village, Nephew?"

Thrown off-balance by the switch in subjects, Browser stammered, "I—I should gather the elders and tell them before I—"

"I do not wish to sway you from your duty, of course, but it might help me to better understand what happened here last night."

"Why? The two events have nothing to do with each other."

Stone Ghost scratched his wrinkled throat, and his gaze lifted to the golden leaves trembling in the wind and the Cloud People sailing through the turquoise sky. "What makes you so certain?"

Browser shifted uncomfortably. The woman on the kiva roof? The "wounded" woman Catkin saw? Could she be the same woman who had murdered their Matron? It didn't seem likely, though a hard run would have brought her to Longtail village last night—as it had them. He and Catkin had made it around midnight, but they hadn't been dragging a little girl along. On the other hand, they'd spent six or seven hands of time sleeping and eating. If the woman had run straight through . . .

Browser looked down and found his uncle staring at him with expectant eyes.

Stone Ghost said, "Did it fit?"

"What?"

"The broken sherds you were piecing together?"

Browser leaned his war club on his shoulder, and considered what he could say without betraying the elders' trust. It was his duty as War Chief to notify them first, but his uncle had a special talent for "putting sherds together," and they all needed that talent today.

Through a taut exhalation, Browser said, "I counted forty-two dead people in the kiva at Aspen village, Uncle. Almost all had been decapitated. We found several of their heads about half a hand of time from the village."

Stone Ghost didn't speak for a time. "What else?"

Browser tied his war club to his belt and reached for his pouch. "I found these." He drew out the three shiny copper bells.

Stone Ghost stared at them unblinking, but awe slackened his face. "Where did you find them?"

"I picked up two in the empty village plaza, but there were three more arranged in a line leading to the kiva."

Stone Ghost's gaze went from the bells to Browser's eyes and stayed there. "You followed the bells and you are still alive?"

"I think our enemy wished to have someone left to tell the tale of his handiwork."

Stone Ghost started walking through the trees again, his eyes focused on the ground. His feather cape swayed with his irregular gait. "Tell me about this handiwork."

"The villagers had been butchered, Uncle, the flesh stripped from their bones and carried away. I don't know where to, but it was not in the kiva. Nor did we find it with the heads."

Stone Ghost's steps faltered. "It would take time to strip that much flesh from the bodies. Even with five or ten people, it would take a few days."

"They had three days, Uncle. And"—Browser tucked the bells back into his pouch—"we found the heads a short distance from the village. They'd been arranged in four concentric circles. We think their Matron had been sitting in the center of the heads for some time. The grass had been mashed down and frozen." Browser exhaled hard. "We saw a white-caped man kill her, Uncle. He found her in the forest, dragged her back, and clubbed her to the death."

"What else? Tell me everything you remember."

"There was also a mummy. We found a mummy."

"A mummy? In the kiva?" Stone Ghost turned around to face him.

"No. At the top of the eastern trail leading down to the village. Someone had wrapped a rope around her belly, then looped it over a boulder to hang her there for us to see."

The lines around Stone Ghost's eyes tightened. "For you, Nephew? Why would someone do that?"

He gestured uncertainly. "It just seemed odd that we would return and—"

"If the mummy was placed there for you, Nephew, then the village was destroyed for your benefit. Do you think you and Catkin are that important to your enemies? Would they destroy an entire village to teach you a lesson? They certainly did not do it to lure you in to kill you, because they let both of you go."

Browser felt foolish. He toyed with his belted club. "When you say it that way, I'm sure I'm wrong, Uncle. But why else would they leave the mummy and then take it away with them?"

Stone Ghost frowned. "They took it away?"

"Well, yes." Browser ran a hand through his hair and nodded. "This is a long story, Uncle."

Stone Ghost nodded. "Let us find a place to sit down, Nephew. I must know everything. Even small details you think are not important."

"Like why they did not kill me and Catkin?"

Stone Ghost took Browser by the arm and headed him toward a cottonwood. "If we can determine that, Nephew, I think we will also know why your Matron was killed."

A HAND OF time later, Stone Ghost turned to Browser where they sat with their backs braced against an enormous tree trunk and whispered, "Copper bells, a scarred mummy with spirals on her chin, and a little girl skipping on the roof of a kiva filled with headless people. Fascinating."

"I don't think it's fascinating. I think it's cruel and inhuman."

"On the contrary. It's very human, Browser." A gleam lit his uncle's sharp old eyes. He steepled his fingers beneath his chin, but he wasn't seeing the shadow-dappled river or the glint of rocks beneath the water. He seemed to be gazing into some private memory chamber. "It's also *brilliant*." He looked at Browser. "Come, Nephew. I must see your Matron's body again."

MAUREEN GAZED OUT the window at the passing pinyon-and juniper-clad ridges. Thick layers of brown sandstone jutted up on each side as they dropped down Bondad Hill into the Animas Valley, then the sandstone gave way to tumbled talus slopes and sagebrush-filled bottoms.

Maureen turned to Dusty. "Sylvia said you were supposed to crash in their room last night? She was worried about you."

When Sylvia had pressed him on where he'd disappeared to last night, he'd simply told them he'd forgotten an errand, and given them his "don't mess with me" glare.

Dusty pushed his cowboy hat back on his head. "Yeah, well, that's a long story. I took 550 north, up the canyon to the top of Molas Pass, and spent some time watching the stars wheel around Polaris. When the cold—vicious at a tad shy of eleven thousand feet—finally ate into my bones, I turned the Bronco around and drove back to Durango." Dusty lifted his coffee cup from the compartment between the seats and sipped at it, driving with one hand. "Sometime after three, I slipped into the hotel room and found Sylvia and Steve sound asleep in the same bed. I backed out of the room, got into the Bronco, and piled my old Pendleton blanket over myself. I slept pretty good."

"You could have come to my room. I would have let you have my floor."

Dusty smiled. "Thanks, but it didn't seem like a good idea."

Maureen shrugged. He was right, of course. It would have been very awkward if he'd come knocking on her door at midnight. She would have invited him in, and they'd have both spent the night with one eye open, watching the other—and wondering about things they shouldn't wonder about.

A few kilometers ahead, rain fell from the cloudy sky in wavering gray sheets.

Maureen kept glancing at Dusty as they passed the fallow farms that dotted the Animas floodplain. Lines had formed around the corners of his eyes, giving his tanned skin a weathered look. His beard, a darker shade of blond, caught the light. A strong straight nose accented his jawline. The crumpled cowboy hat, with the sunglasses perched atop it, reminded her of pictures she'd seen of Jerry Jeff Walker in his heyday. Stewart had a magnetism, a sense of rugged reliability belied by the stories people told about him.

"What river is this?" Maureen asked as they crossed the bridge below the junction with the Florida.

"The same one that flows past the Doubletree where you stayed last night. Originally it was called *El Rio de las Animas Perdidas*. Loosely translated that means 'The River of the Lost Souls,' as in 'The Souls of the Damned.' "

"Such a hard name for such a beautiful river."

"That's why the White guys dropped the 'Damned' part and left it as the Animas, the 'River of Souls.' " He frowned. "Though I'm not sure that was the right decision."

"What do you mean?"

"A lot of the souls in this country were damned. Consider," he said and lifted a finger.

Maureen smiled. She could feel the lecture coming.

"At about A.D. 1000 there were hundreds of pueblos, small and large, scattered over the Four Corners region of Colorado, New Mexico, Utah, and Arizona. By 1300, almost everyone was living in twenty-seven settlements consisting of about a hundred and twenty large defensive pueblos. By A.D. 1400, twenty-four of those twenty-seven settlements had been abandoned. The thirteenth century was a period of annihilation-oriented warfare. At the end, only three settlement clusters were left in the original western Anasazi homeland: the Hopi villages in Arizona, the Zuni pueblos in New Mexico, and the Keres at Acoma, New Mexico. In between those settlements were vast no-man's-lands where, apparently, no one dared to live."

She cocked her head. "Okay, I'll bite. What do you think happened?"

"I think it was a vicious holy war that lasted for two centuries, Doctor."

"Holy war?"

"Yes. We know the Katchina religion starts right after the fall of Chaco Canyon at the end of the twelfth century. The kiva murals in the 1300s are filled with battle images. Why do you paint war scenes on the walls of your church?"

Maureen gazed out at a grove of what looked like apple trees, their leaves just turning yellow. "To show your zeal for killing heretics? The 'God is on my side' thing?"

He nodded. "I think so."

"Well, if your idea about holy war holds up, the 'enemy' should be doing the same thing to the new katchina believers that they did to the Christians during the first century after Jesus died, and to the Jews in thirteenth-century Spain, the Muslims in Bosnia. Did they label them as evil and burn them in their churches and temples?"

Dusty lifted his plastic coffee cup in a silent toast to her. "That, my dear doctor, is an understatement. I personally know of over thirty kivas, subterranean ceremonial chambers, filled with dead bodies. Many of them are children."

A sudden feeling of deep sadness filled Maureen. When a soldier could kill a child, there was more going on than just warfare. Hatred and fear had to be at work. "You've found several children in the kiva you're digging now, right?"

"Right." Dusty sipped his coffee, and steam curled into his mustache. "I think this kiva is one of the tragedies of the holy war. There are a lot of others. At Sand Canyon Pueblo in Colorado, they found forty people burned in the kiva. The kiva at the Snider's Well site in southwestern Colorado had ninety bodies in it. At Te-ewi in New Mexico, twenty-four men and six infants were left unburied on the ground outside. Just south of us is Aztec Ruins. When Earl Morris excavated the site in the twenties, he found a mass burial of fifteen children. At Salmon Ruins, south of Aztec, they found a kiva filled with burned children, most under the age of five. That's just a sampling of the grisly events of the thirteenth and fourteenth centuries. Believe me, there are plenty more."

Maureen watched the rolling hills for a while, then said, "Couldn't the deaths be ritual sacrifices rather than warfare?"

"One doesn't preclude the other, Doctor. Try to see it from the attackers' side. It takes a lot more than hatred to force men to capture children and burn them to death in their parents' churches. They have to *believe* very powerfully that what they're doing is right. I'm sure somebody convinced them that every child was a ritual sacrifice, an offering to the true God—or gods."

Maureen shifted in her seat to face Dusty. "I was just thinking about that. Killing someone in their place of worship is a potent symbol. It's a warning to others that if they share the heretics' beliefs, they'll be next." She studied him with her eyes narrowed. "What else?"

"Oh, lots of things. We find a number of infants stuffed into air shafts. But I don't get that symbolism."

"So, who are the factions. What's the war about? The katchinas versus . . . whom?"

"Good question," Dusty answered, and grimaced as rain speckled the windshield. After a moment, the whole glass was covered.

"Time for wipers, Stewart?" she suggested, squinting through the grimy mess in an attempt to see the road.

"In a bit, Doctor."

She tried not to look worried as the world disappeared into a smear. She impulsively reached for the seat belt, remembering too late the story Dusty had told her about using it for a tow strap once when he got stuck out in the desert. She sank her fingers into the armrest instead.

"All right," Dusty muttered and rotated the switch on the lever. The wipers groaned and popped, as if the rubber had stuck to the glass. To Maureen's horror, the smear grew worse. Mud and bug guts streaked the glass in a semi-opaque film.

"Come on, rain!" Dusty called with the same rising inflection as a gambler tossing dice in a crap game.

"Does this improve?" Maureen asked. Dear God, he had to be driving by guess and by golly. She couldn't see a thing through the sludge on the windshield.

The rain picked up, hammering down in a blizzard of large drops. The view cleared as water sluiced away the grime.

Dusty sank back in his seat. "The rubber hardens up in this high-altitude sun. We get a lot more UV here. Then you get it blown full of dust and the bug guts get baked on the glass. Cooked, you know. It takes a lot of water to soak everything up enough to clean the windshield."

She lifted an eyebrow. "Isn't there something called windshield washer fluid? And don't gas stations in this country have those little squeegees? The ones in the plastic bins?"

"Yeah." He scowled out at the falling rain. "Somewhere along the line the pump for the window washer got full of dust and plugged up. I think it was during the Kayenta project in 'ninety-seven. I mean, God, mechanics want real money to fix those things."

Amazed, she said, "Stewart, you could get killed driving around with a dirty windshield. What if the rain didn't pick up and wash it clean?"

"Well," he said with a nod, "we could pull over and piss on it."

Maureen tried to imagine the positions "we" would have to adopt to accomplish that feat. She said, "You're on your own there, Stewart."

"Women have no sense of adventure." Dusty glanced up at the sky and grimaced. "I hope the tarps over the excavation units hold. We chucked the mattock and shovels over them, but you never know in a storm like this."

She exhaled and it condensed into a white cloud. "You know, it might be about time to see what kind of disaster happens when you turn on the heater."

"Disaster, Doctor?" He reached for the knob.

"I remember my first ride in this truck, Stewart. You had to hammer the dash to get the oil pressure gauge to work. The window crank fell off and disappeared into an alternate universe under my seat."

He smiled, amused, and began rolling his window down.

"That does not improve our situation, Stewart. What are you doing?" she asked.

"Trust me. Roll yours down, too. Oh, and be careful. The—"

"Yeah, yeah, the knob comes off." She carefully cranked the window down, and icy air and spatters of cold rain insulted her cheeks and hair.

The moment Dusty reached over and flipped the heater fan on, a blast of dust blew from the heater vents and fogged the interior in musty-smelling clouds. Dusty used a finger to lower the rear window and the draft sucked the dust through and out the back. That dropped the pressure just enough that a snowstorm of confettied paper shot from the heater vents.

"Good Lord!" Maureen coughed and waved to clear the chaff in front of her face. "What is this?"

"The little assholes!" Stewart roared, and pounded the dash with a knotted fist.

Maureen grimaced as the wind and rain came buffeting through the lowered window, and bits of shredded paper circled and danced, until they settled on her hair and clothing. It looked like chewed-up toilet paper.

"Stewart?"

Dusty hammered the dash one last time. "I *hate* mice!"

"That's what this is?" she said as she plucked at the bits of paper that stuck to her rain-damp skin.

"Yeah, mouse nest," he muttered. "The little bastards crawl into the heater ducts. I mean, if you're a mouse, they're perfect, right? Just mouse-sized little tubes inside a truck where people eat donuts and crackers and sunflower seeds and all those things a mouse loves. Then there's the stuffing under the seats, and, of course, if you're an archaeologist who spends a lot of time in the boonies, you've got a roll of bun wad. TP and seat upholstery make perfect nesting materials."

Stewart rolled up the rear window, and Maureen watched the rush of paper dwindle to an occasional bit of white shooting from the vents and twirling around before it settled on the seats, dash, and her. With the rising temperature of the air, tiny little brown projectiles clattered out of the heater vents and stuck to her wet shoes.

"Stewart"—she kicked one off—"is this . . . ?"

"Mouse shit. Yeah."

"Good Lord, Stewart. Have you ever heard of the Hanta virus? It's big in this part of the world, isn't it?"

Dusty shrugged. "Hasn't killed me yet."

She could imagine beady-eyed little mice, their vibrissae quivering, as they made hex signs and peed Hanta virus all over the inside of Dusty's heater vents. In defense, she hung her head out the window and breathed. The rain felt like shotgun pellets.

"Stewart, can't you, say, poison them, or something?"

"Yeah, but then they crawl in the vents and die, and when the hot sun heats the vehicle to about one hundred and forty, their little bodies swell up and bust. You have no idea—"

"Enough!" She raised a hand, waving for him to desist.

"Well," he said mildly, rolling his window up, "you asked why I didn't poison them."

"Doesn't the Hanta virus scare you?"

"Sure, but out here, you kind of get used to mice. I mean, they're everywhere. You don't hear so much about the virus on the radio these days, so I guess the disease has pretty much run its course."

"I'm so relieved," she wheezed, trying to find a halfway place where she could suck clean air from outside without drowning in the cold downpour.

"Almost there, Doctor." Stewart slowed and turned off the pavement onto a dirt ranch road. "Pueblo Animas is just ahead."

The Bronco rumbled across the Texas gate, known as a cattle guard down here, and along the graveled section of road. She wasn't ready for the left onto the two-track that led up the ridge and across the terrace toward the site.

The Bronco slipped sideways as Dusty steered rapidly into the skid and stopped. "You want to get the hub on that side?" he asked.

"What just happened?" She was clinging to the seat.

Dusty studied her for a few seconds, then opened his door. "This dirt has a high silt and clay content. Have you ever heard the term 'gumbo' before, Doctor?"

Confused, Maureen said, "Not unless it relates to Cajun food."

"Well, it's kind of a generic term in the West. It means slick, sticky, gooey mud." His blue-eyed stare took in her pale expression, and the bits of white toilet paper stuck to her face. "Never mind," he said. "You sit tight. I'll put both hubs in."

He stepped out into the rain, minced his way to the front wheel, and bent down. Then he waded around to her side. She stuck her head out just far enough to see him turn something on the wheel. He slopped his way back to the driver's side, got in, and slipped the four-wheel drive shifter knob forward.

Dusty said, "Just hang on and pretend you're a kid again."

"You mean, I'm going to be scared."

"Just trust me. I promise that no matter what it feels like, we're not going to crash and die."

At the look in his eyes, she braced her hands and feet, and nodded. "Go for it, Stewart."

CHAPTER 18

REDCROP SAT ON the east side of the bench that circled the tower kiva, staring down at her long white ritual dress. Red spirals painted the bodice and collar. Two body lengths above her, late afternoon sunlight poured through the entry and shone on the use-polished rungs of the ladder.

She lifted her gaze and scanned the room. Dancing yellow flames burned in the middle of the kiva floor, but she felt cold. Every time air filled her lungs, an icy tingle filtered outward from her heart and rolled through her body.

The sacred Hero Twins stood on the wall across the kiva, watching her with gleaming black eyes. When she looked at them, fear prickled her belly. The priest-painters always breathed life into their artistry, and she could feel the twins' souls; their presence permeated the chamber like a silent roar of thunder.

Redcrop looked at them from the corner of her eyes. During the Age of Emergence, monsters had ruled the world. They had eaten humans all the time. The Great Warriors had climbed to Father Sun to ask him how to kill the monsters, and Father Sun had given them lightning bolts to use as lances. The twins had saved the First People. Redcrop did not know why she feared the saviours so much, but she did. There was something scary about their fierce expressions and the lightning bolts they held in their upraised hands. No matter where she moved in the room, the lances always seemed to be pointed at her heart.

She lowered her eyes and examined the eight katsina masks that hung above the wall niches. Tufts of eagle down crowned several of the masks. Beards made from buffalo, rabbit, or coyote fur hung from their chins. Her gaze went from mask to mask, staring at the sharp fangs and polished wooden beaks, lingering on the dark, empty eyes. The amber gleam of the fire flickered in the hollow sockets and gave them a strange haunting glow. But the katsinas didn't scare Redcrop. They comforted her. If she concentrated, she could almost hear their voices whispering to her, trying to guide her through the grief and pain.

She exhaled, and her head tottered on her neck. All of her strength had vanished. The picture of a dried-out insect husk painted the fabric behind her eyes. She felt hollow, brittle. The only thing she had ever wanted in life was to be free, to marry a man she loved, and to have children. Now, none of that seemed to matter.

To her right, Cloudblower prepared Flame Carrier's body for the journey to the afterlife. The Matron's gray hair had been freshly washed with yucca soap. It spread around her face in a glistening wreath. A beautiful red macaw feather cape covered her from the waist down. The hideous stab wounds in her grandmother's chest resembled gaping mouths.

In the past seven hands of time, Flame Carrier's skinned face had turned a hideous bluish-purple color. Redcrop didn't even recognize her.

Cloudblower caught the expression on Redcrop's face. Her long white dress flashed in the firelight as she turned and gently said, "Are you all right, Redcrop? You do not have to stay for this."

Redcrop tried to find the breath to speak. She watched the *Kokwimu*; the sacred Man-Woman, paint a line of white stars on Flame Carrier's left arm. "I have to stay, Cloudblower. She might need me."

Flame Carrier had needed her for more than thirteen sun cycles. Redcrop could not get over the feeling that she still did.

Cloudblower used her sleeve to wipe perspiration from her long nose. "You know that each person has two souls, a soul that stays with the body forever, and the breath-heart soul that keeps the lungs moving and the heart beating. At death, the breath-heart soul leaves the body, but it's always near until the body is buried. Both of her souls are here in the room with us, Redcrop. She's probably more worried about you than you are about her."

Redcrop searched the firelit kiva with blurry eyes, praying to glimpse Flame Carrier moving about in her stiff elderly gait, but she saw only fierce warriors and empty-eyed masks.

Cloudblower turned to the array of objects laid out on the bench above Flame Carrier's head: paint pots, yucca cords, carefully folded clothing. She reached for the blue paint pot and swished the human-hair paintbrush around the interior. When she pulled the brush out, the bristles shone the deeply bruised color of storm clouds.

Cloudblower bent over Flame Carrier's bony chest and painted an inverted pyramid of thunderheads above each breast. The blue-gray squares grew smaller as they neared the Matron's nipples. Thunderheads gave people rain in much the same way that a mother gave an infant milk. Both were life.

Cloudblower set the blue pot down, and pulled the red-feathered cape away from Flame Carrier's lower body. Stringy muscles mottled her thighs and calves. Her hip bones stuck out sharply. A sparse mat of gray hair frosted her groin.

Cloudblower gave Redcrop a sympathetic look. "Do you wish to help me with the cornmeal purification, Redcrop?"

Redcrop studied the leather pouches on Cloudblower's belt. Tiny fangs nibbled at her backbone and belly, eating her from the inside out. She was afraid to move. She shook her head.

Cloudblower removed three leather pouches from her belt, loosened the laces of the largest one, and poured a small amount of red cornmeal into her palm; then she picked up the two lengths of yucca cord that lay on the bench and draped them over her wrists.

"W-wait." Redcrop slid off the bench and unsteadily walked toward Cloudblower. "Please, I would like to help."

Cloudblower smiled. A few sweat-drenched strands of graying black hair had escaped her bun and fringed her face. "I think the Matron will be glad to feel your touch."

Redcrop held out her left hand, and Cloudblower gave her two of the pouches, then draped the cords over Redcrop's wrists.

Redcrop stood numbly. She had helped Flame Carrier with this ritual many times, but the dead had always been acquaintances, never someone truly close to Redcrop. Flame Carrier's eyes, the eyes that had looked at Redcrop with such love last night, had turned a dull milky gray. Redcrop could barely stand it.

She took Flame Carrier's rigid left hand and held it for a long moment before murmuring, "For our Blessed Ancestors," then she tucked one of the pouches into Flame Carrier's palm. The flesh had gone cold and clammy.

Redcrop removed a yucca cord and tenderly wove it through Flame Carrier's fingers and around her wrist. Finally, she pulled it tight and knotted it, tying up the hand so that the leather pouch would not fall out. It would be Flame Carrier's offering to the ancestors when she reached the Land of the Dead.

Redcrop repeated the ritual with Flame Carrier's right hand, then weakly sank down on the bench.

Cloudblower stood beside Redcrop, her hands filled with yellow cornmeal. "For our Matron's heart," she said and sprinkled yellow cornmeal into Flame Carrier's eyes and over the purpled flesh of her face, cleansing away the anger and suffering that had marred the last moments of her life. Now Flame Carrier would be able to greet her Blessed relatives with a clean and open heart.

Redcrop lowered her shaking hands to her lap.

Last night, before they'd crawled into their bedding, Flame Carrier had smoothed her warm old fingers down Redcrop's arm and said, *"I love you, child. I will see you at daybreak."*

Tears flooded silently down Redcrop's cheeks.

Cloudblower said, "Try to see us through the Matron's eyes, Redcrop. She is standing right here watching you cry and it's breaking her heart."

Redcrop reached out for her grandmother's hand and held it in a crushing grip, fighting the grief that twisted her belly.

Cloudblower pulled a pale blue dress from the bench. The burial dress had been designed so that the entire front was open. With great care, Cloudblower slipped it beneath Flame Carrier, then worked the wide sleeve openings up over her stiff arms, straightened the dress, and began tying the front laces. The chunks of jet and polished slate around the collar gleamed. "Do you wish to help me put on her jewelry, Redcrop?"

Cloudblower reached for a bag on the bench and pulled out a handful of Flame Carrier's favorite shell bracelets, necklaces, hairpins. Redcrop took several of the bracelets and slipped them over Flame Carrier's wrists. Flame Carrier would love her new dress. Sky blue had been her favorite color.

Cloudblower tenderly touched Redcrop's hand. "Now, please follow me." She walked to the fire pit.

A pot of warm juniper-scented water nestled in the ashes at the edge of the flames. "Please take off your clothing, Redcrop. There are many evil Spirits who are drawn by the scent of death. They secrete themselves in the clothing of the living and cause disease or even death. We must make certain we have killed them all."

Redcrop pulled her dress over her head and handed it to Cloudblower. The sacred Man-Woman took it without a word and dropped it onto the fire. Yellow tongues of flame licked up around the cotton cloth, and a cloud of smoke rose toward the sunlit roof opening.

Redcrop hugged herself. Despite the warmth of the fire, a cool breeze blew down from above, fanning the flames and taunting her bare skin.

"Cloudblower, why did she have to go out last night? Why didn't she wake me? I always go out with her at night. She didn't see very well. She liked to hold my arm to steady her steps. If she had wakened me, maybe I would have seen or—or heard something before . . ." Her voice dwindled to nothing.

A taut expression creased Cloudblower's face while she waited for Redcrop to finish.

Redcrop said, "Do you think she tried to wake me? Maybe I was sleeping deeply and didn't—"

"No, Redcrop. No, I don't. I think she quietly rose from her blankets and went out alone because she wished to. None of us can say why, but she did not die because you did anything wrong. You spent every moment trying to help her. She knew that and loved you very much for it."

Blood pulsed in Redcrop's ears. She still had to gather the things Flame Carrier would need for the journey to the Land of the Dead: a pot of corn to eat, an extra pair of sandals, warm turkey feather socks, and a jar of water.

Cloudblower rattled the pots around the fire, and Redcrop smelled the sweet fragrance of juniper.

Cloudblower pulled the pot from the ashes and handed it to Redcrop. "There's a strip of red fabric soaking in the bottom. Please, wash thoroughly."

Redcrop reached into the warm water and pulled out the cloth. As she ran it over her legs and arms, she watched Cloudblower undress. She had seen the holy Man-Woman naked many times at the bathing pool, but the sight of her penis always caught Redcrop's attention. She stared at it as she wrung out the scented cloth and rubbed it over her face and chest.

Cloudblower placed her white dress on the flames and saw Redcrop watching her. She smiled. "Are you finished with the water?"

"Yes." Redcrop handed the pot around the fire and stood quietly while Cloudblower scrubbed her tall, muscular body.

People had gathered in the plaza outside. Redcrop could hear bits of conversation and flute music. Down by the river, a dog barked.

Cloudblower finished scrubbing the taint of death from her flesh and lifted the pot over her head. "Are you ready?"

Redcrop nodded and stood back.

Cloudblower smashed the pot down on the hearthstones. Broken sherds wheeled across the floor of the kiva.

"Now let us sanctify our souls."

Cloudblower tossed several shiny globs of pinyon pine sap onto the coals. When they sizzled and burst into flame, she cupped the smoke in her hands and rubbed it over her freshly washed chest and face, working her way down her tall body.

Redcrop rubbed smoke over her own naked flesh. It felt warm and smelled sweetly aromatic. Smoke was a cousin to the Blessed Cloud People who brought the rain that watered their crops. Smoke consecrated.

"Good. Now come." Cloudblower held out a hand.

Redcrop followed her to the bench where Flame Carrier rested.

Cloudblower picked up the new dress lying folded on the bench above Flame Carrier's head and handed it to Redcrop. Beautiful, the buttery doehide had chevrons of red-and-blue porcupine quills sewn around the collar. Redcrop slipped it over her head.

Cloudblower put on a deep blue dress. Bands of white shell beads decorated the long sleeves. They glittered wildly in the firelight.

"We have done all we can for the Matron today, Redcrop. Tomorrow, we will place her on her burial ladder and Sing her to the Land of the Dead. I have a pot of venison stew warming in my chamber. Will you share it with me?"

In her entire life, Redcrop had never eaten supper without Flame Carrier. Not even once.

An unexpected sob tightened Redcrop's throat. She reached out to stroke Flame Carrier's tied hand.

"She would wish you to eat, Redcrop. Tomorrow will be a very long day."

Redcrop gazed down at Flame Carrier, and the black hole inside her seemed to swallow her heart and lungs. "I wish to stay with her for a time, Cloudblower. Is that all right?"

Cloudblower nodded. "Yes, of course. I'll keep supper ready for you in my chamber."

She went to the ladder and climbed into the last slanting rays of sunlight. Redcrop heard Cloudblower speak to someone; the soft voices carried.

Steps thumped the roof, and the War Chief called, "Redcrop? My uncle and I wish to see the Matron. Will it disturb you?"

"No, War Chief. Come, please."

Browser and Stone Ghost climbed down the ladder and crossed the room.

Redcrop sank to the floor beside Flame Carrier and rested her head on the old woman's bony shoulder, as she had done a hundred times. When she'd been a little girl and frightened, this had been the only place in the world where she'd felt safe.

"I'm here, Grandmother," she whispered and nuzzled her cheek against Flame Carrier's new dress. "I'm right here."

Stone Ghost gently lifted the Matron's stiff arm and looked at it, then he unlaced and opened the front of her blue dress to examine her chest; he seemed to be searching the deepest wounds. The War Chief stood back with his arms folded, watching. He appeared confused, but curious.

To Redcrop's horror, Stone Ghost parted Flame Carrier's freshly washed gray hair, lifted her severed scalp, and stuck his finger into the hole in her skull. Blood welled into her hair again.

Redcrop said, "Elder? We just washed her. What are you doing?"

Stone Ghost made a small sound, then dug out a bloody object.

Redcrop leaped from the bench with her hand to her mouth in horror. Witches shot objects into people to kill them! She had seen Healers suck them from the bodies of sick people and spit them onto the floor. Is that what this was? A witch pellet?

"Oh, gods, what is it?" Redcrop cried.

Stone Ghost replied, "It is not what I expected. I thought I might find a copper bell." He held the object up to the firelight. "This is a tiny turquoise wolf. Crudely carved, but a wolf just the same."

"What?" Browser rushed forward. "I don't understand. Why would someone place a fetish inside a dead woman's skull?"

Stone Ghost placed the bloody wolf in the War Chief's palm, then wiped his hand on his turkey feather cape. "She must have felt remorse, Nephew."

"You mean, the murderer?" Browser asked as he turned the wolf in his hand.

"Yes. After she killed your Matron, she carved this wolf and gave it to her to make sure the Matron's afterlife soul would find its way to the Land of the Dead." Stone Ghost tilted his head and his eyes moved as though deep in thought. "But why did she think it would work? Wolves carved by the First People had the Power to guide a soul, but wolves carved by Made People don't . . ." His voice drifted away.

Browser said, "Don't what?"

Stone Ghost stared sightlessly at the floor, as if deep in thought.

Browser pressed, "Do you think she sees herself as a saviour? As some sort of deity who can breathe Power into objects like the First People used to?"

As if he had not heard, Stone Ghost stared out at nothing, his eyes unfocused. "Perhaps," he whispered, then relaced the Matron's sky blue dress. "Or maybe the murderer is trying desperately to save her own soul."

Redcrop wet her dry lips and said, "Please tell me what you are speaking about."

Stone Ghost walked over, took Redcrop's hands, and held them tightly, while his black eyes searched her face. He talked to her as if she were an adult, not a child. "I'm not sure yet, Redcrop. All I know is that the woman who murdered your grandmother is in great pain. Her souls have loosened. When I see things more clearly, I will tell you. I promise." Stone Ghost patted her hands. "Do you have a place to sleep tonight?"

"I—I was thinking I would sleep on the bench next to Grandmother. Cloudblower will be here all night tending the ritual fire. I thought she might like the company."

"I'm sure she would." He released her hands. "I will hope to see you later then."

Redcrop nodded. "Yes, I'll be out. Soon."

As he and Browser walked toward the kiva ladder, Redcrop heard Stone Ghost whisper, "I would like to go with you when you tell the elders about Aspen village, Nephew."

"Of course, Uncle, but—why?"

"Because I want to see their expressions."

Browser's steps faltered. He stared hard at the back of Stone Ghost's white head as the elder started climbing the ladder, and Redcrop saw the War Chief's eyes narrow. Browser stood at the base of the ladder for several instants, not moving, not even blinking. Though he stared at Stone Ghost, he did not seem to see him. He appeared to be deep in thought, as though Stone Ghost's words had stirred suspicions he'd never considered.

Finally, he climbed out into the sunlight after Stone Ghost, and Redcrop sank down on the bench above Flame Carrier's head and began gently stroking her bloody hair.

PIPER LIES ON her back in a tunnel the rabbits made through the brush. Thunder rumbles. She listens. Vines weave around her, some as thick as her arms. Through the holes she can see golden leaves wiggling and hear them whispering to each other. She can also see Mother.

This is a Bead Day. Mother came home with blood on her hands. She sits on the ground, turning bones into beads, grumbling to herself. It is the grumbling that sounds like thunder in Piper's ears. This is not Mother's usual voice, but deep and filled with storms. It is her Bead Day voice.

Piper takes the tiny Turquoise Wolf and stone tool from her pocket and quietly continues carving. The wolf has a muzzle now. Tomorrow, it will have a tail.

"Do you hear her?" Mother shouts. "I hear her. She's calling me. She won't leave me alone!"

The thunder is louder, it rolls across the world and shakes Piper's chest.

She looks up at the vines. They are hard and cold, dying. That's why the leaves are yellow. Mother told her this.

The worst thing would be if Mother grew dead flying squirrel eyes. They are huge and empty. Mother does bad things when the dead squirrel sneaks inside her.

Piper feels the joint-stiffening disease tingle her hands. Her fingers curl over and her nails dig into her palms like knives. The wolf and tool drop to the ground. Only old people are supposed to get the joint stiffening, but sometimes it happens to Piper.

She looks down and sees the fists on her stomach and thinks: These are not my hands, not little girl hands.

Flying squirrels have hands. She has seen them. Hands with claws. Maybe the dead squirrel has sneaked inside her, too?

Piper rolls to her side and tucks her crooked fingers between her knees. Tangled black hair flows around her like water.

From somewhere far away a deep voice is saying, "Piper, Piper, Piper . . ."

She hears, but she doesn't really. The voice is too far away to answer.

Piper closes her eyes and falls into the dark place inside.

The place with arms that hold her.

CHAPTER 19

THE BRONCO CAREENED down the dirt road, slithering and spinning its way along, while Dusty rapidly cranked the steering wheel back and forth.

After the first frantic sensations of panic, Maureen realized that while they were indeed sliding this way and that, Dusty was keeping them on the road. She forced herself to relax, and actually smiled as they scrambled up a slope and over the top of a low ridge. The Bronco yawed and pitched on the way down, sliding more than steering, and then Dusty skated them across the flats to the stand of juniper where Dale's battered old camp trailer stood shining in the rain.

Sylvia's Jeep pulled in behind them. Camp looked gray, wet, and cold under the low clouds. Rain continued to patter.

She looked over at Dusty. "Nice driving, Stewart. I take it you've had a little practice at this sort of thing."

"A little."

Maureen gestured toward the overgrown mound of rubble in front of them. It rose eight or nine meters from the desert floor. "I take it that's Pueblo Animas?"

"That's it."

Maureen opened the door and stepped out. The mud was slicker than she would have imagined. Cold rain patted her hair and shoulders as she made her way toward the site.

Dusty caught up and walked beside her.

From behind them, Sylvia called, "Hey, boss? While you guys check out Pueblo Animas, I'll unload the supplies, okay?"

Maureen and Dusty turned. Steve was walking toward them, but Sylvia stood by the Jeep, her freckled face shining with rain, and her brown hair fluttering in the breeze.

Dusty said, "Great, Sylvia. Thanks."

Dusty led the way to the edge of the kiva.

When they reached the ladder, he made a sweeping gesture and said, "After you, Doctor."

Maureen climbed down the ladder and looked around while Dusty and Steve pulled back the rain-drenched black plastic sheeting that covered the kiva floor. The plastic crackled and billowed in the cold wind.

The soil caught her attention first: black, loamy, with scattered chunks of fire-reddened sandstone, the color coming from the oxidation caused by a hot fire.

Dusty and Steve picked their ways carefully as they rolled back more of the protective plastic sheets.

The round structure was built into the middle of the large E-shaped pueblo. The internal diameter of the kiva was roughly seven meters. She could see the square rock pilasters that had once supported the roof cribbing. Though a slanting layer of soil still obscured the northern portion of the kiva, the kiva bench lay exposed in the southern half. Bits of bone littered the floor. She could see skeletal elements from just about every part of the body. And, at first glance, none of it looked adult.

"Stewart, why does the floor slope? Aren't you the one who kept telling me I had to dig a level pit floor back at 10K3?"

Dusty turned, his face shaded by the brim of his ratty felt cowboy hat, and gave her one of those "I expected more of you" stares.

"Doctor, there's a difference between testing—that is, putting in a pit to determine what's under the ground when you don't know—and excavation. We were testing at 10K3. What we're doing here is called digging by natural levels. That means that we found the bone bed. Now, through careful excavation, we'll expose that entire level based on its actual physiology."

"I see. Well, at least tell me why it slopes?"

Dusty released his corner of plastic and gestured to the south side of the structure. "The burned layer of bones slopes because the south side of the kiva roof burned through, and hinged slightly as it fell. The bodies tumbled to the lowest spot. Which is why you can see the bench along the southern wall, and that's also why the burned timbers are sticking up on the north."

She frowned at the blackened logs. "Is that a core hole for a C-14 date?" It looked like the sort of hole a carpenter would drill in a log.

"Actually, Doctor, that's where we took a sample for dendrochronology—but a date is what we're after, yes. We pulled that core three days ago. The same with the other beam to your left. Dale took both cores to the tree-ring lab at the University of Arizona. He's going to put them under the microscope, and see if we can get a good date on the kiva."

"Right." Maureen bent down and frowned at the fragments of bone that littered the floor. Dusty, or his crew, had located them, barely exposing the surface, and stopped. That showed prudence. The soil kept the fragile bone from desiccating and decomposing.

At her feet lay a mandible, the jawbone of a child. "I'd say from the eruption of the incisors, this child was about eight." She pointed to the discolored and broken incisors. "See how the teeth are heat-stained and cracked? When this place burned, it burned hot. The fire seared the lips, pulling them back, exposing the teeth to the extreme heat. That's why they cracked and the front part of the mandible is charred. Back here, where the cheeks protected the molars, see these little ridges in the enamel? That's dental hypoplasia. It usually occurs due to poor nutrition. The kid had a pretty tough time of it."

"That makes sense, Doctor. From the different styles of masonry and the decoration and manufacturing techniques of the pottery, I'm guessing that this site was occupied in the mid-twelve hundreds by Mesa Verdean peoples. They were probably raided often, their food stores stolen, and their crops burned."

"So this dates to the same time period as the 10K3 site in Chaco Canyon?"

He nodded, reached into his pocket, and pulled out a Ziploc. It contained a three-by-five index card covered with Dusty's irregular writing and a piece of broken Anasazi pottery. As he handed it to her, he said, "I just finished the preliminary analysis of the 10K3 stuff that we dug last year, so I'm pretty familiar with the ceramics. I recovered this potsherd yesterday from this kiva under your feet. Except for the dirt it was in, I'd swear it was made by the same potter whose work we found at 10K3."

The rain had dwindled to a few icy drops. Maureen studied the angular fragment of black-on-white pottery. "Do you know how improbable it is that these would be the same people?" Maureen looked up and caught the apprehension in Dusty's eyes. That haunted look had returned. She paused, then said, "So, you *do* know what a long shot it would be."

Steve Sanders tipped his head in silent warning, then walked a few steps away and crouched to study the bone bed.

In an edgy voice, Dusty said, "It would help if you would tell me what you see in the bones, Doctor."

She surveyed the fragments around her feet. "Well, I see a lot of mixed human bone, Stewart." She pointed. "That's a child's humerus there, the arm bone, right side. From the size, the lack of epiphyses—those are the growth caps—I'd say that the kid was about seven. There's a piece of frontal bone there at your feet. Even without brushing dirt away from the teeth in the maxilla, I can tell you the child was about five. That fractured innominate bone by Steve's foot comes from a child's pelvis. The state of ossification would lead me to guess the kid was eight or nine. That skull over there belonged to an infant." Her practiced eye continued the inventory of visible bone.

"Jesus," Steve said, "they are all children, just like we thought."

"So far," Maureen said, "and from the heat spalling, it looks like they burned in the flesh. If you're right that the south half fell in first, there's going to be a whole lot more material down there where the bodies rolled as the roof fell."

"Yes, Doctor, we're in agreement there." Dusty gazed thoughtfully at the thick deposits clustered in front of the southern kiva bench. "We wanted you here before we opened that up."

Maureen shook her head at the cremated bodies. "What happened here?"

"We don't know, except that the children were on the roof when it burned. They may have been dead—killed in warfare, killed by a plague—and this was some sort of burial ritual. Or they may have been standing up here alive and screaming. Either way, it must have been a terrible sight for those down below."

"Who would burn a bunch of children?"

Steve said, "Ask the Nazis. I'm sure they actually believed they had good reasons. Which means, in the final analysis, people stink."

Maureen said, "Given the history of the twentieth century—Hitler, Stalin, Pol Pot, Milosevic—I'd say that's a valid assessment."

"The fire might have been accidental," Dusty pointed out, but his gaze darted around the kiva uneasily, noting the locations of the timbers and the bones. As he pulled his trowel from his back pocket, he added, "Only excavation will tell."

The rain picked up again, splashing off Dusty's felt hat and beading on Maureen's face.

Dusty said, "Why don't we cover this again, go make a hot pot of coffee, and drink it in the trailer until this lets up."

Maureen nodded. "Sounds good to me. I'd like to take a look at that skull you found, the one with the hole in it?"

"I was thinking we'd do that over dinner. After we get your tent set up, etcetera."

"Fine."

Maureen took one corner of plastic, and watched Stewart and Steve as they grabbed other corners. Stewart was nervous, jumpy. Even though the chances were astronomical, he really did seem to believe this site had been occupied by the same people who'd lived at 10K3.

The plastic billowed in the wind as Maureen covered one of the children's staring skulls, and a shiver tingled her spine.

CHAPTER 20

AS THE AFTERNOON waned, shadows stretched across Longtail village and the world turned cold and gray. The scents of freshly split cedar logs and roasting corn cakes filled the air. People crowded the plaza, speaking softly to each other. Sobs occasionally broke through the general din of voices.

Catkin stood near the central plaza fire, guarding the village elders. The breeze flapped her long red war shirt around her black leggings. She'd coiled her braid at the base of her head and secured it with a shell pin. The style accented the oval shape of her face and her turned-up nose.

"I can't believe it," Springbank said and shook his white head. He looked so forlorn, as though utterly lost without Flame Carrier. "How could this happen to us?"

His toothless mouth sunk in over his gums. He kept turning his teacup in his hands. He had been with Flame Carrier since the beginning, and her death had devastated him. To make matters worse, less than a hand of time ago Browser had gathered the elders and told them the tale of Aspen village.

No one felt safe. All of the elders had blankets wrapped around their hunched shoulders, which they tugged at constantly, pulling them closed, then opening them, or readjusting them.

Wading Bird sat on the log beside Springbank. Bald, with a lumpy nose, he had severely bowed legs. Catkin couldn't hear his words, but he spoke to Springbank in a soothing voice.

On the opposite side of the fire, Crossbill, the Longtail Clan Matron, hunched over the big, corrugated-ware stew pot propped on a tripod of rocks at the edge of the flames. She'd pulled her black-and-white blanket up over her head, but tufts of snowy hair stuck out around the edges. As she stirred the pot, the delicious fragrance of venison stew, thickened with blue cornmeal, rose. To her left, a teapot sat in the ashes, surrounded by nests of pottery cups, bowls, and horn spoons.

Catkin's stomach growled. She'd eaten a huge meal at noon, but after the long run home, her body couldn't seem to get enough food. It didn't help that her nerves still hummed. Like a war prisoner, she found herself waiting for the next blow to land.

Guards crouched on the walls, two to her left and two to her right. Another six stood on high points in the distance. Many people sat eating supper around the plaza, their voices low and somber. Others stood near the walls and the safety of doorways.

The elderly Trader, Old Pigeontail, had come through at noon. While he'd bargained for corn and pots, he'd reported the latest news from other villages and asked about happenings here in Longtail. Dozens of upset people had poured out their grief to him. The Trader had listened with wide eyes. Once word of Flame Carrier's death reached the nearby villages, a flood of mourners would start arriving, and their enemies would be alerted. The death of a leader always caused confusion and internal strife. A wise enemy would take advantage of that.

Catkin turned when she saw Stone Ghost and Browser walk around the turkey pen at the southeastern corner of the village. Her eyes clung to Browser. Just seeing him lessened her worry, and allowed her to get a deep breath into her lungs. It did not matter that she could never tell him how she felt about him—her love for him sustained her; it gave her the strength and courage she needed to fight at his side. If his companionship was all he could ever give her, it would be enough.

Browser lifted his head suddenly, glaring over the heads in the crowd, and Catkin followed his gaze.

Five paces to Catkin's right, Obsidian sat on a beautifully tanned elkhide surrounded by several other women and children from her clan. The dark blue hood of her cape covered her face, but the expressions of the other women told Catkin a great deal. Their eyes glittered like those of young warriors listening to a war chief's orders. Obsidian and her people were a curious group. They claimed they'd lived here for ten sun cycles, but few of the rooms in the village had been lived in. Most had collapsed and fallen into disuse, and the members of the Longtail Clan had made no attempt to repair them, not even the beautiful great kiva. They never attempted to join activities, or help the Katsinas' People clean up around the village. They seemed to prefer their own counsel. They hunted, cooked, and prepared their own food. They skinned and tanned their own hides. They wove their own cloth.

Wind Baby whirled through the plaza, and Catkin's knee-length shirt whipped around. She watched Browser clench his teeth and start forward again. He had changed out of his bloody clothing and wore a long buckskin war shirt. His fringed sleeves danced in time with his gait.

Browser's thick black brows drew together over his flat nose as he came to her side. "How is everything?"

"People are grieving and frightened. As they should be. You checked on the guards?"

"Yes. Everyone is fine, holding their positions on the high points around the village. I searched the river again, too. Skink was right. The murderers' tracks vanish a few body lengths from the torture site."

Catkin heard the dread in his voice, and said, "They are experts at vanishing, Browser. They could have walked on the stones at the river's edge. Perhaps they even braved the cold water and waded in the river until they could step out on a sandstone slab and escape. The lack of tracks does not mean they are flying about on rawhide shields."

He propped his hands on his hips and bowed his head. "No, I know. It's just that—"

When he did not finish, Catkin wanted to reach out and touch him to comfort him. But she said only, "Did you ask your uncle about 'The Two' coming home?"

Browser nodded. "He told me that sixty-five summers ago, our bathing pool was called the Witches' Water Pocket."

Catkin tried to figure out what that had to do with The Two. "What does that—"

"Your guess is as good as mine. I assume he was telling me that The Two are witches who lived here in Longtail village sixty or more sun cycles ago."

Catkin frowned. "Then they must be as old as Our Grandmother Earth."

"I've heard my uncle say that Two Hearts is at least sixty. No one really knows his age."

That day outside Talon Town, before Browser rescued her, Catkin had spoken with the monster soul that lived inside Ash Girl. The monster had called himself Yellow Dove. Yellow Dove had talked about Ash Girl's father, a murderous witch who had killed over a dozen women and girls in Straight Path Canyon: *"He's tricky. He disguises himself. He thinks you have his Turquoise Wolf. He has done so many things evil things in his life, he knows he will never find his way to the Land of the Dead without it. He'll be drawn down the Trail of Sorrows, and Spider Woman will burn him up in her pinyon pine fire."*

Catkin said, "Then your uncle did not comment on the man's tracks or the woman's tracks we found this morning?"

"He did not say they belonged to The Two, if that's what you're asking. But I think he believes it, Catkin." Browser's shoulder muscles bulged through his leather war shirt, as if he'd just steeled himself against the truth.

Catkin's gaze held Browser's for a few heartbeats.

Then Browser's eyes shifted to Stone Ghost. The old man had seated himself to Crossbill's left and dipped a cup of tea. His shoulder-length white hair blew around his deeply wrinkled face.

As night settled upon the desert, the autumn leaves on the cottonwoods went from bright yellow to a deep indigo. The chill ate into Catkin's arms. Stone Ghost threw more wood onto the fire, and fragrant coils of cedar smoke drifted into the dusk sky.

Browser said, "When do you expect the search parties to return?"

"Three or four hands after nightfall."

Stone Ghost and Crossbill spoke in low, ominous tones. Browser seemed to be halfheartedly listening to their conversation. "I just saw Redcrop. She does not look well."

"She is fourteen summers, Browser. I spoke to her before she went into the kiva with Cloudblower. She was shaking badly. She could barely walk, and her eyes had almost swollen shut."

"Cloudblower is taking care of her?"

"As well as Cloudblower can, given her other duties. I don't think Redcrop has eaten all day."

"Well, I haven't either. Have you?"

"Yes, but I'm still starving."

"We are no good to anyone if we're concentrating on our rumbling stomachs. Let's see if we can share the elders' pot of venison stew. Come."

Catkin followed Browser around the fire. He crouched to the left of Stone Ghost, and Catkin sat down cross-legged to Browser's left. Springbank and Wading Bird looked up and nodded to them. From across the fire, Crossbill watched Catkin with wise old eyes. Skinny and snowy-haired, she clutched her teacup with knobby hands.

Stone Ghost reached out to touch Browser's arm. "You must both be hungry. Let me fill bowls for you."

Crossbill said, "I seasoned the stew with beeweed and dried onions, then added some blue corn flour to thicken it. It's very tasty."

"I'm sure it is, Matron," Browser said and smiled in gratitude. "We thank you."

Stone Ghost dipped up the first bowl, tucked a spoon into it, and handed it to Catkin. The sweet scents of roasted corn and venison bathed her face.

Stone Ghost handed the next bowl to Browser and continued filling and passing bowls until everyone around the fire had one.

Springbank ate a bite, then gestured at Browser with his spoon. In a strained elderly voice, he said, "Why is it that you two were spared at Aspen village? Don't you think it strange that the white-caped men would kill an entire village and let you live?"

"Yes, Elder, I do," Browser answered.

Wading Bird said, "It does seem curious. Catkin was standing alone at the top of the trail, and you were locked in the kiva. They could have killed either of you at any time."

Browser nodded. "I cannot say why we are alive, Elders, except that I had the feeling they needed us alive, to tell the story."

Springbank uttered a disbelieving grunt. "Even if you hadn't lived, some Trader would have passed through in the next half moon and we all would have known within days."

Catkin stared at the flames, but her souls were seeing the face of the wounded woman again, trying to gaze beneath the thick blood-clotted hair and white powder to get some idea of what she might really have looked like. She'd have been slender, with long black hair, but more than that Catkin couldn't swear to.

Springbank pinned Browser again, shaking his horn spoon. "If these are witches, War Chief, why are they tormenting us? What is it they wish? Have we done something to them?"

Browser shook his head. "I will know more when our warriors return tonight."

Springbank said, "*If* our warriors return. I pray they do not meet the same fate as the Aspen village warriors."

Catkin's stomach muscles clenched. She stared at the flames dancing around the bottom of the stew pot. The same worry plagued her.

Browser said, "My prayers are with them also, Elder."

Stone Ghost blew on his stew and gazed across the fire at Springbank. "Why is it, Springbank, that you think the witches are tormenting us? I have always thought it curious that people see themselves as the tormented, never as the tormentors. Why do you suppose that is?"

Springbank stopped with his spoon halfway to his toothless mouth. A look of incomprehension rearranged his wrinkles. "What does that mean? Are you saying that our Matron tormented someone? Or that we, the Katsinas' People, did? And that's why our Matron was killed?"

Stone Ghost gummed a bite of venison, swallowed, and said, "Killing is a form of grieving, Springbank. The killer must have thought your Matron responsible for her pain. I do not know what the killer is mourning, but if we can determine that, we may be able to find her before she strikes again."

Springbank dropped his spoon into his bowl where it clattered, and gave Stone Ghost a surprised look. "Our Matron was a woman of great charity and compassion. She never tormented anyone! It was not in her nature!"

Stone Ghost lifted a crooked finger. "Ah, that is the truth we see through our eyes, Springbank. I suspect the killer would not agree."

Wading Bird studied Stone Ghost. His bald head reflected the firelight like a mirror. "You looked at the Matron's body, yes?"

Stone Ghost nodded. "Yes, twice."

"What did you discover?"

This time, Springbank leveled his spoon at Stone Ghost. "If you know something, you should have already told us. We have a right to know—"

Stone Ghost interrupted, "Springbank, have you ever wished to kill someone? I don't mean in war or self-defense, but in anger or hatred? Have you ever watched yourself kill someone on the fabric of your souls?"

Springbank lowered his head. "I regret that I have."

"What were your reasons?"

Springbank propped his sandal on one of the warm hearthstones, and his turkey feather sock shimmered in the light. "Oh, more than twenty summers ago, there was an old woman who liked to chase my children around with a stick. One day she beat my ten-summers-old daughter severely. I wished to kill her. I never did, of course, except in my dreams. Why did you ask?"

Stone Ghost tipped his head. "Because I suspect that you, like many people, think there is a difference between committing murder in your souls and actually killing someone."

Everyone at the fire went silent, but their confused gazes riveted on Stone Ghost.

Springbank made a disgusted sound. "Of course there's a difference. A dead body!"

"But that is a minor point, after all," Stone Ghost said, his eyes wide and shining. "Don't you see? It is only because we view soul-murders as lesser crimes that real murders are worth committing. If we openly discussed and judged the reasons for soul-murders, perhaps there would be no real murders."

Wading Bird and Springbank exchanged a look, then Springbank said, "What I see is that you are addled, old man."

"Well, that is another minor point, if you don't mind me—"

"Great Spirits!" Springbank cried. "After the terrible happenings of the last few days, how can you sit here and blather like a fool? Can't you just once try to think like a sane person?"

Stone Ghost's eyes flared. "I could, yes. But then I'd never catch the murderer, would I?"

Apparently exasperated, Springbank shoved to his feet. "I am heartsick and tired. I'm going where I can talk with people whose souls don't flit about like moths. Good evening to you."

He hobbled toward a group of children playing dice on the eastern side of the plaza. Springbank loved children. He often went into the tower kiva during their teachings to regale the children with the great stories of the Hero Twins. Springbank sat down beside a little girl, smiled, and put his arm around her.

Catkin kept her head down and ate more stew. She wasn't sure whose side she was on in the argument. While she had learned that Stone Ghost's peculiar opinions usually proved to have merit, even she had to admit that Springbank had made a good point about the dead body.

A woman laughed, high and throaty, and Catkin clutched her spoon like a knife.

Obsidian's hood had fallen back, revealing a thick wealth of black hair studded with jeweled pins. Turquoise, coral, and jet beads flashed. Obsidian shook her hair out, then sensuously pulled it away from her long neck, twisted it into a bun, and pinned it on the left side of her head. The women around her smiled, and Obsidian laughed again and looked over her shoulder at Browser.

Browser stiffened, then seemed to force himself to relax.

Catkin could not describe the gut-wrenching loathing she felt for Obsidian. It was more than just Obsidian's obvious interest in Browser. The woman had a taint, a malignant element that Catkin could not define, but she *felt* it like a cold stone in her belly.

Stone Ghost said, "There are many old stories about this place"—he waved a hand at the village. "Have you heard them, Crossbill? Wading Bird?"

Crossbill set her teacup on her knee and frowned at Stone Ghost. She used her free hand to clutch her black-and-white blanket beneath her chin. "I know one."

Stone Ghost smiled. "Please, tell us, Matron."

Catkin had the sense that Stone Ghost had just initiated a game of bobcat and rabbit. He was circling, maneuvering his prey into position before striking.

Crossbill took a moment, as though gathering her memories, then said, "My mother once told me about a strange Trader who lived here. She said he came home to his family only three times a sun cycle. I remember there was a cursed little girl in the story. A girl who was banished from the village." She stopped and cocked her head. "No. No, I think the village moved and left the little girl."

Stone Ghost nodded. "That is the version I heard."

Browser sipped his tea and, in the silence, took the opportunity to check the guards on the village walls. Then he said, "Who were they, Uncle?"

"I never knew, Nephew. I first heard the story about thirty summers ago. People who stopped at my house in the south told me fragments. Each person related the tale a little differently. The one thing I remember," he said and scooped up his last bite of stew, "is that the girl was cast out of her clan for incest."

Catkin's heart seemed to stop. Her thoughts went to the little girl on the kiva roof in Aspen village, but of course that was ridiculous. The girl Stone Ghost and Crossbill spoke about would have seen more than thirty summers now. "With her father?"

"That is what the storytellers claimed," Stone Ghost answered. "I don't know if they were right, however. Tales get confused over time and distances. It may have been something else entirely."

"No," Crossbill said and nodded. "That's what I recall as well."

The blue vein in Browser's temple pulsed. "You think the man in the story was Two Hearts? Ash Girl's father?"

Stone Ghost lifted a shoulder, and his ratty turkey feather cape shimmered in the firelight. "Possibly."

Catkin said, "But how could that be, Elder? If Two Hearts was Ash Girl's father, then he lived in the Green Mesa villages far to the north—"

"Traders often have many families, Catkin. They move constantly and suffer great loneliness. They mate at one village, leave, and return when they can. In the meantime, they have mated at another village and must return there occasionally, too."

Crossbill said, "That may be why the Trader here only returned three times a sun cycle."

Wading Bird said, "I was a Trader once. So was Springbank, I think. But I had only one family. I don't know about Springbank."

Catkin cupped her warm bowl in her cold hands. Since she had come to the Katsinas' People, she had seen only deeply holy men. Wading Bird and Springbank spent their time praying and Singing to the gods, begging them to help the Katsinas' People. Often, Wading Bird and Springbank were gone for days at a time. Traders occasionally reported seeing one of them sitting on a hilltop with his arms extended to the sky gods—crying for a vision.

"I remember hearing stories about Two Hearts," Wading Bird said. "He was also known as the Wolf Witch. His Power was legendary."

Stone Ghost nodded. "Yes. The Wolf Katsina was supposedly his Spirit Helper."

Crossbill snugged the front of her blanket closed. "Why would the Wolf Katsina help a witch? I don't believe it."

"Nor do I," Stone Ghost admitted, "but I think that's what the Wolf Witch believed."

Crossbill tugged her blanket down around her hips, and paused for a time, before saying, "Twenty-five sun cycles ago, my grandmother dispatched a war party to hunt him down for his crimes. Many other clans joined hers. No one ever found him, of course. He was supposed to be very clever and very evil. My grandmother said he made a special corpse powder."

"I remember that." Wading Bird nodded. "Ordinary witches make corpse powder by gathering and drying the flesh of the dead. Two Hearts made his from the bones of First People. Isn't that right?"

Stone Ghost said, "Yes, he ravaged the ruins of their towns, stealing whatever he could find, digging up their graves."

Crossbill's breath frosted in the cold air. "I recall my grandmother saying that when he sprinkled his powder in someone's water, or on their food, they died screaming." She held Stone Ghost's gaze. "If he is alive, he must be getting old."

"Sixty summers, perhaps. He could be older. No one knows much about him."

"Yes," Wading Bird whispered, and looked around uncomfortably, surveying the village. "Witches often remove their relatives' hearts with a spindle and put it in their own chests to extend their lives. If he has done that, he may live another sixty summers."

Catkin set her bowl down and spread her hands pleadingly. "Elders, please tell me how we fight the most powerful witch in the land? Does anyone know?"

Wading Bird shook his bald head. "I cannot imagine."

Firelight sheathed Stone Ghost's eyes, turning them into pools of gold. "We can't fight him, Catkin."

"Then how do we stop him?" Catkin asked.

Stone Ghost frowned down into his tea. Grimly, he said, "Oh, I think we know what he wants more than anything in the world. Don't we, Nephew?"

Browser jerked as though surprised. "What, Uncle?"

Obsidian's group suddenly went quiet, and all of the elders turned in unison. Obsidian calmly prodded her fire with a branch, but she appeared to be listening to their every word.

Crossbill glanced at Obsidian, then leaned toward Stone Ghost and whispered, "Her mother once confided to me that she'd given birth to two daughters, but only Obsidian had lived. Imagine what it would be like to have two of her around?"

Catkin stifled a chuckle.

Stone Ghost didn't respond. His gaze had locked with Browser's. They appeared to be engaged in some form of silent communication.

Finally, as though Browser understood, he straightened. Wind teased his black hair around his face, tangling it with his eyelashes. "Uncle, you can't mean that I should—I would not ask that of anyone! Let alone a child who has just lost the only person . . ."

Voices rose from the dimly lit trees beyond the plaza.

Browser and Catkin leaped to their feet in less than a heartbeat, their war clubs in their hands. The village dogs barked and raced toward the river. Women grabbed children and ducked into the closest doorways, while men secreted themselves in the shadows, their weapons up and ready. The elders hobbled for the village as fast as they could.

Catkin said, "The guards would have signaled us—"

"If they saw them," Browser answered. "It's dark. They may have come up through the brush in the river bottom."

Catkin trotted out toward the edge of the light and shouted, "Who comes?"

Skink answered, "It's us, Catkin!"

Catkin flattened her body against the wall of Cloudblower's chamber at the southwestern corner of the village. Browser came up behind her, breathing hard.

She said, "Do you think it's them?"

"Yes, but we mustn't take chances. Our enemies may have captured Skink."

They waited until Skink and the rest of the search party trotted into the orange halo of the plaza fire, then Browser lowered his war club. "We're all right. It's them."

"Maybe. They are back much sooner than they should be."

Browser walked forward. "You are early. Did you find something, Skink?"

Skink shook his head, panting, his round face covered with sweat. "No, War Chief." Mud filled the crow's-feet at the corners of his eyes. The other warriors gathered around them, and people began to emerge from the safety of the village. Women and children ran forward to greet their husbands and fathers. A bustling crowd formed.

"You found nothing at all?" Catkin asked.

"No." Skink bent over and sucked in deep breaths. "We looked everywhere. There were no tracks, no threads of clothing, no grass bent by footsteps."

Water Snake shouldered through the crowd. His dirt-coated face had flushed from the run. "Truly, War Chief. It is as though they never touched the ground!"

Skink nodded vigorously. "I swear they must be witches. That's why we couldn't track them. They are flying about on rawhide shields!"

CHAPTER 21

REDCROP JERKED AWAKE and stared wide-eyed around the kiva. She could hear shouts in the plaza.

Her body felt numb, leaden. Her head ached.

The Matron watched Redcrop through cornmeal-covered eyes, eyes drained of all warmth and love. Redcrop smoothed her hand over Flame Carrier's bony old arm. It felt like a dead branch.

"I think they're back, Grandmother. I should go and see."

She petted Flame Carrier's clawlike fingers and rose on wobbly legs. "I'll be back."

The kiva fire had burned down to red coals. The *Yamuhakto,* the Hero Twins, seemed to be Dancing, their arms and legs moving in time with the wavering gleam.

Perhaps Straighthorn had tracked down the murderers and brought them back. They may even have gotten into a fight and killed them.

"Maybe it's over, Grandmother. Maybe they're dead and they won't ever hurt anyone again."

Redcrop climbed the ladder with her legs trembling.

After the warmth of the kiva, the cold night air stung her eyes. She climbed out onto the roof and walked to the edge of the kiva. The air carried the rich scents of venison and sweet corn.

A crowd milled in the southwestern corner of the plaza, between Cloudblower's chamber and the great kiva. War Chief Browser stood speaking with Skink, and close behind him, Cloudblower, Catkin, and Straighthorn stood.

Redcrop searched the gathering, her gaze touching on each face. She didn't see any strangers.

"They didn't find them."

Her legs went weak. She sank down onto the roof.

The murderers still roamed the night. They might be watching her right now, from the darkness.

It took all of her strength to fight back tears.

She rocked back and forth. Her doehide dress did little to block the cold, but she couldn't return to her chamber to get her cape. She didn't think she could face Flame Carrier's empty blankets, or the small baskets where she'd kept the things that were most precious to her. Tomorrow, Redcrop would have to. But perhaps tomorrow she could stand it.

Flame Carrier had left strict orders that after her death, Redcrop was to distribute all of her belongings among the Katsinas' People. Redcrop wondered how she would decide who got what? Would people argue over the best items?

She tucked her hands inside her long sleeves and drew her knees up to block the wind.

I'll just carry everything out into the plaza and let people take what they wish.

Would the murderers come to the burial? To gloat over what they'd done? No one knew what Two Hearts looked like. He could say he was a Trader from the far south who just happened to be passing by. He could stand and watch people's reactions. He could watch Redcrop.

She started shaking and couldn't stop.

Below, tired warriors walked away with their wives and children. The elders who had briefly stepped out to speak with Skink and Browser headed back for the warmth of the village. Catkin joined Browser and Stone Ghost's circle, leaving Straighthorn alone with the sacred Man-Woman, Cloudblower.

As though Cloudblower had told Straighthorn where Redcrop was, he turned and looked at the tower kiva.

Redcrop gazed down at him yearningly. He was a warrior. He had duties to perform, but he'd told Catkin he would come to see her when he returned, and she longed to have him close.

Strains of conversation drifted on the wind, mostly warriors recounting the day's events. The plaza fire crackled and spat. To her left, in the east wing of the village, a child cried.

Redcrop hugged herself.

STRAIGHTHORN GAZED UP at Redcrop, and his chest felt hollow.

"I think she's been waiting for you to return," Cloudblower said.

"Is she all right?"

A long, gray-streaked braid hung down the front of Cloudblower's blue dress. She had seen perhaps forty summers, but her mass of crisscrossing wrinkles made her look more like sixty. A softness lived in her eyes. People for three-moon's-walk knew her and relied upon her skills as a Healer. Runners often dragged into the village in the middle of the night with a message that someone needed her. Cloudblower never hesitated. She grabbed her Healer's bundle and left. Sometimes, she stayed gone for days.

"I do not think she will be all right for many moons, Straighthorn. She is broken inside."

Straighthorn nodded and hair fell over his eyes. Though he wore a braided leather headband, locks had worked loose and straggled around his thin face. Sweat beaded his hooked nose and created a shiny arc above his full lips. "Please excuse me. I promised I would see her tonight."

Catkin turned as he started to walk away and said, "Do not forget that you and Jackrabbit will be taking Water Snake's guard position at midnight. See that you rest first."

"Yes, I will, Catkin."

His red-and-black cape swayed around his skinny body as he walked across the plaza.

The walk had never seemed this long, or his legs this fatigued. It was as if the day's events had skewed his perspective of distances. The ears of corn stacked on the rooftops, the tan walls of the village, all seemed to be closing in upon him. The evening carried the resinous smells of sage and juniper. Redcrop watched him as he came closer.

Straighthorn climbed the ladder to the kiva roof and Redcrop looked up.

"Oh, my poor girl," he said.

Her eyes and face had swollen. She brushed lamely at her tangled hair.

He crossed the roof. "Are you well, Redcrop?"

"Did you find them?"

"No. I'm sorry." He sat down beside her. "How are you? How is the Matron?"

Redcrop's mouth trembled. "Please, Straighthorn. Tell me what you found. You must have found something?"

As he slipped his bow and quiver from his shoulders, he said, "Four hands of time to the south, I found a place where the man slipped off the stones into the mud. Skink told me it was nothing, but it was, Redcrop. The murderers walked in the water most of the way, but they stepped out onto the river rocks when their feet grew cold." He made an awkward gesture. "They may still be walking on the rocks. We stopped pursuing them three hands of time ago and returned home."

"But I thought . . ." Redcrop's mouth hung open. "I heard Catkin say she had ordered the parties to search both sides of the river until they no longer had enough light to see."

Straighthorn reached out to take her hand. It felt cold in his grip. He cupped it between his palms to warm it. "She did."

All day long Skink had acted imperiously, ordering people about, sneering at anything the other members of the search party found.

"Skink ordered the parties back early?"

Straighthorn nodded. "He said that since we were finding nothing, he saw no reason to continue looking. He may have been right, Redcrop. The killers were taking great care to hide their trail. We probably weren't going to find anything else."

"Did you wish to keep looking?"

He squeezed her hand. "I would have searched all night if Skink had let me."

Redcrop nodded and gazed down at the plaza. From this side view, she looked all the more frail and vulnerable. It touched his heart.

He said, "Did you hear what Skink said when we first entered the village?"

"No."

"He told the War Chief, no one can track witches. They fly about on rawhide shields. He thinks they are the same witches who murdered the women and girls in Straight Path Canyon, Redcrop. I'm certain that's why he ended the search. He was afraid. He could not bear the thought that we might actually find them and he would have to fight witches."

Wind Baby gusted over Longtail village and probed beneath Straighthorn's cape with icy fingers. After the long run, every muscle in his body burned and ached. The cold felt good to him, but he saw Redcrop shiver.

He untied his cape and gently draped it around her shoulders. "Do you think maybe you should go inside, Redcrop?"

"No, I—I don't wish to. I can't go home."

"Perhaps Cloudblower's chamber? I would invite you to my chamber if I could, but—"

"But I am a girl, and you are a man. I know, Straighthorn." She bit her lip.

It wouldn't matter that they would only talk. A man did not take a girl into his chamber alone. Not if he valued his life. Straighthorn would be accused of coupling with her and might even be beaten or driven out of the village.

He smiled and said, "Yes, you are girl. But a very beautiful one."

Redcrop closed her eyes as though the words hurt. "Do you think it's them, Straighthorn? Two Hearts and the other witch from Straight Path Canyon?"

He studied the set of her jaw, and the way her hands tugged at his cape. He missed a woman's company at night. He had been married to Siskin for almost two summers when they'd both come down with the fever that had killed her.

When times got bad, he still heard her musical voice inside him, chiding him, or encouraging him, loving him. He'd never gotten used to living without her.

"I cannot say, Redcrop. They may be."

"But I've never heard of Two Hearts killing old women. Have you?"

"No. Though I do recall hearing of the disappearances of several elders in the past few summers."

"But old people often go away to die by themselves. It doesn't mean someone killed them."

He reached out to touch her long hair where it fell down the back of his cape. "That's true."

She couldn't stand the thought that an insane witch might be wandering about murdering old women, but Straighthorn had been considering the possibility since early morning. Over the sun cycles, he'd spoken with many of the Traders who'd brought them the news of those disappearances. None of the old women had been ill. It didn't seem likely that they'd gone off to die by themselves.

They sat in silence for a time, watching War Chief Browser and old Stone Ghost as they walked across the plaza and sat in front of the central fire pit. The two men had their heads leaned close together, as though discussing things they did not wish overheard. Firelight danced over their somber faces.

Redcrop whispered, "What's happening?"

"The War Chief has been acting strangely since we returned. I heard him tell Catkin that he would speak with her later, and the way he said it sent shivers up my spine. Something terrible happened in Aspen village. No one is speaking of it, but he is desperately worried."

Redcrop swiveled around to face Straighthorn and he saw tears in her eyes.

"Everyone was dead," she said. "Browser found the kiva at Aspen village filled with headless people."

"Blessed gods." He reached out and pulled her into his arms. Her long hair tumbled down the front of his red war shirt. Straighthorn propped his chin on top of her head. "We will find them, Redcrop. I promise you we will."

Redcrop wiped her eyes, and choked out, "Cloudblower told me I—I can't even dream of Grandmother."

"I know." He tenderly patted her back. "It's hard. After my wife's death, I struggled not to dream of her. I didn't wish to pull her back from her journey to the afterlife, but I needed to see her face, to speak with her."

"Cloudblower said that souls who die violently go mad and try to drag the people they love to the Land of the Dead with them." Her face contorted with grief. "Grandmother would never do that to me, Straighthorn. Though if she—if she asked, I would go. If she needed me—"

"Redcrop, please don't say things like that."

"But I miss her so much."

He stroked her hair. "She was a good and kind woman. When she has traveled to the Land of the Dead, the ancestors will be enriched and we will be poorer. But, please, you mustn't speak of dying. It would kill my souls if you died."

"I don't want to hurt you. I've never wished to hurt anyone, but . . ." She sobbed.

She'd said the words in a little girl voice that made his souls twist. He whispered in her ear, "As soon as you are old enough, I am going to shower you with rare Trade goods, and crawl on my belly until you agree to let me court you. Then neither of us will be alone."

The War Chief rose from the fire, said something to Stone Ghost, and strode toward the ladder that led to the tower kiva's roof.

Straighthorn shifted to watch him.

Redcrop looked up. "What is it?"

"The War Chief is coming."

Browser's steps patted the rungs. When he stepped off onto the roof, he stood silhouetted against the firelight. Straighthorn couldn't make out his face.

"War Chief?" he called. "Is everything all right?"

Browser walked forward with his fists clenched at his sides. His buckskin shirt swayed around his legs.

"Forgive me for disturbing you," Browser said. "Redcrop, I would speak with you, if you are not too tired."

"I'm not tired, War Chief. What is it?"

"Alone," he said softly. "I would speak with you alone."

"Oh, forgive me." Straighthorn rose to his feet. "I must get some rest anyway. Redcrop, I will see you tomorrow."

She said, "Thank you, Straighthorn."

Straighthorn bowed to her, then to the War Chief, and walked to the ladder. As he climbed down, he heard the War Chief say:

"I have something important to ask you, Redcrop, but no matter what you decide, you must not speak with anyone of our conversation tonight. Not Straighthorn. Not your best friend. No one. Can you do that?"

There was a hesitation, then, in a small voice, she answered, "Yes, War Chief."

STONE GHOST STOOD up from the fire when Water Snake strode by on his way to his chamber. The youth looked haggard. Long black hair hung around his narrow, weasel-like face in dirty strands, and his leather cape bore a thick coating of dust.

"Forgive me, warrior," Stone Ghost called. "I was hoping we might speak for a time."

Water Snake stopped and turned. He carried his war club in his right hand. "I am very tired, Elder. Perhaps tomorrow."

He started to walk away.

Stone Ghost called, "You were standing guard last night, weren't you?"

Water Snake heaved an irritated breath and turned back. "Yes. What of it?"

"Well, there is something I do not quite understand." Stone Ghost rose and walked toward him. "You see, just now, as your party returned, it sounded as if you called up from the river trail."

Water Snake gripped his war club more tightly. "We did."

"But if I could hear you tonight, how is it that you did not hear your Matron's screams last night?"

Water Snake's face flushed. "I don't know! I just didn't. Perhaps she did not scream."

"Oh, I think she did. I studied her tracks this morning. Her killer knocked her facedown into the dirt not more than one hundred body lengths from the village plaza. If I were running for my life, I would scream. Wouldn't you?"

Angry, Water Snake snapped, "I heard no screams, old man! How many times must I tell you?"

Stone Ghost gestured to the roof of the tower kiva, where Browser knelt beside Redcrop. "Were you standing up there when your Matron left the village?"

Water Snake glanced up. "Yes."

"You saw her leave?"

"I did. What is your point?"

Stone Ghost smiled and walked closer. "Well, it's just that I stood right up there this afternoon, at the very edge of the roof, and was surprised to discover that I could see the place where your Matron was attacked." He stopped two hands from Water Snake and gazed curiously into his brown eyes. "Even if she did not scream, how is it that you didn't see her running for the plaza?"

Water Snake gripped his club in both hands as if to wring the life from it. "It was dark! Are you accusing me of deliberately—"

"I am not accusing, warrior." Stone Ghost said softly. "I was just wondering if perhaps you had left your post? Sometimes it is necessary for a warrior to leave his post, to go explore a strange sound, or examine a place where he saw unusual movement. Did you do that?"

Water Snake tapped his thigh with his club and gave Stone Ghost a withering look. "The tower kiva was my post. I did not leave it. Now, I am tired. I'm going to my chamber. If you have more questions for me, ask them tomorrow."

Stone Ghost bowed and smiled. "Of course. Thank you for speaking with me."

Water Snake stalked away.

Stone Ghost folded his arms beneath his feathered cape and watched Water Snake duck beneath his door curtain. The leather swayed, revealing the deerhides that covered the floor and the array of war clubs hanging on the back wall.

Stone Ghost waited to see if the young warrior would look back, if he feared that Stone Ghost still watched his chamber.

In less than twenty heartbeats, a hand pulled the door curtain aside, and Water Snake's eyes glinted with reflected firelight.

Yes, he's worried, afraid that I know more than I do. Where was he last night? What was he doing?

Stone Ghost turned and hobbled toward his own chamber.

CHAPTER 22

MAUREEN PUSHED THE button on the bottom of the five-gallon water jug that stood on the foldout table, and let the clear stream flow over her left hand to rinse off the dust. She held her right hand under next, then dried off on the towel nailed to the juniper tree.

A single ray of sunlight lanced the clouds and slanted over the camp, cast long shadows across the ruins, and seared the cottonwoods to the east a brilliant yellow.

"It's me, Stewart," she called as she knocked on the door.

"Come on in."

She opened the door and entered the camp trailer, sniffing as she stepped around Stewart, who stood at the stove, cooking. He wore faded blue jeans and a long-sleeved black T-shirt. Gratefully, she slid into the padded booth behind the flimsy table.

"Do you need any help?"

Dusty fiddled with the three pans on the stove. "Nope. I'm just whipping up my usual culinary masterpiece for dinner."

The scent of spices, fried meat, and something green filled the air. "Smells great. What is it?"

"Jalapeño cheeseburgers, Doctor, with beans for vegetables. The hamburger's been in the cooler for about a week so I thought it was time. Nothing like aged meat, you know?"

She watched him suspiciously, unsure what his definition of "aged" was, but decided to change the subject. "Have any coffee?"

"Vee'ola." He made a grand gesture, reached into the overhead cabinet, and produced a plastic cup. A soot-encrusted coffeepot perked lazily on the back burner. Stewart poured with a flourish and set the cup on the veneer tabletop. "Be generous with your tip."

"The French word is *Voilà,* Dusty, so the correct mispronunciation would be *Vo-eela.* And the best tip I can give you is that you shouldn't get your foreign-language instruction from American TV."

Stewart turned to give her a surprised look. "How would you know? You mean you get American TV in Canada?"

"We're drowning in it." She sipped the coffee. "Umm. Stewart, this is wonderful coffee. If your professional career falls apart, I could get you a job at Tim Horton's."

He turned back to his pots and pans. "No, thanks. I'd have to be nice to people. The strain would kill me."

Maureen smiled and looked around the worn interior of the trailer, studying the familiar bleached wood pattern, the sweat-stained cushions, and the battered bench in the front that folded down into a bed. A sleeping bag lay wadded in one corner under a hanging Coleman lantern.

She asked, "So, Dale vanished off to Arizona? Last time I showed up it was a family emergency that drew him away. Maybe he just doesn't like me."

"Actually, he adores you," Dusty said, and glanced at her over his shoulder. "He just has bad timing, that's all."

He retrieved a big Bowie knife from the silverware drawer, whipped it back and forth across his Levi's, as if cleaning the blade, and began dicing jalapeño peppers.

Maureen gazed out the small window at the river flowing lazily below and took a long drink of coffee. She'd been worried about Dale. The last time she'd talked to him, he'd sounded frail, older. "How is Dale?"

"As cantankerous as ever. Last summer he took up anthropological genetics, if you can believe that. He's been working with somebody named Scott Ferris at Colorado State University in Fort Collins. When Dale comes out to the site these days, he spends the entire evening talking about mitochondrial DNA and Y-chromosome research that traces modern humans back two hundred thousand years." He smiled. "Actually, it's great to see. He hasn't been this happy in years. Learning new things has always been his passion."

Dusty's voice softened when he spoke about Dale. "Incidentally, Dale just moved to a new place."

Maureen brushed long strands of dirty black hair away from her face. After the wind today, her braid looked like the tail of a frightened cat. "He moved? I thought he'd been in that house since forever."

"Fifty years, but he said the old place was too big. He bought a one-bedroom house that he swears takes twenty minutes to clean."

Maureen stood and reached for the coffeepot to refill her cup. The rich aroma bathed her face. She sat down again and said, "How's his health? The last time I spoke with him, he was complaining about his knees."

"They're still bad. He's had trouble ever since that old half-breed witch took a dislike to him."

Maureen sipped her coffee. "When did this happen?"

"Let me see," he said thoughtfully. "I think I was twelve or thirteen, which means it must have been around twenty-five years ago." Dusty reached for an almost empty bottle of Guinness and shifted to face Maureen. His blue eyes glittered in the lantern's gleam. "It was Dale's own fault. He's always been too curious for his own good."

"How so?"

Dusty smiled as he remembered. "He'd been out working on a site on the Hopi reservation and befriended an old Hopi medicine man. The elder told Dale about a secret cave on the north side of the Navajo reservation where witches met. The medicine man said that the witches gathered there at night to plot against their victims, have intercourse with dead women, and cannibalize a few babies. Naturally, Dale wanted to take a look."

"Naturally. What did you find?"

"We went up there around midnight. Dale made me stay down the hill near the horses while he sneaked up to the cave. Now, according to him, the witches were standing around a sand painting, nude, except for masks. One of the witches shot an arrow into the sand painting and Dale swears his right knee went out from under him. The pain was unbearable. When he got to his feet again, he discovered the painting was of him—mustache, fedora, even cowboy boots. The witch shot another arrow into the painting, and Dale's left knee went out. He charged stumbling down the hill, white as a sheet, and he's had trouble with his knees ever since." Dusty's blond eyebrows lifted. "I guess he's just lucky the Wolf Witch didn't shoot him anywhere else."

Maureen smiled and eased her cup down to the table. "The Wolf Witch?" She could hear the sudden moan of wind through the junipers, and out the grimy window, could see the tents rippling.

"That's what his victims called him. God, he was a crazy old man. He claimed to have been descended from the most powerful witch in the world—an ancient Anasazi witch. The wolf-hide mask he wore looked old, too. I'd wager it had been in his family for at least a hundred years."

She said, "Did the Wolf Witch really eat babies, like the Hopi medicine man said?"

"Oh, yeah, but that's standard for witches. They're especially renowned for digging babies from fresh graves and boiling them at night. The Wolf Witch's real talent, though, was sucking magic."

"What's sucking magic?"

Stewart flipped the burgers, and grease crackled. "Usually, it's a beneficial form of magic. When someone gets sick, a medicine man or medicine woman will suck the evil out of the body. I've seen holy people remove bullets that way. They suck them out and spit them on the floor, then—"

"Be serious," Maureen scoffed.

Dusty tilted his head, his blue eyes measuring her. "It's something I can't explain, Doctor. I was raised on reservations, and I've seen things that—well, let's just say a lot of people recover from their illnesses and go on their ways happy as larks after being healed through sucking magic."

Maureen gave him an askance look. "All right. Go on. You said that the Wolf Witch had a unique talent for this kind of magic. How so?"

Dusty gestured with his Guinness. "He would go in pretending to be a healer, and when the relatives left the room, he'd suck the sick person's soul out of his body."

This story didn't sound near as funny as it would have a year ago, before she'd met Hail Walking Hawk. "Really? How did he do that? I mean, did he suck the soul out through the nostrils or ears?"

"No. He drilled a hole in the skull, sucked the soul into his mouth, then blew it into a specially charmed pot from which the soul couldn't escape. Then he took it home and forced the soul to do his bidding. This is the evil side of the soul-pot ritual we were discussing in Durango."

Dusty turned suddenly and went to the rear of the trailer. "Speaking of which, you wanted to look at these."

He handed Maureen a bagged skull and the bone "bead" he'd shown her in Durango.

"Definitely female," she said, as she carefully slipped the skull and bead from their bags and set them on the table before her.

"Yeah, I thought so."

Maureen took the "bead" and placed it beside the hole that had been cut into the woman's head. She turned the skull over to look through the foramen magnum. The dendritic patterns of the meningeal grooves matched those on the endocranium. "I'd call that a match, Stewart."

He nodded. "Why do you think the skull was in the burned kiva and the bead was in the room next to the kiva?"

"Maybe the person who lived in the room was a priest or healer and kept the circlet of skull to—" Maureen lifted and turned the skull to the light. "My, my."

"What?" He bent closer.

Maureen could smell the woodsmoke on his clothing and feel his warmth. It felt good. "See these striations?"

Dusty blinked. "Where?"

"Here, and here." She indicated the parallel lines. "They skinned her face. Mortuary preparations?"

Dusty ground his teeth for several moments, his gaze going from the skull, and back to her eyes. "I'd say that it's more likely cannibalism."

Maureen made a skeptical face. "Cannibals usually cook the head, then break open the skull to get to the brains. Her skull is intact. I wager it's part of a burial ceremony that we don't understand yet."

"Hmm," Dusty said and smiled.

"What are you smiling at?"

"It might be witchcraft."

Maureen eased the skull to the table and leaned forward, ready to hear more. "Really? Why?"

Dusty caught the intent expression on her face and stopped. "I don't recall you being particularly interested in witchcraft before."

The last time they'd worked together, they'd argued violently over ghosts and witchcraft. Dusty gave credence to all sorts of superstitions. Maureen insisted upon scientific proof.

"It's a recent fascination, Stewart, is that okay?"

"You bet," he said in ecstatic agreement. "Is it okay if I decide to abandon archaeology and become a stockbroker?"

Maureen's eyes narrowed. "You think I'm lying?"

"I didn't say that. I just meant that given your background, it seems unlikely you'd suddenly develop an attraction to something as unscientific as witchcraft."

Maureen self-consciously lifted one shoulder. "After that last project, I picked up Marc Simmons's book on southwestern witchcraft. Magpie, Sylvia, and Elder Hail Walking Hawk spurred my interest. I've done a little reading. Not enough to qualify as an expert by any means, but a little."

Dusty's eyes bored into hers like blue diamonds, as if trying to see into her soul.

On impulse, she said, "Want to tell me why you didn't leave the basilisk in the ground?"

His face slackened. "It was too scientifically valuable to leave in the sand, Doctor. You should know that. Aren't you the famous Dr. Cole who argued vehemently to study the 10K3 burials, despite the Native religious taboos?"

"That's me."

"Then the reasons I catalogued that artifact should be as clear as the sky."

At the discomfort in his voice, she asked, "You said these witches dig up the bodies of babies and boil them? What do they do with them after they're cooked?"

"Usually, they feed them to unsuspecting victims." He canted his body sideways to peer out the trailer door. "Here come Steve and Sylvia. Uh-oh, from their expressions, they're having a heavy conversation. Probably trying to figure out what to do with each other."

"I noticed that they vanished into the trees down by the river. How long has this been going on?"

Dusty shrugged. "They've been friends for years. I knew they liked each other, but I guess it's become more than that."

She studied him over the rim of her coffee cup. "You seem a little—"

"Concerned?" He smiled. "Sylvia's vulnerable. I worry about her."

"She worries about you, too, you know."

"Yes, I do know. We both have some unpleasant memories from our childhoods. A lot of nightmares. We've had a few midnight talks over the years after one of us woke up bathed in cold sweat. She doesn't sleep with a baseball bat because she's had normal relationships with men."

He didn't have to say more. Sylvia had told Maureen about the men in the foster homes where she'd spent most of the first ten years of her life. Sylvia's descriptions of the abuse still gave Maureen bad dreams. And Dale had told her things about Dusty. About how Dusty's mother used to lock him in the cold dark basement when she wanted to punish him. Dale said he'd come by once and heard Dusty screaming for his mother. She was standing in the kitchen talking to Dale, apparently oblivious. Dusty had been four years old at the time.

He set his beer aside and reached over to slice sharp Cheddar from a block of cheese. "Then there's the distance thing. Sylvia's here in New Mexico. Steve is in Arizona. The University of Arizona just about did back flips to get Steve. He comes from a prominent family in Cincinnati. His dad's a lawyer who can't understand what his bright son is doing living in a tent in the desert when he could be pursuing the capitalist dream. I'm afraid that Steve might go back to Ohio some day. Sylvia would be like a duck out of water back there." He placed the cheese slices on the burgers and covered them with a pie pan. "Want anything besides coffee to drink with dinner?"

"Mango juice would be nice."

Dusty gave her a disbelieving look. "They serve mango juice for dinner in Canada?"

"Mangoes and papayas are staples. We have a large immigrant population from places like India and Pakistan. In fact, Stewart, if you really want an adventurous food tour, come to Toronto. I'll take you out for curried fish that will knock your socks off."

"Can I get them smothered in fresh jalapeños?"

"Umm, maybe not, but we have some remarkable substitutes." She brought her thumb and forefinger together to show him a space of about two centimeters. "We have tiny peppers from Indonesia that are about ten times as hot as your beloved jalapeños."

Dusty leaned his butt against the counter and picked up his Guinness again. "Sounds like heaven. Careful, though. I might just take you up on that invitation."

Maureen read the sincerity in his eyes, and it scared her a little. "I wish you would. I think the people at the ROM would enjoy talking to you about Canadian archaeology."

He smiled, turned around, and scooped her burger onto a plate. As he set it on the table in front of her, he said, "Here's your supper."

"Aged meat, eh? Makes me think of boiled babies dug from fresh graves."

"I'm not a witch. It's cow meat from the City Market in Durango."

She looked down at the burger on the paper plate. The melted cheese was piled with fresh green rounds of jalapeño. He set a pot of refried beans on the table, and she noticed that peppers dotted the beans, too.

"Here's a fork," he said and handed it to her.

"Thanks."

At first bite, she grabbed for her coffee and tried to wash away the burn. After coughing a few times, she choked out, "You may not be a witch, but you still shock unsuspecting victims with what you feed them."

CHAPTER 23

WHEN WIND BABY blew, Sister Moon's gleam slipped around Browser's door curtain and fell across his walls in bars of silver. The fragrance of cedar smoke filled the night. Cloudblower would be up most of the night, tending the sacred fire in the tower kiva. This was the most dangerous time for the village. By now, Flame Carrier's afterlife soul would be desperate. She would be wandering about, grabbing onto people, shouting at them to tell her what was wrong, why they wouldn't speak with her. The ritual fire kept Flame Carrier's dead face lit so that she could see her own body and hopefully realize her life had ended. Some souls never did. They remained on earth as homeless ghosts, wailing, searching forever for loved ones who had died long ago.

Browser sighed and his breath frosted in the cold night air. For the past nine moons he'd felt like a homeless ghost, weary and disheartened. He performed all the duties expected of him, talked to people as if he knew who and what he was, but the appearance was a thin veil over the collapsed wreckage of his life. He had lost the path, and didn't know how to find it again. Every night he lay like this, staring at the ceiling and questioning his worth as a man.

He put an arm over his eyes and tried not to see Grass Moon's little boy smile. *"Father, come and play hoop and stick. I am much better today."*

Images of Ash Girl flared like pine knots in a fire. Ash Girl.

The one hope that fed his heart was the defeat of Ash Girl's father; he had to find and kill Two Hearts.

But what about the woman who seemed to do the witch's bidding? Was she a willing participant? Or a slave? A slave could be freed. A murderous partner, another witch, would have to be destroyed. He couldn't get the white-caped war party out of his mind. He and Catkin had witnessed the passing of an unholy assembly.

Browser rose from his blankets, slipped on a knee-length leather shirt, and reached for his sandals. He laced them up and tied them around his ankles, then sought out his buckskin cape where it hung on the peg by the door. He grabbed it on his way out and swung it around his shoulders.

When he stepped into the plaza, he saw Catkin standing on the tower kiva with Water Snake. Spider Woman's constellation had not yet crawled to the middle of the night sky. Catkin had another hand of time before she had to take Water Snake's guard position. What was she doing up? She should have been sleeping. She had slept for perhaps ten hands of time out of forty. She must feel even more exhausted than he.

Water Snake and Catkin both turned to stare at him. Browser lifted a hand, then walked out to the great kiva at the southern edge of the plaza. He crouched on the eastern side and propped his elbows on his drawn-up knees. The corn on the roof glinted, frosted by the night. Moonlight sheathed the cottonwoods along the river below. Their windblown leaves were a sea of tarnished silver speckles. The juniper-covered bluff in the distance resembled a black wall.

Browser picked up a pebble and threw it out into the darkness. It made a *click-clack* sound when it landed.

Steps approached from behind him, but he did not have to turn to know they belonged to Catkin.

She knelt beside him and stared silently out at the river. The scent of damp autumn leaves rode the breeze.

Browser picked up another pebble and turned it in his hand. "You should be asleep."

"I'm not the only one." Moonlight gilded the arch of her turned-up nose and the war club in her right hand. The long braid that fell down the front of her hide cape shone silver. "What's wrong?"

Browser threw the pebble as far as he could. It tumbled in the moonlight before it vanished. "I don't know if I can explain it, Catkin."

"You mean you don't know if you want to."

He gestured awkwardly. "Yes, probably."

"Tell me." It was an order.

Browser smiled faintly. Despite the fact that he was War Chief, he was certain she gave him far more orders than he gave her.

He reached for another pebble and held the cool smoothness in his palm. "Do you remember in Straight Path Canyon when I told you that I thought my wife was at the heart of all the insanity, all the murders of women and children?"

Catkin's eyes tightened. "I do. Why?"

"I still feel that way. Even though she's dead, I tell you she is central to understanding all of this."

"All of what?"

"Aspen village, why you and I are still alive, our Matron's murder. Everything." He tossed the pebble and it flashed in the moonlight.

Catkin frowned out at the river, and Browser realized how foolish he must sound. He had just blamed his wife for murders committed nine moons after she'd been killed and buried. Perhaps he really was mad.

He dropped his head into his hands and massaged his throbbing temples. "I know how I sound, Catkin. But I also know I'm right."

"Browser, you are obsessed with that woman. Don't tell me you think she's alive? We buried her, placed a stone over her head, and covered her with dirt."

"I—I know that, Catkin. I just—" He shook his hands in frustration.

"Some of this you know, some you don't." It took an act of will to force himself to continue. Catkin knew him better than anyone. She was his closest friend, yet he hesitated to confide this even to her. "You've heard me say a hundred times that my mother arranged my marriage to Ash Girl without consulting me, and that when I found out, I begged her to let me marry Hophorn. I did not have the right to object to the wishes of my clan. Worse, Hophorn was not yet a woman. I couldn't even court her, let alone ask that she be my wife."

"That tells me nothing, Browser. How is Ash Girl connected to Aspen village?"

He let out a breath. "I find it difficult to speak of these things, but please bear with me. I really do have a point."

She sat down beside him and rested her war club across her lap. "Well, if you are going to say it, say it quickly, and then it will be over."

It was good advice. He'd given it to her often enough.

He nodded. "Among the Green Mesa clans it is customary for a young man and woman to spend time together before their marriage, to make certain that the Joining will not be a disaster."

"In my clan, too. So?"

"One moon before our Joining, I crawled under the blankets with Ash Girl for the first time. I had finally resigned myself to the marriage and was eager to touch her, to hold her. She was sound asleep, Catkin. It happened instantly. We had been speaking only moments before. I shook her gently and called to her. It had been a long, tiring day of feasting and dancing for the Longnight Ceremony; I assumed she was exhausted. I tenderly clasped her hand and fell asleep beside her. Just before dawn, I heard her stir and reached over to touch her. My hand came back wet and sticky."

Catkin's fingers curled around her war club. "Blood?"

"Yes, she had used my own knife to slice her throat. Fortunately, she didn't know what she was doing. She missed the big artery, but blood covered everything. By the time I ran from the chamber screaming for help, my body was soaked with it."

Catkin studied his miserable expression, then said, "Why didn't your mother cancel the Joining?"

"She said it was my fault, that I had pushed Ash Girl too fast. She arranged for us to spend another night together, and threatened me to do it right, or else."

"And?"

Browser massaged his temples again. A dull ache pounded behind his eyes. "She cried through the whole thing, Catkin. It broke my heart. After that, she stayed awake long enough to feel my manhood enter her, then she closed her eyes. I think she actually tried to stay awake, but she couldn't. Something inside her forced her to go to sleep when a man touched her."

Browser glanced at Catkin from the corner of his eye. She probably thought his skills as a lover ranked down there with a weasel's. Unfortunately, he didn't have any witnesses to prove otherwise.

Catkin ran her fingers along her war club, as if comforted by the smooth texture of the use-polished wood.

"I'm waiting for you to tell me what this has to do with Aspen village, and the murder of our Matron here."

"I have been wondering about the little girl on the kiva roof. Do you think her mother forced her to watch the slaughter? The butchering?"

She turned and moonlight sheathed her beautiful face. "Are you afraid she may be deranged? As Ash Girl was?"

"Wouldn't you be?" Browser scooped up a handful of pebbles and crushed them in his palm. "I think Ash Girl's father forced her to watch terrible things."

Catkin frowned at the guard on the hill in the distance. Against the starlight, he resembled a black pinnacle of stone.

"Did Ash Girl ever hurt herself again?"

"Once." The pain behind his eyes turned sickening, as though his souls did not wish to remember. "Almost four summers ago. The Katsinas' People had arrived in our village a week earlier. Ash Girl went to every meeting they held. She listened to the Matron like a child. She told me over and over about Poor Singer's prophecy, and how much she longed to find the First People's kiva and restore it. She really believed that a doorway would open to the underworlds and humans would be able to go to the Land of the Dead to seek advice from their ancestors. She wanted the wars to end, Catkin."

Catkin stared him straight in the eyes. "That's why she forced you to join the Katsinas' People?"

"She didn't force me."

"You agreed to leave your home?"

Browser's stomach muscles clenched. "Of course I didn't. After days of shouts and tears, I threw my war club down in front of her and told her she would have to kill me before I would leave my friends and family in Green Mesa villages." Browser shook his head. "I should have known what she would do. But I didn't, I swear it, Catkin."

She did not ask the question, but her eyes glinted.

Browser said, "Late that night, I woke to find her gone. I checked on our son, Grass Moon, to make sure he was well, then I rose and went out to look for her. I saw her ahead of me in the starlight, walking the rim trail. The mountains around Green Mesa villages are filled with deep canyons. My ancestors built in the cliffs for safety. Raiders couldn't reach us as easily. But it's dangerous country, Catkin. One wrong step and a person can plunge to their death before they have time to scream. I ran after Ash Girl. She disappeared into the pines, and I ran harder. I saw her a quarter hand of time later, standing at the edge of the cliff. She was peering over the edge. She looked pale and luminous in the starlight, almost too beautiful to believe. I looked down in the direction where she was gazing, and when I looked back, she was gone."

Catkin watched him expressionlessly, waiting for the rest.

Browser picked up another pebble and rolled it between his cold palms. "I couldn't believe it. I screamed her name and ran after her. I leaped down the cliff like a madman. No one sane would have dived off the edge like that in the darkness. I rolled down the rocky slope until I could grab onto a juniper that grew in the rocks. I saw her lying on a ledge below me. She was sprawled on her back. I thought she was dead. I really did. I made my way to her by holding on to tree limbs and brush. I don't know how I managed it, but I dragged her out of the canyon and carried her back to the Green Mesa villages." He clutched the pebble in his fist and shook it at nothing, or perhaps everything. "That's when I knew..." His voice caught. He swallowed hard and closed his eyes.

"Knew what?"

"I knew she believed in the katsinas, and would rather die than continue believing in the old gods and living in Green Mesa villages with me and our son."

Catkin took a deep breath and looked out at the moonlit hills. Neither of them spoke for a time. The sound of the river, of water flowing over rocks, came to them, and with it the smell of wet earth.

"That's when you joined the Katsinas' People?"

"I had to protect her, Catkin. If a man does not protect his family, he is nothing. I really believe that."

She frowned down at her war club. "I know you do."

Browser waited for her to make some profound comment, but it never came. Finally, he said, "I know that if I can just unravel the mystery of what happened to her, I will understand everything. These events are like knots on a single cord; her madness is one of the knots." His voice came out low and tormented: "If Two Hearts really was her father, and he's alive, he is doing terrible things to people, making them want to die—as Ash Girl did. I must find him, Catkin." He massaged his temples again. "I have to kill him."

"Many have tried before, Browser, and failed."

"I can't fail." Browser found himself toying with the fringes on his sleeve. "There are other things, too—other 'knots.' Did you ever notice that our Matron rarely spoke of herself?"

Catkin shrugged. "I always thought it was because she did not wish anyone to focus on her. She wanted people to concentrate on Poor Singer's prophecy."

"Yes, she spoke of the prophecy and the duties of the Katsinas' People, but I do not even know where she was born. Do you?"

Catkin nodded. "Yes. Dry Creek village. I overhead Ant Woman speak of it one night in the plaza."

Browser's thoughts darted about like swallows on a summer evening. Without realizing it, he turned toward the south. Dry Creek village sat along the Great North Road that led to Straight Path Canyon. They had passed it on their way here. It was a small village, two stories tall, with perhaps forty people.

"What is it?" Catkin asked. "What are you thinking?"

"My uncle told you that 'The Two' had returned home. If Longtail village was their home, and our Matron grew up less than half a day's walk from here . . ."

Catkin slowly straightened. "Blessed Spirits, do you think she knew them?"

"She must have."

Catkin blinked and gazed out at the starlit river below. After inhaling a deep breath, she said, "There's something else I must speak with you about, Browser. It is, perhaps, another of your 'knots.' "

"What?"

"That night at Aspen village when the woman crawled up to me and told me you were in the kiva, she was wearing a pendant I'd seen before."

Browser shrugged. He couldn't fathom why she thought a pendant might be important. "What pendant?"

She stared unblinking into his eyes. "It was carved from jet. A spiral serpent lying in a broken eggshell. I can't swear to it, but—"

"You mean it looked like the pendant Ash Girl found in Talon Town and gave to Hophorn?"

"Yes. It looked *exactly* like the pendant that Ash Girl put around her own throat just before . . ."

Her voice faded and a chill went through Browser. "Just before I killed her. It may have looked the same, Catkin, but it can't be. We buried Ash Girl with that pendant, and no one would rob a burial to steal a fetish from her chest."

"Then the same artisan must have crafted it. If it was not the same pendant, I swear it was an identical twin."

Browser put a hand on Catkin's shoulder, squeezed it in gratitude, and rose to his feet. "Thank you for telling me. I promise I will think more about it."

She looked up at him with shining eyes. "You will never feel safe, Browser, until you learn to let your wife go. You know that, don't you?"

Browser's heart ached. He fumbled with his cold hands. Finally, he said, "I do feel safe, Catkin. Sometimes, when I look into your eyes. I'm sorry I've never told you that before."

She did not reach out, she did not smile or say anything that would require him to say more. She just nodded in understanding and held his gaze.

"Get some sleep, War Chief."

"You, too, my friend. You've had even less than I have."

"I will see you at dawn." She rose and walked toward Water Snake.

Browser gazed out at the dark hills, wondering about the pendant. Ash Girl had found the pendant in Talon Town. Could it have been made by the same artist who crafted the pendant for the woman at Aspen village?

He wearily shook his head and started back for his chamber. Perhaps when he'd rested, he would be able to think more clearly.

As Browser neared the southeastern corner of the village, he saw a man sitting on the ground with his back against the wall. A gray blanket covered his head and bony shoulders, but Browser could see his elderly profile in the moonlight. Springbank stared at the ground as he rocked back and forth. The soft forlorn sounds coming from his throat rode the night wind.

Browser hesitated, not certain he should intrude, then he changed course and walked toward the old man. No one should have to mourn alone. Browser had done enough of it to know.

"Elder?" Browser said as he knelt before Springbank. "Are you all right?"

As though embarrassed to be caught like this, the old man did not look up. If anything, he seemed to retreat more, huddling inside the tent of his blanket, but Browser could see the tears on his wrinkled cheeks.

Browser sank down beside him and leaned against the cold wall. The guard on the hill in the distance had shifted positions. Moments ago he'd resembled a black pillar; now he looked like a hunching animal. He must have crouched down. A wealth of bright stars glittered in the sky above him.

Gently, Browser said, "It would break her heart to see you like this, Elder."

Springbank wiped his eyes on his blanket. The forlorn sounds stopped, but his shoulders shook from the effort. "I know," he whispered in a shaky voice. "I just feel lost without her."

"As do I, Elder. Her presence had become like a second heartbeat in my chest. I always knew her strength was there for me if I needed it. I will miss her very much."

Springbank inhaled a halting breath and let it out in a rush. "Do you think the katsinas have abandoned us, War Chief? Is that why she died?"

Browser gazed into Springbank's moist eyes and wondered how many other people were suffering from the same fear tonight. He replied, "I do not know, Elder. I have never been able to put much faith in gods."

"You are the most solitary man I have ever known, Browser. I do not know how you manage. Do you believe in nothing?"

Browser touched his war club, but he was thinking of Catkin. He believed in her. He believed in himself and his skills as a warrior—but his "faith" didn't go much beyond those things. "You are a holy man, Elder. I am a warrior. I put my faith in the things I can see."

"I used to feel that way, when I was young and strong. Perhaps when a man has the strength to fight his enemies, he does not need to beg a god for help." He frowned out at the moonlit river, and his wrinkled lips sunk in over his toothless gums.

They sat together in silence for a time, listening to Wind Baby whimper around the village.

Tears filled Springbank's eyes again, and he whispered, "It is harder to believe in the katsinas with her gone. That frightens me."

It had not occurred to Browser until now that Flame Carrier's death would wound them so deeply.

"Do you think we should disband the Katsinas' People?" Springbank choked out the words as though he could barely stand to hear them said aloud. "Perhaps we should give up the Dream."

The agony in the old man's eyes implored Browser to say no, but he couldn't find it in him to lie to Springbank, not when the old man spoke to him with such honesty.

"I think we need time to think about this, Elder. Tomorrow, after the burial, we must start thinking about a new Matron. When we have selected a leader, then we can consider our future."

Springbank's head tottered in a nod. He adjusted the blanket over his head and said, "Yes. Wisdom rests in doing what must be done next. If we just take one step at a time, perhaps all will be well."

"I think it will, Elder."

Springbank put a withered old hand on Browser's forearm and held it. After a short interval, he softly asked, "Do you think the old gods would hear me if I prayed to them tonight? The Flute Player and Spider Woman?"

Browser patted Springbank's hand. "Any god should be happy to hear from a deeply holy man like you, Elder."

CHAPTER 24

THE DREAM WAS so real...

Dusty cried out and jerked upright in his sleeping bag. Cold sweat prickled on his skin. He took a deep breath as the fragmenting tendrils of the nightmare broke around him. The inside of the trailer was black as pitch. What time was it? Midnight?

"Goddamn it."

He slung his legs out of the sleeping bag and perched on the edge of the fold-down bunk. Dale's trailer felt like an oversized coffin. In the silence, he could hear the faint sigh of wind through the junipers outside. A mouse skittered along the frame, its tiny claws scratching the metal.

The distant hoot of an owl sent a shiver across his soul. Most southwestern people had a wary respect for Owl. Even the Hispanic population was leery of *el Tecolote.*

Dusty pulled on his pants, slipped into his boots, and shrugged on his worn blue Filson coat. The trailer stairs squeaked as he stepped out into the night and looked up at the late October sky. A three-quarter moon hung in the east, setting the pale cottonwood leaves aglow.

The stories came welling up from his memory. Tales of selfish people jumping through yucca hoops to become witches. How workers of evil would pervert the ways of Power to achieve revenge, or their own ends.

His rootless childhood had been full of stories about witchcraft. While the Navajo skinwalkers tended to be more colorful, the Pueblo witches had a nastier element. For years Dusty had believed that that element of their evil was descended from the Anasazi, particularly the Chacoans; some scholars thought they'd eaten people as a means of terrorizing subordinate villages. A sort of: "Be good or I'll send my elite warriors down to burn your town and eat your wife and children."

The idea wasn't far-fetched. Even the Hopi admitted that they had destroyed the villages of Awatovi and Sikyatki over witchcraft. Hopis killing other Hopis. To this day, Pueblo peoples were circumspect when it came to leaving loose hair, nail clippings, or sweat-soaked garments lying around. The Hopi elder who had been Dusty's mentor had urinated on rocks to prevent witches from later molding a doll out of that damp soil to use against him.

He thought about that as he walked silently through the camp and down into the shadows of the cottonwoods.

He stopped at the river's edge and looked out over the moon-silvered water. It seemed to dance and swirl, alive with the power of life. Like so many of the rivers in the Southwest, it had been flowing here when the Anasazi had devoured themselves like the proverbial snake swallowing its own tail.

That long-ago night when the kiva burned, the gaudy light would have cast a red-orange glow over this water. Here, where he was standing, he would have heard the screams of the children. Were the parents shouting back, desperate to reach their sons and daughters? Or were they silent witnesses to the extinction of their hopes and dreams?

"Stewart?"

He started, wheeling, then sighed. "Jesus! You almost made me jump out of my skin."

Maureen stepped out into the moonlight. Black hair tumbled down her back like a midnight mantle. Her face was ghostly pale, her dark eyes like round holes in white cloth.

He said, "What are you doing up?"

"I think it was the jalapeño cheeseburgers. I didn't dare pick half of those peppers off. I would never have lived it down."

He sucked in a deep breath. "Sorry. I wasn't thinking when I made them. I just made them to my tastes."

She walked closer and examined his face. "Are you all right?"

"Fine. Just out for a walk."

"Uh-huh," she said as she folded her arms over her black coat. "Is something wrong, Dusty? You haven't been normal since I got here."

"The words 'Dusty Stewart' and 'normal' aren't generally joined in the same sentence, Maureen."

"Nightmare?"

He used the toe of his boot to squash a blowing leaf and replied, "I get them on occasion." More lately than ever before.

She paused, took another step toward him, and gazed out over the river. "Well, after looking at the boiled skull, and the kiva filled with bones, I don't doubt it."

Dusty winced and closed his eyes. "Do you mind, Doctor?"

"Is that what you dreamed about? Burning babies?"

He nodded. "I was down in the kiva. The bodies were fresh, charred, the hair melted over the skulls until it looked like glass, lips pulled back to expose cracked blue-black teeth. The eyes, my God, the eyes were popped out where the vitreous humor had boiled inside. I had been chased in there, had fallen among them, and my hand—" He held it out in the moonlight, studying it, feeling it alive and warm. "I kept trying to push myself up, and each time my hand pushed right through rotting bodies. They were all slimy inside."

"Then what happened?"

He rubbed the back of his neck, feeling odd about telling her his dreams. "I searched the kiva for the ladder to get out, and there was Dad, looking down at me, laughing. But the voice wasn't his. It was . . . It was . . ."

"Who?"

He shook his head. "Sorry, Doctor, I'm not about to feed more rumors about the Madman of New Mexico. Besides, I've always secretly been afraid that maybe insanity runs in my family."

"Oh, come on. Granted I didn't know your father, or what would have possessed him to kill himself, but I do know you." The moonlight added its magic to her beautiful face. "I may not always like you, but I've never seen anything that made me doubt your sanity. The quality of your soul, yes. Sanity, no."

He couldn't help it; he laughed. "Yeah, well, the next few sentences will make you reconsider. Do you know why I called you to come to this site?"

"Other than the obvious reason that I'm a physical anthropologist, no."

He bent down, picked up a rounded rock, and pitched it into the river. It splashed liquid silver in the moonlight. "This is really going to sound crazy, so brace yourself."

Maureen gave him a suspicious look. "I'm braced. Go ahead."

He waved a hand at the night. "It's all tied together. Everything. You, me, this site. I showed you that potsherd for a reason. I know it sounds delusional, but this site *is* tied to 10K3. Unless I can lift fingerprints from the pottery, I'll never be able to prove it, but we—you and I—are connected to these sites. And I think I know the reason."

She shivered before she could squelch it. "Okay, why?"

"You liked Magpie Walking Hawk Taylor, didn't you?"

She nodded. "We've been writing letters since I returned to Canada."

"Do you think she's crazy?"

"No, I don't. Why?"

He pitched another rock into the river. "Because she and I believe a lot of the same things. Funny, isn't it? She's an enrolled member of the Keres tribe, and no one thinks she's nuts because she believes in witchcraft. I'm a White guy who's lived on reservations off and on for most of my life, been initiated into a kiva—"

"But if you believe, you're a lunatic."

"The lady wins first prize. Right as rain."

She bowed her head and long black hair spilled around her. The waves rippled platinum where the moonlight touched them. "So, you're telling me you believe these children died because of witchcraft?"

God, she was beautiful, straight and tall, with that perfect Seneca face.

Maureen tilted her head to look at him. "How long did you keep the basilisk in your house, Dusty?"

His stomach tingled. "Too long, I think. I had it in my house for about six months before I finished the excavation report and curated it, along with the other artifacts we found."

She seemed to let it go. She looked out at the river and the full moon shining down. "It's beautiful here."

"It is. Just before you arrived, I was thinking about that, about *El Rio de las Animas Perdidas,* the River of Lost Souls. Just south of here is Aztec Ruins. When Earl Morris dug it in the twenties, it was littered with bodies, and just south of there is Salmon Ruins. Cynthia Irwin-Williams dug it in the seventies. It had another tower kiva like this one. Also filled with children."

"And you think witchcraft was the cause?" She didn't sound so skeptical now.

"One man's belief is another man's heresy. When someone dares to believe differently than you do, it always helps if you can label him as evil; that way people can hate him without feeling guilty. It's very convenient."

Maureen tucked her hands into her pockets and tipped her chin to look at the stars. "I recall that Hail Walking Hawk thought the basilisk was a witch's amulet. She said it was dangerous, filled with evil. Do you think you've been witched?"

Their gazes held.

"That's why you think we're tied to these sites, isn't it?" she whispered as though she feared someone might be listening. "You and I have been witched?" A smile tugged at the corners of her lips.

Dusty didn't see the humor. "Go ahead and laugh, but I recall that you spent a good deal of time touching the bones from that site, and even took home a pot of corpse powder. I'd get rid of that pot *pronto* if I were you. I'm surprised you haven't had the Blair Witch traipsing around your dreams."

Her smile faded.

Dusty caught the tension in the sudden set of her jaw. "Really? And you haven't told me about this before?"

She let out a breath, and it frosted in the air. "Actually, I thought about calling you, or Maggie, but I just couldn't convince myself to do it—and I haven't had the dream since I've been out here."

Dusty studied her taut expression. "Which means you had the dream more than once in Canada? It's a recurrent dream?"

She sternly pointed a finger at him. "Yes, and if you tell anyone, I will mail the pot of corpse powder directly to you."

Dusty crossed himself. "No need to threaten. I'm good at keeping secrets. What's the dream?"

"It's"—she gestured awkwardly—"it's not a witch dream, it's a ghost dream."

"Go on."

She tucked her hair behind her ears, stalling. "A wolf leads me to a cave in the mountains. In the back of the cave, there's a skeleton in a pool of water. While I'm standing there looking at it, four people come in."

"Four. A sacred number. Do they talk to you?"

"The old woman does. She tells me not to be afraid."

"I'm sure that calms you right down, huh?"

Maureen laughed. "Yeah, right. Anyway, it's not a scary dream, it's more like—"

"A Spirit Dream?" Dusty asked. "Like you're being called by a Spirit Helper?"

Maureen frowned at him. "I suppose some would say so."

"Which figure in the dream is calling you?"

"I don't know. Maybe all of them. The old man looks right at me, though."

"I could arrange for you to talk to some Puebloan tribal elders about it."

She gave him an incredulous look. "You're the one who needs a head session, not me."

The clipped tone of voice made Dusty's heart shrivel. "Just can't take the risk, eh? I assure you that nobody I recommend will blab to the American Association of Physical Anthropologists."

She balled her fists in her pockets. "You know what? This has been a lovely chat, but I think it's time to go back to bed."

She spun around and strode away.

Dusty sighed, spent a few seconds staring at the stars, then called, "Hey! Wait up. I'll walk you back."

CHAPTER 25

"THEY'RE COMING," STRAIGHTHORN said and stamped his feet to keep warm.

The cold morning wind whipped Jackrabbit's shoulder-length black hair over his pug nose and into his dark brown eyes as he shifted to look. "Where? I don't see them."

"They are just leaving the plaza."

A purple gleam haloed the eastern horizon. In the distance, he could make out the shape of Longtail village. Gray forms emerged from the great kiva, and flute music drifted up to them, the notes sweet and mournful.

From their guard position on the knoll across the river, they would be able to watch most of the burial ceremony.

Redcrop led the procession, sprinkling the path with cornmeal to sanctify the way. Long black hair draped her white cape.

Behind her, six spectral figures Danced, twenty hands tall, with no arms or legs. They glided forward as if canoeing on air, and the rhythmic clacking of their carved beaks cut the stillness like knives. Buffalo horns curved upward from the enormous empty eyes of their masks. Red-feathered capes covered their misshapen bodies. Part bird, part buffalo, and part man, the katsinas united the worlds of sky and earth, animal and human. They were moments of perfect harmony in a sea of chaos.

"I will miss our Matron," Jackrabbit said.

"She was a good leader. Was she your clan?"

"She was my *family*, Straighthorn." Jackrabbit rubbed his cold arms. "I have no knowledge of my clan. Three summers ago, I woke at the bottom of a cliff with my head bashed and bloody. I could remember nothing. Not even my name. I may have slipped and fallen, or been in a battle. I wandered for days before I saw the Matron standing outside of Flowing Waters Town. She was looking up as if searching for me. I walked down, and she took me in. She fed me and clothed me." His voice turned brittle. "She gave me a home."

"I did not know her for long, but she was always kind to me. I will miss her, too."

The burial procession came slowly down the path toward the river. Cloudblower followed the katsinas, and behind her, Springbank, Wading Bird, and Crossbill marched. On the elders' heels, War Chief Browser and Catkin carried Matron Flame Carrier's burial ladder. A large group of mourners assembled at the rear and fell into line as the procession descended into the cottonwoods.

Thirty people from Dry Creek village had come in for the ceremony late last night. Their campfires gleamed on the outskirts of Longtail village. They walked in the rear. Most wore bright yellow capes that contrasted sharply with the red and white capes of the Katsinas' People. The Dry Creek Matron, Ant Woman, had been a good friend of their Matron.

Straighthorn lost sight of them. Wind Baby shrieked across the desert and blasted the trees until they squeaked and groaned. A hurricane of golden leaves tumbled through the air.

Redcrop reappeared as the burial party moved toward the grave. She walked slowly, solemnly, her right hand extended to the path. The cornmeal falling from her fingers blew away in a glimmering haze.

Straighthorn whispered, "She must be dying inside. I wish I was there."

"Skink will relieve us at dawn. We will be there for the final Songs, my friend."

"I hope so."

Jackrabbit turned to look at him. "Oh, believe me, he will come. Skink may not be happy with you, Straighthorn, but he will not disobey the War Chief's orders. He values his skin too much."

The War Chief had a reputation for explosive anger, though Straighthorn had never seen it. In the past nine moons he had seen only a very solitary man, a man in mourning who dwelled on the deaths of his wife and son. Browser kept to himself, did what had to be done to protect the village, and retreated to his chamber alone at night. Many of the Longtail Clan widows had initially viewed Browser with interest, but he had politely shied away from them. The only woman he spent time with was Catkin.

Straighthorn had heard the story of how, two summers ago, Browser had sneaked into an enemy camp where she was being held prisoner and rescued her. She'd been injured, and was dazed. He killed the men raping her and carried Catkin out on his back. He'd rescued her again in Straight Path Canyon. Straighthorn wondered at that. Browser had risked his life at least twice to save Catkin, but he did not appear to be in love with her. Rather, she seemed to be his best friend.

Straighthorn said, "I should have kept my temper yesterday, Jackrabbit. I embarrassed Skink—"

"Everyone knew you were right. You had found the murderers' tracks. We should have followed them until we couldn't see our own feet in the darkness. Most of us wished to continue the search. The fact that you argued with Skink about it only improved your reputation."

Straighthorn gestured lamely. "Yes, but the argument diminished his. I fear he will find a hundred small ways to punish me."

"He is a very powerful man, my friend. You should be worried about the big ways he can get you. He is as cruel as a weasel, and you know it. If you turn up dead some morning, I'll be very disappointed in you."

Straighthorn sighed and looked up at the last of the Evening People who glittered on the western horizon. Wolf Slayer and his brother Raven were always the last to go to sleep. They watched over the world until Father Sun rose into the sky and could guard it himself.

"You have only known Skink for a few moons, Straighthorn," Jackrabbit said. "He is very clever. If he decides to kill you, he'll make it look like an accident. 'Oh, poor Straighthorn, he slipped and fell on his own knife. I swear there was nothing I could do!' " Jackrabbit nodded for effect.

"That's not amusing. You just sent chills up my neck."

"Good."

Straighthorn glanced over his shoulder, examining the path at the base of the knoll.

"You're going to have me jumping at my own breathing. Let's speak of something else."

Jackrabbit remained silent for a time, then he gestured to the rolling hills in front of them. "Do you think they're out there?"

"Who?"

"The murderers."

"No! Why would you think that?"

Jackrabbit shrugged. "I was in Talon Town when my friend Whiproot was killed. I heard his death screams. Later, the War Chief told me that Stone Ghost said murderers always come to watch if they can. I guess it gives them some"—he waved a hand—"thrill."

Straighthorn felt as if a nest of wriggling baby snakes had hatched in his hair. He pulled his war club from his belt and gripped it in a hard fist.

"I thank you, Jackrabbit. I was getting tired. Now I'm fully awake."

"Just in time. Skink is coming."

Straighthorn turned.

A shadow emerged from the brush and came toward them. The sound of feet crunching sand rode the wind.

Straighthorn sucked in a deep breath to prepare himself, and called, "A Blessed morning to you, Skink."

Jackrabbit lifted a hand and smiled. "We're glad to see you. It's been a bitter night."

Skink's buckskin cape swayed around his tall, lean body as he climbed to the top of the knoll. The pale morning gleam sheathed his catlike face. He did not even glance at Jackrabbit. He stopped in front of Straighthorn and looked down through dark cold eyes. "You saw nothing?"

"Nothing unusual," Straighthorn replied.

"Well," Jackrabbit clarified, "we saw the burial party leave the village and walk to the gravesite. That's a little unusual, but these days not—"

"Then leave. You are no longer needed here."

Straighthorn bowed respectfully, and he and Jackrabbit marched down the hill. They didn't speak until they had passed beyond the brush at the base of the knoll.

Jackrabbit said, "I don't think he likes us."

"It's me he doesn't like."

A sliver of brilliant pink light painted the east.

"It's almost dawn," Straighthorn said. "We'd better hurry if we're going to make it for the last Songs."

Straighthorn broke into a trot, and Jackrabbit followed him down onto the leaf-choked path by the river.

PIPER CLUTCHES HER corn-husk doll to her chest and slides forward on her belly, inching her way to the top of the hill where she can look down at the

hole in the ground. All of the people are shiny birds, red, white, and yellow. They can't talk. They squeak and squeal. Mother wears white, and stands beside another woman in white, but they are surrounded by yellow birds.

Piper puts her dirty finger in her mouth and sucks on it; it tastes bright and bitter, like licking a pyrite mirror.

New people come. Two men. They walk up from the river bottom and stand at the edge of the crowd, right behind Mother. But Mother does not see them. She is crying, her shoulders shaking apart. Or maybe it is laughing. Sometimes laughing looks like crying.

People lift the dead woman from the burial ladder and lower her into the hole. The Songs start. Human Songs. She can hear them. People live inside the squeals. As the masked Dancers spin around the edge of the grave, an old man lowers the burial ladder into the hole so that the woman's afterlife soul can climb out and go to the Land of the Dead.

Piper watches the children come forward, get down on their knees, and begin shoving dirt into the hole. There are many children. More than Piper has ever seen in one place.

The Songs stop. People hug each other and start to walk away. The old people move closer to the grave. Their hair is the color of rain clouds and snowflakes.

As if Mother knows Piper is spying on her, she lifts her head and stares at the hilltop.

Piper cannot move. Her body is frozen. She clutches her doll to her chest.

Mother has dead flying squirrel eyes. Black and bulging.

A small, terrible cry escapes Piper's lips.

She forces her legs to slide her backward down the hill, then she gets to her feet and runs, runs away fast, down the hill.

She stumbles through a tangle of rabbitbrush and takes a deer trail into the bottom of the drainage. The sand is wet; it squishes around her sandals. She runs, searching, her eyes moving until she sees a hole. An old coyote den dug into the wall.

Piper squirms in headfirst. It is big inside, big enough for her to turn around and stare out of the hole at the sunlight.

She listens. The birds have gone quiet. Not even Wind Baby dares to breathe.

"No one yet," she whispers to her doll. "It's all right. We're all right."

CHAPTER 26

DUSTY LEVERED ANOTHER shovelful of dirt from his excavation unit and tossed it into Sylvia's wheelbarrow. Despite the fact that the late afternoon temperature hovered around sixty-two degrees, he wore a short-sleeved gray T-shirt. Sweat matted his blond hair to his cheeks and soaked his armpits. October in the high desert was like nowhere else on earth. The patches of blue showing through the clouds glistened, and the air smelled like freshly plowed earth.

"Anything yet?" he called up from his meter-deep pit. To either side, the classic Chacoan walls of the structure caught the afternoon sun. The interior of the walls were rubble-filled, but the outer layer of stone consisted of flat slabs, carefully fitted together. Each layer was of a varying thickness, creating a pattern. More than once, while looking at such walls, it had struck him that they resembled the weft of weaving, as if the patterns were similar to those reflected in the occasional specimens of blankets recovered from dry cave sites. The masonry workmanship was spectacular. During the time when the pueblo was occupied, that beautiful stonework would have been covered by thick mud plaster, and painted with designs. Despite what modern people thought about brick and stonework, bare rock was anything but beautiful to the Anasazi.

"*Nada*, boss," Sylvia replied as she fingered through the dirt. A sweaty lock of brown hair curled over her forehead. She wiped a hand on her dirt-caked blue jeans and tugged at the battered canvas hat on her head.

"Have I ever told you how much I hate clearing out room fill?" he asked.

"Maybe once or twice."

He bent down and tugged to remove another weathered chunk of toppled sandstone and heaved it into the wheelbarrow.

"Whoa!" Sylvia said. "That's a load!"

"Oops. Sorry."

She artfully turned the wheelbarrow and trundled it down the line of planks that crossed the rubble on the collapsed pueblo. At the edge of the ruin, she separated the rock and tipped the wheelbarrow to spill the dirt into a wooden-framed screen. He heard the unforgettable *shish-shish* as she worked it back and forth.

Dusty wiped his dirty face on his sleeve and took the opportunity to stretch his aching back muscles. "God, I think age is catching up with me."

"Yeah, I've heard thirty-seven is a real turning point. Like the storm surge before the hurricane. Just wait till next year." Sylvia lowered her screen and tossed the dregs—roots, insect hulls, and a few rocks—out onto the back-dirt pile. "Okay, hit me again."

Dusty pried more of the tumbled stone loose and tossed it up into the wheelbarrow. Across from him, he heard Maureen and Steve talking in low voices as they worked over the bone bed in the bottom of the kiva. One by one, Maureen was mapping in the bits of bone, painting the more fragile pieces with polyvinyl acetate preservative, and removing them, many on their pedestals of dirt, to be cleaned later in the lab.

Dusty heaved another stone into the wheelbarrow and gazed out to the east. Beyond the cottonwoods, the Animas River flowed through the floodplain like a winding brown serpent. In every direction, hills rolled until they butted against golden sandstone cliffs. Just to the south, the land turned a drab shade of gray as the Animas wound its way southwest toward the town of Aztec.

He bent to the task of freeing more head-sized blocks of sandstone and tossed them up into the wheelbarrow. The work couldn't be called anything other than nasty, but doing it by hand was the only way to be certain nothing important got damaged.

As Sylvia wheeled another load away, Dusty propped himself so that he could look over the wall. Steve was drawing in his field notebook. The bottom of the tower kiva had been cordoned off into a grid, yellow nylon string crisscrossing the floor in one-meter squares.

Dusty's gaze lingered on Maureen. She'd pulled her long black hair up and pinned it under her hat. The oversized black sweatshirt she wore declared an emphatic OH, CANADA! But his attention was on the way it conformed to her shoulders, and stretched down to accent her slim waist. Her butt did really nice things to the black jeans she wore.

"Uh, Boss Man? You working, or building up to a cardiac condition?" Sylvia asked.

Dusty turned. Sylvia stood behind the wheelbarrow, her arms crossed, green eyes amused.

"I didn't hear you come back."

"No shit?" She cocked her head. "You want Steve and me to cart rocks while you go hold the tape measure for Maureen?"

He pitched a rock into her wheelbarrow with enough vigor to make the steel ring. "Careful. I might start asking questions about your personal life."

"I don't have a personal life."

Dusty scratched the back of his neck. "Right. Sure. At dinner last night, I was afraid to seat you two next to each other."

She rolled the chunks of sandstone to the back of the wheelbarrow. "Yeah, well, we went down to the river to talk. That's all. I mean, we didn't really plan... You know, that thing in Durango? It just sort of happened. We were trying to..." She shook her head. "I don't know, Dusty, it's just all so quick."

"Yep."

"Well, what do you think? I mean, about Steve and me."

"Not a thing. If you make it work, more power to you. If you don't, it's none of my business, and whatever you do is what you do."

"Gee, thanks, Dusty. That was really helpful."

He gave her a sidelong look. "I don't have to worry about assigning you to the same pit, do I? If that will be uncomfortable for either of you, just pull me aside and tell me, and I'll figure something out."

"Naw, we're cool. We're just going to take some time. See if we really like each other as much as we think we do. I mean, God, we've been friends for years. We've always liked each other, but Steve's not sure—"

"You didn't hit him with the baseball bat, did you?"

Sylvia grinned. "No, but I keep having to remind myself. You know, I'll wake up at night and catch myself about to brain him, but so far so good."

Sylvia hauled off another load of rock and dumped it. Dusty had just about picked the floor clean enough to shovel again. Using a broom, he swept the shovel full, waited for Sylvia to return, and pitched it up into her empty wheelbarrow, then frowned at the hard-packed clay. He had finally found the room floor, the original living surface.

He had just bent over to began troweling when Sylvia called: "Yo!"

"What?" He looked up.

Sylvia brushed the twigs and rocks to the side in her screen and picked up a tiny bone fragment. As she held it up to the yellow light, she said, "Looks human to me." She brought it over and handed it to him.

"Looks like a deer skull to me, but let's ask the expert." He stepped over to the wall and called. "Dr. Cole, would you grace us with your opinion, please?"

Maureen said something to Steve, straightened her back, and tiptoed to the edge of the kiva. She stood in the shadow cast by the wall. He could see her Seneca heritage in every line of her face, her straight nose, full lips, the breadth of her cheekbones.

"Catch," he said, and tossed it to her. "And be careful."

She snagged it out of the air and frowned at the flat fragment of bone.

Steve watched Maureen thumb soil from the bone. His blue jeans had turned gray from the charcoal and soot, and the splotches of dirt-caked sweat on his brown shirt made it look as though it had been tie-dyed.

Sylvia said, "Dusty says deer bone. I say human. What's the verdict, Washais?"

Maureen turned the bone over in her hand. "I think, Sylvia, you're a better archaeologist than your boss."

Dusty's brows lifted. "Yeah, why?"

Steve looked up mildly. "Don' I get to guess, massa?"

"No," Dusty said. "I'm not letting you make any more guesses until you learn to speak twentieth-century English."

"You mean like Ebonics?" Sylvia asked.

Dusty scowled. "Okay, Maureen, what part of the human body is it?"

"The same part as your big 'bead,' Stewart: the skull." She leaned over the pit and frowned. "Where's the rest of it?"

"That's all we've uncovered, but hold on."

Dusty jumped down into the excavation unit and picked up his trowel again. He didn't see anything on the surface, but he scraped around the place where he'd taken his last shovelful of dirt. The earth smelled damp and rich. In the corner, the soft soil indicated an intrusion in the prehistoric floor.

"Got a hole here."

Maureen and Steve climbed the aluminum ladder out of the kiva and perched on the wall next to Sylvia. All of them stared down at Dusty like vultures.

Dusty's trowel clanked on what sounded like a rock. He scraped the top of it clean, frowned, and began excavating around the object. Oblong, the quartzite river cobble had been battered on both ends. "Hammerstone," he said, then translated for Maureen's benefit. "The ends took quite a bit of beating. Probably crushing acorns."

"What do you mean, probably?" Maureen asked.

Sylvia answered, "Well, we just found a crushed piece of skull, Washais." Maureen's Seneca name meant something scary like "ritual knife." "Somebody might have used that hammerstone to whack bone instead of acorns."

As he pulled dirt away from the artifact, Dusty added, "Don't forget that people ate each other down here, Doctor."

"*Probably* ate each other," Maureen corrected.

"Mark this one down in the books. She sort of agrees with me."

His trowel clicked in that distinctive way of metal meeting bone. Dusty reached for the brush sticking out of his back pocket and carefully whisked earth from around the smooth stone. A ring of bone beads, twenty centimeters wide, emerged.

He propped his elbows on his knees. "Well. Welcome to feature four. Sylvia, grab a handful of Ziplocs, the Sharpie pen, and the camera."

"On my way!"

Steve rubbed his jaw. "More evidence to support the cannibalism theory?"

"Not necessarily," Maureen said as she crouched on the wall. "Someone may have made beads out of the cranial bones, but that doesn't prove he ate the meat attached to the bones."

"Hmm," Steve said. "What do we have to find to prove the Anasazi ate somebody?"

"Two types of human blood in human feces would be nice. Fragments of human bone would be even better."

Dusty said, "I always thought finding an intact foot in somebody's stomach would prove it conclusively."

Sylvia trotted up with the camera dangling from her neck, a wad of Ziplocs stuffed in her coat pocket, and the Sharpie pen hooked to her belt. "Here you go, Boss Man." She lifted the camera over her head and handed it down to him, then lowered the "feature kit" in its metal ammo box.

"Thanks." Dusty took the articles and positioned himself in front of the ring. He placed a stick, painted black-and-white in centimeters, beside the feature for scale, arranged the north arrow, then jotted the details on the little chalkboard before adjusting the camera's focus. He took several bracketing shots.

Sylvia said, "That's a really strange feature. I mean, it looks symbolic, you know?"

"Symbolic?" Steve wiped his face on his sleeve. "You mean religious?"

"Yeah. Definitely religious."

Dusty handed the camera back to Sylvia, and said, "Plastic, please."

Sylvia pulled the Ziplocs from her pocket, gave him the wad, then handed Dusty the Sharpie pen.

Dusty troweled fresh dirt into a plastic bag and measured in the location. He reached for his line level and took the depth from the pit datum stake. As he pulled the cap off the Sharpie and labeled the bag, he said, "What makes you two think this is religious symbolism?"

Sylvia's freckled face seemed to light up. "Didn't you ever read Mircea Eliade's book, *Patterns in Comparative Religion*? There's this really weird history of people connecting stones and bones. I mean, like, we all know that southwestern tribes put rocks over the heads of people they don't like to keep their souls locked in the earth forever, but did you know that the Gonds tribe in India place a big rock on a grave to fasten down the dead person's soul? There are even people who speculate that we originally set a headstone on a grave to keep the soul in the body until the Second Coming, when the stone would be rolled away, à la Jesus, and the person resurrected." Sylvia glanced around the pit. "Cool, huh?"

Steve gave her a deadpan look. "You took another philosophy class last semester, didn't you, Sylvia?"

"Religious studies," she corrected. "Anyway, this feature is even neater because many people associate stones with giving birth. Childless women among the Maidu tribe in California touch a rock shaped like a pregnant woman to get knocked up, and in parts of Europe young couples have to walk on certain stones to make their union fruitful. In Madagascar, women who want to have a child smear stones with grease."

Steve paused, and his bushy black brows pulled together. "Then what?"

Sylvia frowned. "What do you mean?"

"After they smear the stones. Then what?"

As his meaning dawned, Sylvia said, "Naw, I don't think so. I mean, if they do, nobody's ever recorded it. And somebody would have. Anthropologists are kinky."

"Yassuh!" Steve raised a fist, then jerked it downwards in approval. "By now they would have been nicknamed Mazola Rocks."

Maureen made a disgusted sound, jumped down into the room with Dusty, and edged him aside. "If you don't mind, could I take a look?"

"Why, certainly, Doctor. Besides, you're already here." He leaned back against the pit wall.

Maureen's hair caught the sunlight. He took a moment to admire the way it glistened and wondered what it would be like to touch silky hair like that.

Her brows lowered. "These are virtually identical to the bone bead you showed me in Durango, Stewart, including the ground edges." She took his paintbrush, bent over the bone beads, and carefully whisked dirt away from the edges. "I'd say the bones were not cooked, though there are distinct cut marks on the larger fragments. I—"

"You don't have to cook the bones to be a cannibal," Steve said. "You can crack the skull, shake out the brain, eat it, and toss the bones."

Dusty nodded. "He's right."

"Yes, well, you've still got to convince me this is a cannibal act," Maureen responded. "Even more curious is a cannibal who smashes the skull, grinds fragments into beads, then reassembles them around a large stone."

Dusty's smile faded. He dropped to one knee and stared at the bone fragments. "What are you talking about? The circle isn't in the shape of a skull."

"He didn't use all of the pieces, Stewart, just the callot, the upper part of the braincase." She drew a line across her own eyebrows and then around the back of her skull.

Sylvia's green eyes widened. "Wow. I wonder what that means? Maybe the stone symbolizes a child in the womb."

"Or a rock for a brain," Dusty said.

"I'd guess a penis in a vagina," Steve suggested.

Sylvia squinted at the rock. "Boy, if so, that guy had real delusions of grandeur."

Maureen stood up. "I don't think we have enough information to speculate, folks. We need to finish the excavation. We've just uncovered the top."

"That's the first sensible thing I've heard." Dusty stuck his thumbs in his back pockets. "This has been here for eight hundred years. It could just be that freeze-thaw cycles moved the bone out from the stone."

Sylvia rose and dusted her pants off. "Why don't you let me dig for a while, Dusty? You've been pitching rock out of there all day."

Dusty braced his hands on the wall and climbed out over the unexcavated rubble filling the rest of the room. As he reached for his camo vest, he said, "Just keep in mind that the good doctor is going to be hanging over the pit. If you chip a single bone, I'll have to shove a stick in her mouth to keep her from biting off her tongue."

"I'll be careful." Sylvia leaped into the pit and pulled her trowel from her back pocket.

Dusty smiled across at Maureen, but she didn't see him. Two upright lines formed between her brows as she studied the ring of beads.

Dusty turned to Steve. "Hand me that bucket, Steve. Sylvia can trowel the dirt into it and hand the bucket up instead of using the shovel."

"On my way."

Steve followed the line of planks to where the bucket sat canted at the edge of the back-dirt pile.

Sylvia spent a few minutes carefully troweling down around the rock inside the bone ring. No one said anything until Sylvia's trowel struck something beneath the stone.

"Whoa, Sylvia," Dusty said, kneeling to get a closer look. "What did you hit?"

Sylvia reached for the brush and gently removed the dirt clinging to the object. "Looks like a pot rim to me, boss."

Steve bent forward and braced his hands on his knees. "The rock is resting on top of a pot?"

Dusty and Maureen exchanged a worried glance, memories of 10K3 resurfacing in their minds.

Maureen said, "You don't think—"

"I hope not."

Sylvia looked up. "I'll bet you five bucks it is."

"Is what?" Steve asked in confusion.

"Corpse powder," Sylvia said.

Steve straightened. "You mean, like among the Navajo? The stuff witches use to kill and make people sick? Why would you think that?"

Dusty said, "Remember 10K3? August before last we found a pot in a burial, and it was definitely filled with powdered people. Our local Keres monitor said she thought it was the work of a witch. But"—he pointed a finger at Sylvia—"that's purely speculation right now, Sylvia. You might just have a rim sherd. Keep working."

She gave him a military salute and went back to troweling.

"Powdered people? No kidding?" Steve's ebony face shone with sweat. He wiped his forehead on his sleeve. "None of you died, I notice. Anybody puke their guts out?"

"Nope," Sylvia called up. "Mrs. Walking Hawk cleansed us in pinyon pine smoke. The evil spirits couldn't stick to us—" She stopped suddenly. "Hey, folks, I've definitely got a pot down here. See this?" She used the tip of her trowel to point to the rounded side of the black-on-white pot. "It's a little pot. About ten centimeters across."

Dusty gestured to the tape measure resting to Sylvia's left. "I'd like something a little more definitive, if it won't trouble you, Dr. Rhone."

Sylvia reached for the tape, measured the rim first, then the pot. "Yep! Ten centimeters. Am I a precision instrument or what?"

She set the tape aside, made notes in the unit notebook, and troweled around between the rock and the pot. When she'd moved enough dirt that everyone could clearly see the pot, she said, "I'm not sure, but I think the rock is stuck to the top of the pot."

"Son of a bitch!" Dusty leaped into the pit with his trowel and said, "Move over, I need some room."

Sylvia shrank back against the fitted stone wall. "Careful," she warned. "That looks like pine pitch glue."

Dusty gently troweled and brushed until he'd exposed the base of the pot. "Come on, people. I need light." He went through the ritual of recording, then carefully lifted the small round pot out with the rock intact. "Sylvia, bag this," he said, and handed it to her.

"Gotcha." Sylvia slipped it into a Ziploc and used a Sharpie pen to write the provenience on the outside of the bag.

Dusty climbed out and took the bag. Everyone around the partially excavated room went quiet, staring at him.

"What do you think it is?" Steve asked.

"I don't know," Sylvia said, "but I'm not sure we should open it up out here. You know, without adult supervision. Maybe we should call Magpie and have her bring out an elder—"

"I think we'll be safe on our own," Dusty told her. "This is probably a cache of beads or projectile points, something harmless. Until we have evidence that it's a dangerous artifact, I'm sure we can handle it."

Sylvia whispered something to Steve from the corner of her mouth, and Steve's brows went up.

Dusty asked, "What was that, Sylvia?"

"Oh, I was just telling Steve about that time in Wyoming when you said you could handle big Bob Deercapture. Remember? He said he could pee farther than you, and you told him he couldn't. The problem was, it was fifty-six below zero, and Dusty turned kind of fast before he zipped and accidentally touched the side of the Bronco. I mean, who in the Southwest knows that warm wet parts will stick to metal when it's that cold?"

Steve shuddered. "Ouch. When I was little, my mother told me not to stick my tongue to ice trays or my head would freeze solid. I bet it's kind of the same thing."

"I *don't* think so," Dusty said.

Sylvia tucked a tendril of stray brown hair up under her woolen cap. "Actually, it was no big deal. We just heated up a teapot and steamed it off. It would have gone a lot faster if Dusty hadn't been such a crybaby—"

"Good God, Sylvia," Dusty said. "Do you really have to go into the details?"

"But people can learn real-life lessons from stuff like this, Dusty. I mean, if your mother had told you about ice trays when you were a child, you'd have one less scar."

Maureen folded her arms. "A little like the incident in Cortez, eh, Stewart?"

Steve looked inquisitively from one person to the next. "She knows about Muffet?"

"Oh, come on!" Sylvia said. "Everyone in archaeology knows about Muffet."

Dusty got to his feet. It was the one and only time in his life that he'd danced with a stripper. And the last time he'd touched gin. "It's quitting time. Tarp the pits. Maureen and I will take the pot back to camp and get dinner started while you two clean up and stow gear."

Dusty climbed out of the room and stalked toward camp.

Behind him, he heard Steve whisper, then Sylvia said, "Yeah, well, he's really sensitive about that story. It's kind of the defining moment of his life."

CHAPTER 27

AS EVENING DRAPED the land, the juniper grove behind their field camp went from dark green to black. Maureen sighed as she watched the world change. The long shadows began to disappear, fading into the night. The ancient pueblo became nothing more than a gray mound of rubble dotted with black squares of plastic.

"How are you doing with the lantern?" Dusty asked as he stepped into the trailer.

He had just finished arranging kindling for a fire after dinner. Tall and sun-bronzed, his form filled the doorway.

"I'm working on it, Stewart," she said as she picked up the matchbook. "Don't worry. I've started a few lanterns in my life."

"You pumped it up, right?"

"Right," she answered in irritation, struck a match, and held it below the mantles as she turned up the gas. The mantles caught in a *whoosh* and pulsing white light illuminated the artifacts and bones bagged on the square table. She smiled, suspecting that some of the most precious artifacts in southwestern archaeology had rested on Dale's little Formica table.

"Thanks," Dusty said. "You want to get dinner started? Anything you want."

Maureen's brows lifted. "Anything I want?"

"Well, anything we have. Your selection is somewhat limited due to the fact that we did most of the shopping in Bloomfield. No caviar or escargots, I'm afraid."

She propped a hand on the table. "That's very creative, Stewart. I've never heard it pronounced it *es-car-guts*."

She walked out of the trailer and crossed to the supply tent. Boxes lined the walls. Each brimmed with different shapes and sizes of cans, bottles, bags of chips, and many things she couldn't make out in the dim light. She opened one of the coolers and peered inside. She found a package of meat, sniffed it, and cringed. The celery reminded her of Phil—really limp and sort of slimy. Giving it up as a lost cause, she turned to the cardboard boxes.

Stewart looked up when Maureen climbed into the trailer. Lantern light glinted in his beard, accenting his handsome face. "What did you pick?"

"Something called Dinty Moore's beef stew."

Stewart shuddered. "No wonder you get along with Sylvia."

"You don't like it?" She started to back out of the trailer.

"No, it's all right. I'll eat it. My backbone's rubbing my navel."

Maureen stopped in front of the stove and set the supplies down. As she removed things from the pot and put them on the vinyl counter, Dusty said: "Isn't there a package of pork chops out there?"

"Remember the pot of powdered people from 10K3?"

He gave her a suspicious look. "How could I forget it?"

"The contents of that pot were in better shape than the pork chops in the cooler."

"Ah." Dusty nodded. "Right. We have to get ice the next time we go into town. Like tomorrow. We can wash our clothes at the same time." He looked around the trailer. "Let me see, what do we have to go with this stew? Crackers?"

"Not unless you like those awful little cheesy fishies that Sylvia prizes. That's the closest thing we have to crackers."

He opened the refrigerator and removed a loaf of dark rye bread. "Then I'm going to eat this." He set the loaf on top of the counter. "You can share if you want."

"Looks good to me."

Voices drifted in from the darkness as Sylvia and Steve washed off at the water jug outside. Someone smart, probably Steve, had a flashlight. The beam played around the camp.

Maureen used a match to start the stove burner, found a can opener in the drawer, and poured the stew into an aluminum pot that she had rummaged out of a cupboard. "Here come the hungry hordes."

Stewart nodded. "I see 'em. I'll bet Sylvia wants a Coors Light." He reached into the red ice chest and dredged out a dripping can of Coors Light and a draft Guinness. He set the Coors on the table and popped the top on his Guinness. "Ah, the gift of the gods."

"Canned Guinness, Stewart?" Maureen lifted an eyebrow. "Sacrilege. Your genes should know it even if your tastebuds don't."

Dusty slipped into the booth and studied the black-and-white pot, propped so that the rock didn't overbalance it. He pushed the ratty brown cowboy hat back on his head and said, "Somebody had better get the coffee going."

Maureen's brows lowered. "Just who did you think that would be? I made the stew."

"You did not. Dinty Moore did. You opened cans and poured them into a pot. Besides, you're the coffee drinker."

Maureen sighed. "Good point. Okay, where's the coffee?"

He was staring at the pot, his blue eyes gleaming, but he pointed. "Cupboard to your right. You'll find everything you need on the bottom shelf."

She opened it, took out the battered, soot-coated coffeepot and red bag of New Mexico Pinon Nut Coffee. The water came from a six-gallon blue plastic jug on the floor.

Sylvia and Steve opened the flimsy aluminum door and stepped in.

"Boy, what a day," Steve said. He brushed at his brown nylon coat sleeves, and a sparkling fog floated up.

Sylvia coughed and waved at it as she walked through. "God. Quit that. I feel like Lawrence of Arabia."

"It's down to forty degrees, Rhone," Steve said. "I doubt that."

"Did you get the equipment stowed in the ammo boxes?" Dusty asked.

They used metal ammo boxes to keep most of their equipment safe: the trowels, brushes, dental picks, line levels, compasses, and the camera.

"Yassuh," Steve said. He sank into the booth and pulled a bottle of Anchor Steam beer out of his pocket. Using his Swiss Army knife, he uncapped it.

Sylvia spied the Coors Light on the table. "A beer! I'm saved. Thanks, Dusty." She grabbed it and slid in beside Steve. Brown hair had escaped her gray knit cap and framed her face with damp ringlets. It made her pointed nose look long and sharp.

"Hey!" Sylvia blurted. "Where are my cheezy fishes? Aren't there any in the trailer?"

Dusty called, "Well, I guarantee I'm not the culprit. You'd have to tie me up and poke them down my throat with a stick before I'd eat one of those things."

A pause, then Sylvia said: "God. You don't think I ate them all, do you? There's nothing better than cheezy fishes in beef stew. You know, yellow and brown."

Dusty said, "You're the only woman in the world who evaluates food based on a Munsel color chart."

Steve smiled and turned to Maureen. "Are we going to open the pot tonight?"

"Ask the P.I." Maureen poured coffee into the basket, clamped the lid down, and set the pot on the burner.

Sand sprinkled Steve's neatly trimmed black hair, shimmering in the lantern light. "Massa Principal Investigator, sir?"

Dusty took a swig from his Guinness and said, "I thought once we had dinner going, we'd tend to it."

Sylvia shivered. "Gonna be a cool one tonight. God, I hate climbing into a freezing sleeping bag. The first few minutes are enough to make me change my major to accounting."

Maureen stirred the stew and turned from the stove with the wooden spoon in her hand. She aimed it at Dusty. "I don't understand why we can't go into town on cold nights like this and rent a hotel room. We're getting seventy-five dollars a day per diem, for God's sakes. Wouldn't anybody else like a real shower?"

Sylvia stopped halfway through chugging her beer. "You mean you'd rather sleep in a stucco box, breathing recycled air, than in a tent where you can smell the cedar fire and sage all night?"

Steve added, "You'd rather wake up to the kids next door screaming than birds singing and coyotes howling?"

Dusty smiled at her, as if in victory. "Yes. Just what sort of uncivilized barbarian are you, Dr. Cole?"

Maureen shook her head. "Never mind."

She would never understand archaeologists. Oh, she loved nature, too, but not at the expense of frozen body parts. "It just seems silly to me that we—"

As if to mock her, somewhere out in the desert a lone coyote yipped, paused, then yipped again, and down in the river bottom a whole pack broke into song. Their beautiful lilting voices serenaded the night for several minutes, then the soft evening breeze replaced it.

Everybody at the table gazed at Maureen with wide eyes.

"I don't care," she said. "I'd still like a shower." She pulled at her waistband, feeling sand.

Dusty leaned forward. "I'll make you a deal. We need to pull the bone bed on the kiva roof. If we can do that, and open the kiva floor by Friday, I'll rent us luxurious rooms at the Holiday Inn in Farmington. What do you say?"

"I say, hallelujah."

"I don't know," Steve said. "That's a lot of careful recording to do in three days, boss, and a lot of that bone is burned. Delicate stuff. The old days of chucking bones into paper bags and calling it quits are long gone."

Dusty leaned back. "Yeah. Thank God. I still cringe when I think about the data they wasted back in the good ol' days."

Maureen looked into the pot. "Well, the stew's boiling. I say we let it simmer for a few minutes, and open that pot."

Dusty took a long drink of Guinness, set his empty can down, and lurched to his feet. "I will assist you, Dr. Cole.

Maureen turned to the door. "I have to get my field kit."

She stepped out into the night and walked to her tent. White lantern light cast by the trailer windows threw beautiful patterns on the brown nylon walls. She knelt, reached through the tent flap, and pulled her black field bag from the corner.

As she stepped back into the trailer, Sylvia said, "If we find dried flakes of humans in there, what are we going to do? Notify the regional tribes, or sew our lips shut?"

"My opinion is that we sew our lips shut and do the necessary scientific work to analyze it," Maureen said, and set her field bag on the table beside the small black-and-white pot. "This is private land, right? We don't have to abide by the same insane rules that we would on Crown land."

"That's *public* land here, Washais," Sylvia pointed out.

Dusty made an appeasing gesture with his hands. "Shh. If word ever got out that we'd discovered a pot of corpse powder and didn't tell anyone, I'd be accused by the traditionals of endangering the life of every person I came in contact with. I'd lose a lot of the trust that I've built over the years. People would run when they saw me coming."

"That happens now, Stewart," Maureen said.

He continued as if he hadn't heard: "If we find anything suspicious in that pot, I'm calling Maggie Walking Hawk Taylor."

Maureen opened her field bag. They'd had this argument before. But there was no sense in getting into a shouting match with him. Better to wait and see what happened.

"What?" Dusty said. "No scorching rebuttal from the physical anthropologist?"

"I'll fight that battle *if* the time comes, Stewart. For now, I'm more interested in what's in the pot than arguing with you."

Maureen pulled a stainless-steel scalpel from her bag. She lowered the sharp tip to the black ring of pitch that sealed the rock to the top of the pot, and the metal flashed in the lantern light. "Could you hold the pot still?"

He wrapped both hands around the pot, steadying it while Maureen scraped at the pitch. Their hands touched. Long hours in the dirt and sun had roughened his skin, but it felt warm against her cold hands. When she'd etched a hole through the pitch, she said, "Curtain time."

Steve and Sylvia leaned forward. Anticipation turned the very air electric. Sylvia's green eyes sparkled. Steve looked as if he were holding his breath.

"Well?" Dusty said. "I'm ready for the opening act."

Maureen wedged her scalpel in the hole and slowly worked around the edge, severing the rock from the pot.

"I could just twist that off, you know," Dusty informed her.

"I'm sure you could, Stewart." Very gently, Maureen sawed through the last of the hardened pitch and rested her scalpel on the table. She gripped the big rock with both hands and carefully lifted.

"What is it?" Steve asked, trying to peer inside. "What's in there?"

Dusty's blue eyes narrowed as he scrutinized the interior. He lifted the pot, tipped it sideways, then set it down again. "Nothing."

"What do you mean, nothing?" Sylvia braced her hands on the table and leaned over to look inside.

Maureen frowned at the clay-colored interior. She didn't even see any residue, though the poor light could be hiding many things from her view. She said, "Who's the hunched-over character painted on the bottom of the pot?"

Sylvia answered, "Kokopelli, the humpbacked flute player. He's big in the Southwest, and much older than the katchinas. From about A.D. 200 to 1150, his image was everywhere, etched into rocks, painted on bowls like this one, even carved into kiva floors."

"Okay, but what is he? Is he a god?"

Dusty said, "Kokopelli and Kokopelli Mana, the male and female humpbacked flute players, apparently embody the creative power of the universe."

"Big medicine," Steve said in a quiet reverent voice, "until the katchinas came along."

Maureen looked back at the pot. "I don't understand. They put a big rock on top of this pot, sealed it with pine pitch, and there's nothing inside? Why would someone do that?"

"Kokopelli's inside." Dusty ground his teeth for a few moments. "And maybe he's not alone, or I should say, he *wasn't* alone."

Steve's dark eyes went back and forth between Dusty and Maureen. "Is this some cultural tradition I don't—"

"Oh, I get it," Sylvia said, and grinned. "We just let a ghost out of the pot, right? A ghost that Kokopelli was supposed to be regenerating, or, maybe, reincarnating?"

Dusty fingered his beard thoughtfully. "Maybe."

"God, I love ghost stories," Sylvia said. "I hope it doesn't fly around shrieking and wailing. I'm really tired tonight."

Maureen set the rock down on the table and picked up the pot. She tipped it to the lantern light, studying the interior pot walls. "If you want my opinion, I think that whatever was in this pot evaporated. I'll let you know tomorrow."

"How?" Dusty said. "What are you going to do?"

"I'm going to scrape the interior of the pot and put it under my microscope, Stewart. It's a little scientific process that physical anthropologists use to kill ghosts."

The beef stew bubbled over and started spattering the stove top.

"Stew's ready, folks," Sylvia said. "Let's kill ghosts later."

CHAPTER 28

BROWSER STOOD IN the trees above the river, his eyes on Obsidian. She walked the trail below with another woman and a tall man. She was smiling, her white cape swaying around her tall body. Morning sunlight flashed from the wealth of long black hair that fell from her hood. She walked slowly, her gaze on the trail, but an eerie faraway gleam lit her eyes. The man and woman beside her walked with their heads down, as though grieving. Their white hoods hid their faces, but Browser might not have known them anyway. Many of the people who'd come for the burial were strangers.

Browser removed his white ritual cape and draped it on a branch to his left. His red knee-length war shirt would not keep him warm, but he needed to feel alive this morning. Death breathed all around him, walking the land on silent feet.

Obsidian had stood rigid through the burial. She hadn't joined in the sacred Songs or Dances. She had made no effort to help send the Matron on a safe journey to the Land of the Dead. She'd caught Browser's eye when the katsinas Danced and everyone else had lifted their arms in praise. Obsidian hadn't moved. She'd stared unblinking at the Matron's body on the burial ladder.

Browser leaned a shoulder against the trunk of a towering cottonwood and wondered at that.

Obsidian and her friends passed through the dappled sunlight forty hands below, and the precious stones on her wrists glittered. She moved with uncommon grace for such a tall, slender woman.

As if she felt his gaze, Obsidian stopped, then tipped her pointed chin up. Her dark eyes met his like a clash of war clubs.

"Watching me, War Chief?" she asked in a voice just barely loud enough for him to hear.

"Watching the trail, Obsidian."

"Indeed? I would think any warrior could do that. A great War Chief should limit himself to more important duties, like guarding our village."

"Several of the elders are at the grave. I wish to make certain they have no trouble getting back."

"Then you are alone up there?"

"I am."

Obsidian touched the strange woman's hand, then tugged up the hem of her white cape and climbed the bank toward Browser, her steps as fluid as those of a Dancer. Her hood waffled in the breeze, shielding her face. The strangers continued down the trail toward the village.

Browser straightened and lowered his arms. The idea of being alone with Obsidian tore at his insides like talons. He tried not to rest his hand on his war club. As she approached, he called, "How may I be of service?"

Obsidian halted two paces away, her huge haunted eyes on him, jet black and warm, very warm. He did not know what to think of her. He had never known a woman whose mood could change so quickly. One instant she could look at him like this, and the next instant she could turn to ice. She threw back her hood and tiny turquoise pins twinkled through the endless midnight of her hair.

Browser said, "What is it you wish?"

"Just to talk with you, War Chief."

She walked closer and loosened the ties on her cape, revealing the rich blue dress beneath and the swells of her breasts. Browser felt suddenly starved for air. He could feel the warmth of her body and smell the sweet scent of blazing star petals that clung to her clothing.

"Talk about what, Obsidian?"

Her elegant brows lifted. "You're not afraid of me, are you, War Chief? What have I done to make you feel that way?"

Browser's stomach muscles tightened. There were times, like now, when he swore she was not the same woman he'd spoken to earlier. Her voice had turned deep and husky. Her eyes had a feral glint. "What do you *want*, Obsidian?"

A flock of ravens soared over the treetops, cawing and diving, but neither of them looked up.

Obsidian lowered her eyes to his chest, and her gaze traced the muscles, then moved to his arms and legs, as if seeing beneath his red war shirt.

Browser was burningly aware of her. He clenched his fists. "If you came to speak with me, then speak."

Her eyes returned to his, faintly amused. "Where is it?"

"What?"

"I think you know."

His blood stung as it pulsed through his body. He'd left his buckskin cape in his chamber draped over his bedding hides. She couldn't know. Could she?

"What are you talking about?"

Obsidian moved to less than a hand's breadth from him. Her swaying cape patted his legs as she examined Browser's face in minute detail, and the aching need in her eyes made his breathing go shallow. Her lips parted invitingly.

"I have something I would like to show you, War Chief," she whispered, and toyed with the fringes on his shirt. "Will you accompany me back to my chamber?"

"I have duties, Obsidian."

"Later, then?"

As Wind Baby gusted through the trees, she caught the dark cloud of her flying hair and held it until the gust passed, then she released the hair and let it fall freely over her shoulders.

Browser propped his hands on his hips. Curious, he asked, "Who are you, Obsidian? Where do you come from?"

"I am from here, War Chief. Longtail Clan."

"You were born here?"

She touched Browser's hand, and her fingers felt cool and soft. His skin tingled. "Perhaps we could meet tonight when you return to the village?"

He pulled his hand away. "Perhaps you could answer my question."

"Why do you care where I was born, War Chief?"

"I care because I have never heard you speak about it, and generally if someone does not speak of their home it is because they are hiding something."

"Hmm," she said, and laughed softly. "I never heard your Matron speak of her home. Is that what you really mean? You think she was hiding something?"

The words left Browser floundering. Was that what he'd meant? Perhaps his souls had started down the twists and turns of the maze left by Flame Carrier's death, and he was just taking his anger out on Obsidian? He looked into her eyes and felt a deep swallowing nothingness.

Browser pulled his ritual cape from the branch. "Good day, Obsidian." He walked past her.

Obsidian laughed and called after him, "I will see you later!"

DUSTY STARED DOWN into his coffee, feeling oddly self-conscious. He tapped the table with his fingers and glanced away at the soft pastel colors of the Holiday Inn dining room in Farmington. He and Maureen had spent the morning shopping for the camp and doing their laundry. It had been pleasant. He glanced at her sitting across from him, then looked around the room. The place, like so many in the Southwest, had been decorated in pseudo-adobe with patterned upholstery that echoed indigenous designs. The Navajo waitress was polishing the brass railing on the low adobe wall that separated the buffet from the dining room.

"Boy, I needed this." Maureen cupped the white ceramic cup in her cold fingers and sipped at the hot coffee. Her long black braid fell over her left shoulder. She wore a cream-colored wool sweater over a black turtleneck, with black jeans. "That wind has a bit of a bite, eh?"

Dusty smiled. "The wind doesn't blow in Ontario?"

"On occasion, but not like this."

He settled back in the chair, and stared out the window at the parking lot where grimy pickups had nosed into the spaces.

Dusty lifted a hand. "You get used to the wind after a while. You only get worried when the branches start cracking off the trees."

Maureen laughed. "You know, I've been listening to you all morning, talking about the Anasazi and the modern Puebloan peoples. You speak very passionately for a White guy."

"The Southwest has been the centerpiece of my life. I have a tie to the tribes that not even I understand fully."

She set her coffee cup down and peered across the table at him, studying him with that scientist's eye that he both loved and despised. "You mean because you were initiated into a kiva?"

"Partly, yes. But my fascination goes deeper." How on earth did he tell her about things that lived so quietly in his heart? "I guess it started when I was a kid on Dad's digs. I was always too curious, in trouble a lot, but I learned early that you didn't trip over the grid strings, didn't fool around on the pit walls. Believe me, you don't want to deal with the consequences of collapsing one. Not on Dad's digs—or even worse on one of Dale's. And never ever touch the pottery, let alone pick it up. We still found a lot of whole pots back in those days."

Maureen nodded, as though encouraging him to continue. "So what did you play with when you were out in the field? You were a kid, after all."

"Mostly I wandered around playing with things like grinding stones and flakes. I couldn't break them. I'd pretend I was grinding corn in the mealing bins. I'd build my own little pueblos out of the stones. At least until the walls collapsed. Those Anasazi masons were a lot better builders than I was. Sometimes I'd go into excavated rooms and just sit there in the silence. I'd listen, trying hard to hear them." He slowly shook his head and gave her a hesitant smile. "Maybe it was a kid's imagination, but I could close my eyes and see them. At least they looked like I thought they should. Like the Indians I knew from the pueblos, but wearing different clothes, with different hairstyles."

Maureen's brows lifted. "Really? Did they talk to you?"

"Sometimes."

She frowned down into her coffee. "I thought I heard voices the first time I went to Sainte Marie Among the Huron. They've reconstructed a longhouse at one of the original Jesuit Missions in Ontario. It's magnificent. I swear I could hear them speaking Iroquois, but with a strange accent. I suppose you'd say it was like coming home."

For a moment they were silent, watching each other, measuring each other's responses.

Finally, Dusty said, "That's a curious admission, Doctor. I thought you didn't believe in spooks?" He said it teasingly, but she obviously took it seriously. Her expression tensed.

Maureen smoothed her fingers over the tabletop, as if buying time while she tried to figure out how to answer him. "I don't. But I wonder if some places don't absorb memories in the same way we do. I—"

"You don't have to explain." He lifted a hand to halt her. "The walls in Chaco Canyon often speak to me. I may be a White guy, but my soul is tied to the people here, the old ones. I've tried to explain that I can sense them, but few people believe me."

"Oh, I'll bet that goes over big with the Natives."

"It depends. Some, like Maggie Walking Hawk Taylor, understand. Others, all they see is the skin on the outside and forget that we're all human beings inside. That you can really care who people were five or six hundred, or a thousand years ago. Just because you don't happen to be a direct descendant doesn't mean that they can't talk to you, too. It's, well..." He gave her a probing look. "When I stand over something like that bone bed, I don't see science, Doctor. I see people, and I wonder at their pain and their desperation. I care what happened to them."

The wind hurled itself against the window, and the pane rattled. The trucks in the parking lot seemed to ripple, as though not quite real.

Maureen said, "Do you feel the same way about your European ancestors?"

Dusty thought about that. "I went to a conference in Paris a few years ago. I wandered into Notre-Dame, and I felt nothing. It was sterile. Dead. Sure, it was a beautiful building, and the rose window was stunning, but it wasn't mine. In Brussels, they have this really neat site under the street in front of St. Michael's Church. The bones of the monks are still sticking out of the excavation units. I looked at them, and felt nothing. That connection to those people just isn't there for me. They're strangers. Their spirits don't talk the language of my soul." He paused. "Am I sounding hokey yet?"

"Not yet." She sipped her coffee, and he found himself wishing that they could both let down their guards for just a little while. But he couldn't do it first. She had to.

Maureen slipped two fingers through the handle of her coffee cup and pulled it closer. "Maybe it's because half of me is Seneca, but if there really is a Spirit World, the Spirits should be able to talk to whomever they wish. No matter what your racial or ethnic heritage." Her lips tightened, then she said, "Not everybody agrees with me, of course."

"How's that?"

"Oh, two years ago I got hate mail from some Mohawks. They told me in no uncertain terms that they didn't want any 'science' done on their ancestors' bones." Her fingers traced a pattern on the tabletop. "The thing is, those skeletal 'people' in my lab are important to me. Sure, I measured and took samples, but I had the feeling that they really wanted to teach me about who they were, and tell me what had happened to them. Isn't that what elders do? Teach? I think we should use science as a means of understanding the world. I really believe, unlike a lot of my colleagues in the First Nations, that science is another way of knowing. The best way."

"How Western of you."

"How Indian of you to argue in opposition."

He raised his hands. "Whoa! Remember me? I'm on your side."

"Really?" Her brows quirked as though amazed to hear that. "If you'll recall, you sided with Indian religious fundamentalists and left most of the bodies in the ground at 10K3."

"No, I didn't, Doctor. I sided with Elder Hail Walking Hawk. There's a big difference. If it had been a bunch of angry kids with placards, I would have known they weren't for real and probably would have finished the excavation. Hail Walking Hawk saw something there that I didn't, and

I respected her *knowledge.*" He lowered his voice. "Even if it wasn't scientific knowledge."

Maureen's fingers tightened into a fist on the tabletop. "Science isn't the only way of knowing. I've never said that."

He took a breath and wadded up his paper napkin. "No, but sometimes I think you mean it anyway. I grew up between two worlds, Maureen: mine and yours. When I was kid, this old Hopi—"

"The one who initiated you into the kiva?"

"That's him."

"What happened?"

"In the kiva?"

"Yes. I'd really like to know."

He felt his brow tighten and forced himself to relax. "This may sound funny, but it was a very private, very personal experience. The journey that I went on can't be related to anyone. The rituals that I underwent aren't for the uninitiated. In short, it's not mine to tell. Not only did I take a solemn vow, but it's my compact with the beings who shared their time with me. Have you had an experience like that? A supernatural visitation?"

Maureen touched the crucifix around her throat. She tugged at it, then said, "Four years ago, after the death of my husband, I had terrifying nightmares about the *Gaasyendietha,* the meteor fire dragons of Seneca mythology. The dragons traveled behind me in my dreams, walking as torches of light. Father Gaha, himself a Seneca, but also a Catholic, helped me to decipher the dream, to understand that the *Gaasyendietha* were not chasing me but trying to befriend me, to light my way through the darkness of losing John." She released her crucifix and smoothed her fingers over her cup. "Yes, I think I understand."

A flock of pinyon jaws landed outside the window, cawing and trilling in beautiful voices as they strutted over the dead grass that framed the parking lot.

Dusty fiddled with the napkin on the table, shoving it around. "Do you recall when Hail Walking Hawk told you that she saw a man behind you? A man with light brown hair and green eyes?"

Maureen nodded. "I'll never forget it. She described John perfectly."

"I spoke with Hail about it after you walked out to look at the site. She said that he had loved you very much. Maggie later told me that Hail had seen John moving in a blue glow."

Maureen smiled down into her cup, as though the words comforted her.

Dusty wouldn't tell Maureen the rest. Hail had also said that these things were very hard, but it was too bad John was still in this world. *"His soul ought to be in the Land of the Dead by now."*

Dusty sipped his coffee. "Do you think he's still there, behind you?"

Maureen looked up. "Oh, I don't know. Grief makes you think strange things. Sometimes, I would swear he is. At night just before I fall asleep, I often hear his voice. It's so loud it wakes me." She paused. "I feel him there, too. Watching over me. I can't explain it, but it's a very intimate experience, as though our souls actually touch." Warmth filled her eyes.

"I was once told that death is the most personal experience you will ever have. It's about the only thing in Western culture that isn't shared with other people. It can't be shared. When you die, even if it's in a multitude like a plane crash or a gas chamber at Auschwitz, you're still alone at that final instant." He made a smoothing motion with his hand. "My initiation into the kiva was that way. The most intimate experience I've ever had."

She seemed to absorb that without the skepticism he usually saw in women's eyes. Not that he'd told that many, but the few that he had always wanted to pry away at it, as if he were keeping some secret from them, that true intimacy meant spilling the whole story, betraying the trust of his Spirit Helpers.

"Do you go to your kiva often?"

He tilted his head. "My clan is dead, Doctor."

Her open mouth asked the question.

"My mentor and his uncle were the last of their clan." Dusty took a swig of his coffee. "You have to understand, in this country, among the peoples here, a clan owns certain rituals. Well, 'owns' isn't the right word. Let's say, 'were given certain rituals,' since it was a two-way relationship. Sometimes, because of disease, accidents, infertility, or whatever cause, clans die out. When they do, the rituals, the kivas, the sacred knowledge, die with them."

"That happened when your mentor died?"

He nodded. "There are three of us left. One is in the penitentiary outside of Buckeye, Arizona. He stuck a knife into the man who was living with his wife. The other is sober on those rare occasions when he can't find anything to hock or any White tourists to buy him a drink."

"So, the clan's not dead. There are three of you left."

Dusty gave her a pained smile. God, how he wished that were true. "I was initiated into the kiva, Maureen, not adopted into the clan. Even if I had been adopted, it wouldn't matter. The clan effectively 'died' when the last female died. In this case, my mentor's sister. Hopi are matrilineal."

"Right." Her slim fingers danced on the cup handle. "But you still have the rituals inside you, Dusty."

"I was initiated, Doctor, not trained. I didn't earn the knowledge or permission to conduct the rituals. Neither did the other guys. In fact, I think they were initiated because it was the thing to do. Kind of like a lot of White kids go through confirmation even if they don't believe Jesus is their personal saviour."

Her hand returned to her crucifix. She touched the silver body of Jesus in the same way that Dusty would have touched a katchina mask—as though she could feel the Power there and was grateful. "I understand. In fact, I wish I'd listened more to my mother. Attended more of the dances and prayer meetings. But trying to make time, first as a student, then in the struggle from assistant professor to full professor, not to mention all the other crap you have to do." She shook her head. "Modern life ain't all that it's cracked up to be, Stewart."

"Oh, yes, it is," he told her. "At least for this one golden moment between world wars. You go to bed every night knowing that you'll probably be alive in the morning. You don't spend every day with the knowledge that someone out there is trying to kill you, that your world is about to end in fire, death, or terror. You have health, security, safety, and hope. You know that your stomach will be full tomorrow, and the day after that, and the day after that for as far as you can see. You know that you'll have a roof over your head, that you'll be warm and have plenty to drink. If you break your leg tomorrow, even with a compound fracture, you're not going to die in a month's prolonged agony like you would have even one hundred and fifty years ago. An abscessed tooth won't leave pus dripping into your mouth for six months until it falls out. You can step onto a jet tomorrow that will allow you to attend a seminar halfway across the world. In short, Doctor, it's a wonderful time to be alive." He took a long drink of coffee. "Or would you rather live here in the thirteenth century, when a world was falling into an apocalypse that it would never recover from?"

"You're right, Stewart. Sometimes we lose sight of that fact, don't we? How good life is. We just can't imagine that anything could be worse than our petty little problems, troubled love lives, and financial worries."

"Yeah. If you could ask any one of those kids you've been digging out of Pueblo Animas, I think they'd take McDonald's over starvation any day of the week."

"I'm sure that's true."

The slant of the sunlight changed; it streamed through the window and gave a golden gleam to her dark complexion.

Maureen let out a breath and looked around the restaurant at the other diners. Two other couples huddled over tables, smiling at each other and talking in low voices. "What a wonderful day this has been. We got ice, washed our clothes, filled up the water jugs—and here I am, having the time of my life talking to you about serious things. You, Stewart, of all people."

"What do you mean by that?" He couldn't stop the surprise in his voice.

She laughed again, infectious, overcoming any censure in her words. "Well, you have to admit, we do have a history of despising each other."

He turned his nearly empty cup in his hands. "I was kind of hoping that was over."

Her smile warmed him. "I want to thank you for calling me, even if I spent most of the phone conversation talking to Sylvia. I get lonely at home. After John died, I guess I should have sold the house."

"Maybe, but Dale tells me it's a nice house."

She nodded. "It is. It overlooks the lake. But there are so many memories there."

She had a faraway look in her eyes. He waited to see if she wanted to say more, then said, "Memories are good things."

"Yes. Usually."

"But not always?"

"Of course not," she said, and gave him a skeptical look. "Memories of freezing your penis to the side of a truck in Wyoming can't be all that great, can they?"

Dusty leaned forward, meeting her halfway across the table, and whispered, "True, but I've never exposed my shortcomings to an arctic environment again."

CHAPTER 29

PEOPLE FLOODED AROUND Straighthorn, their colorful capes blazing in the morning sunlight. He did not know most of the people who'd come from Dry Creek village, but many of them wept. Ant Woman, the Dry Creek Clan Matron, sobbed uncontrollably. Two women supported her sticklike old arms as they led her up the trail. He had seen Ant Woman often in the past nine moons. About once a moon, she had come to stay with the Matron of the Katsinas' People. They had laughed and talked well into the night, sharing memories from their childhoods. It must be very difficult to see a friend of seventy summers die.

Redcrop stepped away from the grave and Straighthorn lifted his head. Wind Baby fluttered her long black hair over her white cape. She looked pale and gaunt, her eyes swollen. The village elders surrounded her, speaking softly. Cloudblower gently touched Redcrop's shoulder.

"Warrior?" someone called from behind him.

Straighthorn turned to see the War Chief coming up the trail. He wore a red knee-length shirt and carried his ritual cape over his arm.

Despite the chill in the air, sweat glued his short black hair to his cheeks. His thick brows had pulled together into a single line over his flat nose.

"Yes, War Chief?"

Browser stopped at Straighthorn's side. "Where is Jackrabbit?"

"He stayed for the final Songs, then went back to his chamber to sleep. It was a long, cold night, War Chief. We grabbed for our clubs at every sound."

"You were not alone. People sleeping in the village did the same thing. I don't think any of us will have a peaceful night until we've captured the murderers."

"Captured? Are you going to send out another search party? If so, I would like to volunteer."

"I wish to speak of something else," Browser said in a low voice and spread his legs as if preparing for a long conversation.

"Yes?"

"Tell me about Obsidian? Was she born to Longtail Clan?"

Straighthorn frowned. Browser had never shown any interest in Obsidian before, though she had placed herself within his reach many times. "No, her mother married a Longtail Clan man twenty-five summers ago. His name was Shell Ring. Obsidian was seven at the time. I recall Matron Crossbill saying she was tall for her age, and used her height to threaten the other children."

"But she calls herself Longtail Clan. How did that happen?"

Straighthorn shrugged. "Nothing mysterious. Shell Ring died a few moons after the marriage. Crossbill adopted Obsidian and her mother into the clan."

Browser smoothed his fingers over the war club on his belt, and his gaze drifted over the dispersing crowd.

"Why do you ask, War Chief?"

"What happened to Obsidian's mother?"

"I heard that she was killed, struck in the head by someone, but it happened before I was born. I know little about it. You may wish to speak with Crossbill. She can tell you more."

"Since you have known Obsidian, has she been married, had children?"

"She was married to a man named Ten Hawks for one or two summers, I think. I was very young. They had no children, though. I remember waking one day and finding the entire village gathered around their chamber. Obsidian had moved his belongings out into the plaza and told him to leave. After their divorce, she never married again."

Straighthorn still went cold at the memory. It was the first divorce he'd ever seen. Among their people, women had the right to move a man's belongings out of their house whenever they tired of him. A man, on the other hand, had only the right to leave. He owned almost nothing, not the house, the children, not even his own clothing. He could keep his weapons and whatever else his wife gave him. For a man, divorce meant losing everything.

"Where did Ten Hawks go?"

"I can't say. Why? Do you wish to find him?"

Browser shook his head. "Just curious."

"No one ever spoke of him after he left. Or if they did, I never heard them. It was as though he had never existed at all." Straighthorn frowned. "That is odd, though, isn't it? Usually after a divorce people whisper about the cause for many moons."

"Unless the cause was so terrible no one dares to."

Straighthorn blinked at the ground, wondering. "What could it have been?"

"Incest. Witchery. Something like that."

Redcrop left the grave and came toward them. She looked up at Straighthorn with tired eyes.

Browser said, "One last question. Has Obsidian been gone over the past ten days?"

"No." He shook his head. "No, she was here in the village every day. I would swear to it."

Browser let out a breath. "Thank you, warrior."

Redcrop walked into their circle and Straighthorn reached out to take her cold hand. "The Matron is on her way now, Redcrop. We have done everything we can for her."

"I know. I just—I can't believe she's gone."

Straighthorn lifted her fingers and held them to his cheek while he gazed into her hurt eyes. "It is time you ate something. I was hoping you would share breakfast with me. I thought I would bring out my last venison steaks and cook them over the plaza fire."

Redcrop glanced at Browser, then lowered her gaze. "I wish to be alone for a time, Straighthorn. Please do not be upset with me. I promise I will meet you later this afternoon, if that is all right?"

"Of course," he said, but couldn't hide his disappointment. "When you are ready for company, I'll be waiting."

Redcrop squeezed his hand. "Thank you." She stood awkwardly for a time, then turned and walked toward the knoll to the west.

Straighthorn watched her climb the hillside. As Father Sun rose higher into the sky, every rock on the knoll glimmered and sparkled.

"Strange," Straighthorn whispered. "She usually wishes company when she is sad."

"Many people wish to be alone after burying a loved one, Straighthorn. Give her time to grieve."

He hesitated. "But she shouldn't be going out there, War Chief. Not that direction. It's not safe." He started after Redcrop.

Browser grabbed his sleeve. "Let her go, Straighthorn."

"War Chief, she is not thinking well. She can mourn near the village. That knoll creates a blind spot. You know this to be true. None of our guards will be able to see her."

Browser tightened his grip on Straighthorn's sleeve. I said, "Let her go."

Straighthorn tugged away from Browser's hand and turned around angrily. "Why?"

Browser opened his mouth to answer, then squinted out at the horizon. Cloud People sailed through the blue, their edges gleaming like polished copper.

Straighthorn said, "As I climbed down from the tower kiva last night, I heard you speaking with Redcrop. Is she a part of some plan? What are you doing?"

"Please, I can only tell you that she *is* being watched."

"By whom? I see no guards."

Browser did not answer for a time. Finally, he said, "I hope not, warrior. If you could see guards, they could, too."

Straighthorn felt himself pale.

Browser put a hand on Straighthorn's shoulder and guided him toward the river trail that ran south, away from the village. "Come. Let us speak of this in private."

CHAPTER 30

REDCROP WALKED STRAIGHT up the hill knowing that the farther she went from the village and the safety of other people, the more danger she would be in. She knew it, and it gavc wings to her feet.

She had lain awake in the tower kiva most of the night, watching Cloudblower stoke the ritual fire and thinking about what thc War Chief had told her. He had stressed the danger, whispered over and over that she might not live through it. Their enemy was canny. No one had ever come close to capturing him before. But if they succeeded, the string of mad killings would end. By risking her life, Redcrop might be saving the lives of ten or even twenty people.

As she neared the crest of the hill, she crossed a deer trail covered with small heart-shaped prints. She stopped for a moment to study them. Four deer. Two of them larger. Probably two does and last summer's fawns.

Redcrop followed the trail around a spindly clump of rabbitbrush. To her right, a cloud of woodsmoke rose over Longtail village. The fragrance of burning cottonwood drifted on the wind. Redcrop took it into her lungs and held it. It made her feel closer to her dead grandmother. Flame Carrier had always favored cottonwoods. She could sit for hours watching the trembling interplay of sunlight and shadow in the windblown leaves, her wrinkled lips curled into a smile.

Redcrop continued her climb to the top of the rocky hill, where she eased down on a crumbling sandstone slab and watched the molten streamers that wavered around Father Sun's golden face. A rumpled tan-and-gray world spread before her, dotted here and there with bright splashes of autumn trees. To her left, the snow-covered peaks of the Great Bear Mountains formed a jagged blue line.

She heaved a sigh and watched a flock of pinyon jays flap over her head. Their slender blue-gray bodies sparkled in the sun.

She wondered where her grandmother would be now.

Once a soul passed the traps and monsters that dogged the road to the underworlds, the trail split. The Sun Trail on the left was a broad shining path of corn pollen. Good people took it. But bad people, people who had caused much pain in their lives, saw a coil of smoke rising down the right-hand trail, the Trail of Sorrows, and thought it was a village. Since they loved people and got pleasure from the harm they caused others, they hurried down the right-hand trail. At the end of the Trail of Sorrows, Spider Woman waited. She kept her sacred pinyon pine fire blazing. Spider Woman listened to the travelers' tales of woe. Some she cleansed in pinyon smoke and sent back to the Sun Trail. Others were cast into the fire and burned to ashes. As the ashes fell upon the ground, Spider Woman tramped them down into the dirt, where they stayed forever. Dirt under the feet of the gods.

Redcrop hunched forward, braced her elbows on her knees, and rocked back and forth to ease the pain in her belly. Wind Baby taunted her, gentle one instant, snatching at her long hair the next.

"You must be strong, girl."

The clarity of Grandmother's voice startled her. Redcrop spun around and stared for a long moment at the sunlit slope, expecting to see her. Only the fresh dirt of the grave met her eyes.

Those were the first words she remembered hearing Flame Carrier say. Redcrop had seen barely three summers. The Matron had found Redcrop in the plaza helping the women grind corn, taken her by the hand, and led her to her chamber where she had gently told Redcrop of her mother's death. Her mother had died quarrying stone from a cliff. A boulder had tumbled down and crushed her.

Dust gusted across the desert in the distance. Redcrop focused on it. She had no memory of her mother now, but she remembered screaming her mother's name and had tried to run out of the chamber. Flame Carrier had caught Redcrop, pulled her against her chest, and hugged her tightly, whispering, "You must be strong, girl. Be strong and do your duty. Those things mean survival in our world."

Looking back, she knew that's when her life had truly begun. The person Redcrop was now had been born at that instant, and everything she had known about her own people, even her family, had died.

She'd never looked back, never indulged in resentment or anger, because it drained her strength, and nothing had seemed too great a price for the happiness and love Flame Carrier gave her.

The cloud of smoke hovering over Longtail village billowed as though someone had added more wood to the plaza fire. Redcrop reached beneath her cape and pulled her chert knife from her belt. The red blade glinted as she lowered it to her long hair and began sawing. She lifted each handful and let Wind Baby feather it from her fingers and scatter it across the hilltop.

By now, all of the Matron's closest friends would have cut their hair in mourning. It was a sign of their grief, a way of openly acknowledging the loss and inviting the healing words of others. Those who had not been as close to the Matron would be filling their bowls with succulent robins, grass-seed cakes smeared with roasted bone marrow, boiled beans, and corn on the cob. After the feasting, Cloudblower would pass around baskets of pine nuts and toasted squash seeds, and people would tell wonderful stories of Grandmother's life and generosity.

Red, white, and yellow capes flashed in the cottonwoods along the river, probably people who needed time away from the crowd. She saw Obsidian standing in the cottonwoods. Her wind-swept white cape flapped around her like huge wings. Redcrop couldn't see her face, but she gazed in Redcrop's direction. Was she looking at her? Or the bluff to the southwest? Redcrop turned. The sandstone shone golden against the sere blue sky. Eroded terraces dropped away from the flat top and descended into the river valley like a giant's staircase.

Redcrop frowned and looked back at Obsidian. She hadn't moved. She seemed to see something there that Redcrop did not.

Redcrop turned away. Jagged locks of hair patted her face. She wished Straighthorn were here. She needed him. But he would be safer in the village than with her.

When she opened her eyes, she noticed strange impressions in the sand below the crest of the hill. At first she couldn't fathom what they might be, then it came to her: a child's arms. The points of the elbows had dimpled the ground, and the forearms had smoothed the sand. Three body lengths down the slope she saw sandal prints. She followed them.

In several places the child had tripped over brush and stumbled, leaving overturned pebbles and mashed grass. As she followed the trail down the hill, the child's stride lengthened into a run.

He was alone and running.

On an ordinary morning a mother might not know exactly where her child was, but not today. Whenever the village adults were occupied—for example, when someone spotted a war party, and every person who could wield a bow had to take up a position on the walls or in the hills—all of the children under eight were gathered into the tower kiva, the safest place in the village. Redcrop had seen the children go into the kiva with old Black Lace before dawn. Black Lace had a reputation for being fiercely protective of the younger members of the village. None of those children could have escaped her watchful eye.

Redcrop paralleled the child's path down into the drainage bottom and sand oozed up around her sandals. The tracks grew erratic, weaving back and forth across the drainage, running, stopping, running again.

Redcrop's pulse increased when she saw the coyote den in the drainage wall. About four hands wide, the opening yawned like a dark toothless mouth. The tracks led straight to it.

Redcrop hurried.

CATKIN LURCHED TO her feet when Redcrop disappeared into the drainage. Her long buckskin war shirt snagged on the brush that had been hiding her, and the slender limbs snapped and cracked.

What's she doing? Browser told her to stay on the hilltop!

Catkin waited for a few instants, long enough to realize that Redcrop was not immediately coming back to her perch on the sandstone slab. What could have lured the girl into the drainage? Had someone called to her? Had she seen something that demanded her attention? But how could that be? Redcrop knew the danger. Browser had explained it to her in excruciating detail. Perhaps grief had taken the girl's senses?

Catkin had lost her senses when her husband, Wind Born, died. Every moment had been a nightmare of loneliness. Was that how Redcrop was feeling?

Catkin pulled her war club from her belt and broke into a dead run.

IN THE BRUSH-CLOTTED drainage near the grave, I move through their burial offerings, bowls of food, bits of colored cloth. I lick the side of a bowl,

and sniff the fresh dirt where they stood. One of the females dropped a tear-soaked piece of cloth. I take it into my mouth and chew, tasting her salty taste.

I whirl at the sound of pounding feet and see the warrior Catkin dash by like the wind . . . and I know they are watching the girl.

I duck back into the shadows, breathing hard.

REDCROP FROWNED AT the coyote den. Had the child been looking for a place to hide, perhaps being chased? Orphans often sneaked up this drainage to get to Longtail village, and the raiders who'd murdered their parents frequently ran right behind them.

Redcrop knelt before the opening, and the sharp tang of coyote urine stung her nose.

"Hello?"

She glanced over her shoulder, then moved closer, her face inside the opening. A dank coolness coated her skin. "Hello? Don't be afraid. I won't hurt you."

As her eyes adjusted to the darkness, she saw a corn-husk doll lying in the rear, six hands away.

Redcrop stuck her arm into the opening, but couldn't reach the doll. She twisted sideways, slipped her arm in first, then tucked her head through the opening. As she grasped the doll, she noticed the scratches that lined the walls and floor.

Redcrop backed out of the den with the corn-husk doll. The painted lips and eyes had faded, but the doll's long black braid hung to the middle of her back. She wore a grimy white deerskin dress.

A little girl's doll.

Redcrop examined the ground. In her haste to peer inside the den, she'd disturbed many of the tracks. The War Chief would not be happy with her carelessness. She looked for the best place to stand, a place away from the sign left by the child, and spied a small boulder about two paces away. When she stood on it, her eyes widened. From this vantage she could see many things she had not seen before. Most of the small prints near the den had been covered with larger prints.

She swung around, searching for an intruder. As Father Sun rose higher into the sky, the sand shimmered with a blinding intensity. Redcrop lifted a hand to shield her eyes and squinted back toward the hill that overlooked the grave. Shiny filaments of yellow Cloud People trailed across the sky.

If she was in trouble, why didn't she come down to us? Or call for help?

A Straight Path Nation child would have run down as quickly as her legs could carry her. Perhaps the girl with the corn-husk doll had been born to the Flute Player Believers, or the Fire Dogs?

She looked into the faded brown eyes of the doll. Many of the orphans who wandered into Longtail village carried toys clutched to their chests and would utter inhuman shrieks if you tried to take them away even for an instant, to dress the child, or bathe him. It must have broken the little girl's heart to leave her doll behind.

Redcrop slipped the doll into her belt and bent over the large sandal prints. The depressions cast shadows. The man's feet had sunk deeply into the wet sand.

Her gaze followed them down the eroded drainage to the south. Twenty paces ahead, a deer trail cut the bank. The tracks headed toward it, but she no longer saw the child's prints.

Had he carried her?

It was probably just a father who'd come to find his wayward daughter, but it might have been a raider tracking down an escaped child, or . . . or worse.

The War Chief had told her to stay on top of the hill and within sight of the guards. She'd disobeyed by coming down into the drainage. Could the guards still see her? Would they come if she started to follow the man's trail? She stepped—

"What are you doing?"

Redcrop jerked around so fast that she stumbled and had to catch her balance.

Obsidian stared at her with slitted eyes. The wind had torn locks of long hair loose from their jeweled pins and spilled them down the front of her white cape.

"Obsidian! I didn't hear you. Where did you come from?"

"What are you doing out here?" She walked forward with her fists clenched at her sides.

The anger in her voice stunned Redcrop. She stammered, "I—I wished to be alone for a time." She folded her arms across her chest like a shield. "When I reached the hilltop, I found a child's footprints. They led down to this old coyote den."

"A child?" The lines around Obsidian's beautiful mouth tightened. "What did she look like? How old was she?"

"I didn't see her, Obsidian. Just her tracks." Redcrop gestured to the sand. "It looks like a man came to get her."

Obsidian knelt and her white cape spread around her in sculpted folds. She stared at the man's sandal prints for a long while, as though thinking. When she rose to her feet, her voiced had changed, grown soft and guarded. "Did you see him?"

Redcrop shook her head. "No. I didn't see anyone after I got into the drainage. Why? Did you see him?"

"Don't be a fool. How could I have seen him? Why would you think that?"

"Well, I heard fear in your voice, and I thought maybe you—"

"Where do the tracks go?" She glared at Redcrop. "Did you follow them?"

"No. I—I thought it would be wiser to go and tell the War Chief, in case the man was a raider."

Obsidian's mouth curled into a smile. "Yes, that was wise." She reached out and stroked Redcrop's hair in a way that made her shiver. "Go. Tell Browser I'm waiting for him. I'll remain to make sure nothing is disturbed."

Redcrop backed away, but her gaze remained locked with Obsidian's. The woman's eyes had a savage glitter. They reminded Redcrop of a weasel she'd seen last summer. He'd trotted by her with a dove in his mouth. Just before he sank his teeth into the dove's skull, his eyes had glittered like that.

"I—I'll return as soon as I can."

Redcrop ran.

CATKIN RACED TOWARD the hill, panting, her war club clutched in a tight fist. Blood pounded in her ears as she sprinted over the crest and lunged down the slope toward the drainage. Tracks covered the hillside, but she didn't have the luxury of studying them. She threw every shred of energy into pushing her legs harder, praying she wasn't too late . . .

"Redcrop!" she called when the girl climbed up out of the drainage.

"Catkin? Oh, Catkin, thank the gods you saw me! I was going to find the War Chief. I—"

"What's wrong?" Catkin halted in front of Redcrop and gazed down at her, furious. "Why did you leave the hilltop?"

Redcrop's eyes widened. "I'm sorry. I found a little girl's tracks, and I followed them. I know I shouldn't have, but I—"

Catkin fought to control the fear surging through her body. "You walked out of my sight because of a child's tracks!"

Redcrop jerked a nod. "Yes, I'm sorry, Catkin. Truly. But, please"—she gestured down at the drainage—"come and see. I think a little girl was trying to get to us and was captured by a raider."

"Do not ever do that again!" Catkin ordered through gritted teeth. "Do you understand me?"

"Yes," Redcrop answered in a small voice.

She'd cut her hair and it hung around her chin in irregular black locks. Her eyes were still red-rimmed from crying.

Catkin said, "I'm just worried about you, Redcrop. My duty is to keep you safe."

"I know. I'm sorry."

Catkin relented. "All right. How do you know it was a girl?"

Redcrop shoved her cape aside and pulled a tattered corn-husk doll from her belt. She held it out to Catkin. "I found this in the coyote den where the child was hiding. Don't you think it looks like a girl's doll?"

Catkin stared at the faded eyes and grimy white dress, then handed it back to Redcrop. "Yes, it does. I will go and check the tracks, but I want you to run down to the river trail. There are many people there. You will be safe. Take it back to the village and tell Browser what you found and where I am."

"Yes, Catkin."

She turned to run, and Catkin grabbed her hand and stared hard into her fragile young eyes. "I know you are hurting, Redcrop. But you must listen to me. Grief can take a person's ability to think. I want you to do exactly as I say. Do you understand me?"

"I—I do. I'll run all the way. I promise. I won't even stop if someone calls out to me."

"Good." Catkin released her hand. "Hurry. Remember that while I am in the drainage, no one can see me. I may be in danger."

"You won't be alone, Catkin," Redcrop told her. "Obsidian is down there. She saw me go over the hill, too, and came looking for me. She said she would stay and make sure no one disturbed the tracks while I went to find the War Chief."

A strange floating sensation possessed Catkin, as if her souls hovered high above and could see things that her human body could not. She stared unblinking at Redcrop.

"How long after you climbed down the hill did Obsidian arrive?"

"I can't say. I . . ." Redcrop shook her head uncertainly. "Less than a hundred heartbeats, maybe? I'm sorry. I guess I've been living in my souls with Grandmother."

Catkin's heart twinged. Wind Born had called it "mourning time." Intense pain turned thousands of moments into one single terrible instant. Time had no meaning for the grieving.

More gently, Catkin said, "Thank you for telling me about Obsidian. Now go. Find Browser."

"Yes, Catkin."

Redcrop pulled up her long hem and dashed down the hill toward the river trail.

Catkin waited until she saw Redcrop moving among the people clustered in the trees, and knew she would be in someone's sight the rest of the way to Longtail village, then she walked down the trail to the edge of the drainage.

It surprised her to see Obsidian standing on the opposite bank, not in the drainage at all. Obsidian was leaning over something. Her white hood covered her face.

Catkin worked her way down the trail slowly, studying the tracks. Redcrop's prints covered many of the child's, but in places she could see the girl's prints clearly. They were small, the size a child seven or eight summers would make.

What would a child this young be doing out here alone?

Redcrop was probably right; another orphan had tried to get to them, and the safety the Katsinas' People promised.

Catkin made her way toward the coyote den, and Obsidian gracefully walked down the deer trail on the opposite side. Catkin's stomach churned. Just the thought of having to deal with Obsidian made her wish she'd waited for Browser. When Obsidian spoke with a man, she exuded warmth and charm. She treated other women like dung beetles.

Catkin halted three paces in front of the den. Four sets of tracks marred the ground. Redcrop's and Obsidian's, a little girl's, and a man's—a tall man from the length of his stride.

Catkin edged forward and crouched at the side of the den to examine the man's prints more closely. Her stomach muscles knotted when she saw the distinctive weave. She heard Obsidian coming, but did not look up. *Blessed gods. He was here, this close, and we didn't know it. But who is the little girl?*

Obsidian stopped and the spicy scent of blazing star petals filled the air. "One over, three under. An unusual weave, wouldn't you agree?"

Calmly, Catkin answered, "Many people use that weave, Obsidian. Just because we don't doesn't mean it isn't common elsewhere."

"Where? I've never seen it before."

Catkin straddled the tracks and peered inside the den where Redcrop said the girl had been hiding. She waited until her eyes adjusted to the darkness, then frowned at the scratches that covered the walls and floor. A wet splotch darkened the dirt in the rear. Catkin leaned inside. She touched the splotch, smelled its coppery odor, then frowned at the right wall. Footprints marked the wall two hands up from the floor. Her gaze went to the left wall, and she saw tiny handprints.

"What do you see in there?" Obsidian asked.

Catkin backed out of the den and examined the fresh claw marks on the lip of the opening.

Obsidian smiled and in a friendly tone said, "It looks like a coyote was in there this morning, doesn't it?"

"A coyote's claws are sharp and pointed, Obsidian. They leave deep, narrow grooves. These are broad and shallow."

"Well, what else could they be but coyote claws?"

Catkin rose and clutched her war club more tightly. "The work of frantic fingernails. The girl was dragged out of the den by her feet."

"Oh, really," Obsidian said smugly, "and how can you tell that?"

Catkin paused. She longed to use her war club to beat some respect into Obsidian, and it took real effort not to. "She tried to wedge herself on the roof to avoid the man's grasping hands, but he pulled her down hard. There's blood in the back where her chin struck the floor before he dragged her out. That's probably when she dropped the doll. The impact must have knocked it from her hands, and she didn't have time to—"

"What doll?" Obsidian said, as if indignant that no one had told her about it. "There's a doll in there?"

Catkin turned away and followed the man's tracks toward the deer trail that cut up the wall of the drainage. It was not easy going. Redcrop had disturbed a few of the tracks, but Obsidian had obliterated most of the rest.

Obsidian hurried to catch up with Catkin. "I noticed there weren't any small prints here."

"He was carrying her, probably afraid she'd try to run away again."

"Do you think it was a raider chasing down an escaped slave?"

Catkin stopped in the middle of the deer trail. The steps vanished. She spun around, studying the rocks at the edges of the trail. Had he walked on them? Or . . .

Catkin turned to Obsidian. "Did you see any tracks here when you first walked up?"

"No. Not even one."

"You're certain you didn't accidentally erase them? I see the places where your cape dragged the ground."

Obsidian blinked as though shocked to hear that. "I suppose I might have. I'm not a warrior, after all. But if they were here, I didn't see them."

Voices rose from the opposite side of the drainage. Catkin looked up and saw Browser coming over the hill with Jackrabbit and Straighthorn behind him. He stopped when he saw Catkin and Obsidian, surveyed the drainage, then cupped a hand to his mouth to call, "Are you all right?"

Obsidian shouted, "Yes, War Chief. Come and let me show you what I've found!"

Catkin could see Browser's hesitance. He'd cut his hair in mourning. Ragged tufts covered his head. Browser led the way down, slowly, probably placing his feet on Catkin's tracks so as not to disturb any other sign. Jackrabbit and Straighthorn fell in line behind him.

Catkin and Obsidian walked back down the deer trail to the coyote den. Obsidian leaned a shoulder against the drainage wall and watched Browser as a hawk does a juicy mouse.

As he approached, Browser's red war shirt flapped around his tanned legs. A sheen of sweat covered his handsome face. He must have run as hard as he could to get here.

Browser deliberately passed Obsidian without a glance and came to stand beside Catkin. "What did you find, Catkin?"

Obsidian let out a low laugh and Browser's shoulder muscles bulged through his shirt. He kept his eyes on Catkin.

Catkin said, "He has a little girl, Browser. Seven or eight summers."

"He? Redcrop said a raider—"

"This is no raider."

Catkin knelt and pointed to one of the large sandal prints.

Browser bent over and propped his hands on his knees. It took less than five instants for understanding to slacken his face. "The child is a captive?"

Catkin met his worried eyes. "I've never heard of Two Hearts taking slaves, Browser. Have you?"

He straightened. "No, but . . ."

Catkin could see the horror rising behind his eyes, coalescing into a monstrous possibility.

"We can't be sure, Browser, but we must speak with Cloudblower when we return."

"Cloudblower? Why? What could she—"

"Just believe me, she knows."

Browser stared hard into her eyes, silently questioning what she meant.

Obsidian's white cape flashed in the sunlight as she stalked up the hillside trail.

They all watched her, but no one said anything. Straighthorn didn't even seem to notice she'd left. He looked preoccupied, his forehead lined and his eyes far way.

When Obsidian had passed beyond hearing range, Jackrabbit whispered, "Why did she leave?"

Browser said, "The gods must have heard me."

"Or maybe they heard your stomach," Jackrabbit said. "Ever since you crested the hill and saw her, it's sounded like a dog fight in there."

Browser put a hand on his belly and grimaced. "That's what it feels like, too."

Straighthorn said, "The man must have seen Redcrop. Why didn't he come after her?"

"Perhaps he had more pressing considerations," Browser answered. "He clearly wanted to get the little girl away from here."

"Because he feared for her safety?" Straighthorn asked. "Or because she was trying to reach us, and he didn't wish her to?"

"Maybe both. He feared what would happen to her if we found out who she was." Browser knelt in front of the den and examined the claw marks on the lip.

Catkin knelt beside him. "Yes. Fingernails."

"She did not go willingly, that much we can tell. Did anyone hear her scream?"

"I didn't," Catkin answered, "but he may have had a hand clamped over her mouth."

Straighthorn said, "Even if she had managed to scream, with all of the Singing and Dancing surrounding the burial, I doubt anyone would have heard her."

Browser leaned into the den. He stayed inside for thirty heartbeats, then backed out and gazed around the circle. Dread darkened his face. "I doubt that she screamed," he said. "From the way he treated her, I think she knew better than to scream."

PIPER LIES ON her belly, a stuffed girl skin with eyes. If she does not move, he won't see her.

But she sees him.

Her grandfather's shadow moves on the opposite wall. He walks on knees that slip and slide. His mouth is a dying bird's beak. It opens and closes, opens and closes, but the words are all dead bubbles breaking in the dirt.

From beneath the corner of her blanket, she sees his shadow coming closer, bending down. Piper does not even blink. Firelight lives in his spiderweb hair, shooting about like Meteor People.

His whisper is old blood. "For us it is always daybreak on the second day of the world, child. We live suspended between Father Sun's first and second coming. Remember the daybreak beast. You cannot kill him, but you can tame him and use his Power."

Piper squeezes her eyelids together and her head shakes. The joint-stiffening disease turns her hands into eagle's feet. She tries to find the place inside with arms that hold her, but it is too deep and dark, very dark, and a man's hand clamps over her mouth, crushing her lips, and her lungs are dying.

She's dying.

And somewhere far away a woman cries.

CHAPTER 31

MAUREEN BENT OVER her work. The temperature had dropped to ten degrees Centigrade, but the kiva bottom was warm, barely caressed by the breeze that blew above. Sunlight flecked the red sandstone walls with gold.

She used a sliver of bamboo to pick moist black soil away from the femur and tibia of what looked like a four-year-old child. The bones lay articulated, the epiphyseal caps still in place where the joints had come together. Above the leg lay a confusing mass of bone, as if several children had been piled atop one another. She had started on the single leg, deciding to remove it in order to have a place to sit while she worked on untangling the mess of intertwined bodies.

The mottled upper leg was dark, stained by the ash-filled soil. The lower limb, however, had been charred, the bone spalled in the characteristic pattern caused by the marrow boiling inside. The distal portions of the fibula, the slim bone in the lower leg, had been completely burned. Tarsals, or ankle bones, were badly calcined from the heat. The foot seemed to be missing.

"Why bamboo?" Sylvia asked as she knelt beside Maureen with a clipboard in her hands. She had pulled her brown hair back into a short ponytail.

"It doesn't scratch the bone the way a dental pick does." Maureen probed carefully and dug out around the bottom of the bone.

"So, what's the latest?" Sylvia started sketching the bone on the draft paper.

"This child burned whole. That's why the ankle and lower leg are in such bad condition."

Sylvia studied the tangle of bones. "Do you think they were alive when the kiva went up?"

Maureen shrugged. "Hard to say. Without lab analysis, all I can tell you is that they were either alive or hadn't been dead for very long. The meat around the bones still had a lot of water in it."

Sylvia's nose wrinkled. "Gruesome."

"Yes, it is."

"I can't believe it was an accident. I've dug pithouses in Colorado that burned. We were pretty sure in those cases that a spark set the wooden roof on fire, and they couldn't get out through the rooftop entry." Sylvia gestured around. "This is an arid climate. Wood dries out. Sometimes a spark is all it takes, and *whoosh!* The whole thing goes. A fire turns the ventilator shaft into an inferno. Most of the skeletal material is in pretty good shape because when the roof collapsed, the dirt covered everyone and sealed the draft from the ventilator. These kids, though, God. I mean it must have been an awesome fire. Why would forty or fifty children be on the roof of a kiva?"

"Good question." Maureen shook her head. "I don't suppose we can ever prove it, but I'd say someone did this on purpose, set the fire with the intent to burn these children."

Sylvia eyeballed the bone, sketched on her pad for a time longer, then said, "How could anyone do that? Most of these kids were under five."

Maureen took a deep breath and paused to pull back several loose strands of hair that were tickling her nose. "I've seen it before, Sylvia. The massacres in El Salvador, Bosnia, Kosovo, Rwanda. Even the dead from Indian battlefields in America, like Sand Creek, Bear River, and Wounded Knee. It happens when people hate each other. In Russia, Nazi soldiers herded women and children into barns and churches and burned them alive." She paused. "It's part of who we are as human beings. One of the many images you see in your reflection when you look into a mirror."

"Makes me glad I sleep with my baseball bat."

"Yes, but on the other hand we're the same species that spends tens of thousands of dollars to rescue beached whales, or to provide food and medicine to people halfway around the globe that we don't know." Maureen cocked her head, and her long black braid fell over her shoulder. "That's the magic of anthropology, Sylvia. We get to study people in all of their many different forms, characteristics, their diverse cultures, languages, and their physical variation. But we're all the same animal."

"Kind of wonderful and horrifying at once, isn't it?"

Maureen smiled. "Sounds like a description of Dusty."

She used her bamboo sliver to pull dirt back as far as the femur's *linea aspera*, the line of muscle attachment on the back of the bone.

"That's for sure," Sylvia replied, and her green eyes turned thoughtful. "Speaking of which, if you're right that these children were torched on purpose, it would support Dusty's suspicion of holy war."

"Not necessarily. The children could also have been plague victims, or something similar. Sometimes, when illness breaks out, bodies are burned in mass graves. That's also what this might have been."

Sylvia made a face. "Maybe. But if that was the case, why burn the kiva, too? I mean, it's the centerpiece for the entire pueblo."

"Maybe there was an epidemic. They took the children into the kiva and prayed and sang over them, trying to heal them in their holiest place, but it didn't work. One by one, the children died. Heartsick, they carried them all onto the roof and burned the entire kiva. They cremated their children to kill the evil spirits that had caused the illness. Then they abandoned the pueblo."

"In an epidemic, the kids wouldn't have died all at once, though. To prove it was disease, you would have to show that some of the kids had been dead for a while."

Maureen nodded. "That's right. I'll try to discern that in the lab." She resettled where her leg was going to sleep and continued whisking dirt away from the brittle bone.

"We haven't found many grave goods either," Sylvia pointed out. "If they'd died because of warfare or illness, somebody would have prepared them for the journey to the afterlife, left pots of food, new sandals, precious belongings."

"Grave goods would definitely weight the evidence more toward a funeral than a massacre."

A crow sailed over them, his black wings canted to catch the air currents.

Sylvia chewed her lip for a moment. "If the other sites in the area are any indication, it's going to turn out to be a massacre site."

"You think Dusty's right?"

"I haven't seen him wrong very often, Washais."

Maureen frowned at the tangled bones. "I'm sure that's true."

Sylvia paused, then said, "You know, I don't get you two."

"How's that?"

Sylvia shrugged. "You have a unique relationship, that's all. After you left 10K3, Dusty was glum. I mean, really glum. He spent a lot of time moping. Then, after we packed up, and he went back to Santa Fe, I'd get calls. Maybe about once a week. You know, 'How ya doin'?' sorts of things. Then he'd ask, 'So, you heard from Dr. Cole?' as if it had just slipped into the conversation."

Maureen hesitated, stopped what she was doing, and rocked back on her haunches to get a better look at Sylvia. "He could have called me, you know."

"Not Dusty. It would have been an admission."

"Of what? That he wanted to know how I was doing? My God, I was doing the analysis of those burials we found. It wasn't like he needed an excuse. I thought the reason Dale was always calling for updates on the data was because Stewart wasn't interested. That, or he'd get what he needed when I wrote the final report."

Sylvia finished her sketch, set her clipboard aside, and sat down cross-legged. "I've never seen him this way over a woman before. I mean, when we cut this bone bed? He was practically phobic about picking up the phone to call you. Then, when he did, you heard him. He said hello, fumbled around sounding like an idiot, and handed the phone to me, for God's sake."

Maureen turned her head when a gust of wind whirled around the kiva. When she turned back, she said, "Dale called him a *Kokwimu* once. I had to look it up to discover it meant a Man-Woman. I don't think Dale meant it, since Stewart certainly has a male body and soul."

"Yeah, he just can't get them together."

"Because of his mother and father?" Maureen raised her face to the sun, thinking.

Sylvia said, "Dale told me that in all the years since Ruth Ann Sullivan left Samuel Stewart, she has never once tried to get in touch with Dusty. I think the fact that old Samuel committed suicide made matters worse for Dusty. I mean, God, talk about traumatic. He was a child." She indicated the delicate bones spread around the kiva room. "Like these kids."

"But he's almost forty now, Sylvia. He should have figured out that not all women are Ruth Ann Sullivan."

"Yeah, and I should have figured out that not all men want to hurt me; but outgrowing your childhood is tougher than normal people think." She shook her head. "Things that happen to you as a kid can really screw up the rest of your life."

"Thinking about Steve?"

"No. Thinking about *him*—my foster father when I was four years old. I still have nightmares about his breath and hair. Isn't that funny? That sight of all that black, curly hair on his chest terrified me." She stared off into nothingness. "Each time I thought I was smothering. And the smell ... of his breath ... his body."

"That was a long time ago."

"Only to you. I relive every moment every day." Sylvia seemed to come back to this world. She gave Maureen a cautious look. "How about you?"

"What do you mean?"

"I mean you're haunted, too. Do you still have nightmares about your husband?"

Maureen nodded. "I have one dream. John and I are walking along the beach, it's morning, and the waves are coming in off the lake and splashing. The water is turquoise. Gulls are hanging on the breeze, bobbing, and the sun is slanting in from the east through the clouds. I'm holding John's hand, and dear God, Sylvia, I'm so happy, as if my heart is about to burst through my chest. Then I look into John's face, expecting him to be smiling, happy, as full of life as I am at that moment, but I see his face as he looked lying on the kitchen floor, and I can smell the burning spaghetti sauce."

Sylvia stared at her with kind eyes.

Maureen shrugged. "I wake up and there's a huge gaping hole inside me. The empty feeling is so intense, I just lay there in the dark, in the bed I used to share with him, and ache."

Sylvia's eyes tightened. She stared out at the clouds on the southern horizon. "That sounds pretty lonely, Washais."

They were silent for a moment, then Maureen leaned forward and resumed her excavation of the child's leg. "I just about have this femur ready to be removed."

"Okay. I've sketched the bone to scale. Let me get a photo and a box ready." Sylvia retrieved the camera from the ammo box that sat on the lip of the unit and snapped several shots.

Maureen rocked the small femur back and forth with her fingertips to ensure it was loose, then lifted it free. Sylvia began wrapping it in tissue while Maureen removed the epiphyses and wrapped them.

"You've worked with Dusty for years, right?"

"Sometimes it seems like forever. I was just a student. Went to the Pecos Conference that year. It was being held back in Pecos, sort of a reunion kind of thing. I walked around the trucks and there was Dusty, drinking beer with Dale. I can still remember, they were arguing about contamination of a C-14 sample, and Dusty was reaming Dale for letting a big drop of sweat fall from the end of his nose onto this piece of charcoal. The date they got back from Beta Analytic said that their site had been built yesterday." Sylvia shook her head, smiling. "I couldn't believe I was standing that close to Dale Emerson Robertson! As an anthropology student, I was blown away. I kept wondering who the blond asshole was, and how dare he blame someone like Robertson for screwing up a C-14 date!"

"So you launched into Dusty?"

"God, no. I was just standing there with my eyes bugged out, when Dusty turned. He made this gesture with his hand. Like, 'come here.' I stepped forward and Dusty said, 'Do you promise not to sweat into my charcoal samples?' Well, Jeez, what would a sophomore anthropology student say? I answered, 'Yes, sir.' And Dusty said, 'All right, you're hired, Mary. We're blowing out of here at noon tomorrow.'

" 'Sir,' I said, 'My name is Sylvia.'

" 'Okay,' he answered, 'whatever. We're digging a late P-One site that they're running a pipeline through. We've got three weeks. I'll meet you at the old mission at noon tomorrow. You can ride out with me, or Dale, assuming you want to be sweated on.'

" 'William,' Dale said in this imperious voice, 'one drop of sweat wouldn't have ruined your sample. They *wash* the material before they run it. I suggest that you see to how you record and package your materials before you send them off to the lab,' and Dale stalked off."

Maureen chuckled. "What an introduction."

"Yeah." Sylvia placed the wrapped bone in the box. "And there I was, hired onto a field crew. I asked Dusty, 'What about my classes?'

" 'What about them?' he asked.

" 'Well, they're supposed to start in—'

"He cut me off, and said, 'Kid, are you going to be an archaeologist or an academician?' " She made a face. "It was the way he said 'academician,' as if it was something really foul. Then he added, 'Why didn't you say you were still in school on your *vitae*?' "

Sylvia rubbed her nose. "I was so dumb I didn't know a *vitae* was a résumé. So, I shrugged. And Dusty says, 'Where are you going to school?'

" 'University of New Mexico.'

" 'Don't sweat it,' he says. 'Dale will fix it.' And, of course, he did. I got credits for my fieldwork."

"So you had a job?"

"Right. Doing real archaeology with Dale Emerson Robertson. We'd been working on the project for three days before Dusty figured out he'd hired me by mistake. He thought I was some girl named Mary who had wanted to talk to him about a job. She was supposed to meet him that night. I dug that entire semester, doing archaeology instead of sitting in a classroom learning about it."

Maureen returned her attention to the burned tibia. "So, where did Dusty's reputation as a ladies' man come from?"

Sylvia appraised Maureen. "That's an interesting question, Washais. Worried about him?"

"No, just wondering."

"Uh-huh." Sylvia rubbed her chin with the back of her dirty hand. "Women like Dusty's looks, that's where the reputation comes from. The problem is that as soon as they start getting close, he sort of self-destructs. Says and does things that are really bizarre. You ask him about it later, and he doesn't know why he did what he did."

"We all have our little disasters, don't we?"

Sylvia nodded. "It's only when you get to digging something like this, all these children, and you realize that no matter how screwed up your life seems, it's nothing compared to what these people went through." She stared at the piles of bones. "Imagine how they must have felt. Their children incinerated. How did they survive that?"

"I don't know," Maureen whispered, and chipped away another piece of dirt from the delicate bone.

CHAPTER 32

BROWSER KEPT HIS eyes on Catkin as she shouldered through the crowded plaza on her way to Cloudblower's chamber. She had her right hand propped on her belted war club. She probably wasn't even conscious of it, but Browser knew what it meant.

Danger here.

As they passed the great kiva, to their left, Stone Ghost said, "What did Catkin tell you, Nephew?" Thin white hair blew around his face as he looked up at Browser.

"Nothing, Uncle, except that Cloudblower knows things about Two Hearts that I do not."

Thin white hair blew around his uncle's wrinkled face. "I'm sure she does. After all, she knew the monster soul that lived inside your wife. Yellow Dove must have told her many things."

Browser ducked his head as they passed Springbank and Wading Bird. He didn't want to answer any questions before he'd heard what Cloudblower had to say. "What things, Uncle? Do you know? You sound like you know."

Stone Ghost stuck a hand through a hole in his ratty turkey feather cape and grasped Browser's elbow. To the people in the plaza it would appear that he was seeking support for his elderly steps, but he squeezed Browser's arm, and Browser realized he was actually offering support, not asking for it.

"Cloudblower told me a few things nine moons ago in Straight Path Canyon, Nephew, but I do not know what she will tell us today."

"Why didn't you tell me, Uncle?"

"The story was not mine to give. It belongs to her. I discovered long ago that if people wished to tell others the same things they told me, they would."

They veered around a group of mourners, and Browser whispered, "I am War Chief, Uncle. To protect our people, I must know everything."

"Then ask her, Nephew. I think she will answer you."

Catkin stopped in front of Cloudblower's door and turned to watch their approach. Her red shirt clung to every curve of her tall body. Her beautiful oval face had flushed, as though she feared what the next hand of time would bring.

Browser could feel his uncle's finger bones through the thin veneer of translucent skin; they felt like knotted twigs.

When they stood before the door curtain, Stone Ghost called, "Healer? We are here."

"Come," Cloudblower said softly. "I think I am ready for you."

Stone Ghost held the leather curtain aside and stepped into the chamber. Catkin and Browser followed.

As the door curtain swung behind them, bright yellow light splashed the dim interior. The chamber spread three-by-three body lengths. Cloudblower stood two paces away, to Browser's left. She'd braided her gray-streaked black hair and coiled it on top of her head, then fastened it with bone pins. The style accentuated the triangular shape of her face. The shell beads on her long blue dress shimmered with her movements.

Gray pots lined the walls, and the sweet scents of herbs and dried flowers pervaded the air. Katsinas Danced on the white walls with their hands linked and their masked faces tipped toward the smokehole in the roof, Singing. In the ruddy glow cast by the hearth coals, their painted bodies wavered. Their white kirtles seemed to sway as though touched by a wind Browser could not feel. He watched them from the corner of his eye, half expecting them to suddenly look down at him.

"Please, sit," Cloudblower said, and extended a hand to the opposite wall where deerhides covered the floor.

"We thank you, Elder." Browser sat down cross-legged, and Catkin and Stone Ghost sat to his left.

The tension seemed to have sucked the air from the room. Browser had to remind himself to breathe.

Cloudblower touched the pot that hung on the tripod at the edge of the coals, and the beads on her blue sleeve twinkled. "I think this tea is still warm. May I fill cups for you?"

Stone Ghost smiled. "Yes, thank you, Healer. It has been a chilly day. My aching bones could use the warmth."

Cloudblower dipped up the first cup and handed it to Stone Ghost, then she filled cups for Catkin and Browser. Finally, she tipped the pot and poured her own cup full. She did not move for a long time. She just clutched her cup and stared blindly at the glowing coals.

Browser said, "Elder, I—"

"Yes," Cloudblower responded and sank back on the floor as though uttering that one word had drained her last bit of strength. Her soft brown eyes filled with sadness.

Catkin said, "He must know the things you told me that day long ago, Cloudblower."

She jerked a nod. "I just did not wish to be the one to tell him." She looked at Browser. "These things will hurt you, War Chief. That is why I haven't told you about them before now. You have had many other burdens to consider."

"If Catkin believes I must hear them, Elder, then our lives may depend upon it. I assure you that I can stand it."

Browser twisted his teacup in his hands and prayed that was true. For six moons after he'd killed his wife, no matter where he was, or what he'd been doing, Ash Girl's face had lived before his eyes. The instant before she'd died, she had gazed up at him with all the love she could muster and tried to warn him that Two Hearts was close. Despite the anger and hatred they had inflicted upon each other over the summers, at the last, even knowing that he had killed her, she had loved him.

"Please, Elder, go on."

Cloudblower nodded, but her voice came out low. "He was a terrible boy, Browser, the monster that lived inside your wife. But he tried to protect her from her father."

Browser said, "I spoke with Yellow Dove the day I killed Ash Girl's body, Elder. I know something of his madness. Please, continue."

He had never told anyone that. Catkin knew because she'd been there. Browser had shot an arrow through the boy's chest, then ripped off the wolf mask he wore, and stood frozen, looking down into Ash Girl's face. The horror of that moment still lived in his heart.

Cloudblower sat down again and laced her fingers in her lap. "Stone Ghost helped me to understand monster souls." She nodded respectfully at the old man. "He told me that murderers are not born, but molded as children. He said it takes repeated intolerable pain to chase away a child's souls and make a nest where a monster can be born." Her eyes shifted to Browser. "That's what happened to Ash Girl. Her father chased away her human souls and in their places a hideous creature was born."

Browser sat quietly, listening.

Stone Ghost shifted. "I have seen only two monster souls in my life, Nephew. Both were born when the frightened children had given up hope, when they could no longer endure the pain alone. Someone stronger was born inside them, a protector who would never leave them, who could stand up to the tormentor and shield the child from the terror. Protecting the child often includes murder."

The popping of the fire seemed to fill the world.

Browser said, "What else?"

Cloudblower bowed her head. "I know it hurt you deeply that your wife fell asleep every time you started loving her, Browser, but she couldn't help it. That's how Yellow Dove shielded Ash Girl from the pain. Her father—he—he started lying with her when she was two."

Browser's grip tightened around his cup. For the first three summers of their marriage, he'd desperately tried to speak with her about it. He could still hear her husky voice shouting, *"I do not know what you're talking about, and it angers me that you would accuse me of such a thing!"*

Browser frowned down into his tea. His reflection stared back with anxious eyes. Jagged black locks fell around his face. He looked like a man who'd been running for summers, scrambling to escape a foe he could not see. That's how he'd felt throughout their marriage, like he was fighting an invisible foe. Every day he could smell the enemy closing in, but never saw him until the very end when Ash Girl died in his arms.

Cloudblower stared at the red coals in the hearth. "If little Ash Girl cried, her father made her play a game he called 'beetle.' He forced her to lie on her back, then push up with her arms and legs until she'd arched her back as far as she could. When she weakened and fell, he beat her in the head with a fire-hardened digging stick. By the time she had seen four summers, she fell asleep every time he walked into their chamber. She went somewhere deep inside her souls to hide. That's when Yellow Dove woke up. He saw what happened. He took the beatings. He endured the agony."

Browser felt as though he were seeing Ash Girl for the first time, and it twisted his insides. "Why didn't my wife tell me these things, Elder? Was she afraid to? Afraid that I would cast her out for being tainted with incest?"

He must have failed her in some way that made her unable to trust him. What had he done? Perhaps he had not shown her enough love, or cared enough about her problems. Or maybe she realized that his family would have forced him to leave her if they had known about her father.

Cloudblower said, "Ash Girl didn't speak with you about these things because she didn't remember them. Truly. I know about them because Yellow Dove told me."

Browser kept his voice even. "How could she not know, Elder? These things happened to her."

Stone Ghost put a gentle hand on Browser's wrist. "Tortured children rarely recall what their tormentors do to them. It is the monster soul who keeps those memories."

Cloudblower reached for a stick of wood in the pile to her right and placed it on the coals. Smoke curled up, then delicate yellow flames licked around the fresh tinder. The rich tang of sage filled the chamber.

"Did Ash Girl's mother know?" Browser asked.

Cloudblower nodded. "Yes, but not until much later. Ash Girl was five when her mother discovered the truth. Her father ran away to escape being punished for incest. He was a Trader. No one in Green Mesa villages even missed him for two summers. Her mother never told anyone. She loved Ash Girl. She couldn't bear the thought that her daughter might be Outcast from the clan, or even killed to cleanse the village."

"And no one else knew? How could that be?" Browser said in a strained voice. "Children say things without thinking. Ash Girl's strange behavior must have roused someone's suspicions."

Cloudblower shook her head. "Not that I know of. Though I cannot prove it, but I always thought our Matron knew."

The fire crackled and a wreath of sparks spun toward the roof's smokehole.

Catkin said, "How could our Matron have known? She did not even meet Ash Girl until three summers before her death. Surely Ash Girl would not have told her."

"Ash Girl *could* not have told her," Stone Ghost reminded her. "She didn't carry the memories, Yellow Dove did. And I doubt that your Matron had the privilege of speaking with Yellow Dove. Monsters are very secretive. They may reveal themselves during times of great stress, but even then it is rare that people recognize them for what they are." He cocked his elderly head at Cloudblower. "What did the Matron say that made you think she knew?"

The shell beads on Cloudblower's blue sleeves twinkled as she folded her arms. "About six moons before her death, Ash Girl started acted very strangely, screaming and lashing out at people for no reason. I remember our Matron whispering that it was her father's fault. I didn't understand what she meant and asked her about it. Our Matron just shook her head. She wouldn't tell me anything else."

Browser unconsciously touched the soft hides beside his sandals. For the last seven or eight moons of her life, Ash Girl had awakened swinging her fists and crying from nightmares she would not discuss. Browser had slept with Grass Moon in his arms, just to be certain Ash Girl didn't hurt him.

Stone Ghost's thick white brows pulled together. "Ash Girl's father left the family when she was barely five summers. That's probably what your Matron meant."

"Perhaps," Cloudblower whispered. "But I don't think so."

Stone Ghost's dark eyes glinted. "Why?"

"Our Matron told me once that many summers ago she had spoken with Ash Girl's grandmother. That struck me as odd. Flame Carrier was born in Dry Creek village, not far from here. With the warfare over the past fifty summers, why would she have risked traveling to the far north? Green Mesa is a dangerous place, filled with canyons where raiders ambush travelers."

"Did she say when this trip took place?"

"No. But I thought she meant a long time ago, perhaps fifteen or twenty summers."

Stone Ghost sipped his tea and steam curled around his wrinkled face. "Perhaps, Healer, your Matron did not do the traveling. Ash Girl's grandmother could have come to Dry Creek village. We should ask Ant Woman."

"Yes," Cloudblower murmured. "She might know."

Catkin's eyes caught the firelight as she leaned forward. "We found something today, Cloudblower. The tracks of a little girl."

"A girl?" Cloudblower frowned. "What girl?"

Browser said, "We don't know, Elder. She had been lying on the hilltop to the west of the grave, apparently watching us. She—"

"One of our children? Or another war orphan?"

Browser sipped his tea, and the sweet flavor of fireweed blossoms coated his tongue.

Catkin answered, "Not one of ours, but we're not sure she was an orphan, either. Something frightened her. She ran down the hill into the drainage and hid in an old coyote den in the bank. A man found her. The girl tried everything to avoid his grasping hands. She clawed the walls and floor of the den before he dragged her out on her belly and carried her away."

Cloudblower's soft brown eyes widened. "How old was she? Could you tell?"

"Seven or eight summers."

Catkin said, "Redcrop discovered the tracks. She also found a cornhusk doll in the rear of the den."

Cloudblower's gaze lifted to Catkin. "What does this girl have to do with Ash Girl? You don't think she . . . ?" Her lips parted with words she did not speak.

Catkin said, "She may be the same girl whose footprints Stone Ghost found at the torture site. The same girl Browser heard at Aspen village. All we know for certain is that the man who found the little girl was wearing the same sandals as the man who helped to murder our Matron."

"Is that why you wished me to hear this?" Browser asked Catkin. "You think the little girl may be suffering the way Ash Girl did?"

Catkin said, "There are three of them, Browser: a man, a woman, and a little girl. I fear it is possible that she is his daughter."

"Blessed gods." Cloudblower bowed her head and closed her eyes for a long moment. "I pray not."

Stone Ghost's deep wrinkles rearranged themselves into sad lines. "We all do, Healer. But we must make plans in case Catkin is right."

"Yes." She stared at Stone Ghost with tear-filled eyes. "I will do whatever you wish me to."

Stone Ghost nodded. "I am grateful, Healer. Where is Redcrop?"

"At the grave, Uncle," Browser said.

Stone Ghost braced a hand on Browser's shoulder and rose unsteadily to his feet. "Please bring her. I want her to be there when we speak with Ant Woman. Your Matron may have told Redcrop things in the past thirteen summers that no one else knows."

I LAY ON my belly on a sandstone terrace halfway down the side of the eroded bluff. My buckskin clothing blends with the tan rock. Father crouches five hundred body lengths below me. He is invisible to my eyes, like a serpent coiled among the sage, but I know he is there, watching. I feel him there.

The girl sits alone by the grave. She rocks back and forth.

The tension in Father's tall body must be unbearable, like a starving cougar with a rabbit in sight, afraid to leap for fear the rabbit will escape.

He has barely slept since he first saw her out there by herself. He wants her badly.

My gaze drifts over the rolling hills. Somewhere, warriors hide, waiting for him to strike.

Father knows this, of course. He must be trembling, his whole body fit to burst from the longing, but he will not give them what they expect. He will bide his time until he can no longer stand it, then he will trick them into turning away, into looking in the opposite direction for one brief instant, and when they do . . .

"Mother?" the whisper is barely audible. "I have been good. Can we go? I want to go."

A man in a red shirt walks the river trail toward the girl below. He is tall, with broad shoulders, and carries a club in his hand. The War Chief, Browser.

"Mother? My legs hurt, please?"

I pull my buckskin hood up to cover my hair and flatten my body against the sandstone ledge. I have not been afraid of being seen before now. The other warriors require only ordinary precautions, but this War Chief scares me. He has eyes like an antelope. No matter how far away I am, or how well hidden, his eyes always find me. I must be some curious color or shape to him. He has not yet realized what he is seeing, but he always takes the time to look more closely. Someday, he will see me, and then one of us will die.

Yes, but first I will play with him as a ferret does a rabbit. We are entwined in the old gods' web. We will Dance together, casting shadows in the moonlight until his shadow is devoured by mine. In the end the only laughter will be the Blue God's—echoing in the empty rooms of empty places.

"Mother?"

"Shh. Your grandfather is coming back. I feel him coming."

She seems to turn to stone, her eyes huge.

"Now?" she asks in a trembling voice. "Is he coming now?"

"Yes."

She grabs my hand and tugs with all her strength. "Let's run away! Hurry, let's run!"

I jerk her to the ground. My voice is ice. "He is the only one in the world who loves us. Do you understand?"

Her mouth opens with silent cries. She lies down beside me in the dirt and hides her face in her hands.

I stroke her back. "The *only* one."

CHAPTER 33

DUSTY CRIED OUT and bolted upright, gasping. He batted the top of his sleeping bag out of the way and gulped air. "Good God, not again." He bent over in the cold darkness and cradled his head in his hands.

The creak of the trailer floor shot sudden adrenaline through him. He tensed, sensing a presence, feeling the faint shift of the springs. His tongue had gone dry in his mouth.

"Dusty?" the voice asked softly from the metal stairs outside.

"I—I'm okay, Maureen. Just a dream."

The latch on the door clicked and a sliver of light widened across the room. She wore a gray sweatshirt and sweatpants and held a flashlight in her hand. Long black hair draped her shoulders, falling to her waist. "You're sure you're okay?"

He shivered. "I said I'm fine. It was just a bad dream."

She stood uncertainly in the doorway. The flashlight beam illuminated her face and her black eyes shimmered. "The same one?"

"I wish I'd never seen that little son of a bitch." Maybe it was the hour, the lingering aftereffects of the dream, but he actually wanted company.

"The basilisk?"

He made a gesture and squinted up into the light. "If this is an interrogation, I'm supposed to be in a wooden chair. But I think you've got the light about right."

"Uh, sorry." She lowered the beam. "The basilisk from 10K3?"

He rubbed his bearded face. "I swear it belonged to someone insane."

She stepped into the room and leaned against the stove. The sweatshirt looked two sizes too big, but it must have been warm to sleep in. "That thing really has a handle on your subconscious."

"Yeah, fancy that." He rubbed his face and exhaled. His breath fogged in the cold air.

"It's just an artifact. A piece of stone." She sounded so sure of herself.

He frowned. "Part of me believes that—the part that went to the university. But the part of me that went down into that kiva when I was twelve thinks you're really naive."

She bowed her head, and her hair fell over her shoulders in thick black waves. "That's possible, but I want you to consider the possibility that the dream is trying to tell you something. Are you struggling with guilt because Elder Walking Hawk wanted that basilisk reburied, or are you torturing yourself over something else?"

He shivered again, mostly from cold this time. "The other explanation is that evil exists and I touched it. Somehow or another, it got its hooks into me. Not all the way, but just enough." He rubbed his cold arms. "Remember the cleansing that Elder Walking Hawk did for us?"

She nodded. "Very well."

"I did that again the night I packed the *basilisco.* You know, just to be sure. God knows, if I hadn't, I might have cut your head off or something today."

She crossed her arms against the cold. "You're not the type, Stewart, despite what I originally thought about you."

"How nice of you to keep an open mind."

She tilted her head and smiled. "Tell me about the dream. Was it vivid?"

"Clear and sharp—even the smell."

"The smell?"

"The odor of burned skin and meat. I'm awake and I can still smell it."

She leaned against the counter. "Why don't you start from the beginning."

He swallowed hard. "I was sitting on a bench in the kiva. It was beautiful, the walls painted in white on the top, and bright red on the bottom. Bundles—net bags, I think—hung from the rafters. And really peculiar paintings. I think they were katchinas; they each had holes gouged in their chests. You could see the stone walls where the plaster had been chopped right out of the paintings, as if they'd cut their hearts out."

"Who did? Did they look like anyone you know in real life?"

"No. I didn't recognize any of the faces. They wore white capes, and carried war clubs and axes. Men, all of them. Lots of jewelry. Turquoise and jet bracelets. Colored feathers. Some wore what looked like necklaces made from bone disks." He shook his head. "They were insane, Maureen. Angry and filled with hatred. I'll never forget those bronzed faces, their black eyes enraged as they grouped around the woman."

"What woman?"

He frowned. "I don't know who she was. Proud, though. Stately. She just seemed to radiate authority and poise. She was someone important. Someone who had lived all of her life respected and obeyed. You could tell by the way she carried herself. And she despised the men around her."

A gust of wind rattled the trailer, and mice scrambled in the walls.

"They weren't her men?"

"No. Anything but. Her face twisted with pain as she watched them set fire to the pile of katchina masks in the middle of the floor. I could feel her fear growing with each beat of my heart."

"What does that mean, burning katchina masks?"

"It's a sacrilege. That's what they were doing. Destroying the katchinas."

Maureen brushed her long hair over her shoulders and braced a hand against the counter. "What happened to the woman?"

"She was dressed in blue, and she had gray hair, long, hanging down like yours. She wore a turquoise and eagle-bone breastplate, a beautiful thing that caught the light. Around her throat she had a choker covered with beads. And I remember a wolf pendant, hanging down over her chest, but separate from the breastplate."

He exhaled hard and his breath glimmered in the light. "The men prodded her forward. She turned her head, just far enough to glare at them like they were something she'd scraped off her foot. One of the men shoved her into the fire." Dusty shivered. "That's when the smell came. She pulled up the hem of her skirt and tottered around in that burning mass of katchina masks. I could see the skin on her calves blistering and wrinkling in the flames. When she could no longer stand, she fell and rolled against a big painted olla, a jar. She just lay there, writhing."

Maureen's eyes tightened. "She was dead?"

"No. One of the men leaned forward. It was like he knew the others were losing their will. He jammed his foot down on her burned feet, tramped on them. The burned skin split and peeled back; blood seeped through. Her toes came off, Maureen. I mean, my God, the meat, the muscles, were cooked." He took another breath. "Each time I huddled back on the bench, hoping, praying that they wouldn't see me. That they wouldn't turn and throw me into that fire."

Maureen rested the flashlight on the counter and aimed the beam at the back of the wall. "Did they?"

He shook his head. "They were interested in her. She tried to stand, and . . . and she fell, because her legs wouldn't hold her. So she tried crawling away, dragging herself. Her skin peeled away on the dirt floor, leaving a smear of blood and fluid."

"That sounds horrible."

He closed his eyes. "It was. That's when the big guy turned and looked right into my eyes."

"Is that when you woke up?"

"No." His tongue felt swollen. "The big guy shouted something. I couldn't understand the words. It wasn't in Hopi, or Zuni, or any of the languages I know. But there he was, looking at me, while the old woman clawed at his legs, and tears ran down her cheeks."

"You're sure you don't know who this man was?" she gently asked.

"No. He was Indian, brown, broad-cheeked, with his hair done up in a bun like in the pictographs."

"Okay. What happened next?"

"I looked back at the old woman. She had wrapped her fingers in her beaded choker and twisted it so that the weight of her arm hung on it." He paused. "She was dead, Maureen. She had strangled herself."

"What did the big guy do?"

Dusty shifted uneasily, crumpling his sleeping bag with his hand. "He laughed, and—and when he looked back at me, it wasn't the big guy."

Maureen shifted and flashlight beam bobbed around the trailer.

"Who was he?"

His voice cracked. "An old man! A toothless elder. He was wearing *el Basilisco* on his chest."

Maureen cautiously came over and sat down across from him. "You know what I think?"

"What?" He looked up into her dark confident eyes.

"I think you need another cleansing. One performed by an elder who knows what she's doing. Someone like Hail Walking Hawk."

"I thought you didn't believe in such things?"

Maureen leaned toward him and softly replied, "The point is that you do."

Dusty ran a hand through his sweat-drenched blond hair. "You think I've talked myself into this, don't you? I believe the basilisk was evil and so I'm acting as though I've been witched, right?" He actually wanted her to say yes. It would have made him feel better, like the basilisk really wasn't evil and all of his fears were for nothing.

Instead, she surprised him by reaching out to touch his hand. Her fingers felt cool on his. She said, "No matter what I say, Dusty, you won't believe me. You *believe* you've been witched. The only way you'll know for certain is by talking about this with an elder that you trust."

He turned his hand up and gripped her fingers. "Thanks for coming." He squeezed her hand and let it go. "But I feel better now. Why don't you go back to bed and get some sleep. We'll talk more tomorrow, okay?"

"You're sure?"

"I am."

"Okay." She straightened and headed for the door. She looked back just once, before she stepped outside.

Dusty dropped his head in his hands and tried to figure out what the hell was happening to him. Was it just his own mind playing tricks? Could Maureen be right? Or could an ancient witch from the past be tormenting him?

He flopped back on his blankets and stared at the ceiling.

CHAPTER 34

WIND BABY PLAYED on the ridge tops, kicking up dust and whirling it high into the air. In the afternoon sunlight, the tall streamers bobbed across the distances, glistening like powdered amber.

Ant Woman watched them for a moment, then let out a breath and looked back at the crowded plaza. Most of the mourners had settled into groups. They huddled around the plaza with food bowls in their hands, whispering, weeping. Some laughed at stories told about Flame Carrier. There had to be more than one hundred adults and perhaps that many children. Colorful blankets lay spread across the ground, filled with food pots, baskets of nuts and breads, steaming bowls of meats, and piles of roasted corn on the cob. Children hovered around them. They knew they shouldn't play today, but it must be difficult, especially for the youngest.

"We're sorry to disturb you, Matron."

The voice jerked Ant Woman from her thoughts. She turned to see old Stone Ghost, Browser, and Flame Carrier's slave, Redcrop, standing before her.

"Yes, what is it?"

Stone Ghost gestured to the logs pulled up around Ant Woman's small fire. "May we sit? We would like to speak with you about our dead Matron."

"That is what this day is all about, old fool. Of course you may sit with me."

Stone Ghost grunted as he sat down by her side. His sparse white hair looked as if it hadn't been combed in moons. It stuck out at odd angles. Through the holes in his mangy turkey feather cape, she could see a threadbare tan shirt. War Chief Browser knelt at the old man's side.

"What is it you wish to know?" she asked.

Stone Ghost answered, "We are hoping you can help us find your friend's murderer."

"Me?" she said in surprise. "How can I do that?"

Browser said, "We wish to know things about her early life, Matron. Things that only you may know."

Redcrop knelt to Ant Woman's left, and her white cape draped around her. The girl looked as broken as Ant Woman felt. Her nose glowed like a ripe chokecherry.

Ant Woman tugged her brown-and-yellow blanket more tightly around her shoulders and gave Redcrop a sympathetic look. The girl didn't notice. She gazed down at her hands as though her entire world lay there now. What had they done? Dragged her away from the grave?

Softly, Ant Woman said, "Are you well, child?"

"Yes, I—I am, Matron. Well enough."

"It's all right to miss her, girl. I miss her, too. She was my friend for seventy summers. I don't know how I will get along without her wisdom."

Redcrop's mouth quivered. She had to swallow before she could say, "She loved you very much, Ant Woman. She told me many times."

"She loved you, too."

Ant Woman placed a bony hand on Redcrop's arm, and tears welled in the girl's eyes. "We'll manage. It will take many lonely nights of wishing and waking to find the wishes unfulfilled, but when the wishes have worn themselves out, we'll both be all right."

Redcrop whispered, "Thank you, Matron."

Ant Woman squeezed her arm and released it, then reached for the bowl of corn bread filled with giant wild rye seeds that sat on the hearthstones before her. She had been picking at the bread for over a hand of time. It was delicious, but she felt sick without Flame Carrier. Sick and lost. Even when they'd been separated by great distances, Ant Woman had relied on Flame Carrier's memory to carry her through. She'd had imaginary conversations with Flame Carrier, asking her what she would do in her position, or what she thought about this problem or that person. All of her strength had come from her friend.

But she's gone. Flame Carrier is gone.

Ant Woman broke off a chunk of corn bread and put it in her toothless mouth. While she gummed it, she watched Stone Ghost and War Chief Browser. They whispered to each other. Stone Ghost nodded, and his mouth tightened. His long hooked nose had a slight bend to it, as though it had been broken some time during his long life. Probably from a fist. Ant Woman squinted one eye at him. Half the world thought he was a powerful witch. The other half thought he was an old fool. She straddled the line. There were many stories about his foolishness, and many more about how clever he was. She figured he was probably a clever fool. She glanced down at the holes in the toes of his moccasins. Whatever the truth, his cleverness certainly hadn't gained him much wealth.

"Well?" she said. "What is it?"

The War Chief leaned forward. He had a round face, with a flat nose and thick black eyebrows. Handsome, in a rough-hewn sort of way. "Our Matron rarely spoke about her parents or her childhood."

Ant Woman's souls drifted, seeing faces she had not seen in seventy summers. "Well, I never knew your Matron's father, Ravenfire, but I knew her—"

"I knew Ravenfire, or I should say I met him once." Stone Ghost waved a hand apologetically. "But forgive me. Please go on."

"I was just going to say that I knew her mother well. Spider Silk came to our village eight moons pregnant. She had the child and lived with us for the rest of her life. Spider Silk was running at the time. She never said so, but she must have been."

"Running?" Stone Ghost cocked his head. "From what?"

Ant Woman made a helpless gesture. "I never knew. But only a desperate woman would run away from her people eight moons pregnant, and chance traveling the roads alone. That was back after the Straight Path Nation collapsed. War had just broken out. Villages were being burned."

Stone Ghost stared at her with unnerving intensity. "What of her parents? Did you ever meet them?"

"On occasion Spider Silk's parents came to visit her, and then everyone knew why Spider Silk was strange. Her father, Born-of-Water, had pink eyes and the skin of a corpse, white and shiny. He looked just like a wolf—a human wolf. I swear it. His face was long and pointed, like a muzzle." Ant Woman lifted her hands to her own face and showed them how it was shaped. "Her mother, Golden Fawn, seemed fairly ordinary, but—sad. Even when she smiled, despair lived in her eyes. I remember those two very well. They claimed to have been raised with the Blessed prophets, Cornsilk and Poor Singer. I don't know if that was true, but that's what Born-of-Water told people."

Stone Ghost's white brows drew together, and Ant Woman frowned. "What's wrong?"

Stone Ghost laced his fingers around one knee, and his cape fell back, revealing the threadbare brown shirt he wore. She could see his ribs through the fabric.

Stone Ghost said, "It's just curious. You see, my own grandmother, Orenda, was raised with Cornsilk and Poor Singer. I wonder if she knew Spider Silk or her parents?"

Ant Woman took another drink of tea and wiped her mouth with the back of her hand. "Perhaps Orenda and Spider Silk grew up together?"

Stone Ghost shrugged. "Who can say? Every person alive wishes to be associated with the most important holy people in our history. I often thought that—"

Ant Woman broke in: "Did Orenda ever mention a turquoise cave to you?"

Stone Ghost's eyes went wide. "The Turquoise Cave! Why, yes. After my grandmother left the land of the Mountain Builders and came to the Straight Path Nation, she lived in the Turquoise Cave for a time, before moving to Green Mesa."

Ant Woman broke off another piece of corn bread and ate it. The giant wild rye seeds hurt her gums, but they had a rich earthy flavor that tasted delicious. "Spider Silk said she was born in that cave. Maybe your grandmother, Orenda, was related to Spider Silk."

Stone Ghost relaced the crooked blue-veined fingers around his knee. "Maybe, but I don't recall my grandmother ever mentioning her name."

Browser said, "If there is a connection between your grandmother and our Matron's mother, could it have something to do with her murder? Perhaps the murderers are hunting down the children of people who knew the Blessed Poor Singer and the Blessed Cornsilk?"

Stone Ghost peered unblinking at the leaping flames before responding, "Everything is connected to everything, Nephew, but that would seem very odd. After all, I've been living alone in the middle of nowhere for most of my life. If someone had wished to kill me, it would have taken little effort."

Ant Woman made a disgusted sound. "You old fool. You're either senile or stupid."

Stone Ghost gave her a genuinely interested look. "Why would you say that?"

"Think of the amount of courage it would have taken! Most people think you're a witch. No sane human would willingly walk into your lair."

Stone Ghost's white brows lowered. "Well, they wouldn't have had to 'walk into my lair,' Ant Woman. They could have shot me in the back when I was out gathering prickly pear cactus fruit, or clubbed me to death while I was dozing in the summer sunshine. And your Matron has been wandering about gathering followers for the Katsinas' People for almost four summers. If someone had wished to kill her, they could have done it easily long ago. Why now?"

Redcrop shifted and toyed with the hands in her lap.

"What is it, child?" Ant Woman asked.

"I was wondering if maybe the murderers just discovered something they did not know before."

"What?"

Redcrop shook her head and raggedly chopped locks of hair fell over her face. "I don't know, Matron. I'm sorry I'm not more help."

"You're grieving, child," Ant Woman said and touched Redcrop's knee. "I'm surprised you can think at all."

Browser lifted his gaze to Ant Woman. "Perhaps our murderers are simply patient. They may have waited many sun cycles for the right moment to strike."

Ant Woman pointed a knobby finger at Stone Ghost. "If that is the case, you had better start walking backwards so you can see who's sneaking up on you."

Stone Ghost smiled. "Don't you think it would be easier if I just borrowed the eyes of a big cat and used pine pitch to glue them to the back of my skull?"

Ant Woman stared at him. On night excursions, witches often used an animal's eyes to see better, then they left the eyes to spy on people. Ant Woman had known a young man who woke up one morning to see a bobcat's eyes watching him from his ceiling rafters. They'd been there for quite a while because nests of maggots had hatched in them. That's what had awakened the man, maggots dropping onto his face.

Ant Woman said, "I wouldn't joke about such doings if I were you, Stone Ghost. You might find yourself dead at the hand of a friend, rather than one of your many enemies."

Stone Ghost chuckled, but didn't respond.

"Matron," Browser said, "I must ask you about something that happened long ago. Do you recall a woman from the Green Mesa clans coming to see our Matron when she lived in your village?"

Ant Woman ate another mouthful of bread and reached for her teacup to wash it down. "When would that have been?"

"I can't say for certain, perhaps fifteen or twenty summers ago?"

"Twenty summers ago," Ant Woman whispered, trying to remember. She sipped her tea. The flavors of dried mint and shooting star petals mixed deliciously. "I would have seen forty or fifty summers. During that time, many people came to see your Matron and her mother. Spider Silk was getting old, but she had a reputation as a Powerful Healer. Your Matron helped her mother with surgeries and applying poultices, mixing herbs. Those two saved many lives. People genuinely loved them." She gestured lightly. "They also feared them, of course. Anyone who is skilled with plants is a little frightening, because she can kill as well as cure."

Redcrop said, "Grandmother knew a great deal about plants. She taught me."

Ant Woman nodded. "She got that from her mother, who claimed she got it from her mother, and she said she got it from her mother, and on back forever, I suppose."

Browser touched Stone Ghost's hand. "Uncle? Who was Orenda's mother? What was her name?"

Stone Ghost shook his head, but Ant Woman could see his hesitation. He said, "She never spoke about her real mother, but a woman of the Hollow Hoof Clan, named Nightshade, raised my grandmother."

Browser looked back at Ant Woman. "Do you recall the name of Born-of-Water's mother, or Golden Fawn's? Was it Nightshade?"

"I don't think I ever heard their names. If I did, I've forgotten."

Redcrop murmured, "Grandmother talked about Badgertail and Nightshade."

Everyone turned in her direction.

Firelight glazed Redcrop's wide eyes.

Ant Woman gently said, "Go on, child. What do you remember?"

"Not very much, Matron. I recall that she said Badgertail had been a great War Chief somewhere far to the east near a huge river. Nightshade was supposed to have been a very Powerful Dreamer."

Browser said, "Then our Matron had at least heard stories of the woman who raised Orenda. Did she say anything else, Redcrop?"

Redcrop touched her temple, as though her head ached. "I remember that Grandmother had an older brother—"

"Yes." Ant Woman nodded. "Bear Dancer. I remember him. He was an odd one. Many summers ago I heard he was killed in a raid. I recall hearing that she had a half brother, too, but I don't think she ever knew him."

Stone Ghost tilted his head and frowned at the fire. "Bear Dancer, gods, I have not thought about him in many summers. He was a violent man, always provoking fights just so he could hurt someone—much like his father."

"What about his father?" Browser said. "Did you ever hear our Matron talk about him?"

"No," Stone Ghost answered. "I heard many rumors from other people, but—"

Redcrop said, "I asked Grandmother about him once, and she just smiled and said that she did not wish to remember him. I don't think she liked him very much."

Ant Woman brushed corn-bread crumbs from her crooked fingers onto her yellow cape and tried to see through the hazy veil between the present and the past. Contemplatively, she said, "A woman from the Green Mesa villages. Twenty summers ago. I don't recall anyone coming down from Green Mesa, except Traders, of course. But there weren't any women Traders from Green Mesa at that time."

Stone Ghost said, "Perhaps a man from Green Mesa, then. He may have been carrying a message for the woman."

Ant Woman rubbed her wrinkled jaw. "Old Pigeontail was from somewhere near Green Mesa. He frequented our village. He's still around, charging outrageous prices for his trinkets. He may know. And your Matron was married to him for a few summers. He—"

"What?" Redcrop said, stunned. "Grandmother was married to Old Pigeontail? I never knew that!"

Browser added, "Great Ancestors, that's like corralling a buffalo bull with a wolf! What battles they must have waged against each other."

Ant Woman grinned. "That's why the marriage did not last long. She was always chewing at his throat, and he was always trying to kick her senseless—but Spider Silk ordered her to marry him. I never knew why."

Redcrop laughed. She had tears in her eyes, but a smile turned her lips. "When was that, Elder? How old was Grandmother?"

"Oh, let me see." Ant Woman rubbed her wrinkled throat. "It seems like that was forty summers ago. Maybe a little longer. Pigeontail was younger than your Matron. That was part of the problem. She'd seen a lot more of life than he had, but he didn't like it when she pointed that out."

"How strange," Browser said. "Old Pigeontail has often visited our villages, but our Matron always went out of her way to avoid him. I used to wonder why."

Ant Woman could feel Stone Ghost's gaze. She turned, and found him staring at her with unwavering eyes. White wisps of hair had glued themselves to his wrinkled cheeks.

"What are you staring at?"

Stone Ghost lowered his voice. "I was remembering a tragedy that happened twenty summers ago in the Green Mesa villages. Four old women were murdered." He rubbed his thumb over the black-on-white geometric paintings on the side of his teacup. "One of them was my sister."

Browser said, "That would be about the time the woman from Green Mesa supposedly came to see our Matron."

Ant Woman nodded. "I remember those murders. Your reputation soared after you found your sister's killer. Everyone wanted you to come and solve crimes in their village."

Stone Ghost answered, "That is exactly why I've spent the last twenty summers living alone in the middle of nowhere."

"But you have helped many villages."

"Yes. The ones I could."

Ant Woman brought up her aching right knee and rubbed it. On cold damp days like this, a fire built in the joint. She'd have to brew up a cup of willow bark tea before she'd be able to sleep tonight. "Whatever happened to your house down at Smoking Mirror Butte?" She used her chin to point southward. "Is it still there?"

Stone Ghost turned to the south and longing filled his old eyes. His white hair fluttered in the wind. "I hope so. I plan on going back."

"Not until after you've found the people who murdered my friend, I hope."

"That is my first duty, Matron."

Flame Carrier's smiling face appeared on the fabric of Ant Woman's souls and the pain in her heart expanded to fill her whole chest.

"Well," she said, "if you have no more questions for me, I would like to go to my camp where I can be with my family."

"I understand," Stone Ghost said. "Thank you for speaking with us, Ant Woman. How long will you be staying in Longtail village?"

"Perhaps another day. I need to speak with Crossbill about trading some of our pots for her pretty red blankets. Then we'll be going."

Stone Ghost rose unsteadily to his feet, and Browser grabbed his elbow to help support him.

Stone Ghost said, "If we have more questions, I hope you will speak with us again?"

"I will do whatever I can to help. Just don't interrupt me when I'm haggling for blankets."

"I promise not to." Stone Ghost smiled and bowed to her. "A pleasant evening to you, Matron."

"And to you, Stone Ghost."

The old man hobbled away with Browser and Redcrop behind him.

Ant Woman watched them with narrowed eyes as they walked through the crowd. Stone Ghost knew something he wasn't telling. She could feel it in her squirming belly. What was he hiding? The reason for Flame Carrier's murder? Maybe the reason for a number of murders that had happened in the past twenty summers?

Ant Woman shook her head, finished her tea, and struggled to her feet. As she walked across the plaza, she saw the pain on the faces of others, and it made her own grief worse.

Could Browser be right? The murderers were hunting down those who'd known the Blessed prophets. Why would someone do that? Cornsilk and Poor Singer had never harmed anyone. Legends said they'd spent their lives teaching and Healing, moving from village to village. They had claimed to have no clans, or families, which made them members of all clans and all families. That was their greatest strength.

Ant Woman sighed, too tired and grief-stricken to think more about it today. As she rounded the southeastern corner of Longtail village and looked down at Dry Creek village's camp, a sea of yellow capes flashed. Her people drifted from one fire to the next, speaking in hushed tones. Her daughter, Rock Dove, knelt before her own fire, nursing her baby. The beautiful boy had been born less than four moons ago. Rock Dove waved at Ant Woman.

Ant Woman lifted a hand and smiled. If she could just lie down for a time before the evening Dances, she might be able to stand it.

She forced her aching knees to walk.

CHAPTER 35

THE SOUND OF rain drumming on her tent roof woke Maureen.

She opened her eyes and stared at the darkness until she realized that the bottom of her sleeping bag was soaked clear through, as were her favorite pair of wool socks.

"No wonder I froze all night."

She shoved out of her bag and looked around. Even in the storm light, she could see pools of water glistening on the tent floor around her.

She tugged off her drenched socks and reached into her suitcase for a clean pair. She had to be a magician to dress beneath the bowed, waterlogged tent walls, but she managed. The aroma of coffee perking and breakfast cooking drifted from the trailer, encouraging her. Dusty must be up.

Maureen shrugged on her black down coat and ducked out of her tent. In the light from the trailer windows, she could see the water puddles. While the supply tent, Steve's, and Sylvia's, stood resolute against the storm, Maureen's had become a pathetic pond. The sides sloped inward as though ready to collapse. It took an act of will not to pull the stakes and let the rest of it collapse.

Maureen shoved her hands into her pockets and ran for the trailer. As she stamped the mud off her boots on the stairs, Dusty called, "Come on in. Coffee's on!"

Maureen pulled the door open and stepped into the warmth. "Oh, this feels good. My tent leaked last night."

Dusty turned from the frying pan on the stove to give her a knowing look. The white light of the lantern pulsed, giving his blond hair and beard a silver sheen. "I noticed. Sylvia bet me ten bucks that it would collapse on top of you before you got up."

"How nice. You win." Maureen took off her coat and hung it on the peg by the door. Wet splotches darkened her jeans. There must have been more water on her sleeping bag than she'd realized. "You're ten dollars richer. Speaking of Sylvia, where is she?"

Dusty handed her a note with rain-smeared ink:

> Boss Man! The skies opened. Since it doesn't look like this is going to quit, we're making a town run. We promise to do the shopping *before* we find a couple of cold brews. See you late

tonight or first thing tomorrow depending on how fuzzed up we get.

Love and Kisses,
S^2

Dusty's version of *huevos rancheros* simmered on the stove, made with a local brand of salsa, fresh jalapeños, canned beans, and tortillas; it smelled wonderful. They'd eaten it three days in a row, but she hadn't grown tired of it, yet.

"This is going to take a while," he said. "Why don't you sit down and I'll pour you a cup of coffee."

"Thanks."

Maureen shivered and walked over to the table piled high with specimen boxes. Dusty's neatly piled stacks of papers sat on the opposite side of the table.

"Sometime," he said, gesturing at her with the spatula, "you ought to have my specialty. I make my own refritos. Two parts black beans to three parts Anasazi beans."

"Anasazi beans?"

"Yeah. The same kind the Anasazi grew here eight hundred years ago. It's the single biggest industry up in Dove Creek, Colorado."

"This is a joke, right?"

"No. Fact. If we have time, we can drive up to Dove Creek and look at their bean elevator. That, and the café and gas station, *are* Dove Creek. See that and you've seen it all. Unless, of course, you've got a thing for tractors."

Last night after dinner, she'd spread her first collection of bone—a child's femur, a skull fragment, and what looked like an adult's tibia—out onto the little square table and set up her microscope. She started rearranging things so she would have a place to put her elbows. She slid her microscope to the right and blew dust from the table.

"You don't think Sylvia will get her Jeep stuck in the mud getting back in here, do you?"

"No, I know those two. They'll get a hotel room and watch the weather report. They'll linger, enjoying town life until this lifts."

Dusty set a steaming cup of coffee in front of her, and Maureen cradled it in her cold hands. "Oh, that smells great." She took a swallow and said, "My tent and sleeping bag look grim. Maybe I'd better go in and get a motel room tonight, too."

Dusty leaned against the counter and picked up his own coffee cup, one of those insulated travel mugs. "Dale keeps extra blankets in the cabinet over the couch. It's mouseproof up there. Why don't I move to the rear of the trailer, and you can have the front. That'll save me a trip into town tonight and another one to go get you in the morning."

She hesitated. "I guess you won't come crawling into my bed in the middle of the night."

Amusement twisted his lips. "No, probably not. Not that it would be such a bad bed to crawl into."

Maureen gave him a skeptical look. "You're such a sweet talker, Stewart."

He smiled and took another drink of coffee. "I was thinking I'd go back to work while I waited for the *huevos* to cook. Will you mind?"

"No. I'll just do the same."

"Okay."

Dusty slid into the booth opposite her and huddled behind piles of photo logs, feature records, artifact lists, field specimen forms, and the other minutiae of a well-run archaeological dig.

Maureen had begun her cataloguing with the partially burned child's femur she and Sylvia had recovered. It lay before her on the table, next to her notebook.

Dusty didn't seem much inclined to talk this morning, which was unusual. Dark circles filled the hollows beneath his blue eyes. More bad dreams?

She glanced at him, set her coffee down, and picked up her hand lens and pen. As she examined the bone, she wrote in her notebook, remarking on the scalloping and charring, the overall preservation, the fact that the epiphyseal lines were unossified—meaning it was a young child's leg bone.

"Uh, Doctor?"

She glanced up from measuring the mid-diaphyseal diameter—the middle of the long bone—and hesitated, calipers in one hand.

He was watching her with uncertain eyes.

"What?"

"About my nightmare." Dusty seemed to be fighting the urge to cringe. "I just wanted you to know that—"

"You're not a raving lunatic?"

"That, too. But, no, I was just going to say thanks for listening to me. I appreciated it."

"No problem."

She bent back to her work. After several minutes, she could feel his unrelenting blue-eyed stare boring into her. She looked up.

Dusty said, "You don't think I'm on the verge of a mental breakdown of catastrophic proportions, do you?"

Maureen could read the rest in his eyes—*like my father?* "No. I think you're stronger than that."

He fiddled with his pen. "I've been trying to figure out who the old woman is in the dream. The brain cooks up strange things. Maybe it was something I saw in a movie, or on TV. Something that clicked, got a reaction, and stayed buried until the *basilisco* called it up."

She reached for her coffee cup where it steamed next to a dirt-encrusted child's skull. She took a sip, and ran a finger over the curve of the frontal bone. "Do basilisks have a reputation for doing that? Calling things up?"

He frowned down at a field specimen list. "Frankly, Doctor, I don't know. They had a lot of trouble over in the Valley early in the last century. *Basiliscos* didn't show up much after World War II." He shook his head. "I keep telling myself I don't believe in them."

"We could call Maggie. Find out how to destroy the evil."

"No," he said, and ran a hand through his blond hair. "She has enough problems herding tourists for the Park Service without us exposing her to some sort of ancient Anasazi evil. Let's leave Maggie out of this. Besides, I know how to deal with the little son of a bitch. You're supposed to force the basilisk to look into a mirror. It creates a sort of feedback loop that makes the evil feed on itself and kills the wicked creature."

Dusty leaned over his specimen list again, his brow furrowed.

Maureen went back to her bones. She studied the curved length of femur, puzzled for a moment, and then lifted it, hefting the light tube of bone and sighting down the shaft. "Stewart, I think this child had rickets."

"Huh?"

"Vitamin deficiency. I can't prove that here, in the field, but I probably can in the lab. That, or some soil pressure has caused deformation of the diaphysis."

"In English, please, Doctor."

"Vitamin D fixes calcium in the bones. Without it, bones go soft. This bone curves. See it?"

"Yeah, I do."

Having completed her measurements, taken notes, and made a preliminary description, she rewrapped the bone in tissue and newspaper and replaced it in the box. Then she turned to the skull. The fragment consisted of a child's frontal bone, both orbits—eye sockets—and the maxillary bones. She carefully studied the heat-damaged incisors, cracked and broken by the fire. The alveolar area, the part of the upper jaw just under the nose, had been calcined where the lip had pulled back in response to extreme heat. This, she noted, and then used a bamboo pick to break soil loose from the inside of the orbits.

"It was just so real," Dusty said absently. He was staring off into space, and she could almost see the dream playing behind his eyes. Dusty shook his head. "They must have ritually killed the katchinas, that's why they chopped the hearts out of the paintings and burned the masks."

Throwing caution to the winds, Maureen said, "Maybe the woman was a witch and that's why they burned her in the fire with the masks."

"Possibly. That's a universal way of handling evil."

Maureen paused when she noticed the roughness inside the child's orbits. She turned the thin fragment of skull and squinted at it in the gray light. Reaching for her brush, she carefully whisked dirt out of what should have been the smooth top of the orbit. "I'll be—"

"Be what?"

"I've got *cribra orbitalia* here."

"Why is it that every time I talk to you, I have to keep mentioning that the language of the realm is English, not Latin?"

"Science uses its own language, Stewart." She lifted her hand lens as Dusty rose and crossed to watch her. She smiled at the frothy look of the bone, little holes visible across the concave top of the orbit. She pointed as he leaned over. "Look here. See, this is just above where the eyeball is set. This porosity and irregular bone. That's *cribra orbitalia.*"

"Okay, so it looks like someone boiled the top of the kid's eyeballs. Was that from the fire?"

"No." She cocked her head, glanced at him, and then turned her attention back to the broken piece of skull. "Remember the hypoplasia, the ripples, I saw in the teeth that first day?"

"Yes, the burned mandible."

"That's the one." She indicated the wrapped femur. "Then I see rickets in that femur, and now *cribra* in this skull."

"Which means?"

"These children were really sick. We're seeing nutritional deficiencies everywhere. A lack of vitamin D causes rickets. Iron deficiency is one of the suspected causes of *cribra orbitalia,* and I'm betting I'll get thickening of the cranial vault, uh—the skull bones—as well as *cribra cranii*: holes in the inner table of the braincase. This whole population was under stress."

He braced a hand on the tabletop. "That fits. If my pottery is correct, if these are like the same people we found at 10K3—" He seemed suddenly stunned.

"What is it?"

For a moment, he was silent. "At 10K3, you found tuberculosis among some of those women. Remember? You told me that for there to be that many cases of tuberculosis in the bones, the disease's attack rate had to be through the roof."

She nodded. "That's right."

"Okay," he said, excited. "Then, like 10K3, this site dates to the period about one hundred years after the fall of Chaco. These folks are making Mesa Verdean–style pottery, they're sick, and running, moving from place to place in search of a sanctuary. They're rebuilding the kivas, right? And, I'm willing to bet that once we get through the bone bed and the kiva roof, we're going to find that they remodeled this tower kiva, too."

"Okay. So?"

"Of course they're malnourished. Entire sections of the Southwest were being abandoned at that time. People were fleeing the warfare and crowding into the remaining villages, swelling the population. There had to be a lot of hungry people. Agriculture depends on a predictable workforce."

Dusty picked up the bit of skull and looked into the empty orbits, as if seeing the bright brown eyes that might have once stared back at him. "The poor little guy never had a chance. His whole world was plunging itself into a holocaust."

Maureen unwrapped the fragment of adult femur Sylvia had found. The specimen consisted of the upper, proximal portion, the head, neck, trochanters, and perhaps fifteen centimeters of shaft that ended in a badly calcined end. She couldn't tell if it had been broken, or just burned so badly that the bone had crumbled.

Stewart was still studying the child's face when Maureen bent and took a close look at the femoral neck. Using her hand lens, she squinted in the poor light, studying the bone's exterior, then stopped short. "My, my, look at this."

"What?" He put the skull fragment down and dropped one knee onto the booth's padded seat beside her.

She used her bamboo pick to indicate the irregular grooves that incised the bone just under the femoral neck and above the trochanters. "That's where you cut to sever the ligaments." She turned the bone, exposing the round ball of the femoral head to the light. At the top, where the tendon inserted, the bone was marred, as if it had been sawed at. "I'd say they cut the teres tendon." She looked up. "My first guess, based on the diameter of the shaft, and the smooth surface of the *linea aspera*, is that this is a woman. From the light weight, compared to bone size, I'd say an old woman."

She paused to get his full attention. "Dusty, someone cut this woman apart *before* the kiva burned. An adult femur, surrounded by thick muscle, would not have burned away in mid-shaft."

He looked at her intently. "What does that mean?"

"I'm saying that someone threw those bones on the kiva roof before it burned. She was disarticulated—cut apart—and then her bones were scattered over the roof. The only reason we have this section of bone is that a child's body was lying on top of it, protecting it from the heat."

Dusty slid into the booth beside her, forcing her to move over, and took the bone from her hand. "So the children were marched to the roof and forced to stand in the middle of the bloody bones of one of their elders?"

Maureen sank back against the seat. "That's what it looks like."

CHAPTER 36

THE RITUAL JEWELRY on the people in the plaza winked as they turned to watch Browser pass. He refused to meet their eyes. He walked purposefully, hoping no one would stop him to offer condolences, or to question him about the murder. He was dead tired and needed to be alone.

Ant Woman's words had stirred his souls. Flame Carrier's marriage to Pigeontail disturbed him. If Ant Woman was right, then by the time of the marriage, Flame Carrier must have been greatly revered by her people. She could have had her choice of powerful and esteemed men. Why would Spider Silk order her to marry a young lowly Trader?

A man in a yellow cape took a step toward Browser with his mouth open, and Browser held up a hand and shook his head.

The man called, "Perhaps later, War Chief?"

"Yes. Thank you for your understanding."

The unknown man turned back to his friends.

Browser watched his feet. Stone Ghost and Redcrop spoke softly behind him, but he ignored their words. His own mother had ordered him to marry Ash Girl, but he had understood her reasons. Spider Silk's order made no sense.

Children sat with their backs to the western wall, plucking food from the array of baskets, stew pots hanging from tripods, and platters of fried breads. Most of the village elders had gathered on the roof of the great kiva. The drying ears of corn had been stacked around the rim of the roof, creating a speckled, many-colored circle four hands high. Wading Bird's scratchy old voice carried, then he laughed.

Springbank shoved through the crowd, his age-spotted face taut, his toothless mouth sucked in as though he was upset. He wore a beautiful white ritual cape covered with glistening circlets of seashells. He called, "War Chief?"

Browser stopped. This one, he could not refuse. "Yes, Elder?"

"Have you seen Obsidian?"

"No, Elder. Why?"

Anger strained his ancient face. "Ant Woman asked me to make certain that Obsidian remembers she is bringing food to the tower kiva for the children tonight, but I haven't seen her since midday. Nor has anyone else. Where can she be?"

Browser shrugged. Fatigue made him less cautious than he would ordinarily have been. He said: "She tells me nothing, Elder. She turns even simple questions like 'Where were you born?' into a game. Perhaps that's what she's doing today. Playing a game of hide-and-seek."

Springbank balled his fists and drew them beneath his cape. "As for where she was born, she once told me she was born here. As for whether or not she's playing a game, I promise to find out. If you see her, tell her we have things to discuss, and I want her to come to me immediately."

"Yes, Elder."

Springbank dipped his head to Stone Ghost, then marched across the plaza like a warrior on a mission.

"War Chief?" Redcrop called.

Browser turned. "Yes?"

"If you are finished with me, I think I will start sorting through the Matron's things, trying to decide what she would wish people to have."

"You are free to go, Redcrop. Thank you for accompanying us to speak with Ant Woman."

Stone Ghost reached out and lightly placed a hand on her shoulder. "Come for me if you need help. I did not know her as you did, but I can carry things and place them where you tell me to."

Her pretty face looked pale and gaunt. "Thank you, Elder, but you must have many more important things to do. Straighthorn told me he would help me tonight."

Browser said, "I saw him go into his chamber just before I went to fetch you from the burial. I think he's still there."

Redcrop turned toward the ground-floor room where Straighthorn lived at the base of the tower kiva. Water Snake stood guard on the kiva roof. He held his war club in his hand. "I do not wish to disturb Straighthorn if he is sleeping. He has to stand guard from midnight to dawn."

Browser said, "He's spent most of the day in his chamber, Redcrop. I suspect he's slept for several hands of time. Why don't you go and see."

She smiled. "Yes, thank you. I will. I wish you both a pleasant burial feast."

"And you, also," Stone Ghost said.

They watched Redcrop make her way through the crowd toward Straighthorn's chamber. Several people stopped her to speak with her.

Stone Ghost looked at Browser from the corner of his eye. Wind Baby's voice had eased to a whisper, fluttering people's capes and tousling their hair. Stone Ghost kept his voice down. "Pigeontail seems an odd choice, doesn't he, Nephew? Is that what you were thinking?"

Browser nodded. "Yes, Uncle."

As the afternoon light swelled, slow and gold, over the village, the walls shimmered.

Stone Ghost said, "You should try to rest for as long as you can. People will be clamoring to speak with you when the nightly Dances begin."

"I know, Uncle."

Every bit of his strength had been focused upon organizing their guards to best protect the surviving villagers and guests, while at the same time struggling to understand why their Matron had been murdered, and by whom. All the while, the mystery of Aspen village lay buried in his souls. Weariness had numbed his wits as well as his body. He needed rest.

"I will speak with you later, Nephew," Stone Ghost said, and he hobbled across the plaza for the great kiva.

Wading Bird, Cloudblower, and the other elders sat in the center with blankets clutched about their shoulders. Another thirty people crouched around them, listening to the tales they told. In the sky above the elders, flocks of Cloud People billowed, glowing the purest white Browser had ever seen.

He glanced over his shoulder toward Catkin's chamber. She would be sound asleep by now. He wished she'd heard the conversation with Ant Woman, but he would tell her every detail later. With everything that had been happening, he'd had little time to really sit and talk with her. He missed the soft sound of her voice.

Browser walked toward his chamber. As he slipped beneath his door curtain, the sweetness of blazing star petals struck him. He glanced around at the darkness. Had she been here?

"Obsidian?"

A shadow moved on his bedding hides, and in the light that streamed around his door curtain, he caught a glimmer of blue dress. A hundred tiny jeweled pins winked through her hair as she lazily rolled to her back.

Browser stiffened. For an instant he thought she was Ash Girl, his dead wife—and it wasn't the first time that had happened. Three or four times in the past nine moons he'd caught himself replacing Obsidian's face with Ash Girl's. He shook himself and clenched his fists. "What are you doing here?"

"Waiting for you, War Chief."

"Why?"

She stretched like a bobcat in warm sunlight, her arms over her head, her back arching, forcing her full breasts to strain against the fabric of her dress. "You know why."

Browser hesitated, then removed his cape under that dark intense gaze and hung it on the peg by the door. "You have been dogging my steps for moons, Obsidian. No matter where I am, I expect to see you watching me. Do I entertain you that much?"

"Let us speak for a time, Browser. Perhaps we can overcome this—this unpleasantness."

"I don't think so, Obsidian. And if I were you, I would rush outside. Elder Springbank is searching for you, and he isn't happy. He told me to tell you he has things to discuss with you and wishes to see you immediately."

She waved a hand. "He is never happy with me. He spends half his days watching me like a hawk, and the other half ordering me about as though I were his daughter, or worse, his slave. The old man can wait."

She tipped her chin and gazed at him with those warm black eyes, and Browser had to fight to control his emotions. He genuinely disliked her, but that meant nothing to his body. His manhood responded to her beauty whether he wished it to or not.

"All right," he said, exhaling hard. "I grant you one finger of time. But speak quickly."

Browser walked to his warming bowl in the middle of the room and pulled a twig from the woodpile. As he laid it on the coals, smoke drifted up. He lightly blew on the fresh tinder. It took a few moments for the twig to catch, then a pale wavering light flickered over the white walls, and danced in her black eyes.

She said, "I heard that you asked Straighthorn about me."

Browser didn't look up, but he wondered at that. He doubted Straighthorn had told her about their conversation. Calmly, he answered, "You have a mysterious background, Obsidian."

"Is that what Straighthorn told you?"

"He told me that twenty-five summers ago your mother married a Longtail man named Shell Ring. After his death, Crossbill adopted you and your mother into the clan. You were seven at the time."

She propped herself up on one elbow, and a wealth of thick hair tumbled around her shoulders. "Straighthorn had not even been born yet. How would he know?"

Sparks crackled and whirled through the air that separated them.

Browser replied, "People hear stories, Obsidian. He's lived in the same village as you for sixteen summers."

"Few people speak about those days. I'm surprised he knows that much."

"Why does no one speak of it? How long were you married to Ten Hawks?"

Her graceful brows lifted. "How long were you married to Ash Girl?"

"That's not an answer."

"But 'people hear stories,' War Chief. I would like to know. How long?"

Grudgingly, he said, "Five summers. We—"

"You lived with her for five summers and did not know she had a monster soul inside her?" Her eyes gleamed at his expression. The words affected him like the blows of a war club. She'd done it deliberately, taking control of the conversation. "You must have seen it peeking out at you when you fought with her."

Browser toyed with the woodpile, rearranging the twigs. "I suppose, but I did not realize what I was seeing, Obsidian."

With mock compassion, she said, "Poor Browser. He didn't have the courage to gaze into the murderous eyes of the woman he loved."

Browser gave her a thin smile. "Feel better?"

"A bit."

"Good. I've answered some questions for you. Now do me the same honor. I am confused by the stories your people tell about you. When we first arrived, Crossbill told me that you were not human, that you had flown down from the skyworld as a meteorite. She said that your mother had caught you, and when she opened her hands, she found a baby girl there."

Obsidian rolled to her side to face him. "Yes, my mother told me the same ridiculous story."

Browser tilted his head. "Did you ask her about your father?"

She toyed with the hide. "Of course I asked. Many times. She would tell me nothing, and I could see the pain in her eyes when she spoke of him."

"Do you recall him at all?"

Obsidian ran a jeweled hand through her long hair and her voice turned soft. "Sometimes. But I'm not sure if they are real memories or the longings of a lonely child for a father."

Browser added another twig to the fire. "What do you recall?"

"In my dreams, I often feel hands upon me, smoothing my skin like warm fur. I think they are his hands."

Browser looked up sharply. "I don't understand."

She rose to her knees, tipped her chin up, and closed her eyes. "Like this," she whispered.

She ran her hands over her arms and throat, as though showing him her dreams, then her hands moved lower. She caressed her breasts and let her fingers slowly glide down her narrow waist to her groin. It was the most sensual display Browser had ever seen. Even if he had wished to, he could not have taken his eyes from her.

"Obsidian—"

She opened her eyes. "You asked if I recalled anything about him. That is what I remember."

He paused, not certain if he should make the accusation. ". . . Incest?"

"No, I don't think so. I only recall his hands. If he'd taken me, I think I would recall much more. Wouldn't you?"

Browser inclined his head. "I don't know. I've heard that children often don't recall such violations."

She lay back down and curled on her side on his buffalo hide, watching him with onyx eyes. "Because your wife didn't?"

Browser clenched his fists. "Yes. That is one reason."

Her gaze moved leisurely, tracing the line of his broad shoulders, then his chest, and finally dropping to his manhood. She moaned softly. Without taking her gaze from him, she stood and walked around the fire toward him.

He lurched to his feet.

As though reaching for a frightened child, Obsidian extended her hands until her fingers almost touched his knotted stomach muscles. The firelight glimmered through her magnificent hair. "Take my hands. It is not as difficult as you imagine, War Chief."

"I don't wish this, Obsidian."

"You do. You know you do."

She placed her hands on his sides and smoothed them down over his hips.

He grabbed her hands and held them. He could imagine himself gently removing each turquoise pin that adorned her hair, slipping her blue dress over her head, pulling her naked body against his.

"What was his name, Obsidian? Your father's name? Did your mother ever tell you?"

Her mouth twisted into a pout again. "What difference does it make?"

"If you came here twenty-five summers ago, do you remember hearing stories about Two Hearts?"

"The legendary witch?"

Browser nodded. "Crossbill's grandmother and many other clan matrons had dispatched war parties to hunt him down for his crimes."

"I had seen seven summers, Browser. I may have heard about it, but I do not recall—"

"What about the stories of the cursed little girl who lived in this village thirty summers ago? You must have heard about that."

She leaned forward until her breasts pressed against his hands. The sensation was akin to being struck by lightning. His whole body throbbed.

"That wasn't me, Browser. Is that what you fear? That I have been tainted by incest, like your wife? Is that why you won't touch me?"

"I won't touch you because I don't wish to, Obsidian. I—"

She bent to kiss his hands, and he abruptly released her and backed into the wall. Before he could avoid it, Obsidian stepped forward, slipped one arm around his waist, and with the other hand reached for his manhood.

He roughly shoved her toward the door curtain. "Enough. Leave!"

She stumbled, grasped the leather curtain to steady herself, and turned. Her smile mocked him.

"You were close, War Chief. A hair's breadth. The next time, this will end differently. You know that, don't you?"

"There won't be a next time."

She laughed and ducked under the curtain into the afternoon sunlight.

Browser stood for a moment, breathing hard, then he pulled his red war shirt over his head and threw it on the floor.

He paced his chamber like a caged lion, wondering what she wanted, what game she played. She apparently needed Browser to win. But how could that be? What did he have that she...

His gaze went to his buckskin cape hanging on the peg by the door.

That morning she'd asked him where "it" was.

The turquoise wolf would be a prize for anyone, but how could she know he possessed it? No one knew, except Uncle Stone Ghost and Catkin.

And the man who lost it.

CHAPTER 37

REDCROP'S WHITE CAPE whipped around her legs as she climbed the ladder to the tower kiva and stepped onto the plastered roof. Straighthorn's chamber sat to her left, sandwiched between Elder Springbank's chamber and Obsidian's. Her feet thudded hollowly as she walked from the kiva roof, onto the elder's roof, and toward the ladder that stood in Straighthorn's roof entry.

People in the plaza turned to watch her. The kind looks, the tears, went straight to her heart. The din of conversations died down, then picked up again.

Straighthorn called, "Redcrop? Is that you?"

"Yes. Were you sleeping? I don't wish to disturb you. I know you have to stand guard—"

"I'm coming up," he said, and his steps patted the ladder.

As he stepped onto the roof, he gave her a desperate look. He'd changed into his ritual clothing, a pale green knee-length shirt studded with circlets of polished buffalo horn, black leather leggings, and sandals. When Wind Baby pressed his shirt against his body, she could see his muscles.

"Come with me."

The urgency in his voice made her stutter, "W-why? What is it?"

He took her by the arm. "We must find a place to speak alone."

"But I was going to sort through Grandmother's belongings—"

"I'll help you later. This can't wait."

"What's wrong, Straighthorn?"

He dragged her toward the ladder propped against the village's long northern wall. Behind the village, a grove of junipers covered the hillside. The villagers hadn't cut them down for firewood because they collected the juniper berries to make teas and to season meats. If they stayed here long enough, however, they would cut them down. It always happened. A bad winter would come along and they would need the wood more than they needed next year's berry crop.

"You go first," Straighthorn said, and steadied the ladder for her.

Redcrop climbed down into the lacy shade of the trees. Sunlight gleamed from the brown bed of dried juniper needles. "Please tell me? What is it?"

Straighthorn jumped to the ground. "Let's sit in the shade over there."

Redcrop followed him to the fragrant spot between the trees and sat down at his side. Sweat gleamed on his long hooked nose and above his full lips. His shoulder-length hair had been freshly washed, and blue glints danced through the strands.

"Straighthorn?"

He knotted his fists. "The War Chief told me why you insisted on being alone this morning. I want to know why you agreed to do it?"

Redcrop felt the blood rise into her cheeks. "I—I wish to help catch them."

Straighthorn massaged his forehead. "I accompanied the War Chief down into the drainage to look at the little girl's tracks. Redcrop, the man who helped murder your grandmother was there. I saw his tracks! I know—"

"I know, too, Straighthorn. The War Chief told me."

He stared at her. "You know that the murderer was that close to you, and you don't care?"

"That's why I was out there. To be seen."

His mouth fell open. He looked as though he wished to shout at her, but his voice came out unnaturally quiet: "Blessed gods, do you realize what might happen? If he captures you—"

"I'm being closely guarded, Straighthorn. Catkin was watching me the whole time. When I went over the crest of the hill into the drainage, she came running as fast as she could."

"How long did it take her to get there?"

Redcrop shrugged. "Less than five hundred heartbeats."

"Do you know what can happen in five hundred heartbeats? He could have killed you and left you for Catkin to find! He could have clubbed you and carried you off somewhere to torment for days!"

Redcrop squirmed. "I know I shouldn't have followed the tracks. Catkin already shouted at me and made me promise never to leave her sight again, and I won't, Straighthorn. I'll stay just where the War Chief tells me to. But I—"

"I don't want you out there at all!"

"But Straighthorn, please, I—"

He took her by the shoulders in a move that startled her. "Listen to me. I have been too worried to sleep, or eat. I could barely contain myself long enough to dress for the sunset Dances. The War Chief is using you! Why can't he use someone else? A woman warrior would work just as well, and she would be able to—"

"I asked to do it, Straighthorn."

In a soft, agonized voice, he said, "Blessed gods. Why?"

"I want to help the War Chief catch him."

"There are other ways for you to help, Redcrop. You could—"

"Straighthorn, nine moons ago we often heard that a woman or girl was missing. We assumed raiders had caught them and taken them as slaves, but later we found their bodies. Most of them still wore the jewelry they'd had on the day they disappeared. Grandmother sent word to the nearby villages, and people came to see if they could find their missing loved ones. Some did." Her voice fell to a whisper. "It was terrible. If the same man killed my grandmother, I have to help the War Chief stop him."

"That's why I'm frightened for you, Redcrop. If he catches you—"

"He won't. After today, the War Chief said he's going to put many more guards on me. All I have to do is sit alone and wait for him to try to take me, Straighthorn. Then, when he does, we'll capture him." Redcrop gazed down at the towering walls of the village. As Father Sun sank below the western mountains, shadows crawled over Longtail, turning the walls a deep gray.

Straighthorn took her hands in a hard grip. "I know you wish to help find the murderer, but this is madness. If this man is the famed witch named Two Hearts, he has escaped every trap ever laid for him. Twenty-five summers ago, dozens of villages banded together to hunt him down. They sent their best warriors, burned every hole he might be hiding in, questioned every person who might have spoken to him or known him before he became a witch. None of it worked. He's still killing!"

Wind gusted over the hill and whipped Redcrop's shorn hair into her eyes. She shivered. "It's not just us I wish to help, Straighthorn. I'm afraid for the little girl. I was stolen from my people. I know how it feels."

"She may not be a slave, Redcrop."

"If she is his daughter, she needs my help even more."

Straighthorn suddenly wrapped his arms around Redcrop and hugged her. "Gods, I'm afraid you'll be hurt!"

He smelled of yucca soap and woodsmoke, things she found comforting. The first tendril of relief crept through her. It felt like cool salve on a fevered wound. "I'll be careful, Straighthorn. I will."

"Tomorrow, I'm going to the War Chief, Redcrop. I want to guard you myself. That's the only way I'll be able to carry out my duties. If you are out of my sight, I'll think of nothing else."

Redcrop lifted her head to look into his concerned eyes. "Thank you. I won't be afraid if I know you are watching me."

He gave her a pained smile. "When are you supposed to go back out?"

"He wants me on the hill overlooking the grave at dusk."

Straighthorn shook his head. "I am supposed to be standing guard east of the village tonight. Perhaps I can switch with someone . . ."

"Speak with the War Chief tomorrow, Straighthorn. That will be soon enough. I don't think anything will happen tonight, not with the Death Dances going on."

Straighthorn looked at the eastern horizon. A thin layer of dust blew over the hills and feathered the sky like delicate brush strokes. She could tell he didn't agree with her words.

In a worried voice, he said, "I pray you are right," and hugged her so hard his arms shook.

He had never held her like this before. The feel of his arms made the world go away. Redcrop closed her eyes and leaned against him.

CHAPTER 38

"TRUCK COMING," SYLVIA said, and lifted her head over the rim of the excavation unit where she worked with Steve. He rose beside her and squinted down the road.

The chatter of a diesel could be heard over the afternoon stillness.

Maureen straightened and stretched her aching back muscles. The bright candy red truck motored over the hill and down toward the camp.

"'Bout time," Sylvia said. "We've been out of beer for over twenty-four hours."

"A tragedy of biblical proportions," Maureen said and smiled. She wiped her dirty face on the sleeve of her black sweatshirt and smoothed sweaty, tangled hair away from her face. "I've been looking forward to this. I haven't seen Dale in over a year."

"Go give him a bear hug," Sylvia said, "and ask him where the hell he and the beer have been."

Maureen followed the planks off the kiva rubble and walked to the camp trailer. Dusty had already jumped out and was watching the big

Dodge pickup park behind the Bronco. Sweat darkened the armpits and chest of his long-sleeved green T-shirt. He brushed futilely at the grime on his pants as he walked down toward the road.

When Maureen caught up with Dusty, he said, "You think we ought to tell him that while he was gone, we got engaged? You know, just to see what his reaction is?"

Maureen's mouth dropped open. "Not on your life."

"Oh, come on. Then we could both say, 'Trick-or-treat,' and walk off."

"You are a sick man, Stewart."

Dale turned off the engine and opened the door. He put one foot on the sculptured running board and then lowered himself to the ground. He wore khaki pants with a gray shirt and his battered old brown fedora. Wiry steel-colored hair stuck out beneath the brim.

Maureen walked forward. "Hey, Dale! It's been a long time."

"Maureen! You look beautiful."

She stepped into his arms and he hugged her fiercely. Through his coat, she could feel his bones and stringy old muscles. No matter that he kept himself in good shape, the fact remained that he was seventy-three this year. She patted his back, stepped away, then resettled his fedora.

A happy glow filled his eyes. "How have you been?"

"I'm better, thanks. I really needed this break. Thanks for easing the way. I think the department would have let me come anyway, but a call from you never hurts a thing."

"My pleasure." He smiled, and the action rearranged the wrinkles that a thousand suns had burned into his face. He glanced suspiciously at Dusty, who stood by the trailer corner, his arms crossed. The battered brim of the brown cowboy hat and the mirror sunglasses hid any expression above his grim mouth. "And William? Has he been treating you well?"

"Sticking me with dental picks and roasting me at every opportunity. 'Doctor' this, 'Doctor' that."

Dale sighed. "Well, what can I say?"

"Actually, I'm joking," she whispered. "Miracles do happen. We've done fine. Although on my off moments I contemplate dousing his truck with gasoline and setting fire to it and all of its little inhabitants."

Dale frowned. "I don't follow you."

"It's a long story. Just trust me. Don't turn on the heater."

"Oh," he said with an exaggerated nod. "I *do* follow you."

He smiled, took Maureen's arm, and started toward Dusty. "Hello, William. I don't suppose that you have any coffee in there? I left Zuni before the crows cawed. I thought about stopping at Farmington, and then again at Aztec, but I wanted to get here."

Dusty cocked his head. "I'll trade you a cup of coffee for what they told you in Tucson."

Dale smiled. "Sample one, taken from the big log, dated to A.D. 1108. Sample two, from the little log, dated to A.D. 1258."

Dusty smacked a fist into his hand. "Am I good, or what? I knew the pottery matched."

"Matched what?" Dale asked on the way to the trailer door.

"A hunch the good Doctor and I will let you in on once we get caught up." Dusty held the door while Dale stepped inside. The trailer rocked and squeaked as they followed him in. Dale stopped short when he saw Maureen's sleeping bag on the foldout couch in the front.

"My tent blew down in the storm, Dale," Maureen told him. "Dusty let me sleep on the couch."

Dale's bristly mustache twitched. "What did you do, Doctor, slip him a little Prozac when he wasn't watching his beer bottle?"

Dusty answered for her: "Given the nightmares I've been having, a little Prozac sounds really good."

"What nightmares?" Dale asked as he slid into the booth behind the table. His khaki pants and gray shirt matched the colors of the dirt on the table.

Maureen slid into the booth opposite Dale and looked at Dusty, wondering if he'd actually tell Dale.

"Nothing. Just kidding," Dusty said. He rolled up the long sleeves of his green T-shirt, reached for the water jug, and went about fixing a pot of coffee.

Dale turned to Maureen, and his brows lifted questioningly. She shook her head. It was Dusty's place to share that information, not hers. She figured he'd tell Dale when he couldn't stand it any longer.

As he poured grounds into the basket, Dusty said, "I'm surprised they let you run the samples that quickly."

Dale cleaned off a small spot and propped his elbows on the table. "Oh, of course, William. When I was a kid I used to core samples. Half of the reference specimens in the lab are there because I provided them. All those years of sending them little cylinders of wood ought to be worth something." He gave Dusty a curious look. "But, outside of the rain, which is why I assume you shut down, what have you found?"

"We have a kiva filled with burned children, and at least one adult. We found another old woman's skull."

"The one with the hole in it?" Dale asked, as he smoothed his fingers over his mustache.

"No, this one had burned in the kiva fire. So that makes two adult female skulls—one burned, one not. Then, yesterday, Maureen identified an adult femur. Probably female. She was cut up, her flesh stripped, and the bone tossed onto the roof before it burned."

Dale grunted to himself, then glanced at Maureen. "What do you think?"

"I'll know more when I get the specimens to the lab. You don't have any more Butvar, do you? Or polyvinyl acetate, to stabilize the bone for transport? I've used all of mine. Some of the bone is very fragile. The calcined stuff is like dust. Touch it and it falls apart."

"I got Dusty's message to bring you some. It's in the truck." He smiled at her. Then his expression turned dour. "I'm going to tell you immediately so we can get this out of the way. I've been in touch with the Wirths. I must say, I gave them the preliminary report that we had a great number of bodies coming out of the kiva. My impression was that they were a little stunned."

"So am I," Maureen said. "What's the—"

"What's wrong?" Dusty set the coffeepot on the burner and turned from the stove with a dreadful expression. "I've heard that tone in your voice before, Dale. It usually spells disaster. What's the problem with the Wirths?"

Dale took off his fedora and smoothed a hand over his gray hair. "Well, they want to make a housing development here. A subdivision based on an Anasazi theme. You know, touch the past, take a moonlight stroll through the ruins. Own your own little piece of prehistory. That was the marketing plan."

"Yeah, so?"

Dale sighed. "It would seem they're having problems with the data, William. What we are finding here isn't what they had expected. They wanted a clean kiva, maybe with some intact murals. They're nice people, but they're modern Americans. They purchased this land with the notion of selling romantic home sites. The romance of the Anasazi, William."

"The truth isn't quite so romantic? Is that what you mean?"

"Well, yes. I mean, we're not playing according to the American myth. This is a new age of hope and prosperity. The baby boomers, who don't believe in war, who believe that Indians were saints before the coming of Columbus, are filling this country. That's what the Wirths were banking on. How do you sell a seven-hundred-and-fifty-year-old mass grave? How do you convince buyers to come and build million-dollar houses on land where someone incinerated a group of children?"

Dusty slumped against the counter and hung his head. "Okay, give me the bottom line, Dale. Are they going to shut down the excavation?"

Dale spread his hands. "You'll know in a few days. They're getting on a plane tomorrow morning."

Dusty paled. He glanced at Maureen and she could see his fear. "Great. That's just great."

CHAPTER 39

BILLOWING CLOUD PEOPLE drifted through the lavender sky, their hearts blazing as though aflame, while their edges glowed like eiderdown.

Stone Ghost stopped to look at them, and inhaled the mingled fragrances of roasted pumpkin seeds and cedar smoke that filled the village.

Dusk seemed to magnify sounds. He could hear turkeys gobbling and macaws squawking. Dogs snarled at each other as they trotted around in search of dropped bits of food. Hungry infants wailed on the northern side of the plaza where mothers had retreated to talk and nurse their babies, and a general hum came from the crowded plaza.

A little while ago, Ant Woman had taken fifty or sixty children into the tower kiva to tell them stories. Death Dances often lasted all night. If the children listened to the Creation stories and napped for a time before the Dances began, they did not complain as much.

Stone Ghost propped his walking stick and searched the gathering.

Three young women moved around the village, lighting shredded yucca bark torches. With each new torch, more faces were illuminated in the plaza, but he did not see Obsidian. The shining white heads of the elders sitting along the western wall reflected the yellow light.

Warriors seemed to be everywhere: on the roofs, around the perimeter of the plaza; several stood guard on the high points around the village. A group of ten men huddled outside the great kiva in front of Stone Ghost, whispering with about twenty people from Dry Creek village. The Dry Creek villagers could be easily identified because most wore yellow ritual capes. Bows and quivers hung from every warrior's shoulder.

Obsidian emerged from her chamber on the western side of the plaza, and Stone Ghost nodded to himself. She saw him, glared, and looked away.

He cupped a hand to his mouth and called, "Obsidian?" then waved to get her attention. "May I speak with you?"

Everyone in the village turned to gaze at him, including Obsidian. He gestured for her to come over, and throughout the crowd people whispered and shook their heads.

Obsidian glanced around. She couldn't refuse such a request from one of the village elders, but she clearly did not wish to comply. She gathered her long blue skirt in her hands and swept across the plaza with the grace of a dancer. She'd tied her long white ritual cape at the throat, but through the front opening he could see the intricately decorated bodice of her blue dress; it glittered with red-and-white beads. Every man in the village watched as she passed, as did several of the women.

"Ah, Obsidian," Stone Ghost said when she stopped before him. "You look especially lovely tonight. I hope that you—"

"Tell me what you want, old man. Water Snake said you questioned him. Is that why you waved me over? You wish to blister me with your tongue?"

Stone Ghost pointed to the shining coral beads that netted her hair and flickered like sparks when she moved. "That is a very old and beautiful style, beads in a woman's hair. I haven't seen a woman wear her hair that way in sixty summers or more. Did your mother wear her hair that way?"

"Yes," she said suspiciously, as though fearing ulterior motives for the question. "But I doubt that you called me over to discuss beads. *What do you want?*"

Stone Ghost moved the point of his walking stick and shifted his weight to his left hip. It didn't hurt as badly on cold nights like this. "Forgive me for disturbing you. I realize this is a difficult time for you. You must be grieving." She did not, however, appear to be. "I promise my questions will be short."

"Then begin."

Stone Ghost rocked against his walking stick. "I wished to speak with you because Water Snake's story confused me. He said—"

"He confuses everyone," she replied as if bored by the thought of Water Snake. "It is his way."

"Really? Well, he told me he did not hear the Matron's screams, and I—"

"Of course he didn't. He heard nothing but his own squealing."

As her implications seeped in, his brows arched. "I've never known a man who could 'squeal' loud enough to cover death screams, Obsidian. Surely there must be more."

Obsidian folded her arms beneath her full breasts, and looked at Stone Ghost with cold eyes. "Do you wish me to tell you straightly, or shall I smooth the edges for your elderly ears?"

"Straightly, please. At my age, time is too valuable for smooth edges."

"Very well. Water Snake is a fool. He did not wish to couple on the roof where anyone might see us. He insisted we go inside. I didn't wish to. I like to feel the fresh night air on my skin."

"I see. Where did you go? To your chamber? To his?"

She laughed as though he'd said something ludicrous. "I would never invite Water Snake to my chamber. He's a slug." She gave him a sly smile. "I would, however, be very pleased to have your nephew in my chamber."

She obviously expected Stone Ghost to deliver that message, which, of course, meant he would go out of his way not to.

Stone Ghost pressed, "Where did you and Water Snake go to couple, Obsidian?"

She smoothed her jeweled hands down over her cape and said, "Inside the tower kiva."

She smiled, apparently pleased with herself. Not only had she lured Water Snake from his guard duties, she had desecrated the kiva.

"Ah, well, that makes everything clearer. How long were you in the kiva?"

"Less than a finger of time. Water Snake couples like a mouse. He squirms, squeals, and runs away."

Singing rose from the great kiva, accompanied by the faint heartbeat of a drum. Soon the drummer would emerge, the flute players would follow, then the katsinas would rise up from the underworlds and spread out across the plaza. He didn't have much time.

Stone Ghost said, "I would like to know why you did not marry again after you divorced Ten Hawks."

Obsidian frowned at the sudden change of topic. "Why do you care? I didn't marry again because I didn't wish to."

"But you are a striking woman. Surely you could have married any man you wished. A war chief, a wealthy Trader, perhaps a powerful—"

"Yes. I could have."

Stone Ghost held her hot gaze. "I spoke with Crossbill today. She said you were plagued by suitors after Ten Hawks left, but you rejected them all without even speaking with them."

As though impatient, she snapped, "My life is none of your concern, old man! If you wish to question me about the night of the Matron's murder, well enough, but I have duties. I am supposed to deliver sweet corn cakes to the tower kiva—"

"Yes, I know I'm delaying you, and ordinarily I wouldn't. But, you see, I started wondering about you after Matron Crossbill said that you had a sister. Since then, I have been quietly asking around. How old are you?"

Her glare turned icy. "I have seen thirty-two summers."

"Are you certain? Is that what your mother told you?"

"Of course I'm sure! Why would my mother lie to me about my age?"

Stone Ghost smiled in a harmless elderly way. "I doubt that she would, I was just curious. How did your father die?"

"Great Ancestors, these are silly questions! There is no secret about that! He was standing guard one night and someone shot an arrow through his heart."

Many eyes turned to them when Obsidian raised her voice, but they stood far enough away from the other mourners that Stone Ghost did not think they could be overheard. He kept his voice low anyway. "What about your mother? How long after Shell Ring's death was she killed?"

Obsidian searched his face, as though trying to ferret out his real meaning. "Six or seven moons. You may ask anyone. They will tell you the same thing. Why do you care?"

"Oh," he answered mildly, "it is just a problem I have been considering. What clan was your mother?"

Obsidian tightened her arms beneath her breasts, and the flesh swelled against the blue fabric. "She was Ant Clan, why?"

"And Shell Ring?"

"I think he was Buffalo Clan. What difference does it make?"

"None really. Old people like me are just curious about family. Perhaps because family is all we have left, and we cherish it so much. That's why I'm happy you like my nephew. He and I are the last living members of our family."

The Cloud People had turned a fine gossamer shade of purple. As Wind Baby pushed them, thin threads stretched across the southern horizon.

Stone Ghost said, "My grandmother Orenda once told me that the Blessed Cornsilk was Ant Clan. Perhaps you are related to her. That would be a great honor, wouldn't it? Everyone wishes to be—"

"If you have nothing of importance to say to me, I have duties, Elder."

"Yes, I'm sure you do. Forgive me. There is just one other thing that has been troubling me. Crossbill told me that you had seen seven summers when you and your mother joined the Longtail Clan."

"Yes. What of it?"

"That would have been twenty-five summers ago, yes?"

"Yes," she answered irritably.

Stone Ghost scratched at his wrinkled chin. "Well, I'm confused. You see, Longtail Clan has only lived here for about ten summers, but Elder Springbank told my nephew he had heard you say that you were born here, in this village. That leads me to wonder how old you were when you and your mother left here and headed south to find the Longtail Clan? Five, perhaps? Six?"

Obsidian went still. Her gaze searched the crowd as though trying to find Springbank, then it landed on Stone Ghost's chin. She didn't seem to be breathing, as though his words had knocked the air out of her lungs.

"Did I say something wrong?" he asked.

She spun around and ran across the plaza with her white cape flapping.

Stone Ghost touched his chin. Few people these days knew what the spirals meant, thank the gods. His mother had been the last person who dared to identify her children, and she had lived to regret it. All of Stone Ghost's sisters had been murdered. He did not know why he had been spared.

Yes, few people knew what the spirals meant, but at least two did. He and Obsidian.

Stone Ghost blinked suddenly. "Oh, Blessed gods, that's why her mother was killed. And—and that's why Obsidian did not remarry!"

A cold shiver went through him.

Could it be true?

Stone Ghost glanced around the plaza. Over the heads of two shorter men, he saw Skink watching him. When Stone Ghost looked directly at Skink, the warrior's gaze immediately dropped, and he spoke to one of the men in his circle. He couldn't have overheard the discussion with Obsidian, could he? Obsidian had raised her voice often enough that a careful listener might have been able to piece together some of the conversation. Though very few people would have grasped its dire significance.

Stone Ghost turned away.

Cornsilk and Poor Singer had escaped the wrath of the Made People because they were raised by Made People and adopted into Made People clans—though they later disowned those clans. Stone Ghost's great-grandmother, Night Sun, had not been that lucky. As the last great Matron of Talon Town, the most magnificent and powerful town in the Straight Path Nation, she had been quite a prize. Made People had captured her and tortured her to death in front of her husband, Ironwood. Legends said that she had never cried out, not even once, because she couldn't bear his tears.

Like Night Sun, Obsidian's mother had married one of the Made People, and thereby violated a sacred trust: *First People only marry other First People.*

Stone Ghost propped his walking stick and rubbed his forehead.

"Is it possible?"

Was someone tracking down the last of the First People, studying their lives, and meting out punishment for their transgressions?

The thought sickened Stone Ghost.

Before Obsidian made it to her chamber, Springbank cut her off. The old man lifted a fist and shook it in Obsidian's face. Stone Ghost couldn't hear the words, but he could tell from Springbank's expression that they were not kind words. Obsidian stood like an indignant clan Matron, her breast heaving.

Though Stone Ghost had been looking forward to the Dances, he walked in the opposite direction, away from the village plaza, and out into the growing darkness.

THE LANTERN HISSED, its white light illuminating the inside of the trailer. Maureen fought a yawn as she removed her measuring tools from her field kit and spread newspaper across the table.

Dusty stood with his back to her, his hands in the dishwater, scrubbing the pot they'd used to make chili. Dale sat to her right, one elbow propped on the booth's backrest, his pipe clenched between his teeth as he puffed. His soft dark eyes were focused somewhere in the distance, perhaps on a memory of another long-ago field camp.

Dusty shook the silverware off and set it in the drainer. Then he pulled a dishtowel from the oven door and used it to dry the big aluminum pot. "You know, you can't leave chili in an aluminum pot."

"Why's that?" Dale asked absently.

"I made a batch of chili once back when they used to hold the Little Snake Rendezvous in Wyoming. Won the chili cook-off, but I didn't clean the pot. Left it in the back of the Bronco. By the time I got back to Craig, Colorado—I was working up there that year, doing Fremont stuff—the chili had eaten a thousand pinholes in the aluminum. You could hold it up and see light through it."

Dale grunted in assent, one hand cupping the bowl of his pipe.

"So, what's in chili that dissolves aluminum?" Maureen looked up. "And doesn't the same thing also eat the human stomach?"

"Relax," Dusty said. "Have you ever known a hard-core Mexican to have an ulcer?"

"We don't have a whole lot of hard-core Mexicans in Ontario, Stewart."

"Well, believe me. It's only the Anglos that get ulcers in New Mexico. That and the coconuts."

Maureen arched an eyebrow. Forget it. She didn't want to know. Instead, she opened the cardboard box that contained the old woman's skull. Unwrapping it from the bubblewrap, Maureen withdrew a fabric donut from her kit and rested the skull carefully on it. The donut shape not only cushioned the delicate bone, it kept it from rolling.

"How is the room beside the kiva coming?" Dale asked, glancing Dusty's way. "Have you and Steve finished removing the rubble?"

Dusty stuffed the pan into a drawer and dried his hands on the dishtowel. He turned, drying his hand. His muscles bunched and corded under his tanned forearms. She watched his fingers, twining with the fabric as they worked the towel.

"We ran two screenloads." Dusty said. "We'll be down to floor fill by noon, I'd say. If there's anything there, we ought to be into it."

"And then?" Dale puffed out a blue cloud. The tobacco had a sweet aroma, one that, if Maureen *had* to suffer through, could at least be tolerated.

"Open another room, I guess." Dusty tilted his head, questioningly.

"I'd say it would be best to move into the kiva with Maureen and Sylvia." Dale pointed at Dusty with his pipe stem. "Call it a hunch. I'd say we'd best finish that. Recover the osteological remains, pull that floor, and get a handle on the architectural history of the kiva."

"I can already write that report." Dusty bent, flipped open the battered blue-and-white cooler, and fished out a Guinness. He used a foot to push the lid closed and dug a bottle opener from the drawer. Popping the top, he sucked off the oozing brown foam, eyes on Dale's.

"Fascinating. Most archaeologists I know have to excavate. Something about recovering the data before they describe it. I don't know why we have to pay you to excavate, if you can just do it off the top of your head."

Dusty ran fingers through his dirty blond hair. "Okay, let me ask it this way. Do you want us to stop with the Mesa Verdean renovation, or go through it to expose the Chacoan architecture underneath?"

"I'll be happy with the Mesa Verdean occupation." Dale levered himself up, and grunted as he picked his way to the door.

"Need a steadying hand?" Maureen asked, starting to rise. "It's dark out there."

Dale gave her a chastising look. "Maureen, I've been going to the bathroom outside for almost *two* of your lifetimes. I can find my way to the latrine."

"Right. Sorry." Maureen lowered herself back into the bench.

Dale winked at her and stepped out into the darkness. The metal steps complained under his weight. Maureen turned her head. Through the window she could see Sylvia and Steve sitting in lawn chairs around a low fire. The flickering light shone off their faces. Sylvia held a Coors can, Steve had a Guinness. They seemed to be deadly serious, apparently happy to be left alone to talk their way through their shaky relationship.

"Is Dale going to be all right?" Maureen turned back to Dusty. "Should you go check on him?"

Dusty slid onto the bench beside her. "I cannot tell you how much trouble I'd be in if I did. If he falls down and breaks a leg, we'll deal with it. The other way would subject me to days of cutting comments, the total brunt of his acid ire, if you will."

"I get the point."

Dusty smoothed his fingers over the tabletop. "On the other hand, you could probably get away with it. He thinks you walk on water. Enjoy your sainthood while it lasts, Doctor. Eventually, he's going to figure out that you're just as human as the next person, and then—*whoosh*, you'll drop to my level in the Robertson cosmology."

She smiled and stared at the old woman's skull. "Oh, I don't know. It's different between the two of you. You're his son, Dusty. Face it, fathers and sons have a different relationship than anyone else in the world."

He smiled at that. "I suppose." After a pause, he indicated the skull. "What can you tell me about her?"

Maureen turned her attention to the brown globe of bone. "Well, to start with, she's definitely female. At least, we can be about ninety percent sure, based on the bossing of the frontal bone, the small mastoid processes, and the almost knifelike sharpness of the superior borders of the orbits. She had a shallow palate even before her teeth fell out." She lifted the skull, holding it between her and the lantern. "Looking through the foramen magnum—that's the hole the spinal chord passes through—I can see a series of defects in the endocranial vault. In short, she also has *cribra cranii*."

"So she was stressed like the rest of them?"

Maureen nodded. "The cranial deformation of the skull is interesting. It reminds me a lot of the women at 10K3."

He pointed to the back of her head. "That flatness back there is caused by the baby's head being bound against a cradle board to flatten it."

"Right. This woman has more than her share of it. This goes beyond the usual flattening. This is more severe. Falls into the category that we call lambdoidal deformation; it's higher on the skull. You can see that the back of her head is almost concave."

Dusty smoothed his beard with one hand, while the other clutched the Guinness bottle. "Yeah, we really don't know what that means. Cradleboard deformation shows up in the seven hundreds, at the transition from Basketmaker Three to Pueblo One. This is also the time they start making pottery and building free-standing pueblos. From there on out, we see a lot of cranial deformation."

Maureen turned the skull to the light, exposing the hole that had been cut into the woman's head just back of the coronal suture. She took her hand lens and looked closely at it. "Drilled and scribed," she said softly.

"Huh?"

Maureen held the lens close to the curve of the skull. "Fascinating."

"Yes, Dr. Spock?"

"If you look closely, you can see the initial incision on the outer table. Well, that pretty much answers that. The trephination was done perimortally. From the look of the incision, the scalp was cut when it was soft and pliable."

"I'm not following you."

For a moment, she just stared into Dusty's blue eyes. They seemed to look right inside her soul and, oddly, that knowledge bothered her. She took a breath. "Well, if the scalp was dry, say several days after death, it would take sawing to cut through it with stone tools. We'd see deeper incisions into the bone where the scalp was peeled back. Now, if the incision were made antemortally, before she died, we'd know it."

"Why?"

"Because bone is living tissue. When it's damaged, it immediately begins to heal itself. Looking closely with the hand lens, I can see no evidence that any remodeling took place. I can clarify that with electron microscopy in the lab. The same with the incisions."

He frowned. "Any evidence of a wound? Any reason they'd trephine her? Maybe a brain tumor?"

Maureen did a careful inspection. "Not that I can see from the gross morphology. But a brain tumor, stroke, or anything similar wouldn't leave its signature in the bone. That's a soft tissue defect that . . . Whoa."

"What have you got?"

She bent closer, slowly turning the skull so that the lantern light cast shadows along the outside of the skull. "Someone scraped this, Stewart."

"Huh?"

"This isn't scalping; this is scraping, like cleaning off the tissue that was stuck to the bone." She turned the skull so that the toothless upper jaw faced the light and focused her hand lens on the alveolar bone. "My God."

"What?" Dusty was glancing back and forth between her and the skull.

"Polish, Stewart." She cocked her head. "I've seen this before. In the micrographs that both Christy Turner and Tim White documented in their works on cannibalism. 'Pot polish.' They boiled her skull. As they stirred, the bone rubbed the side of the ceramic pot and was 'polished.' " She held the lens for him. "Here, look."

Steward took the lens and leaned over her. She could feel the heat from his body, and her nostrils caught the subtle musk of his sweat. He shifted slightly, and her arm tingled as he brushed it.

"That shiny stuff?" he asked, peering through the lens.

It took her a moment before she could refocus and answer. "That's it. At least I think it is. In all honesty, we're going to need to put it under the microscope." She took the lens back, experiencing a tinge of anxiety as he resettled himself and stared thoughtfully at the skull. He resumed that pensive stroking of his beard.

"How do you know that's pot polish? I mean, what if someone carried her head around in a leather sack? What if there was fine sand in it? Wouldn't that leave the same kind of microscopic surface abrasion?"

She shook her head. "No. If that is indeed the case, the micrograph will show a random scratching of the bone surface. Pot polish resembles microscopic rasping. Lots of parallel striations in the bone. And we should see it all around the skull, places where it was scraped against the inside of the pot."

"You can tell this?"

She nodded, squinting at the facial bones as Dusty turned the skull.

Maureen took the skull and positioned it so that the light struck the left malar, or cheekbone. "Look at this." She used her pen to indicate a shallow cut across the bone. "And here." She slowly turned the skull, the light accenting additional cut marks. Maureen held her hand lens up, studying the V-shaped groove. "My God, what did they do to her?"

Dusty was frowning. "What are you seeing, Doctor?"

She turned the skull upside down, following the hollow bridge of the zygomatic arch from the cheek to the temporal bone. "Someone cut the masseter muscle—that's the big one in your cheek that bunches when you tighten your jaw—right off the bone."

She turned the skull back to where the lantern light shone into the big hole cut into the side of the cranial vault. The lightning bolts incised into the bone caught the light.

"Okay, so put this together for me." Dusty sipped his stout, eyes on the skull.

"Well, remember that what I'm about to say is a shot in the dark that I'll have to prove or disprove in the lab, but I think someone cut the hole in her skull when she was alive or just freshly dead. Then they skinned and defleshed the skull, and finally boiled it. Probably to completely clean the bone."

"How do you know they didn't boil it and then deflesh it?"

She frowned. "Well, I won't really know until I put it under a scanning electron microscope, but I don't think so. For one thing, you wouldn't have pot polish on the alveolar bone. The lips would cushion the skull from abrasion. And you wouldn't have these cut marks." She indicated the nicks in the bone. "Cooked meat would simply peel away in these areas."

He folded his arms. "Cannibalism?"

"Maybe." She pushed herself back and took a deep breath. "Do you think this skull is related to the stripped femur we were looking at the other night? Both specimens are elderly, female, and found in the kiva."

As he considered that, the lantern shot light through his beard and hair. "If it's the same person, the leg was burned in the fire, and the skull was placed in the kiva after the fire. That would be curious." He gave her that careful inspection again and asked: "Can you test the bone? Determine if it's the same individual?"

She shrugged. "I *might* get a blood type out of the skull. It was boiled, Stewart. Heat denatures protein and DNA. The only thing we can do is an exclusionary test."

"What's that?"

"If we test both bones for blood type, and one comes out type A and the other type B, then you can postulate with some confidence that you've got two individuals. If both come out type A, then you can postulate that it *might* be one individual."

"Or two individuals that just happen to have type A," he supplied.

"Right. It all becomes a matter of probabilities and potential contamination."

"Sorry, Grandmother," Dusty said respectfully. "Whatever happened to you, it must have been terrible."

Maureen considered the sadness in Dusty's eyes, then asked: "The woman in your dreams?"

His handsome face turned stony. "I don't believe in astral archaeology, Doctor. I have to tell myself that was only a dream. I'm hardly going to write an article for publication proclaiming—"

Dale's heavy step sounded on the trailer stairs. He entered, and nodded to them, shooting a glance at the skull. "Finding anything interesting?"

"Just the enigmatic and magical lure of archaeology," Dusty replied. "She was skinned, drilled, scraped, and boiled."

Dale paused. "Well, tell me the details in the morning. I'm off to bed." He raised an eyebrow. "I take it that you'll want me to pull the overhead bunk down in the back, William?"

Dusty nodded, eyes still on the skull. "Given the wreckage of the good doctor's tent, I think that's a good idea. Besides, it's going to be cold out there tonight."

"Good night, Dale," Maureen called as he stepped back, opened the flimsy door, and entered the cramped little bedroom.

"There's a bed that folds out from the roof over mine," Dusty explained. "I'm used to Dale's snoring. I hope you survive it."

She smiled and rubbed her face, feeling tired as well. "I think Dale's right. We ought to call it a night."

For a moment he didn't move, attention still on the skull. In a voice barely above a whisper, he said, "It's not her. I can feel it. She's—someone different. She doesn't call out to me."

Maureen watched him, and a sudden shiver played along her spine.

Dusty tossed off the last of his beer and got to his feet. "I'll be back."

He opened the door, and the stairs rattled and creaked as he stepped to the ground.

For a long moment she sat, staring at the skull. "Who were you, Grandmother? Why did someone do this to you?"

CHAPTER 40

FLUTE MUSIC ROSE from the depths of the great kiva, and streamed over Longtail village like colorful ribbons. Redcrop listened to it as she walked by the kiva and took the trail down to the river. The plaza bonfire had been stoked to a blaze. Waves of orange light washed the plastered walls and illuminated the faces in the crowd.

The farther she walked from the village, the lighter her steps became. She would not have to stand bravely while people patted her arms or took her hands to share their misery. She would be spared the torment.

Redcrop trotted down the leaf-choked trail. As the cold deepened, mist curled from the river and twined through the cottonwood branches. Her long white cape rustled as it trailed over the glistening bed of leaves.

She did not look across the river at the place where her grandmother had been tortured and killed. She paused only a moment at the spot where the murderer had attacked the Matron, then hurried on toward the grave. Somewhere out there in the growing darkness, Browser and Catkin watched her. She trusted them to keep her safe.

When the trail turned damp and slick, she slowed down and placed her knee-length white moccasins with care, bracing her hands on tree trunks to steady herself.

She felt no fear. In the past two days, she had eaten her own heart, leaving her chest hollow and numb. Tomorrow, when Straighthorn came to watch her, perhaps she would feel something. She would be able to look out across the rolling hills and imagine that she saw him standing tall and straight, his bow and quiver slung over his shoulder.

She would not actually see him, of course. He was much too fine a warrior to let anyone see him. But she would dream, and inside, he would be with her.

The thought comforted her.

Redcrop gathered up her cape to step over a log that lay in the path. The beautiful curving trails of worms decorated the bark. As she stepped across, she saw the heart-shaped prints that sank into the mud at the river's edge. The doe had come down to drink, then bounded away into the brush. The tracks were fresh. Redcrop's movements had probably spooked her.

A drum boomed, and Redcrop turned to look back at the village. She could picture the drummer emerging from the kiva and trotting into the plaza. He would be wearing a buffalo-hide cape painted with red wolves, coyotes, eagles, and ravens, the special Spirit Helpers of the Katsinas'

People. Two flutes joined the drumbeat, and a wave of coughing went through the crowd as people readied themselves to greet the sacred beings.

Redcrop turned back to the trail. Sister Moon perched on the eastern horizon. Huge and perfectly round, her pale gold face floated in a gauzy layer of clouds.

She rounded the final bend in the trail and noticed the fresh pile of dirt, darker than the other soil. But it wasn't over the grave; it formed a hump to the right.

Redcrop stood motionless, listening to the gurgling of the water running over the river rocks, and Wind Baby rustling the trees. Tendrils of mist trailed across the fresh dirt like ghostly iridescent fingers.

"What happened?" she whispered.

Had wolves dug up the grave?

In the distance, a dog barked. A frightened bark, as though the katsina Dancers had climbed out of the kiva and begun to whirl, their sacred feet pounding out the heartbeat of the world. Then all the dogs started barking, and an enormous roar filled the night. From the corner of her eye, she could see a bubble of light swelling over Longtail village. Light filled with gouts of black smoke. Someone must have heaped wood on the...

Panting. Very close.

Redcrop jerked to her right and stared wide-eyed at the brush. Something moved in there, parting the brush as it came. A low growl rumbled.

"Hello?"

She backed away a step at a time: *one, two, three, four* . . .

She saw the long ears first, shining in the moonlight. Then eyes rose above the brush, and a painted muzzle. The jaws opened slowly, and rows of sharp teeth gleamed.

Redcrop's knees went weak.

"WHAT'S SHE DOING?" Browser asked, squinting across the river into the gathering dusk.

He lay on his belly next to Catkin in a thicket of rabbitbrush three hundred body-lengths to the west of the grave. They'd chosen this hill because it was covered with brush, but they could not see the village, or much of the surrounding country, unless they stood up. Through the brush, they had one good view: Redcrop. Her white cape blazed in the moonlight. She had stopped abruptly a few moments ago and hadn't moved since.

"I don't know," Catkin answered.

Browser brought his club up and turned it in his hands. He wore his bow and quiver over his left shoulder. He might have enough light to shoot tonight, but a war club would prove better in a close fight. He glanced at Catkin. She had rubbed soot over her oval face to keep it from shining in the moonlight. Her eyes resembled two black holes cut into a gray blanket.

"What's she looking at?" he whispered.

"She's probably praying, or speaking with her dead grandmother."

"Maybe, but she turned toward Longtail village."

"Or away from the grave," Catkin pointed out, her voice sympathetic.

Browser silently pulled himself forward on his elbows.

Catkin whispered, "Where are you going?"

"Closer. I want to—"

"The brush thins out down there, Browser. If we go any closer, we will be visible."

He stopped, turned, twisted his club in his hands. "All right. I will give her a few more instants."

He had enough guards posted in the village, around the village, and along the trails that led to the village, that nothing could possibly happen without an alarm going up. But something about Redcrop's stiff posture ate at him. He'd been studying her for four summers. It wasn't like her...

Redcrop collapsed to the ground and put her hands over her face.

Catkin whispered, "See. She's grieving, Browser. That's all."

Browser released his stranglehold on his club and sank to his belly in the grass. As the cold intensified, the mist along the river crawled across the ground like shiny white fingers.

Catkin pulled herself forward until she could look Browser in the eyes. Her plain buckskin coat and pants blended with the darkness. She whispered, "Why are you so anxious tonight?"

He lifted a shoulder. A strange, terrible sense of dread had entered his bones and would not leave. "It's the mist. If it keeps moving like this, in less than a finger of time we won't be able to see Redcrop. Perhaps we should go and escort her back to the village now."

"Give her a little while longer, Browser. There are four guards watching—"

"How much longer?"

She rolled to her side to face him, and her long braid dragged the ground like a glistening black serpent. "Are you sorry she's out there, Browser? Is that why you're so jumpy? You think that you—"

"I know what I'm doing," he answered sharply, and started to slide forward again, away from her.

Catkin caught his hand, and he stopped and looked back at her.

"This wasn't your idea, was it?" she said.

He hesitated for a long time before answering. "It doesn't matter. Two

Hearts must be stopped, Catkin. I just—" His stomach twisted. He struggled with himself, trying to shove away the guilt. "She is just so young. I wish we did not have to do this."

Browser anxiously started to move again, but Catkin entwined her fingers with his to keep him still.

"She may be young, but Redcrop understands what she is doing, Browser. No one ordered her to do this. She is out there because she wants the killing to stop, too. And Redcrop is not the only one risking her life tonight. Every warrior on guard is a target."

Browser gazed down at her fingers. They looked small and frail against his big hand. He tightened his grip and could feel the slender bones of her hand, and the steady rhythm of her pulse where her wrist touched his arm. For just a moment—just a few heartbeats—he closed his eyes and allowed himself the comfort of her closeness.

"Browser, I have wanted to . . . to tell you . . ."

He heard the longing in her voice and opened his eyes. She looked vulnerable and frightened, her love for him very plain on her face. Tenderly, he brushed a lock of black hair from her cheek, and they stared at each other for a long time, listening to the sounds of the night, the wind in the brush, the river splashing over rocks below.

Through a taut exhalation, Browser said, "That tone in your voice scared me, Catkin. Are you certain that you wish to tell me things that you may not be able to take back?"

She suddenly went rigid, and Browser instinctively gripped his war club. Catkin was staring over his head, in the direction of the village.

Browser flipped over to follow her gaze.

A strange haunting shimmer lit the sky above Longtail village. He stared at it, trying to decide what it was.

"What is that?" Catkin asked.

He shook his head. "Even if they piled the entire wood supply onto the ritual bonfire, the glow wouldn't rise that high into the sky."

"A lightning strike? Maybe a grass fire?"

"Maybe." Browser propped himself on his elbows and eased up to get a better look.

Before his head cleared the tufts of rabbitbrush, he heard a thin, high-pitched sound. It rose and slipped away, like someone playing a wooden comb with a juniper stick. He got on his hands and knees—and gaped at the halo of red sparks that swelled in the sky.

"Catkin, there's a fire in the village!"

He leaped to his feet and ran to the crest of the hill. The ground seemed to drop away from beneath his feet. "Oh, gods."

"What is it?" she demanded as she ran up beside him.

A billowing pillar of flame and smoke rose above Longtail village. When the smoke shifted, Browser saw dozens of children huddled together on the roof of the tower kiva, apparently trapped by the flames. In the plaza below, people raced through the smoke with bowls of water, threw them on the fire, then ran back toward the river.

Catkin cried, "Was it an attack? Do you see enemy warriors?"

"No."

Browser lunged down the hill, his legs pumping as hard as they could.

Catkin shouted, "Maybe the ritual fire burned out of control?"

"Or sparks landed on the exposed roof timbers and caught before anyone knew it!"

Breathless squeals pierced the night.

The children! Gods, not the children!

He jumped a rock and stumbled out of control, his arms flailing until he reached the base of the hill, then he ran flat out, leaving Catkin behind.

"Browser?" she shouted. "*Redcrop!* I'm going after Redcrop!"

"Go!"

Ant Woman appeared out of the smoke and started throwing children off the kiva roof into the arms of people below. They had to fall through a wall of flames, and their terrified screams split the night. A crowd of thirty or forty men and woman jostled on the ground, shouting, crying, and leaping to catch each child that fell. Several of the older children ran to the edge of the roof and bravely leaped off by themselves. Ant Woman pulled a blanket-wrapped infant from the arms of a little girl and threw the baby over the edge. The child seemed to hover in the air for a moment, then he came tumbling down end-over-end. A woman snatched the shrieking bundle out of the air and ran through the firelit darkness toward the river.

As Browser neared the river, he saw Ant Woman grab the arm of a little girl with long shining hair. The terrified girl struggled to break free, throwing all her weight against Ant Woman's grip. Ant Woman's mouth opened in what must have been a shout of rage, then she jerked the child forward so hard Ant Woman almost toppled over the edge herself. She pulled the screaming girl into her arms and heaved her over the edge. As the girl fell through the fire, her hair caught and burst into flame. In less than two heartbeats, the girl's head blazed like a torch.

A man on the ground caught her, threw her to the dirt, and began beating the fire out with his bare hands while the panicked little girl shrieked and clawed at his face and arms.

Browser hit the river running. Injured people filled the water; many sat soaking burns, others nursed broken arms or legs. Some just appeared to be sitting in the water, weeping.

As he splashed across, Browser shouted, "What happened? Did anyone see what happened? How did the fire start?"

Wading Bird, twenty paces downstream, cupped a hand to his mouth and half-sobbing, half-yelling, called, "We were Dancing when the entire village seemed to go up at once! There were flames everywhere! The entire back wall blazed!"

"Are you all right, Elder?"

Wading Bird dipped his head in a weary nod. "I will live. Go and help those who are still in danger!"

Browser splashed out onto the bank and ran.

Just as he reached the plaza, the kiva roof collapsed, and a thunderous explosion of cracking timbers and roaring flames shook the world. Ant Woman's arms flew up and she staggered backward into the flames. Several children leaped off the roof. Others clung to the edge as long as they could, but when their clothes caught fire, they let go, and fell into the inferno.

"No!" Browser cried, as the blast of heat hit him.

Burning splinters flew through the air and wheeled across the ground around him.

The screams died. For a single terrible instant, no one made a sound. People stood like carved wooden statues, their eyes fixed on the flames that flapped across the sky like blazing wings.

Then a deep-throated groan began, low and anguished, and swiftly built to a deafening crescendo of shrieks and cries. The crowd surged forward, shouting and shoving each other to get to the children who'd been thrown from the roof.

Straighthorn dashed around the southeastern corner of the village with his bow up, an arrow nocked, his gaze searching for a target. "War Chief!" he shouted when he spied Browser. "Blessed Katsinas, was it a raid? What happened?"

Browser came to his senses. He yelled, "Straighthorn, help me clear the plaza. We have to get people away from here!"

Browser ran forward like a madman, waving his arms, crying, "Get out of the village! Move! Let it burn! There's nothing more we can do. Go on, get out! *Get out now!*"

Straighthorn raced along the eastern side of the plaza, shouting, "Hurry! Run! There's no time! Move!"

Retreating people flooded around Browser, weeping, carrying injured children in their arms.

Browser and Straighthorn, caught up in the rush, were carried down to the river. People waded in and sat down in the water with their children in their laps, washing soot-coated faces, dripping cold water over burns while children sobbed.

Twenty paces away, Cloudblower splashed into water up to her waist and raced about, examining wounds, touching people gently. Locks of graying-black hair had torn loose from her bun and straggled around her triangular face. From the thick layer of white face powder she wore, he guessed she must have played the role of White Shell Woman tonight, grandmother of Father Sun, the creator of light and warmth. Raven feathers and seed beads dotted the fringes on the sleeves of her red dress.

Straighthorn stopped in front of Browser and looked up with terrified eyes. "War Chief? Redcrop. Where is she? Did she return with you or—"

"Catkin went to get her, Straighthorn, but I suspect that Redcrop saw the fire just as we did and rushed back on her own. She's probably here in the crowd somewhere."

Straighthorn exhaled hard in relief and said, "Thank the gods."

Browser's gaze darted through the crowd, and for a long moment he couldn't speak. Then he spun around in the water, and shouted, "Uncle Stone Ghost? Uncle? Uncle, where are you? *Has anyone seen my uncle?"*

CHAPTER 41

ASH FELL AROUND Stone Ghost, coating his white hair and tattered turkey-feather cape like black snow. In the firelit darkness below, he saw Browser running, calling out to someone, but Stone Ghost couldn't hear over the dwindling roar of the flames.

He'd just seated himself on this small hilltop one hundred body lengths from the village when the first tongues of flame crackled to life. Before he realized what was happening, the fire had turned into an inferno.

Stone Ghost cupped a hand to his mouth and shouted, "Nephew? Up here!"

Browser did not seem to hear. He ran along the trail behind the village.

Didn't matter. If Browser was looking for Stone Ghost, he would wind up here eventually. He came here frequently to rest and think.

Everyone knew that.

Stone Ghost turned to the new painting that adorned the sandstone boulder to his left. Someone had painted a white spiral. Two people, a man and woman, stood at the entry to the spiral with their arms extended toward Longtail village.

"Gods," Stone Ghost whispered in agony. "They have lost their souls."

He clutched his shaking fists in his lap and hunched forward to ease the pain in his heart.

Browser trotted up the trail toward Stone Ghost. Dirt coated the front of his knee-length buckskin war shirt, and ash sprinkled his short black hair.

"Uncle, thank the Spirits! I was worried you had been caught in the fire." Browser dropped to one knee at Stone Ghost's feet, breathing hard. "Are you well?"

Stone Ghost reached out to touch Browser's arm and his gaze traced the line of his nephew's square jaw, and lingered on Browser's worried eyes. Stone Ghost had always planned on telling Browser the truth, but the moment had never seemed right.

"I'm well, Nephew. How is everyone else?"

Browser shook his head. "In shock. No one seems to know how the fire started. Cloudblower told me the Dancers had just emerged from the kiva when the first flames licked into the air. She said the fire grew so rapidly they had no chance to get the children out of the tower kiva. It seems impossible to me, but—"

"That's the way it happened, Nephew. I've never seen an accidental fire roar to life as this one did."

Browser stopped breathing. His eyes darted over Stone Ghost's expression. "What are you saying. That—that it was not accidental?"

Stone Ghost lifted his beaked nose and sniffed the air. Browser, taking the cue, did the same. His nostrils flared several times, as if to make certain.

His voice came out strained. "Pine pitch, Uncle? Someone threw pine pitch around the village and set it on fire? But I—I," he stammered. "I looked for raiders, Uncle! Most of my guards have come in and they saw no one!"

Stone Ghost nodded. "They weren't raiders. At least, not in the way you mean."

"Tell me. Quickly."

Stone Ghost gestured to the boulder at his side. The white spiral gleamed golden in the firelight. "I found this tonight."

Browser's eyes slitted. He tilted his head and examined the painting with care. "What is it, Uncle? We found a similar painting on a boulder outside Aspen village, except it was a black spiral. We thought the injured woman had left it for us, to tell us we were walking a path into darkness."

Stone Ghost traced the four rings of the spiral with his crooked index finger and tapped the two white figures who stood on the right side. "Each ring represents one of the underworlds, Nephew—"

"But"—Browser shook his head—"there are only three underworlds, Uncle. There should be three rings."

Stone Ghost smiled weakly. "The Katsinas' People believe there are three underworlds, Nephew. The First People speak of four. To them, this world of light is the fifth world."

"Is?" Browser leaned forward as though he had not heard right. But Stone Ghost could see him putting the pieces together. The vein in his nephew's temple started to pulse.

Stone Ghost gestured to the spiral again. "Our enemies are too bold for their own good. They do not think that anyone among the Made People will know this symbol. They left the spiral here to identify themselves to a select few."

Browser's gaze flicked to the spiral and back to Stone Ghost's wrinkled face. "What is the symbol? What does it mean?"

"The two people you see on the right side are just emerging from the underworlds. They are First People. *The* First People."

Browser stared at Stone Ghost unblinking. "But the First People died out long ago, Uncle."

Stone Ghost took a deep breath. The fire had died down enough that he could see the people along the river and hear the faint cries of children. A determined group of men stood a short distance from the tower kiva, probably waiting for the flames to die completely before beginning the grisly work of sorting through the dead.

Stone Ghost closed his eyes to block the view. "You will not understand unless I start at the beginning, Nephew, so please forgive me if I seem to be speaking about things that have no relevance to tonight. Trust me. They do."

"I trust you," Browser said softly.

Stone Ghost opened his eyes and tried to smile. Love for his nephew swelled in his breast. "Over one hundred and ten sun cycles ago, the Blessed Matron of Talon Town, Night Sun, abandoned her people and married one of the Made People, her former War Chief, Ironwood. Night Sun and Ironwood fled the Straight Path Nation with her daughter, Cornsilk, and the man who would become Cornsilk's husband."

"The Blessed Poor Singer."

"Yes." Stone Ghost bent forward to hold his great-nephew's gaze.

Browser searched his face as though fearing the world might end after this discussion. "And after they left?"

"You must understand that we are talking about the final scramble for power in a dying civilization, Nephew. The First People were desperate, and terrified of each other. They started hiring assassins to take each other's lives. They called them the White Moccasins and considered them to be sacred warriors. My grandmother, Orenda, told me about it many times. She said that the surviving rulers selected their best warriors, groups of no more than ten, and sent them out to destroy anyone who might threaten them. They paid these assassins too handsomely to believe, with baskets of turquoise, coral pendants, rare shells from the distant oceans. The fools did not realize what would happen next. When you give men such unrestrained power and wealth, it is like a Spirit plant in their veins. The assassins quickly amassed enough wealth that they could adopt their own rules for who should live and who should die. Night Sun had been wise enough to flee before the White Moccasins got to her, but they cut down people like the Blessed Sun, Webworm, and Matrons Weedblossom and Moon Bright. Few escaped."

Was it possible that groups of White Moccasins still existed? It didn't seem likely, but . . .

Browser sat back. "Are you telling me that you believe this spiral was painted by one of these White Moccasins?"

Stone Ghost nodded. "I fear that may be the case, and if it is, we are in grave danger."

"We? You mean—"

"I mean you and me, Nephew."

"I don't understand."

Stone Ghost held Browser's gaze as he whispered, "My grandmother, Orenda, married . . ."

Stone Ghost hesitated when he saw Catkin sprinting up the trail with Straighthorn at her side. Their faces appeared stark in the firelight.

Browser whirled around, then lurched to his feet, as though he saw more in Catkin's expression than Stone Ghost did.

"Catkin?" Browser shouted. "What is it?"

Catkin clenched her fists at her sides. "We've searched everywhere," she said. "Redcrop is gone."

"What?" Browser blurted. "Are you certain? Did you look—"

"That's not all," Catkin interrupted in a stern voice. "Our Matron's grave was dug up, Browser. Someone took her body."

Browser stood unmoving for several heartbeats, then turned around to stare at Stone Ghost. The fear in his nephew's eyes twisted Stone Ghost's belly.

"Go, Nephew. Hurry!"

CHAPTER 42

PIPER IS DOWN on her hands and knees, throwing up in the sand. Through blurry eyes, she sees Mother add more wood to the fire. The big pot hanging from the tripod steams. The boiling has been going on for a long time. Another spasm shakes Piper and she rocks forward and retches up the last of her supper. Her nose burns and runs.

"Piper," Mother says sharply. "Go away."

"I can't . . . stop." The smell from the pot blows to her on the night wind, and she retches again.

"Go on! Get away from here!"

Piper drags herself to her feet and trots away from the rock shelter out into the darkness. Her knees are wobbly and she trips many times in the soft sand before she sits down fifty paces from Mother. The smell from the boiling pot is fainter, the damp scent of the creek bottom stronger.

She does not know where Grandfather is. He carried the hurt girl into camp, tied her up, then left without a word. The girl still sleeps near Mother. Grandfather must have gone away to pray and prepare himself for the sacred bowl of life, which they will eat at dawn. He has told Piper many times that the Katsina Believers must be bathed in blood to be saved.

Piper breathes deeply and is grateful when her belly does not heave. She wipes her cheeks on her coat sleeve and can see the skull bobbing in Mother's pot. One cooked eye stares at Piper. Gray foam bubbles around it.

Piper can't help it. She flops onto her hands and knees and throws up until she can't breathe.

"Piper!" Mother's voice warns. "For the sake of the gods!"

Piper hangs her head and cries, but the sound is locked behind her teeth.

She stretches out on her stomach and places her hot cheek against the cool sand. The boiling smell almost goes away. Piper wishes she had a cold drink of water to wash the sour taste from her mouth, but the water pots are back in camp.

Evening People sparkle above her and Piper wonders which of her ancestors might be watching tonight. Only the greatest of the First People get to climb into the sky and become stars. She looks at the biggest, brightest one and wonders if it is her grandfather's grandmother, the Blessed Cornsilk. She was a great Healer.

Piper hugs herself and whispers, "Cornsilk, can you Heal me?"

Piper feels herself splitting inside, rotting, like fabric that's been left out in the sunshine too long.

Mother grunts, and Piper turns.

Mother uses a long stick to lift the steaming pot from the fire, then sets it on the ground and kicks it over. Boiling water splashes out. The skull rolls and rocks in the firelight. Mother upends the pot, and when the last trickle drains out, she hangs the pot back on the tripod and lets the heat dry it. The steam Spirits will carry the message to their ancestors in the sky: Another lost soul has been freed. Soon the Cloud People will come and the dead Matron will be able to use them as stepping stones to get to the skyworlds.

Piper searches the darkness. Two Cloud People sail far to the south. Are they coming for the dead Matron? She hopes so.

Mother takes a hafted chert scraper from her pack and goes to work on the wet skull, carving out the boiled eyes, peeling off the last bits of cooked meat.

Piper gasps and chokes, but nothing comes up.

She closes her eyes and watches the lights flash behind her lids. They flit like the spark flies she saw four summers ago on a journey to the lands of the Swamp People with her grandfather. At sunset the spark flies started to wink and glow and, before she knew it, flocks were Dancing together in the trees. Happiness had left Piper weak. She'd chased the spark flies through the tall grass for half the night.

Mother has finished scraping off the meat. Piper knows because the sound has changed. Mother's scraper makes the rattle of chert on bare bone.

Piper opens her eyes. Mother puts her scraper on the ground and studies the gleaming skull.

Piper's eyes slide to the girl, wondering what her name is. She usually finds out, but not until after the bowl of life.

Wind Baby gusts up the sandy wash, thin and cold, and Piper's teeth chatter. Only a moment ago, when she'd been throwing up, she'd felt too hot to touch. Now she is afraid she might be freezing solid.

She glances at Mother and tries to decide if she wants to go back and crawl into her bedding hides, or stay here. Her hides lay rolled up near the girl. Grandfather makes her sleep close to them. He says it calms the girls to see Piper when they wake up. Often Mother and Grandfather leave so that the only person the girls see is Piper.

Piper's souls always die when they first look at her.

Piper quickly pulls sand over her legs, then lies down and covers her stomach and chest.

"Piper?" Mother calls.

Piper's fingers curl into the sand and shake.

"Piper? Where are you?"

Mother stands up and lifts an arm to block the firelight. "Piper?"

Piper pulls more sand up around her face and neck, covering everything but her eyes.

"Piper! If you do not tell me where you are, I will send your grandfather to find you!"

A burning flood shoots up Piper's throat. She bursts from her bed of sand and runs back to camp, throwing up on her moccasins, her pants, her hands.

Mother stands by the fire, holding the skull.

Piper flies past her, crawls into her hides, and covers her head.

She can feel pieces of her souls breaking off and flying away, like autumn leaves in a strong wind.

Soon her body will be empty and dead.

When she gathers the courage, Piper pulls her hides down and peeks out, searching the starry sky for Cloud People, afraid they are coming to take her away.

Praying they are coming.

STRAIGHTHORN PICKED UP a leaf from the river's edge and turned it in his hands, as he listened to the heated words coming from the crowd ten paces away.

"Who were they, War Chief?" Crossbill demanded to know. "Who did this?"

The Longtail Matron sat on the ground near Browser with her bandaged hands in her lap. She had dragged a little boy from beneath a burning pile of timbers. Singed white hair matted her freckled scalp and blisters bubbled over her wrinkled face. A red blanket draped her shoulders. "Was it raiders? A war party?"

Browser crouched beside Crossbill. Dirt and ash coated his buckskin cape and streaked his round face. He quietly answered, "We know that someone poured pine pitch over the roof of the tower kiva and splashed it on the rear wall of the village. They also piled brush along the rear wall, then set it on fire. That's why the village burned so quickly."

"But who did it?" Crossbill stabbed one of her bandaged hands at him. "Flute Player Believers? Fire Dogs?"

Browser hesitated, as though he knew more than he wished to say. He glanced at his uncle, Stone Ghost, who stood alone at the edge of the crowd, then looked at the ground. "It may have been enemy raiders, or even a war party, but both seem unlikely."

The crowd murmured and clothing rustled as they shifted. Several people turned to Stone Ghost, but the old man said nothing. He just watched his nephew with tight eyes.

Crossbill sobbed, "Why do you say that? Surely this was an enemy attack!"

"Matron, we had guards posted on every trail and on the high points around the village. Many more stood guard in the village itself. None of them saw anything unusual. They saw no dust from approaching refugees or other strangers. Straighthorn saw Old Pigeontail running the Great North Road in the distance, but that's all." Browser ran a hand through his shorn black hair and shook his head. "In the morning, when we can see better, I promise you we will know more."

Windblown ash piled around Straighthorn's feet. He glared at it, threw his leaf down, and stood up.

Up the hill, the gutted black walls of Longtail village smoldered. When the wind gusted, the charred roof beams glowed like a thousand red eyes. Now that the fire was out, the panic had turned to shock. Sobbing people filtered through the plaza, kicking over burned debris in search of belongings, calling out to lost loved ones.

They had laid the dead and dying on the roof of the great kiva. Seven sick people had suffocated in their beds from breathing the smoke. Three women and one man had been crushed by falling walls. Five more had mortal burns. Their moans filled the night. Occasionally, a terrible cry escaped someone's lips.

Ant Woman's daughter, Rock Dove, walked among the dying, holding cups of water to their lips, or gently smoothing hair from a burned brow. Her yellow cape flashed as she moved. She had accepted the duties of village Matron in a way that would have made her mother proud. As soon as her people had acknowledged Ant Woman's death and cast their voices in her favor, she had begun giving orders, softly, clearly, with no hesitation. Every Dry Creek villager had a duty, carrying water, gathering wood, cooking food, standing guard—it gave them something more important to worry about than their own lives.

Crossbill had performed the same function for the Longtail villagers. She had ordered the injured people to be carried into the undamaged great kiva and then built up the fire to keep them warm while Cloudblower tended their wounds. But several hurt adults stood in the crowd, people with blistered bodies, and broken arms and legs, injuries received when they jumped from the upper story. Three men supported themselves on makeshift cottonwood-branch crutches.

The acrid scents of burned pitch and scorched hair were so strong they almost gagged Straighthorn.

No one knew the whereabouts of Springbank, and Straighthorn feared the worst.

Browser said, "Matron Crossbill, I have ordered twenty warriors to stay here to guard the village, and assigned ten more to the high points around the village. Matron Rock Dove assigned ten of her own warriors to guard the roads. What more do you wish me to do?"

Crossbill closed her eyes and lowered her forehead to her bandaged hand. She didn't say anything for a long time. Finally, she murmured, "I want you to lead the party that goes to search for Springbank."

"Yes, Matron."

"That is all I can think of. I will organize people to start packing our few belongings so that we can leave this forsaken place. The ghosts of those who died will be wandering about all night, tormenting the dreams of the survivors, trying to drag them away to the Land of the Dead. We must leave soon."

Browser nodded and asked, "Where will we go?"

"Rock Dove has asked us to come to Dry Creek village. She says they will feel safer with us there. I think we should go, but I will place the decision before the village tomorrow morning." Crossbill looked up and her wrinkled mouth trembled. "I wish all of you to be thinking about her offer. It is a good offer."

Someone down the river shouted, "Springbank told me that the katsinas had abandoned us, but I did not believe him! Now look! We have nothing! Our families are dead. Our homes are gone. I hate the katsinas!" Several people nodded. Most appeared too stunned to think.

Browser called out, "I will cast my vote with Matron Crossbill. I think Dry Creek village will be a fine home for us. Now, please help me. I must decide what to do about Redcrop. I wish to form a search party—"

"A search party! For her?" Water Snake shouted. A thick black bar of soot coated the left side of his weasel's face. "We will find nothing in the darkness!" Water Snake gazed defiantly at Browser.

Browser met the threat with a lethal glare, and a hand on his war club, silently daring Water Snake to challenge his authority.

Skink stepped forward and calmly said, "I think we should search around the village for missing people and wait until morning to search elsewhere."

Straighthorn exploded, "By morning, Redcrop could be dead!"

Water Snake thundered, "By morning, Springbank could be dead! Who do you think is more important? One of our elders, or a slave girl?"

Straighthorn drew himself up and glared at Water Snake. In a trembling voice, he said, "She is not a slave, Water Snake. She is free."

"It makes little difference," Skink replied tiredly. "I think it would be better for everyone if we used all of our resources to protect the village tonight and care for the injured and dying. I, for one, do not wish to go out into the darkness with search torches. If there are enemy warriors out there, they will be able to shoot us down like dogs."

Matron Crossbill lifted a hand and the gathering went deathly silent. "People have so many concerns tonight, let us call for volunteers for both search parties, War Chief."

"Yes, Matron," Browser dipped his head respectfully, then looked around the gathering. "Who will go with me to look for Elder Springbank?"

"I will." Catkin stepped to Browser's side. Tall and beautiful in the firelight, her hard eyes gazed straight at Skink. She called: "Who else will come with us?"

Skink's mouth puckered as though he'd eaten something bitter. He could not refuse with everyone looking at him. "I will," he said, and grudgingly pulled his war club from his belt.

"So will I," Jackrabbit said, and pushed through the crowd. The ash that filled the lines around his eyes made him look much older than fifteen summers.

"Good enough," Browser said. "And who will search for Redcrop?"

People muttered and milled about. Several men waved their hands dismissively and drifted away from the gathering.

Straighthorn shouldered through the crowd, feeling sick. *"I will."*

When no one else came forward, Straighthorn suddenly hated everyone in the village. He couldn't even bear to look at them. He walked away, cut down to the river trail, and headed for the Matron's burial site with blood pulsing painfully in his ears.

I'm coming, Redcrop.

He had searched through the Longtail survivors, then raced around the Dry Creek village camp, calling her name, looking for her, asking everyone he came across if they'd seen Redcrop.

After talking with Catkin, he feared that she might have seen the fire and run back into the heart of the blaze to help someone. His belly twisted. She could be lying beneath a fallen wall, or trapped under the weight of a collapsed roof, alive, praying he would find her.

His steps faltered, but only for an instant. If she were in the village, eventually someone would hear her, or see her, and pull her out. But if she'd been captured, she had no one but him . . .

"Straighthorn?"

He looked over his shoulder.

Browser caught up with him and matched his stride. "Straighthorn, wait. There are things I wish to tell you before you go."

Straighthorn kept walking, his head down, eyes on the trail.

Browser clasped his shoulder and forced Straighthorn to stop and look at him. He handed Straighthorn an unlit yucca bark torch. "You may need this."

Straighthorn took it, but glowered.

Fear and sympathy tightened the War Chief's eyes. "First, I wish you to know that as soon as we have finished our search for Springbank, I will be on your trail. Expect me."

Straighthorn swallowed hard and nodded. *You should be, since you got her into this.* "What else, War Chief?"

Browser seemed to read Straighthorn's souls. He lowered his eyes. "Your foes are not merely warriors. You must understand—"

"I don't have to understand them, War Chief. I just have to find them and kill them." He lifted his war club and shook it.

Browser pushed Straighthorn's club aside. "Listen to me. I *know* who set the fire tonight, and I know why they did it."

Straighthorn stared at him. "It was the same people who killed her grandmother, wasn't it?"

Browser's gaze did not waver. "Yes, but the important part is that the killers are First People. They are fighting for—"

"First People?" Straighthorn laughed out loud. "They died long ago!

My mother used to tell me stories about the great war they fought with the Made People. The last of the First People were killed more than one hundred sun cycles—"

"They are First People, Straighthorn," Browser said, and looked around to make sure no one stood nearby. "If you are captured, tell them—"

"How do you know they are First People?"

Browser searched Straighthorn's face. He seemed to be struggling with himself. He said, "Did you see the symbol painted on the boulder where my uncle Stone Ghost sat tonight?"

Straighthorn's brows drew together. "Yes. I thought your uncle had painted it. It was a spiral, wasn't it? A spiral with two people?"

Browser nodded. "We found a similar painting at Aspen village. It depicts the First People emerging from the underworlds. Apparently it is the murderers' way of claiming responsibility and sending a message to other First People—"

"*Other* First People?"

"They exist, Straighthorn. They live in hiding, but they exist."

Straighthorn turned and marched down the trail again, his war club over his shoulder.

"Straighthorn?" Browser trotted to catch up. "I told you those things for a reason. If you are captured, tell them that you and Redcrop are not Made People. Tell them you are both Fire Dogs or Tower Builders, or anything else you wish. I don't think they will kill you if you are not Made People."

Straighthorn found himself chuckling. "So they only kill Made People? Why? In retribution for a war that ended—"

"The war hasn't ended, Straighthorn. Not for them. And it isn't just against Made People. They hate anyone who believes in the katsinas. You do not have to believe me, just remember the things I told you tonight. Remember also that I will not be far behind you. Do not cover your trail too well."

"I am a one-man search party, War Chief. I won't have time to cover it at all."

Straighthorn couldn't stand it any longer. Angry, feeling betrayed, he broke into a run, his feet pounding the damp leaves.

The War Chief ran after him for several steps, then stopped and called, "I'll find you tomorrow!"

Straighthorn looked back and saw Browser standing in the trail with his fists clenched at his sides.

He ran harder.

CHAPTER 43

BROWSER'S BUCKSKIN CAPE flapped around his long legs as he swiftly walked back along the river trail. The crowd had begun to disperse. A line of people headed toward the Dry Creek camp and the shelter it offered, while others curled into borrowed blankets and laid down on the river bank with weeping children clutched in their arms. Catkin, Jackrabbit, and Skink huddled together a short distance from Crossbill and Rock Dove.

The two matrons knelt before a little boy of perhaps eight summers. The child was from Dry Creek village. Browser did not know him, but the boy must have been hurt in the fire. He wore a splint on his left wrist and his hair and eyebrows had been singed off. As the two matrons conversed, he glanced back and forth.

"War Chief," Crossbill called when she saw him. "You must hear this."

Browser walked into their circle, and the acrid scent of smoke rose from the boy's scorched clothing. "What is it, Matron?"

Crossbill placed a hand on the boy's head and said, "This is Tadpole. He was in the tower kiva tonight."

The boy looked wide-eyed at Browser.

Browser noticed that even his eyelashes had been burned away, and said, "You are a very brave boy, Tadpole."

"I—I cried, though," Tadpole admitted and ducked his head.

"That's all right," Browser replied. "If I'd had to fall through a wall of flame, I would have cried, too."

The hairless boy looked up at Browser with shining eyes and smiled.

Crossbill said, "Tell the War Chief what you saw, Tadpole."

Tadpole took a breath and let it out, then said, "Just before the fire started, we heard things being dropped on the roof of the kiva. They make hard knocks, like someone throwing rocks."

Browser frowned. He had no idea what that meant. "Go on, Tadpole."

Tadpole lifted his good hand and pointed up at the sky. "Then, a little while later, we saw a woman look down at us. She was pretty."

The boy paused, and Rock Dove softly coached, "And what did my mother say?"

"Matron Ant—" Tadpole seemed to realize of a sudden that he wasn't supposed to say her name. "Our former Matron said, 'You are late, Obsidian.' Then we saw fire behind the woman's head, and the woman ran away. We heard her steps go across the roof. Our Matron screamed her name, but she didn't come back. No one came."

The boy shivered, and Browser's souls ached, like stiletto wounds taken in the heat of battle. He looked up. "Where is Obsidian?"

Rock Dove answered, "In our camp. Her chamber was burned, so she—"

Browser stalked away.

Crossbill called, "War Chief, wait! There is more!"

Browser kept going, straight toward the Dry Creek camp. He seemed to be walking through some nightmare country where time had ceased to exist.

He strode through the center of the camp, then weaved around the hide shelters and cooking fires. Almost two hundred people had taken refuge here. They looked up as he passed, but no one called out to him. They concentrated on feeding the hungry, and rocking sobbing children to sleep.

Browser's steps froze when he saw Obsidian standing alone under a huge cottonwood at the edge of the camp. A beautiful red blanket with white spirals draped her shoulders. She leaned against the trunk, gazing up at the Evening People.

When she heard Browser's steps, she turned and fear lit her black eyes. She started to walk away.

"Yes!" he called after her. "Keep walking! Straight up the hill to that boulder with the white painting."

Obsidian's pace quickened. "Leave me alone. I don't wish to speak with you tonight!"

She rushed up the hill, not so much obeying his order as trying to get away from him.

Browser ran after her.

When she started to pass the boulder and continue up the hill into the grove of junipers, Browser lunged for her hand, grabbed it, and dragged her backward.

"Let me go!" she shouted and tried to wrench free. "You're hurting me!"

Browser shoved her against the boulder and placed his hands on either side of her narrow shoulders, trapping her there. "Where were you tonight? Were you looking for me?"

"What are you talking about?"

He reached down with one hand, ripped open the seam in his cape, and held the turquoise wolf up before her eyes.

"Is this what you want? Is this why you destroyed our village?"

She glared at him. "You've lost your senses!"

"Don't lie to me! You as much as asked me about this yesterday! You said, 'Where is it?' Don't tell me you didn't mean this wolf!"

Obsidian hissed, "Of course I did! I wanted to see it, you fool!"

"Why? Are you working with the murderer? With Two Hearts? He wants it back, is that it?"

She looked as though he'd struck her in the face. When she could finally manage to close her mouth, she whispered, "I wanted to see it because it proves you are who I thought you were. It proves you are *suitable!*"

Browser threw the wolf at her. "Take it! It has only brought me misery!"

Obsidian gasped and her hand flew to her cheek where the turquoise had drawn blood. She looked at her bloody fingers, and snapped, "I don't want it! Why do you think *I* want it?"

Breathing hard, Browser knelt and picked up the wolf. As he rubbed the dirt away, he said, "I thought you were trying to get it back for him, or—or maybe for yourself. I don't know, I—"

"You fool!" Obsidian jerked the necklace from around her throat and held up her own magnificent turquoise wolf. It swung back and forth in front of his eyes. "Why would I need yours?"

Obsidian slipped her necklace back over her head and marched down the trail.

"Wait!" Browser called.

"No!"

He stuffed the wolf into his belt pouch and ran after her. "Obsidian, wait!"

"Leave me alone!"

He grabbed her arm and whirled her around. She fought, but he refused to let go. The coral beads in her long dark hair glittered like sparks, and he could see her breast heaving beneath her white cape.

"Tell me what you were doing on the roof of the tower kiva tonight."

She looked at him as though he were mad. "I had duties! The Dry Creek Matron asked me to bring sweet cakes to the children. I had just walked to the kiva ladder when I heard the flames. I whirled around and saw them racing toward me—"

"You didn't see the pine pitch on the roof?"

She frowned and shook her head. "No. I—I mean there may have been pitch there, but I was so taken aback by the bones scattered over the roof that I hardly noticed anything else, I just—"

"What bones?"

"*I don't know!* There were bloody bones all over the roof! As though someone had just butchered a deer and thrown the bones up there! Except"—she wet her full lips—"they didn't look like animal bones. I didn't have time to really look, but I thought—"

"You thought they were human?" He let her go.

Obsidian nodded.

Browser's arm muscles tightened, bulging through his war shirt. "Did you know our dead Matron's grave was robbed?"

Obsidian seemed to go weak. She backed up and leaned against a cottonwood trunk. "When did that happen?"

Browser shook his head. "I don't know for certain. Before sunset, I think."

Obsidian reached out and let her hand hover in the air over his shoulder. When Browser didn't pull away, she touched his arm.

He shivered and her voice turned soft. "I know you are crazy with worry, Browser. So am I. Ever since your uncle questioned me, I've been terrified that someone else may know, and I—"

"My uncle questioned you? Today?"

"Just before the Dances. It was only after speaking with him that I knew for certain you were—"

"What?"

She pulled her hand away. "It is not safe to say it out loud, and you know it."

In the Dry Creek camp, people stood up and shielded their eyes against the glow of the fires to watch Browser and Obsidian. A low hum of concerned voices rose.

"What? What is not safe to say?" Browser shook his fists at her. "Obsidian, for the sake of the gods, tell me that you know nothing about these murders!"

"I don't!" she shouted. "I do not know how you could even think that I would do something so—"

"Fine!" He strode down the hill.

"Browser?" she called and ran after him. "Let's talk. Please! Perhaps now that we understand each other—"

"No, and *no!*"

He ignored the questioning glances of the onlookers in the Dry Creek camp and trotted to meet Catkin where she stood alone near the river. Behind her, people lay rolled in blankets and hides, trying to sleep. A chorus of whimpers rose.

Browser stopped in front of Catkin. Her soot-blackened face had an eerie sheen in the smoky light. "Where are Jackrabbit and Skink?"

"After hearing the rest of Tadpole's story, I told them to return to their former guard positions in the hills."

Browser knew that tone. "What else did the boy say?"

"Tadpole said that the Dry Creek Matron and Springbank made a deal: she would climb onto the roof and try to figure out how to get the children to safety, while Springbank remained inside and made certain every child got out of the kiva. Tadpole saw Springbank climb up through the entry just before the Dry Creek Matron threw the boy off the roof and into his father's arms." Catkin inhaled and let it out in a rush of words, "That was moments before the roof collapsed."

"You think he was inside?"

"He must have been."

Browser braced his hand on his belted war club. Another elder lost. His heart ached. What would the Katsinas' People do without Flame Carrier and Springbank? Perhaps when they reached Dry Creek village, Browser could quietly begin moving through the people, suggesting they cast their voices in favor of Cloudblower as their new Matron. Cloudblower would know what to do, whether they should stay at Dry Creek village or continue moving, searching for the First People's kiva and the tunnel to the underworlds.

He looked up at the smoldering village, the windblown piles of ash heaped against the toppled walls, and wondered if any of them still believed in Poor Singer's prophecy after this.

Maybe Springbank had been right. They should disband the Katsinas' People and give up the dream.

Catkin said, "I filled our canteens." She tapped the two pots tied to her belt. The black-and-red geometric designs gleamed in the flickering light. "Straighthorn can't be too far ahead of us. If you grab your bow and we hurry, we may catch him before he leaves the burial site."

"No, I—I wish you to speak with my uncle first. There are things you must know before we leave, Catkin."

"What things?"

Browser squared his shoulders. "About our enemies."

SYLVIA SAID, "WHOA, what's this?"

Golden sunshine streamed out of the cool autumn sky, a pleasant companion to the smell of wet earth. The temperature was in the fifties, forecast for a high of sixty that afternoon, and into the seventies tomorrow.

Dusty looked up from the two-by-two he was digging with Maureen. "What have you got?"

"Maybe a storage cyst, but it looks bigger. Hang on, Steve's taking photos and notes while I excavate around the edges."

Maureen turned to Dusty. She'd pinned her braid up in back, but strands had worked loose and fluttered around her face when the wind blew. She used her sleeve to wipe her sweaty forehead. "How big are these cysts? I mean, they were just used to store corn, beans, and squash, weren't they? How much space can that take?"

"Some of their storage cysts were huge, Doctor." Dusty braced his hands on the lip of the pit and climbed out.

A thin layer of high clouds filtered the afternoon sunlight, turning it a flaxen shade. Where it struck bone or potsherds, it sparked a blaze.

He brushed his hands off on his jeans as he walked across the kiva floor, and dust clouded the air around him. "Okay, tell me what you've got?" He knelt beside the excavation unit.

Sylvia and Steve backed to the edge of the unit to give him a clear view. "I take it back," Sylvia said. Her freckles had almost merged with her tan. "Now it looks more like a trap door."

Steve used the hem of his blue T-shirt to sop up the sweat on his face, and said, "A kiva tunnel?"

"We'll see." Dusty jumped into the pit and crouched over the floor feature. The three-foot square opening had a layer of intact, though charred, poles over it. "You've taken all your measurements, photos, written everything down in the log?"

"Of course," Sylvia said. "What do you think we are, government archaeologists?"

Dusty gave her an annoyed look, pulled his trowel from his back pocket, and carefully began excavating around the closest pole. When he'd cleared the edges, he wedged his trowel beneath the tip of the pole and gently levered it out of the ground. Darkness, not dirt, met his gaze. A musty scent rose.

Sylvia said, "I have the feeling you may have just inhaled the same air the Anasazi were breathing seven hundred and fifty years ago."

Dusty said, "Sylvia, you and Steve help me with the other poles. This could also be a burial pit. We need to be very careful removing the 'lid.' "

Maureen came over and stood beside the unit with her hands on her hips. "How deep is it?"

"Can't tell yet," Dusty answered and worked another pole loose. As he turned it over, he frowned. "Curious."

"What is?" Maureen asked and knelt.

"The pole is charred on the top but not the bottom."

"Which means?"

Dusty placed the pole to the side and started working on the next one. "Which means that soon after the fire started, the oxygen needed to burn through the poles vanished."

"Snuffed when the roof collapsed?" Steve asked.

Dusty nodded. "I would say so, yes."

Steve eased two poles out and laid them to the side, then helped Sylvia remove the pole she'd been working on.

Dusty got down on his stomach and leaned into the opening. He twisted, looking around at the beautiful masonry-lined walls, and the stairs leading down. "This is classic Chacoan stonework. I'd guess circa A.D. 1090 to A.D. 1100. *Gorgeous.*"

"How deep is it?" Maureen repeated.

Dusty said, "If you will hand me the flashlight from my dig kit—"

"On the way." Maureen trotted for the green ammo box where Dusty kept his excavation tools. Metal rattled, then she ran back and handed it to him. "Be careful. There could be something fragile in the bottom, like a human body."

"That's *why* I asked for the flashlight, Doctor. Feeling my feet slide off skulls unnerves me."

Dusty pressed the switch and a flood of yellow bathed the opening.

In an awed voice, Steve said, "Yes, indeed. That's Chacoan masonry. Look at those stairs. Every stone was rubbed together until it fitted so tightly they didn't even need mortar. I wonder if the Mesa Verdean folks who came here in the mid-twelve-hundreds knew this opening existed?"

"They must have," Sylvia replied. "The poles burned on the top, which means they weren't covered with dirt when the roof fell."

Dusty said, "I'm going in to get a better look. Be prepared to rescue me if the opening collapses."

"Go for it," Sylvia said.

Dusty put his foot on the first stair and tested it to see if it would hold his weight. Then he walked deeper, one stair at a time.

"What's down there?" Steve called.

Dusty looked up and could see three heads leaning over the opening. Billowing clouds filled the blue sky above them. "Well," Dusty said as he examined the collapsed wall in front of him. "You were right. This was definitely a tunnel."

"A kiva tunnel!" Steve said excitedly. "I've never opened one before."

"You have now." Dusty ran his fingers over the cool stones.

Maureen said, "What was the tunnel used for?"

"During the Chacoan period, they were primarily ceremonial. The priests could emerge from the underworlds right before the eyes of the faithful. Later, after all the kiva burnings started, villages began building escape passageways, just in case their enemies attacked during a ritual and caught them inside the kiva."

Maureen called, "Do you think someone tried to escape through the passageway when this kiva caught fire?"

Dusty examined the walls, then knelt and surveyed the floor. A layer of dark brown earth covered the ground. When the tunnel collapsed, the force had thrown rock and dirt into this part of the passageway, covering up any evidence of usage. He saw no artifacts.

"I doubt that we'll ever know."

CHAPTER 44

SOMEONE PRODDED A fire with a stick, and Redcrop jerked awake, but she kept her eyes closed, listening, trying to learn as much as she could before they knew she had awakened.

Moccasins brushed sand. The steps light.

Dried blood matted the back of Redcrop's skull, and she felt like her head might explode. Was that what had happened? She'd been struck in the head? She remembered little about last night. She'd seen the Wolf Katsina rise from the brush, and for an instant thought it might be one of the sacred Dancers, then the katsina had leaped out with a war club . . .

The sound of breathing. Close. And the smell of vomit and smoked leather.

Redcrop shivered.

"Are you awake?" a child whispered.

Redcrop opened her eyes, and the little girl jumped back as though she'd been struck. She squatted five paces away, breathing hard.

Redcrop looked up at the concave stone ceiling of a rock shelter. The firelit roof stretched ten body lengths over her head. Her gaze followed the sloping rear wall down to the rolls of bedding hides five body lengths away. Two rolls. Firelight swirled over the thick buffalo fur. A third roll of hides, smaller, a child's hides, lay near Redcrop.

Where are the adults?

"Who are you?" Redcrop asked.

The girl didn't answer. She wore a filthy grease-stained hide cape, and her long black hair looked as though it had not been combed in moons. Bits of bark and leaves tangled with the snarls.

Redcrop forced herself to sit up and almost collapsed from the pain in her head. Yucca cords wrapped her ankles, and she could sense that her arms had been tied behind her back, but she couldn't feel them. They might have been dead meat.

"Water?" Redcrop croaked. "Could I have some water?"

The girl twisted her dirty hands in her lap.

Water pots sat near the fire hearth, along with nests of cups, bowls, and horn spoons. An enormous soot-blackened pot hung on a tripod at the edge of the flames. Just to the right of the big pot lay a bundle. An object the size of a large gourd had been carefully wrapped in bright yellow cloth.

A sandy wash ran at the base of the rock shelter. The way out?

"Where is this place?"

Redcrop looked up at the juniper-studded canyon rim thirty body lengths away. Humps of tan sandstone stood silhouetted against the pale blue gleam of dawn. Many shallow canyons cut the desert. She might be anywhere, a hand of time from Longtail village or a day's walk.

"How long did I sleep?"

The girl sucked her lower lip.

On the verge of tears, Redcrop choked out, "My name is Redcrop. What's your name?"

The girl cocked her head as though listening to the darkness. Her eyes darted to the junipers and the popping coals. She looked back at Redcrop, then duck-walked closer.

"Are you a witch?" she whispered.

Redcrop stared at her, then shook her aching head. "No. I'm just a girl, like you."

"Grandfather says all of your people are witches."

"The Katsinas' People aren't witches. We just believe in different gods than you do."

The girl peered at her with glassy, inhuman eyes. The feral eyes of a wolf pup.

Redcrop said, "The katsinas—"

"Eat people's souls!" the girl shouted. "That's what happened to her!" She whirled around and pointed to a dark alcove in the rear of the rock shelter. "Katsinas sucked her souls out through her ears."

Redcrop had to squint against the fire's gleam to see the rounded shape hanging on the wall. "What is that?"

"An old husk."

It took Redcrop several heartbeats to realize she was looking at a mummy, a mummy with a rope around her waist. White hair fluttered in the cold breeze. She murmured, "Blessed Ancestors."

The girl nodded. "She was the first Matron to believe in the katsinas. She made all of her people believe in them, too. That's why she's a mummy. The katsinas—"

"The katsinas are good gods. They bring rain and game animals, and they watch over us to keep us—"

The girl shouted, "They started the war between the First People and the Made People so they would have food!"

Redcrop felt sick. She sank back to the ground and curled onto her side. When the sickening throb in her head dimmed, she repeated, "What's your name? My name is Redcrop."

The girl chewed her lip for several moments, then answered, "Piper's Song, but my people call me Piper."

"Piper," Redcrop said and smiled. "That's a pretty name."

The girl smiled back, a quick, almost horrifying gesture: an animal pretending to be a little girl.

Piper hissed, "Are you one of the Made People?"

Redcrop's heart thudded against her ribs. "No. I was captured when I was younger than you. My people believe we came to this world as wolves made from gouts of Father Sun's fire. We—"

"Oh. You're a Fire Dog."

"Yes, though I've lived with Made People almost my whole life."

"Made People aren't really human," Piper confided. "The Creator made them look human, but they have animal souls. Under their skins they are really buffaloes, and bears, and ants. That's why they worship the katsinas. Katsinas have animal souls, too."

Redcrop lay there, her head splitting, and forced her lungs to slowly breathe in and out.

Piper pointed a dirty finger at the mummy. "My great-great-grandfather was the son of the Blessed Cornsilk and the Blessed Swallowtail."

Redcrop frowned. She'd never heard of Swallowtail. His name had no place in the sacred stories of Cornsilk and Poor Singer. She wondered who he might have been. Perhaps he'd been made an Outcast, and his name deliberately forgotten by his people. Her gaze returned to the mummy.

"What was her name?"

"Hmm?" Piper turned to look. "Oh, she was Matron Night Sun. Grandfather looked for her for many summers."

Night Sun.

The red gleam from the coals danced across Piper's face.

"Where did he find her?"

"In a fallen-down room at Talon Town. Made People captured her and her family and dragged them back there. They kept them as slaves for a while. Then they killed her and walled her up in a room." Piper pounded the air with her fists. "Grandfather had to knock the wall down with a big rock to get to her."

Wind swirled through the shelter and the fire spluttered. Light danced over the mummy's shriveled face.

"He knocked down a lot of walls before he found her," Piper said. "I've been to Talon Town. It's old and dirty. I don't wish to go back. It scares me."

Night Sun had been the last great ruler of the Straight Path Nation. She'd given up everything to marry one of the Made People. After she was gone, the other First People had made her an Outcast. But rather than ordering that her name be forgotten, they had decreed that no one would ever forget her name. It seemed a pathetic irony that Made People had dragged her back to the town she had abandoned, and forced her to live there as a slave before they'd killed her.

Flame Carrier had always told Night Sun's story in a reverent, but pained voice. Redcrop recalled because she'd never understood that pain. It had verged on guilt, and Redcrop couldn't fathom why her grandmother would feel guilty about Night Sun's decision to abandon her people for the love of a man.

Redcrop said, "I've heard stories of Night Sun."

"You have?" Piper said excitedly. "Tell me!"

Redcrop shook her head. If she was going to have any chance of escape, she had to build up her strength. "I need food and water. I'm very thirsty and I haven't really eaten in days."

Piper turned to look back at the pots near the fire. Her young brow furrowed. "I don't think I'd better. Grandfather didn't say you could drink or eat."

"Where is your family?"

"Mother and Grandfather went away to pray. They'll be back soon."

"Where's your father?"

Piper tilted her head as though she didn't understand the question. "Grandfather will be back soon."

"How soon?"

Piper lifted a shoulder. "They usually come back around dawn."

Redcrop surveyed the slice of pale blue sky visible over the canyon rim. Less than a hand of time away.

"Piper, I'm sure your mother would want me to have water. I'm just a girl, like you. Your mother would give you water if you were thirsty, wouldn't she? And food?"

Piper thought about that for a time, then nodded. "Yes."

"Did your mother or grandfather say I couldn't have food or water?"

"No."

"Then I think it would be all right. I would be very grateful if you would bring me a cup of water and some food."

Piper rose uncertainly, hesitated, then trotted to the fire. She dipped up a cup of water and tucked a brown fabric bag under her chin. As she walked around the fire, carrying the cup in both hands so she wouldn't spill it, Piper tripped over the yellow bundle. The bundle started rolling down the slight incline, peeling off the cloth, until a skull tumbled out.

Redcrop saw the toothless mouth and the hole in the bone, and memories of last night came flooding back. Her grandmother's grave had been desecrated, her body stolen . . .

Oh, gods.

Piper set the cup of water in front of Redcrop, and sat down cross-legged at her side. "I can't untie you," the girl said as she placed the brown bag at her feet, "but I can help you."

Piper lifted the cup to Redcrop's lips, and she drank greedily, spilling water down the front of her white cape, but her gaze remained on the skull.

It can't be. Can it?

Redcrop said, "Thank you, Piper. That was good."

Piper nodded and gestured north up the wash. "There's a little pool. It isn't big enough to bathe in, but we fill our water pots there."

Redcrop watched Piper untie the laces on the brown bag and pull out a long strip of jerky. She held it up for Redcrop to take a bite. Redcrop tore off a hunk with her teeth and chewed. Crushed beeweed sprinkled the meat, giving it a delicious peppery taste. Redcrop swallowed and Piper held up the jerky for her to take another bite. As she chewed, her stomach squealed, longing for more.

"Do you live here?" Redcrop asked.

"Sometimes." Piper jerked a nod. "But mostly we live in falling-down villages where Grandfather's people used to live."

"Do you know the names of the villages? Maybe I've been to them."

Piper ate as though she hadn't had food in a moon, chewing swiftly, swallowing, and ripping off more jerky. "We lived in Talon Town for a while, then Center Place, and Sunset Town. Since last spring, we've lived around here. I like it better here than in Straight Path Canyon. Too many bad ghosts live there."

With the food, the pain in Redcrop's head began to ease. She took a deep breath and felt a little better. "Who is your grandfather? What does he do?"

"He's a great Trader. He lives in other villages most of the time." Piper stuffed the last bite of jerky into her own mouth, and pulled out another strip. She let Redcrop take a bite, and slurred, "This is good meat, isn't it?"

"Yes. I like the beeweed flavor."

"Me too. Mother sprinkles the meat with beeweed and dried phlox blossoms. It's the flowers that give the meat the sweet taste."

"It's really good."

Piper smiled, as if proud of her mother. "Yes, Made People have animal souls. That's why we can eat them. They're not really human. They're like buffalo and bear . . . what's wrong?"

Redcrop choked down the meat she'd already started to swallow and sat trembling.

"Do you need water?" Piper asked, her young voice worried.

The more Redcrop shook, the more stunning the pain in her head became. She tried to calm herself by closing her eyes and taking deep breaths. She choked again and Piper scrambled to her feet.

"I'll get you another cup of water!"

Piper ran to the water pots by the fire, filled the cup, and rushed back. "Here," she said as she tipped the cup to Redcrop's lips.

Redcrop drank, cleaning the taste from her mouth.

When Piper lowered the cup, she leaned close and stared deeply into Redcrop's eyes. "More?"

"No. No, thank you."

Piper sat down in front of Redcrop, drew up her knees, and reached for another stick of jerky. She propped her elbows on her knees as she ate, staring at Redcrop with bright curious eyes.

Piper said, "You're pretty."

"You're pretty, too, Piper. Doesn't your mother ever comb your hair?"

Piper stopped eating and looked at the filthy snarls that fell over her shoulders. "There have been a lot of Bead Days."

"What's that? A bead day?"

Piper's shoulders hunched, and she went back to her jerky, chewing, swallowing, chewing, as though she hadn't heard the question.

Redcrop couldn't move her numb arms, but she worked at the cords around her ankles, trying to loosen them.

Piper watched her intently for a time, then said, "You can't get away."

Redcrop twisted her ankles and grimaced as the cords sawed into her flesh. Blood flowed down her feet. "Piper, did your family kill my grandmother?"

Piper cocked her head like a surprised bird. She pointed up at the ceiling. "Her bones went to the clouds. Grandfather cleaned them and turned them into smoke so they could fly."

"You mean he burned—"

"Shh! They're coming." Piper used her chin to gesture northward down the sandy wash. "See."

Redcrop glanced out at the darkness, and fear ran like fire through her veins. "Your family?"

"No." Her voice got very small. Piper sucked in her lower lip and clamped it with her teeth. Her eyes went huge.

Redcrop fell to her side and kicked her feet to stretch the cords. They were going to kill her, just as they had Grandmother. She tried to remember everything Grandmother had taught her about the journey to the afterlife, where the monsters stood, the traps along the trail...

"Closer," Piper whispered. She pulled her knees against her chest and hid everything but her eyes, which stared unblinking at the darkness from a halo of filthy tangles.

"Where?" Redcrop sobbed. "I don't see anything!"

In the barest murmur, Piper said, "There are only two of them. Usually there are ten."

"Who are they?"

Piper's gaze fixed on the darkness. "White Moccasins."

"Who?" Redcrop fought to blink her tears away, and see something, anything, but she saw only the junipers rocking in the wind and the tan sandstone walls shimmering in the azure gleam of approaching dawn.

"Piper, please, help me? Cut me loose!"

Piper hissed, "It's Him."

"Him?"

In an awed whisper, she said, "First Man."

Redcrop wanted to scream, but dared not, not yet. She kept her voice controlled. "Who?"

"Wolf Slayer," Piper replied almost too low to hear.

"He eats wolves."

Redcrop curled into a ball and wept. These were gods she did not know and she feared all the more because of it.

"Who is Wolf Slayer?"

"Your people killed him."

"If he's dead, how can he be coming?"

"He's coming," Piper said and pointed. "Right there."

Two men walked into the rock shelter, their long white capes swaying around their bodies. One of them, the tallest, wore a wolf mask and had long black hair. The other, a head shorter, wore a raven mask. Redcrop should have screamed and scrambled to get away. But she shocked them.

She sat up and started singing in an agonized voice, a voice that resembled a death cry. Flame Carrier had taught her the words as a little girl of barely two or three summers. She had forced Redcrop to learn them:

"Come the brothers, born of Sun! One is slayed. Here by the long trail, his corpse is laid. You, born of Father Sun, laid in the light next to night. Choose my people. Come the brothers, born of Sun!"

The man in the raven mask turned to his companion and whispered, "That is one of our most sacred Songs. How does *she* know it?"

Redcrop sucked in a breath. His voice sounded familiar.

The tall man walked forward.

When he stood over her, he pulled off his wolf mask and stared at Redcrop with haunting eyes, eyes electrifying in their intensity. He had a triangular face, with a long nose. His black hair disappeared with the mask, and she could see that a human scalp had been fitted inside the wolf's fur. His real hair, long and white, tumbled around his shoulders. "My sister taught you that, didn't she?"

Redcrop swallowed hard. "Your sister?"

"The Blessed Flame Carrier."

Redcrop paled at the mention of her name. Had he no fear that he would pull her grandmother back from the Land of the Dead? That she might be trapped here on earth and become a wailing ghost?

"My words can't draw her back," he said, startling Redcrop. "She is already in the skyworlds with our ancestors. She climbed up with the smoke. The greatest of us do not run the road to the underworlds." He gestured expansively to the sky. "We fly."

He stared up at the last of the Evening People, then crouched in front of Redcrop. His eyes gleamed like polished black stones.

"What my foolish sister did not tell you," he said, and smiled at her with broken rotted teeth, "is that coming from your lips, those words were an abomination. You are not one of us, no matter what Songs you know."

He slapped Redcrop across the mouth.

Redcrop cried out and sobbed, "But she told me—"

"She told you the Blessed Ancestors would hear you and save you?"

Redcrop wept. "Yes."

He leaned down very close and whispered, "Only when you have been bathed in blood will you be saved. In less than a hand of time, the Blessed Two Hearts—"

"Bear Dancer!" the man in the raven mask called and furiously waved his war club. "There's someone out there!"

Bear Dancer! Grandmother's older brother?

Bear Dancer stood. "My son?"

"No. I don't think so. I think there's more than one."

"Perhaps my son and my brother. But let us make sure."

Redcrop tried to think. Grandmother had only spoken of one brother. Could Bear Dancer be talking about Grandmother's half brother? The brother she'd never known?

Bear Dancer jerked the cotton sash from around his waist and threw it at Piper. "When I am gone, gag her."

He rose and took three long strides to look at where the other man aimed his club. They spoke softly, and both men sprinted away, up the wash into the dark canyon shadows.

Redcrop rolled to her side, and her belly heaved. Burning liquid seared her throat and nose.

Piper scampered across the ground, glanced repeatedly up the sandy wash, and squatted next to Redcrop. "Are you all right?"

Redcrop nodded.

Piper said, "Here," and pulled a turquoise wolf from her pocket. Tiny, and crudely carved, it looked almost identical to the one that Stone Ghost had found in the hole in Grandmother's head. "I was going to give it to you after they killed you, but they may take you away." She tucked it into the top of Redcrop's left legging.

Redcrop stared at her with blurry eyes. "Piper, did you give one of these to my grandmother?"

Piper nodded, but glanced around as though frightened someone might hear her. "Yes. No one told me they were going to burn her and send her to the clouds. I thought she was one of the Made People."

"And you wanted her to be able to find her way to the Land of the Dead?"

"If you can't find your way, you get lost and the monsters eat you."

As if that young voice had painted perfect images on her souls, Redcrop had a momentary glimpse of a lonely little girl forced to see things no child should ever see, a girl who heard the cries of the victims, watched them die, and could not walk away without making certain their souls were safe. The realization pierced Redcrop's heart.

"Piper, please untie my hands."

She shook her head.

"Do you want to see me dead?"

Piper twisted her hands in her lap.

Redcrop said, "Piper, I have a gift for you. Please look beneath my cape."

"What is it?"

"Please, look. I can't hurt you."

Piper crept forward, flipped Redcrop's cape aside, and jumped backward. Her mouth gaped at the corn-husk doll.

"Where did you find her?" She snatched the doll from Redcrop's belt and scuttled backwards with the doll clutched to her chest.

"I found her in the coyote den where you dropped her when your grandfather Bear Dancer came to get you."

Piper sat on the ground and stroked the doll's hair so roughly that Redcrop feared she might rip off the frail corn-husk head.

It took twenty heartbeats before Piper remembered the sash, grabbed for it, and ran forward.

Before she gagged Redcrop, she looked at her with shining eyes, and said, "He's not my grandfather."

CHAPTER 45

DRY NEEDLES AND fallen berries crackled as Straighthorn crawled through the junipers overlooking the shallow canyon. The brightest of the Evening People sparkled above him, but pale lavender light banded the eastern horizon. He studied it, gauging how much longer he had before the darkness failed him.

A hand of time. Maybe a little less.

He blinked the sweat from his eyes, gripped his war club, and got down on his belly to slide to the edge of the rim.

One hundred hands below, the firelit rock shelter gleamed. Redcrop lay on her side with her white cape spreading around her like a mantle of snow. Dead? A little girl crouched a few hands away, furiously rocking a corn-husk doll in her arms, as if trying to get a stubborn baby to go to sleep. Redcrop lay perfectly still.

Straighthorn pulled himself forward on his elbows and looked along the rim for a trail down. A dark slash cut the canyon wall perhaps two hundred body lengths to the south. It was probably a shadowed crevice, but it might be a trail.

He swiftly backed away from the rim, got to his feet in the thickest junipers, and sprinted headlong toward the slash. His fringed sleeves whipped against the branches as he passed.

It is a trail!

He flopped on his stomach fifty hands away and surveyed the junipers. Dust puffed before his face every time he exhaled, scenting the air. Toppled boulders the height of a man lined the trail down into the canyon. It didn't appear to be guarded, but it must be.

Straighthorn eased forward on his hands and knees.

Just as he rose to his feet and started the run toward the trail, he heard a sound and spun around with his club up.

"*Straighthorn?*" a familiar voice called.

"Who's there?" Junipers rustled as the man pushed through. "Who are you?"

"It's me, you young fool."

Skink ducked beneath an overhanging limb and trotted toward Straighthorn. Tall and lean, he wore a knee-length buckskin shirt and carried a bow and quiver over his shoulder. His flat, heavily lashed face bore a sheen of sweat, as though he'd run all the way to get there.

"Blessed gods, Skink! What are you doing out here? I thought you stayed to help search for Elder Springbank."

Skink grasped Straighthorn's shoulder in a friendly gesture, and whispered, "Our elder died in the fire, my friend, and there's no time to talk. Have you seen Browser or Catkin?"

"No."

"They should be here soon. We left the village at the same time." He turned to the firelit canyon. "What's your plan?"

Straighthorn let out a breath and gestured helplessly with his club. "I was going to run down this trail into the rock shelter and get her."

Skink's mouth tightened. "Oh, very clever. You want to run out in the open so everyone can shoot at you. That should work."

Straighthorn's face reddened. He flapped his arms. "I thought I was alone. I didn't know what else to do."

"You're not alone." Skink's eyes narrowed as he studied the lay of the canyon. "All right, do you see that trail to the north?"

As the day brightened, many things came into view that Straighthorn had not seen before. In the darkness, he'd have run right past the narrow game trail. Shamed, he said, "Yes. I see it."

"You start down this trail. I will go up and come down the northern trail and hide in those trees at the base of the cliff. You won't see me, but I'll be guarding you the whole time. You understand? If something goes wrong, do not look in my direction or you'll give away my position, but that is where my shot will come from. Be ready for it."

Straighthorn jerked a nod. "I understand, Skink."

"Good." Skink slapped his shoulder. "Go."

Skink trotted away into the dark junipers, and Straighthorn began the descent into the canyon.

Loose gravel scritched beneath his feet as he dodged from boulder to boulder.

Redcrop still had not moved, but the little girl skipped around the shelter. Her shrill singing rang out, magnified by the arched ceiling of the rock shelter.

When he reached the sandy wash less than one hundred hands from the rock shelter, he ducked behind a thicket of greasewood and used his sleeve to wipe his forehead. Through the spiky tangle of limbs, he saw Redcrop shift and Straighthorn's heart almost burst through his ribs. She sat up, sobbed, and struggled with the cords around her ankles.

The little girl started running around in circles, faster and faster . . . then suddenly stopped and looked out into the darkness where Straighthorn hid.

Straighthorn frowned. Could she see him?

The girl whispered something to Redcrop, and Redcrop whirled around to look.

Straighthorn searched the canyon bottom, then slowly rose to his feet. "Redcrop?"

She screamed against her gag, fell onto her belly, and struggled to reach him.

Straighthorn ran to her, his feet pounding out a muted rhythm in the sand.

"Gods, I'm glad to see you alive," he said, as he laid his war club down, ripped his knife from his belt, and began sawing through the bindings on her ankles. If someone came, at least she would be able to run.

She kept moaning, shrieking against her gag. He jumped around to free her wrists next.

"Redcrop, hold still! I don't wish to cut you and I—"

"You really are a fool."

Straighthorn's gaze shot up. For a moment, he did not understand. He watched Skink step into the firelight with his bow drawn and aimed at Straighthorn's heart. Two men in white capes flanked Skink. One wore a black raven mask. The other, the taller man, looked to be around seventy summers. He had long spiderweb-thin white hair.

Straighthorn looked from Skink to the others and whispered, "What's happening?"

Skink shook his head disdainfully. "You are about to die, Straighthorn."

The tall old man with white hair smiled at Skink. "Well done, my son. Did you have any problems?"

"No, Father."

The old man stepped around Skink and came toward Straighthorn. He knelt and picked up Straighthorn's club.

Straighthorn glared at Skink, and the tall man ordered, "Throw your knife away, then toss your bow and quiver to the side."

Straighthorn trembled with rage. That's why Skink had ended the search for the murderers after the Matron's death. That's why he hadn't wished to hunt for Redcrop. He'd been spying on them, working against them all the time.

"Was it you," Straighthorn asked Skink, "who set fire to the village tonight?"

Skink smiled.

No one would have thought twice about Skink wandering around the village. He was on guard duty. People expected him to examine every unusual sound. More important, Browser had left Skink in charge of the village guards. He could have ordered everyone else away while he piled up brush and poured pine pitch—

"Drop your knife!" Skink repeated his father's order.

Straighthorn let his knife fall to the ground, and eased his bow and quiver from his shoulder. He tossed them to his right, almost striking the filthy little girl. She let out a shriek and ran to the rear of the rock shelter, where she huddled with her doll pulled to her chest. She looked more like a wild animal than a child.

Straighthorn wrapped his arms around Redcrop. He could feel her working to pull the last threads apart, to free her hands. He had to fight to keep his voice even. "What do you want from us? We've done nothing to you."

Redcrop leaned against him, shuddering, and he tightened his arms. They were going to die, here, now, and the only thing Straighthorn could think of was his indignation that Skink had fooled them all.

"Did you help to murder our Matron? Did the man's tracks belong to you?" Straighthorn asked. "That must have been a challenge, eh? It takes a great warrior to kill an old woman."

"Shut your mouth!"

Redcrop had worked her hands free. Straighthorn could feel them moving beneath her cape.

Please, tell me you hid a weapon . . .

To distract the onlookers, Straighthorn said, "Ah, but I forgot about the woman. Perhaps you grew squeamish and had to let her do your killing for you? Yes, the brave Skink. I hope you live long enough that I can beat your guts out with my club."

"I will," Skink replied and pulled his bowstring taut. "But you won't."

"No, wait." The tall man touched Skink's arm. "We must wait for Two Hearts. He said he—"

A hiss.

The white-haired man staggered and stared wide-eyed at the arrow sticking from his chest. The bright red fletching shimmered in the firelight. A hideous scream broke from his lips. The next arrow hit almost simultaneously, striking the short man in the raven mask in the throat. He clawed at his neck and tried to run, but fell facefirst to the sand, gurgling and rolling, trying to dislodge the arrow.

Straighthorn roared and leaped for Skink, shouting, "Redcrop, run! *Run!*"

As Straighthorn hit Skink, Skink's shot went wild, flying out into the darkness. He grabbed a handful of Straighthorn's hair and slammed Straighthorn in the head with his bow. Straighthorn got his fingers around the bow and screamed, "Give it to me so I can kill you! I'm going to kill you, you traitor!" He jabbed his thumb into Skink's eye, and when Skink shrieked, his grip loosened. Straighthorn ripped the bow from Skink's hand, rolled, and bashed Skink over the head. From the corner of his eye, he saw Redcrop running down the wash.

Skink's head landed squarely in the middle of Straighthorn's chest, knocking the air out of him. They both skidded across the sandy floor of the rock shelter, roaring, kicking, shouting.

Straighthorn managed to get on top and smashed his forehead into Skink's nose twice before Skink brought his knee up into Straighthorn's groin. Straighthorn cried out and grabbed Skink's hands, but Skink, much heavier than Straighthorn, rolled him over, and glared into Straighthorn's eyes.

"You worm," Skink hissed. Clotted blood bubbled from his broken nose. "I always wanted to kill you with my bare hands."

He slammed a fist into Straighthorn's throat and Straighthorn choked and gasped for air. He grabbed Skink's hand again, but he could feel Skink working free and knew he was losing. Had he given Redcrop enough time to get away? As a last resort, Straighthorn roared, lunged, and fastened his teeth onto Skink's broken nose. Skink screamed and beat at Straighthorn's head, but Straighthorn refused to let go. He bit down hard and blood spurted hotly, filling his mouth, running down the sides of his face.

Skink jerked one hand loose, balled his fist, and pounded the side of Straighthorn's head until Straighthorn's teeth tore through Skink's nose.

It came off in Straighthorn's mouth. Skink bellowed and jerked away. Straighthorn spat the rubbery mess out, locked an arm around Skink's head, and gripped his jaw.

As he twisted, Straighthorn shouted, "You were going to kill me? I'm going to cut your eyes out and feed them to the village dogs, then I'm going to boil your miserable testicles—"

Skink slammed his knee into Straighthorn's groin again, and Straighthorn's stomach heaved. He vomited in Skink's hair, but didn't let go. He kept twisting and roaring. He could feel Skink's fingers groping for his windpipe and panic fired his veins. He groaned as he threw all of his weight into twisting Skink's head off.

A loud crack split the night and Skink turned into a limp, quivering mass of flesh. Straighthorn shoved the body off and crawled across the rock shelter. His war club rested beside Skink's dead father.

Straighthorn grabbed the club, stumbled to his feet, and saw Catkin sprinting down the southern trail, coming hard. The dust she kicked up glimmered in the firelight.

"What took you so long?" Straighthorn asked.

"You didn't slide your feet enough." She knelt beside Skink and lifted his eyelids, then put two fingers on his throat to test for a pulse. After a few heartbeats, she rose and ran to the man in the mask. Over her shoulder, she asked, "Are you all right?"

Straighthorn sucked in a breath and staggered after her. "Yes."

Catkin ripped the raven mask from the man's face.

In shock, Straighthorn gasped. "Water Snake!"

"Of course," Catkin hissed and threw the mask into the dirt. She glowered down at the dead man's bloody face. Her voice shook with rage. "I should have known. Obsidian didn't draw him from his duties on the night of the murder. He took her into the kiva and coupled with her so she wouldn't hear our Matron's screams."

"What?" Straighthorn said in confusion. "I know nothing about—"

Catkin interrupted, "Are you well enough to keep up with me?"

He nodded. "I will keep up. Where is the War Chief?"

"He ran ahead. To the trail that cuts down at the head of this canyon."

Straighthorn blinked. "So you know where we are? I've never seen this place."

"We ran up this canyon on the way to Aspen village. Now gather your weapons and follow me. Browser may be in trouble." She sprinted up the wash.

Straighthorn grabbed for his bow and quiver, and the little girl caught his eye. She huddled in a dark corner of the rock shelter, petting her doll, humming loudly to herself. Her eyes resembled those of a suffocating animal, huge and bulging, ready to burst from her skull.

A helpless sensation went through him. Should he take her with him? Would she give away his position to his enemies?

They are her people. Of course she will.

Straighthorn pulled his gaze away and ran after Catkin.

CHAPTER 46

REDCROP STOPPED IN the middle of the wash. The canyon had grown steep and narrow. Pines fringed the rim five hundred hands above her. Despite the pale blue sky, shadows cloaked the canyon bottom. The screams and shouts had died a finger of time ago, leaving her in eerie silence. She didn't know what lay ahead, but she couldn't risk going back.

"He's coming," she whispered, and tears blurred her eyes. "He'll be here soon."

She didn't want to imagine what she would do if it wasn't Straighthorn who came for her.

Redcrop trotted up the winding canyon, searching for a place to hide. She studied the toppled boulders and brush, but nothing moved. Not even a whisper of wind penetrated this deep. After about one hundred paces, the sand started to grow damp, and she could smell water. Her dry throat constricted, longing for a drink.

Mist crept from around the next bend like ghostly serpents, slithering out, then retreating, only to slither out again. A spring?

She pulled up the hem of her cape and ran.

When she rounded the curving canyon wall, she stopped dead in her tracks.

A tall old man moved through the mist, arranging what looked like stones around a tiny black-and-white pot. He grunted as he bent, then straightened and sighed, as if pleased by his work. He wore a brown-and-white turkey feather cape that flashed as he walked. Even in the dim light, Redcrop could see his long hooked nose and white hair.

Something about the way he moved . . .

Redcrop walked closer and frowned as he placed another object. Redcrop's foot slipped off a slick piece of wood, and the old man gasped, and spun around. His wrinkled lips sunk in over toothless gums.

Redcrop blurted, "Elder Springbank! What are you doing out here?"

His black eyes widened. He rushed toward her with his gnarled old hands out. "Blessed gods, child. What are *you* doing here? You must leave immediately! You are in great danger."

"I know, Elder, I just escaped—"

"What you just escaped from is nothing compared to what's coming! Do you understand me? Run, child!"

Springbank's fingers sank into Redcrop's arms like talons and he swung her around and shoved her back the way she'd come.

"Elder, wait! I think there are warriors coming up this canyon. If I go back—"

"There *are* warriors coming!"

Redcrop spun around breathlessly. "You know there are?"

"Of course, I do!"

"How—"

"I know it!" he said furiously. Then, more quietly, he added, "Please believe me. They are coming to meet me. I've been waiting for them since they dragged me out of the burning kiva last night."

"The burning kiva?" she said and horror prickled her veins. "At Longtail village?"

"Yes," he said softly. Beads of sweat glistened on his hooked nose. "If we live through the next hand of time, I will tell you all about it, but for now, we must find a place to hide you."

The village burned? How many of my friends are dead? Is that the glow I saw last night just before . . . ?

"Come with me," he said, and guided Redcrop toward a dark wall of junipers that grew in a pile of boulders. "The problem is, they know about this place, too. In fact, I suspect their people have known about it for hundreds of sun cycles. Every time they find a precious object that belonged to one of the First People, they bring it here to hide it. I can't guarantee they won't follow us inside."

Redcrop followed him. "Where are we going?"

"Over there. Climb up on that slab of sandstone."

Springbank shoved her toward it, and she climbed.

A muffled groan escaped his lips as he stepped up behind her. He wobbled, and Redcrop grabbed his sticklike old arm to keep him from falling.

He steadied himself, patted her hand, and said, "Thank you, child."

The stringy muscles in his neck stood out like cords as he parted the branches and peered into the darkness beyond.

Redcrop cast a glance over her shoulder, but she saw no sign of warriors, not yet.

Springbank stepped through and held the branches aside for her. "Come, child. Hurry."

Redcrop gaped at the cave. The small round opening spread perhaps seven or eight hands wide. She would have to get down on her hands and knees to crawl inside.

"Move, child!"

Redcrop got down and scrambled into the hole. Cool air blew her hair around her face.

Springbank crawled through behind her, and said, "Stand up. It's all right. The tunnel is more than twice your height, but it's less than a body's length wide. Extend your hands and you'll feel the walls."

Terror filled her. She did not know which was worse, the warriors outside or the impenetrable darkness that lay ahead. She extended her arms and her fingers touched cold stone. "Where are we going?"

Springbank gave her shoulder a comforting pat. "Don't you feel the wind? There's another way out."

"How far?"

"Just brace your hands on the walls and walk. The tunnel slopes upward and breaks the surface of the ground about a thousand hands from the canyon. I'll accompany you until you can see daylight, then I must go back."

To Redcrop's surprise, the floor of the tunnel was fairly even. They moved swiftly through the musty darkness.

"There's a bend up here," he whispered. "You are going to curve to your right."

Something skittered in the darkness, and for an instant, cold air bathed her face. Cold air and a strange scent that made her shiver. Something fetid and old, like the dust of lost civilizations. Where had she smelled that odor before?

Redcrop glanced over her shoulder, and Springbank whispered, "We haven't time to dally, Redcrop. Please, *walk.*"

She felt her way around the curve and saw a luminous blur ahead. "I think I see the opening." Relief made her light-headed; she started to run.

"Don't run!" Springbank shouted. "The floor is much more uneven up here. Walk carefully until you can truly see."

"I will, Elder, I just—I'm anxious, I want to—"

The floor dropped away suddenly, and Redcrop cried out and clawed at the walls. Springbank caught her flailing arm and pulled her to her feet. The drop had been little more than two hands deep, but she'd twisted her ankle.

"Are you hurt, child? Can you walk?"

"I don't know!"

Springbank held her arm in a tight grip. "Try it."

Redcrop tested her ankle and had to bite back the cry of pain that worked up her throat. "It—it doesn't want to take my weight, Elder."

"Then you must crawl, child. Believe me, crawling is better than staying here. I promise you that I will try to return for you, but I cannot guarantee you that the next footsteps you hear will be mine. Do you understand?"

Redcrop felt sick. "Yes."

She longed to sit down and weep. Springbank supported her arm until she got down on her hands and knees and started feeling her way along the floor.

"I'm all right, Elder."

"You're certain?"

She felt the same way she had as a child when she'd first learned of her mother's death. As if the world had died. "Yes, I can crawl."

"Good. I should go. I don't think they will take kindly if I'm—"

"Please, go, Elder. Thank you."

He was silent for a moment, then she felt his hand on her back, the touch light. "I pray the Blessed Katsinas keep you safe, child."

"You also, Elder."

She heard his steps going rapidly back down the tunnel.

Redcrop hung her head and fought to regain control. Without him, she felt terrified and alone.

But she crawled.

BROWSER WALKED BY the pond silently, and examined the bone beads that encircled the pot. Large beads. Each had a hole drilled in the center. They looked as if they'd been made from pieces of human skull. What sort of strange ritual was this? He had never seen it before. In the brightening gleam of dawn, he could make out the prints in the damp sand.

He scanned the dark gray cliffs, searching for movement, then followed the man's tracks; he had hurried away from the pond, his stride long, almost running. When the man's tracks connected with a woman's, Browser glanced at the junipers and the toppled boulders.

Gods, is it them?

He gripped his war club and continued on. The steps vanished below a sandstone ledge covered with scrubby junipers. A strange musky scent surrounded the junipers.

Browser stepped up onto the ledge and peered through the dark weave of branches. Someone had passed through the trees, snapping twigs. A turkey feather hung from a tuft of needles.

Browser eased through and saw the cave. Most of the prints had been smoothed away by a dragging cape, or the hem of a long dress, but he saw two handprints pressed into the dust near the cave's mouth.

He whispered, "They crawled inside."

Browser bent to examine the interior. Utter darkness met his gaze. He sniffed at the dank odor of packrats and mold, then got down on his hands and knees.

As he stuck his head through, he glimpsed a fringed white moccasin . . .

The blow came out of nowhere, slammed into his head, and knocked him face-first into the dust. He twisted desperately, trying to look up. A shifting blur of faces swam above him. One face . . . or ten?

CATKIN WALKED CAREFULLY around the pond, studying the tracks. The sky had begun to purple overhead, but the cliffs remained a deep dark gray.

"Browser found the man's tracks first," she said to Straighthorn, who stood guard looking down the canyon. "Then he followed the man's tracks until they met up with Redcrop's."

Straighthorn glanced over his shoulder at her. "And then?"

"Let us find out."

Catkin placed her steps to the side of Browser's and followed them back to where they met Redcrop's tracks. "They veer off," she said, and swerved right toward a tangle of junipers that grew in a boulder pile. "All three of them stepped onto this sandstone slab."

Straighthorn backed over to look at the scuffed dust and the mixture of moccasin and sandal prints. "They pushed through the junipers. See the broken twigs?"

Catkin nodded. "I will let you know what I find."

Straighthorn licked his lips and jerked a nod. Sweat coated his bruised face. A huge black knot had swollen on the left side of his forehead. Catkin sniffed the air and the coppery tang ate at her insides.

She shouldered through the junipers and frowned. The mouth of the small cave was splattered with blood. She knelt and ran her finger over dark spots. Fresh blood. It had just begun to dry. Knee and handprints marked the soil. Her gut tightened. Browser's blood? Redcrop's? She prayed that Browser had caught Two Hearts and the blood belonged to him.

"But if that were true," she whispered to herself, "the man would be lying here dead. Unless Browser wounded him—"

"And had to follow him inside?" Straighthorn asked.

He peered at Catkin through the weave of juniper needles.

She nodded. "I'd say that's our best guess. Browser probably struck the man, and the man ran away and crawled into this cave."

Straighthorn looked at her with soft eyes. "But where are Redcrop's tracks? Where was she when Browser attacked her captor?"

Catkin shook her head. "I see a woman's handprint on the left side of the cave, but—"

"Maybe she went in first?" Fear lined his face. "Perhaps the man forced her to crawl inside?"

Catkin wiped the blood from her finger onto her buckskin war shirt. "There's no sign that she was forced in here, Straighthorn. You can look at the tracks yourself. She met the man and walked here with him. She never stumbled, or dragged her feet as if being forced. She never tried to run. I think she crawled into this cave willingly."

"But"—he gave her a heartsick look—"how could that be? She would never . . ."

Straighthorn's eyes flew open, but before he could spin around, Catkin saw the white capes flash. The warriors crept from behind boulders and trees and glided forward in ghostly silence.

"Oh, gods," Straighthorn whispered.

Catkin shouted, *"Get into the cave!"*

Straighthorn dove through the trees for the hole in the cliff.

CHAPTER 47

THE FLOOR UNDULATED, the dips and protrusions hidden in the darkness. Redcrop crawled on through the black cavern. Every time her injured foot stubbed rock, she wanted to scream.

The strange smell grew in strength: like old bones that had been moldering for sun cycles.

Redcrop's palm struck something small, cold, and round. She lifted it.

It tinkled.

The notes were so pure and beautiful, she rang it again.

"A bell," she whispered to herself. "It's a bell."

She turned it in her palm, smiling, longing to laugh. It had the cold smooth feel of metal. She touched the bell to her tongue. *A copper bell!*

She tucked it into the top of her moccasin, and continued on.

The luminous blur turned into an awl-prick of solid gray light.

Redcrop forced herself to crawl faster. How could the air be getting more foul as she neared the opening? She should be smelling dew-soaked earth and damp trees.

"Ow!" she cried without thinking when her knee ground over a pebble.

Redcrop reached down and had started to throw it away when it clinked.

"What—?"

She turned the object over until she knew for certain that it was another copper bell.

"Gods, how did these get here?"

They must have been left by the First People who had built Longtail village more than a hundred summers ago. Awe prickled her chest. Perhaps this cave had been one of their secret places. A sacred tunnel . . .

From her place in the womb of earth, she looked up suddenly and listened.

A faint voice whispered through the darkness.

"Come the brothers . . . born of Sun . . ."

The words floated across her souls; she wasn't certain if she actually heard them, or was remembering what had happened earlier in the rock shelter. Her grandmother told her that First Woman had spoken those words right after she had emerged from the underworlds.

"One is slayed. Here by the . . . trail . . . his corpse is laid."

A man's voice. Breathless, the words more panted than sung. The voice verged on ecstasy. Or an agony too terrible to be borne.

The voice of a dying man.

Scarcely perceptible footfalls echoed.

"You, born of F-father Sun, laid in the light next to n-night . . ." Sobs.

Elder Springbank's voice!

She had heard him Sing many times at ceremonials. Usually, he had a deep, ringing voice. She would know it, even when whispered in agony.

On her knees, her eyes blind with tears, she turned and started back down the tunnel.

A scream froze her blood. In the middle of the scream, she made out the words: *"Come the brothers, born of Sun! . . ."* The last word ended in a high-pitched wail.

A sudden trembling left her shaking so badly she could barely force herself to breathe. Had they caught him? The warriors he'd been expecting? He said they knew about this tunnel. Perhaps they hadn't found him where they'd expected to and came looking?

In a fit of frenzy, she turned and scrambled toward the light, toward the foul smell.

Hurry. Hurry!

Behind her, feet scuffed stone. She could hear him staggering, as though the man could not find the strength to put one foot before the other.

Tears ran down Redcrop's face. She crawled like a madwoman.

The metallic taint of blood carried on the air. She heard a tortured groan, but couldn't tell if it had come from behind or ahead.

The tunnel opened into a chamber. A yawning maw.

Redcrop's heart expanded at the sight. Her gaze swept the walls and lifted to the towering ceiling. She might have been kneeling in a womb of dove-colored radiance. Pots, hundreds of them, lined the shelves that had been carved into the stone. Pots of all colors and designs, red-on-tan, black-on-white, red-on-black. Some had lids, others did not. Precious shells and carved fetishes packed the open pots. Redcrop gaped at the wealth. One pot held nothing but jet frogs with turquoise eyes, another had a jumble of malachite wolves and red coral birds.

She heard a body thump onto the stone, and a man moaned, then wept, his desperation beyond pain, beyond words.

In a quavering voice, Redcrop whispered: "Elder Springbank?" She looked back.

The dark throat of the tunnel stirred, then fluttered as though filled with black wings—and she realized someone was coming through. Staggering toward her.

The man stepped into the pale gleam.

Crimson splotched Springbank's cape and dotted his white hair. Tears flooded the elder's wrinkled cheeks. He had both fists twined in War Chief Browser's collar, dragging him along behind.

"Help me, child!" he begged. "I found him lying in the cave entrance. He's hurt badly!"

"Oh, gods, what happened?" How on earth had the fragile elder managed to drag the War Chief? Redcrop scrambled back, clenching her teeth against the pain in her ankle.

Springbank eased Browser down and sank to the floor as if he'd used his last bit of energy. A club hung from Springbank's belt. She hadn't seen it earlier. Had it been hidden by his cape?

Springbank said, "The warriors I was supposed to meet—I think they found him." He held blood-soaked hands out to Redcrop. "Your grandmother was a Healer, child. Do something!"

Redcrop slid to Browser's side and brushed the hair from his round face. Blood leaked down his forehead in ropy red lines.

"It may not be as bad as it looks." She reached down to tear a length of cloth from her skirt. The sound of ripping fabric echoed in the still chamber. "Scalp wounds always bleed like this."

Springbank used his sleeve to wipe at the blood speckling his wrinkled face. "I've suffered enough of them to know that, but he's unconscious, and that means the blow was severe enough to make his souls flee."

"Yes, but often they return fairly quickly."

Browser's eyelids jerked. That was a good sign.

Springbank suddenly gasped and slid closer. "Gods, do you think he's wounded anywhere else? I'll search while you tend his head wound."

"Thank you, Elder."

Springbank's gnarled fingers untied the laces on Browser's buckskin cape and pulled it away from his muscular body. "I don't see any blood." He continued searching, pulling up the War Chief's sleeves, scrutinizing his chest and belly. He pulled a bone stiletto from the top of Browser's red leggings and tossed it away. Springbank's eyes narrowed when he saw Browser's small belt pouch. He opened it, and a sharp cry came from his lips.

Redcrop blurted, "What's wrong?"

Springbank pulled out a magnificent turquoise wolf and clutched it to his chest. "I searched for twenty-two summers before I found this. I feared it was gone forever."

Redcrop frowned at the wolf, wondering why the War Chief had been holding something that belonged to Elder Springbank. It resembled the wolf Piper had tucked into the top of her legging. "Twenty-two summers? Where did you find it?"

He peered down at the wolf with blurry eyes. "In a walled-up room in Talon Town. It was hanging around the throat of a hideous mummy."

Redcrop's veins tightened as fear rushed through her. The mummy in the rock shelter? With trembling hands, she used the cloth to wipe blood from Browser's forehead. The long gash began at his hairline and extended back across the middle of his skull. Redcrop folded the cloth, placed it over the wound, and pressed hard, but her eyes sought the daylight streaming through the hole less than fifty body lengths away. Escape. It lay so close.

"The bleeding will stop s-soon, Elder," she stammered.

Springbank put a hand on her hair and stroked it. "I thank you, child. I knew you could help him."

Springbank's hand gently moved down her hair to squeeze her shoulder. "I wish I knew what happened to him. There were no warriors around when I found him."

"He was struck from above, Elder."

Springbank's wrinkled mouth opened. "How do you know?"

"The wound. It's deeper in the front than the back. I think he was on the ground when someone hit him from above."

"You mean Browser may have been crawling away and his attacker straddled him and brought the club down on top of his head?"

Redcrop gave him a sidelong glance. "Yes."

Her hands started to shake. Had the War Chief followed their tracks to the tunnel and been attacked when he got down to crawl inside?

Springbank stroked Redcrop's arm in a way that sent shivers down her spine. "You are very good at helping people."

Redcrop pulled away and stared at him.

Springbank grabbed her hand. His bony fingers closed around her wrist in a viselike grip. "Why did you pull away from me?"

"I'm sorry, Elder. I'm just not accustomed—"

"Don't be frightened," he whispered, and slid closer to her. The sparse white hair that framed his cadaverish face had a blue glint. "I have been watching you for a long time. Unfortunately, you never left the Matron's side. It was impossible to speak with you privately. Now that she is gone, we will have a great deal of time together."

"Run!"

Redcrop saw Browser's fist come up and felt it slam her in the shoulder, knocking her away from Springbank, then he rolled, ripped the war club from Springbank's belt, and brutally slammed the old man in the chest. A sickening thump echoed in the room. "Go!" Browser shouted at her. "Run! *Now!*"

The blow sent Springbank toppling backward. He stumbled into the cavern wall and cried, "Why are you attacking me?"

"War Chief!" Redcrop cried, stunned. "What are you doing?"

Browser staggered as though he could barely stand. His scalp wound had broken open again; blood poured down his face. "Redcrop, *run!*"

"But you struck the elder!" she shouted, and crawled toward Springbank. "He's hurt badly!"

Browser reached down, gripped a handful of her hair, and flung her across the chamber. When she landed hard, a wrenching cry broke from her lips. She screamed, *"I was trying to help!"*

Browser weaved on his feet. Blood coated his round face and clotted his hair. "Who are you?" he shouted at Springbank. "I want to know!"

Springbank cradled his ribs and slid back against the cavern wall. He winced every time he inhaled. Pain glazed his old eyes. "What you really wish to know is . . . if I killed your lover, Hophorn."

Browser nearly collapsed, as if his legs were failing him. He locked his knees and stood silently a moment, as though mustering his strength to ask: "Did you?"

A smile curled Springbank's toothless mouth. "She converted to the Katsina faith . . . as did your wife."

Browser turned to Redcrop again and said, "For the sake of the gods, girl, leave! I don't know how long I can stay on my feet. Someone must run back to the village and tell our people what happened here!"

Redcrop slid toward the exit, but she cried, "But I don't know what's happening! Why are you speaking to Elder Springbank this way?"

Springbank sat back and laughed. "Do you really think I would guide her in here without having a guard posted at the exit? The instant she sticks her head outside, it will be lopped off!"

Redcrop hesitated, her confusion building.

Browser shouted, "He's lying! If there was a guard out there, he would have already heard our shouts and come in!"

Springbank's grin belied the terrible pain in his eyes. "The guard has orders not to enter this chamber until called. I assure you, she's used to hearing screams from in here."

Redcrop's exhausted arms and legs would no longer hold her. She slumped to the floor, a soft mewing in her throat.

Browser shook his head, as though he couldn't think, or perhaps his vision had gone dim. He wasn't going to black out, was he? "Are you descended from the Blessed Cornsilk?"

Springbank watched Browser like a hawk with a wounded mouse in sight, as though waiting for the first moment of weakness to pounce.

Springbank sighed. "Cornsilk is the cause of all this, you young fool. *She should have become the Matron of Talon Town.* When she abandoned her duty, she killed us all. Our nation fell to pieces. My father would have been the Blessed Sun, the ruler of the Straight Path Nation!" He lifted a fist and shook it. "I would be the Blessed Sun this instant!"

Browser put a hand over his left eye, as though to block the light, and squinted through his right eye. The blood streaking his face gave him a fearsome appearance. "Did you kill my grandmother?"

Redcrop gaped at Browser. *His grandmother?*

Springbank chuckled and flinched. A shiver went through him. "Ash Girl was two at the time. She must have said something to Painted Turtle at one of the ceremonial gatherings. I never knew what, but Painted Turtle found me, dragged me aside, and told me she knew what I was doing to the girl."

Tears welled in Browser's eyes. "She should have killed you for what you did to her!"

Springbank's black eyes burned into Browser's. "She would have if she'd had a little more proof. She even sent a messenger to Spider Silk to ask her if my father had hurt my half brother Bear Dancer when he was a boy. She suspected that I was treating my daughter the same way I'd been treated as a boy."

Browser braced his feet, struggling to lift the club. "I curse you, you filthy . . ."

Browser stumbled and almost dropped the war club. He gripped it so hard his fingers went white. "What about the other old women who died at the same time as my grandmother?"

Springbank studied Browser's eyes, then his gaze lowered to Browser's jerky hands. A knowing gleam replaced the pain in his eyes. "Painted Turtle couldn't keep her jaws closed. I could tell from the way those elders looked at me after the ceremonial that she had shared her suspicions. You know what our people do to those who commit incest. It was my life or theirs. What would you have done?"

Incest! Redcrop glanced back and forth between them, struggling to understand.

Browser said, "I wouldn't have hurt my children in the first place."

Springbank smiled, as if gleeful. "Only because you don't know what it's like. If you knew the feel of that young flesh, you—"

"Shut up!" Browser staggered back, trying to prop himself with the war club, while his other hand went to his head. He'd started breathing raggedly. "Gods, how many people have you killed? How many children have you wounded—"

"Ash Girl's mother would have discovered the truth much sooner if it hadn't been for Stone Ghost. I was very grateful when he arrived to 'solve' the crime and found the blood-encrusted knife I hid in that young warrior's chamber. Everyone, including Ash Girl's clan, thought he'd found the murderer."

Browser's knees wobbled, and he nearly pitched over. "I had seen eight summers at the time. I must have known you, or at least seen you at the gatherings. What was your name?"

Springbank glanced at Browser's knees, then at the war club propped on the floor like one leg of a tripod.

Patiently, he answered, "I have had many names. As a boy I was known as Silver Shadow, but when I went through the manhood ritual—"

Browser blurted, "And Obsidian?"

Springbank's eyes widened, as if surprised. "Did she tell you, or are you guessing?"

"I think she helped you to kill our Matron. I think—"

Redcrop shouted, "*What?*"

"She didn't help me, you fool!" Springbank broke into a coughing fit and his whole body spasmed. Blood bubbled at his lips. He wiped his mouth with his sleeve and stared at the blood as though he had expected as much. "You may not need your club. It looks like one of my broken ribs punctured a lung, which means I don't have long—"

Faint voices echoed in the tunnel.

Browser looked up, and Springbank smiled.

"I told you they were coming."

Browser backed away unsteadily and staggered toward the tunnel. He stood to one side with his club up, blinking the blood from his eyes, waiting for the first person to come through. He'd be lucky if he didn't raise the club and fall flat on his face.

Redcrop scrambled for the bone stiletto Springbank had thrown away earlier, and crawled to the opposite side of the tunnel. She braced her hands and dragged herself to her feet with the stiletto in her trembling fist. A stab of agony shot up her leg.

Browser gave her a confident nod, but his eyes kept drifting, as though he couldn't keep them focused. He closed his eyes and sucked in deep breaths. It seemed to help. When he opened them, his fingers tightened around his club. He leaned against the cold cavern wall.

The whispers grew louder.

Redcrop had to fight her own hand to keep hold of the stiletto. Silent sobs shook her.

Feet shuffled, then dust puffed from the tunnel and shimmered in the gray light.

A head appeared.

Browser said, *"Catkin! Thank the katsinas,"* and his strength failed him. He crumpled to the floor.

Catkin crawled out slowly, her eyes glinting like polished stones.

That look told Browser something Redcrop didn't understand. He scrambled to get to his feet and lift his war club...

"Put it down, or she dies!"

Redcrop saw the hand twined in Catkin's red collar. A large, powerful hand.

Browser's club clattered to the stone floor.

As the man emerged from the cavern behind Catkin, he ordered, "Sit down and don't move, or we will kill your friends."

"Don't listen to them!" Straighthorn screamed.

Redcrop straightened, her veins on fire, and clutched the stiletto in both hands.

Catkin knelt just outside the tunnel, facing Browser. The tall, black-haired man straightened behind her. His strong fist knotted in the fabric, he kept Catkin's body between him and Browser.

Browser's voice shook with anger. "Who are you? What do you want?"

The tall warrior gave him a crooked smile. "Didn't Two Hearts tell you? I'm surprised. We came for the ritual feast."

Redcrop felt the words like a blunt fist in her belly. She gaped at Springbank. *Two Hearts?*

Browser said, "I don't know what you're talking about. Who are you?"

Floating, Redcrop waited for the man to turn his broad back to her...

Springbank shouted, *"Ten Hawks, you fool, there's one behind you!"*

The man spun around and Redcrop threw herself forward, all of her weight driving the deer-bone stiletto into his chest. *Have to hold him long enough. Hurry, Straighthorn. Hurry!*

The man flung his arm up and knocked her sideways. Pain, like fire, lanced up her leg, but she lunged again, driving the stiletto into his shoulder, stabbing at his chest, shrieking, sobbing. Blood spattered her face and smeared warmly on her hands.

Ten Hawks screamed, twisted away, and his fist slammed into Redcrop's shoulder, knocking her to the floor. Stunned by the brutality, she had barely managed to get her hands under her when he dove headlong onto her. A woofing sound burst from her lips as his weight drove the air from her lungs, and he wrenched the stiletto from her hand.

She looked up in time to see the primal rage in his black eyes. Then he struck her, blasting lights through her vision. Her head made a sickening, hollow thud as it bounced off the floor. Through the ringing in her ears, she heard his bellow. She blinked to clear her swimming vision, and saw him above her. Like a shimmering mirage, he plunged the stiletto down. Three times, in rapid succession, the white-hot pain pierced her breast. She was gaping, mouth open, when he heaved to his feet.

In the growing river of pain, fear, and shock, she almost didn't see the four white-caped men who crawled through the tunnel.

Redcrop tried to rise, only to collapse onto her side. When she tried to breathe, her lungs gurgled and she coughed up blood. Panic powered her muscles. She writhed onto her side and watched the red pool fill the hollow in the cave floor in front of her. With each labored breath, the red spewed. Blood seemed to explode from her mouth. So much blood!

CATKIN SCRAMBLED TO one side as Redcrop leaped on Ten Hawks. She roared at Browser, "Throw me your club!"

Browser, weaving on his feet, gave her a dumb look, his blood-streaked face oddly pale, his eyes glassy. Gods! How badly was he hurt?

Catkin got her feet under her, leaped, and ripped the club from Browser's hand, tumbling him in the process. She turned just in time to see the four white-caped warriors emerge from the narrow cave. From the corner of her eye, she saw Ten Hawks stand, saw the blood bubbling from Redcrop's mouth. Then she waded into the enemy horde, swinging her club with deadly intent. One man fell immediately, howling and jerking like a clubbed dog.

Browser, down and dazed, but not out, scuttled forward and grabbed the last man out of the tunnel by the ankle. The warrior tried to kick the hand off, then Browser was on him, pummeling him with his fists, kicking, biting. They rolled across the floor.

Inside the tunnel, she could hear Straighthorn's screams and shouts.

Catkin spun in time to parry a blow that would have crushed her skull. Her attacker lifted his club again, but in that instant before he could kill her, she leaped at him, and swung the stone-headed war club into his testicles. She sidestepped as he stumbled forward, his throat bulged from a stifled scream. She caught the barest glimpse of his pained eyes, then twisted, hammering him across the stomach. As he curled around the blow, she pirouetted on tiptoe, and crushed the back of his skull.

Springbank yelled, "For the sake of the true gods, Browser! We shouldn't be fighting! *You are one of us.* Join us and we will let your Made People friends live!"

Catkin whirled, skipped aside as the third warrior's club whistled past her head. With a desperate glance, she could see that Browser was losing—driven back against the wall by a much younger man with a body like a stout tree trunk. Browser's hands were pinned, and blood gushed from his wound. His face resembled a shiny red mask.

Catkin blocked another blow, the sting of it transmitted through the seasoned wood of Browser's club.

"Join us!" Springbank shouted. His bloody fingers dug into the sandstone wall as, ledge by ledge, he pulled himself to his feet. He leaned against the wall, coughing. Blood welled from his wounded lungs and poured down his chin. "You don't believe in the katsinas, do you? I know you don't!"

Catkin danced to the side, avoiding another blow by a fraction. Gods, this man was no callow youth, but a seasoned warrior. Her only hope lay in her agility. Ten Hawks? What had happened to Ten Hawks. She couldn't spare the glance.

Think, Catkin! This man is going to kill you!

PANIC CLEARED BROWSER'S foggy mind as he stared into the warrior's hard black eyes. The man was trying to raise his war club.

Reactions fed by the years of war, Browser kicked his legs out and let himself fall, tearing free of his opponent's hands. He grabbed the man around the waist and hurled him backward.

The rage came boiling up from deep within Browser's souls. As they fell, he twined his fingers into the man's hair and bashed his head into the stone floor. He screamed: "Murderers! You're murderers! You think it is heroic to slaughter innocent people? Like the people in Aspen village!"

He butted his bloody head into the man's face, spattering it into the warrior's eyes. Browser got his hands on the man's war club and twisted it away. The white cape recovered too quickly, and they struggled, Browser intent on forcing the handle down across the man's throat.

"They were witches!" Springbank cried. He had propped himself against the wall. "You know it! In the name of the gods, Browser, *think!* The coughing sickness comes from the katsinas! Good people everywhere are dying from it. As soon as they start to believe in the katsinas, the sickness nests in their lungs and—"

"Ah!" Browser cried as the warrior released his grip, and Browser lost the leverage.

They rolled across the floor, screaming, until Browser managed to get on top. He drove the club down onto the man's throat. Their souls touched as they looked into each other's eyes.

The stiletto flashed out of nowhere. Only Browser's reflexes saved him. He jerked away and the keen point missed his eye by a lash's breadth; the passing fist tore through his hair. Browser bucked, driving his knee into the warrior's groin. With all his weight, he bore down, pressing the war club into the man's windpipe, seeing the throat bulging around the wooden handle.

When the animal scream died in Browser's throat, he was still driving his knee into the man's crotch, still pressing down with all of his weight, glaring into sightless eyes. The man's tongue stuck out between the lips like a bloated worm.

Browser stared at the mangled flesh of his left arm. When had the stiletto found him?

Catkin danced back, fear in her eyes, and Browser saw the triumphant look in her opponent's face. As the man skipped, twisted, and raised his club for the deadly strike, Catkin spit in his face. In the split heartbeat it bought her, she hammered the man in the ribs. Spinning, she swung the stone head of the club in a high arc. The warrior saw, pivoted. The blow caught his shoulder. The collarbone snapped, the sound loud and meaty.

The man cried out and tumbled to his knees, gasping.

The cave, with its pots and piles of wealth, was eerily quiet.

"Join us," Springhank whispered into the silence.

Browser shouted, *"I'll never join you! Never!"*

Springbank coughed and coagulated blood coated his lips. "Yes, you will. It's only a matter of time."

Straighthorn pushed through the tunnel entrance with another man before him. The white-caped warrior was bleeding badly from a belly wound. When Straighthorn saw Redcrop, he cried, "No!"

The youth's reaction was instinctive. He clubbed the captive in the head. A pumpkin made that hollow sound when dropped from a height. The warrior jerked and collapsed in a heap, and Straighthorn ran to Redcrop.

"Redcrop?" He fell to his knees and gathered Redcrop into his arms. *"Redcrop!"* All the pain in the universe might have been in that wounded voice.

Browser glanced at Redcrop and read her dilated pupils, fixed now in death. She seemed to wilt in Straighthorn's arms.

"Oh, gods, no!" Straighthorn cried.

Futility filled Browser. He slammed his fists into the stone floor, and his skull felt as if it might split wide open.

Straighthorn cradled Redcrop in his arms, rose, and started toward the round hole of daylight on the far side of the cavern. "I have to get you out of here."

She hung limply, a dead weight. The blood that leaked down her arms splashed onto the floor in crimson stars.

Browser took his war club back from Catkin, handed her the one from the dead warrior, and surveyed the room. Ten Hawks lay to one side, curled into a fetal ball, blood soaking his white cape.

"Redcrop," Catkin said. "She saved us."

"You're not saved," Springbank wheezed through his blood-clotted windpipe. "Shadow's coming with the rest."

Browser staggered. "The other warriors from Aspen village?"

"Join us, Browser," Springbank said, his voice insidious. "You're one of us. The blood of the First People runs in your veins!"

Browser swallowed hard. He couldn't speak.

"We *will* destroy the katsinas," Springbank gasped. "That was the *true* vision." The old man's clothing scraped as he slid down the wall, his eyes seeming to lose focus. "The true vision..." He coughed weakly. "Think, Browser. When did this begin?" Without waiting for an answer, he said, "With the coming of the katsinas. They came, and within a generation, the First People were hunted down and killed. Forced to run and hide. All we need to do is destroy the katsinas, and the Straight Path Nation will rise... from the ashes... like gods from Spider Woman's web."

Springbank slumped sideways, his body tumbling like a sack of old bones. He lay there, unmoving, with bloody drool leaking from the corner of his mouth onto the stone.

Catkin blinked at Browser with wonder-filled eyes. "Springbank is one of the First People?"

Browser rubbed his face, and found it sticky with blood. He nodded. "Yes."

They heard voices echoing from the mouth of the tunnel. Browser cocked his head. From the sounds of scuffing feet, and the rustle of clothing, it was a large party.

"Shadow?" Catkin asked. "Those other warriors he was talking about?"

"Gods, we don't have much time." Browser fought to pull his thoughts together. "Come on. Our only chance is to get Straighthorn and run. We'll come back, but with all of our warriors. Then we'll clean out this witch's nest once and for all."

Catkin carefully backed away.

"And"—he blinked against the splitting headache—"I'm not good for another fight. The run is going to be hard enough."

Catkin ducked out into the light.

Browser winced at the pain as he bent down and uncurled the old man's hands. He pried the turquoise wolf from his leathery grip. He took two steps toward the opening, and turned. The old man's white hair resembled a glistening blur of snowflakes, but his eyes were pits of darkness.

Springbank seemed to be smiling at him, a gloating smile, as if he knew something...

Browser was raising the war club, ready to go back and cave in the old man's head, when laughter could be heard in the tunnel. Close now.

Browser staggered for the mouth of the cave. The daylight seemed to burn right through his eyes and into his brain.

Catkin was shouting, "Straighthorn, let's go! Hurry!"

"No! I won't leave her!"

Catkin gripped Straighthorn's arm, dragged him to his feet, and shouted in his face, "She's *dead*! Leave her or you will be, too!"

She flung Straighthorn into a shambling trot and raced after him, shoving him hard. He kept screaming and batting at her with his fists, but Catkin fended off every blow and drove him ahead of her with the handle of her war club.

Thank you, Catkin. Thank you. Gods, now, if Browser could just make it back to Longtail village without collapsing. If the White Moccasins didn't chase them down. If . . . if . . .

CHAPTER 48

MAUREEN WORKED ON the next of the carefully pedestaled bones: a child's radius and ulna that ended in a fragile calcined mess. Sylvia had already photographed it, mapped it in, and taken the provenience.

Maureen uncapped the diluted polyvinyl acetate that Dale had brought her, and carefully painted the mixture onto the bones. The tang of acetone carried on the cool morning wind. As an undergraduate, before she'd understood the effects of acetone, she'd cooked a lot of brain cells cleaning specimens.

The rattling of the aluminum ladder alerted her to Dale's long body as he climbed down into the kiva. She watched him pick his careful way across the floor to where Maureen recapped the PVA jar. His gray hair and mustache shone, as if freshly washed.

He cleared his throat. "Um, Sylvia, would you mind going down to the trailer and making me a pot of coffee? If you could fill my thermos, I would appreciate it."

Sylvia tucked brown hair behind her ears and gave Dale a measuring glance. "Sure, Dale. I'm on it." She stood and knocked the dirt from the knees of her jeans. "Probably take me a while."

"Thank you," Dale told her warmly, and watched as Sylvia clattered up the ladder and disappeared over the kiva rim.

"What's up?" Maureen asked.

Dale sighed and retrieved a big plastic bucket. He turned it over to use as a seat and leaned close to Maureen's ear. "Tell me about these dreams William is having. I almost jumped out of my skin when he yelled last night. You've been staying in the trailer; has this happened before?"

Maureen wiped her hands on her black Levi's. "Dale, you need to ask Dusty, not me."

Dale pushed his fedora back on his head. "So. This is a recurring nightmare?"

"I never said that."

"You didn't have to." Dale frowned. "It's something tied to 10K3, isn't it? That's why he's so sure this site is related?"

"Regardless of the dream, I think he's right," Maureen answered.

Dale looked thoughtful. "The dating is correct, the pottery is the same design. We have another trephined skull. But you can't dismiss coincidence. It isn't that unlikely that people in a similar time would have similar pottery motifs. But . . ."

Maureen stiffened at his hesitation. "This is completely off the record. No matter what you tell me, it's between us."

Dale's gaze held hers. "I've spent a good deal of time with the people here. When you're around the Native people long enough, you learn to respect their beliefs. And, in my years, I've seen some pretty curious things."

Maureen pointed and asked, "How are your knees?"

"The damn things hurt," he admitted, eyes widening. "How do you know—ah, William, of course." He shook his head. "I wish I'd never gone up there. But I was young and White."

"You're still White."

"Not as much as I used to be," he answered and smiled.

Maureen released his hand and rose.

Dale looked up at her. "Where are you going?"

Maureen gazed up at the crystal blue sky, then propped her hands on her hips. "To make a phone call. Dusty needs more than either you or I can give him. He won't make the call himself, so somebody has to do it for him."

As she walked for the ladder, Dale called, "Don't tell me you believe in witchcraft?"

She shook her head. "No. But Dusty does."

She ran up the rungs, a new spring in her steps, and started across the planks. To either side, the ruins of Pueblo Animas lay in mounded desolation, only the round ring of the kiva and Dusty's single rectangular room opened in the rubble.

She waved to Dusty as she passed him. He was bent over a screen, one foot propped in the back dirt as he sorted through bits of rock and root mass for ceramics and other artifacts.

Her route took her directly to the Bronco, where she opened the door and dug the cell phone out of the center console. She flipped the cover open and watched the display come to life. Four bars of power, that ought to be enough. She punched in the number and waited through two rings.

At the voice prompt, she said: "I would like the number for Chaco Culture National Historical Park. Maggie Walking Hawk Taylor, please."

"THERE'S A CAR coming," Sylvia called as she carried Dale's thermos of hot coffee back to the kiva.

Dusty stretched his back muscles and propped his elbows on the lip of the pit. "Who is it?"

Sylvia squinted out at the dust on the road. "Blue Mercedes. I think it's the pygmy."

Dale narrowed one eye disapprovingly. "You mean Mr. Wirth?"

"Yeah. Right."

Dusty jumped out of his pit and walked over to stand beside Dale. Steve crawled out behind him, his black face painted with streaks of tan dirt. They both wore faded jeans, but Dusty's red flannel contrasted sharply with Steve's denim shirt. The Mercedes sped up the dirt road, trailing a cloud of dust.

Sylvia added, "He's got somebody in the car with him."

Steve wiped his forehead on his blue sleeve. "His wife?"

"Hard to tell."

The Mercedes pulled up in front of the pueblo. The people inside waited for the dust to clear, then got out.

Sylvia let out a low whistle. "Wow. I'll bet those silk suits cost over a thousand bucks each."

"Fifteen hundred," Dusty guessed. He shoved his cowboy hat back on his head, revealing a thin line of mud where his sweat had mixed with the dust.

Peter Wirth's pale gray suit was shiny enough to blind the average person. The other man, tall, with dark hair, wore a cream-colored suit with a black-and-gray striped tie. They both had on reflective sunglasses.

Dusty brushed the caked dirt off his hands and morosely said, "Time to take a break. Why doesn't everybody grab something cold to drink."

Steve said, "I'll get it. Sylvia, what do you want?"

"A Pepsi, thanks."

"Sure. Dr. Robertson? Dusty? Can I get you something?"

Dale said, "Sylvia just brought me a thermos of fresh coffee, but thank you anyway, Steve."

"Dusty, what about you?"

Dusty shook his head. "Don't worry about me. I'll get my own later, Steve."

"Okay, I'll be back." He walked for the ice chests sitting in the shade outside the camp trailer.

Dusty studied the two men. Wirth's white hair didn't move an inch, despite the fact that the wind had picked up. He must really want to keep that pygmy-mannequin look today. The other man stopped frequently to pick up a potsherd, or a flake, then lay it down very gently, before continuing on up the hill.

As Wirth closed in, Sylvia leaned over and whispered to Dusty, "Tell them we're from Earth and mean them no harm."

Dusty adjusted his sunglasses. "It's not them I'm worried about."

"What do you mean?"

"Well, check out the guy in back. What do you make of him?"

Sylvia's gaze took him in from head to toe. "For what his shoes alone cost, I could pay for my entire college education. I wager Italian mob."

Dale scratched his wrinkled chin. "I wager he's another investment banker."

"Yeah, well," Sylvia granted, "same thing."

Dusty crossed his arms and waited.

As Wirth came up the rubble slope, he called, "Hello, Stewart, Dr. Robertson, how are you? How is everything coming along?"

Sylvia cupped a hand to her mouth and yelled, "We dug up about forty burned babies, a cannibalized old woman, and just yesterday we found a secret passageway to hell."

Dale sighed as Wirth gave her an irritated glare.

"Good day, Peter," Dale said, and stepped forward to shake Wirth's hand.

Dusty examined the other man as he came up and stood to Dusty's left. Sadness filled his eyes, as though he sensed the pain that lingered in the walls of Pueblo Animas. A curious ability for an investment banker.

"Good day, Doctor," Wirth said to Dale. "Just what did the young lady mean?"

Dusty saw Sylvia's mouth open and shot her a warning glance. Wirth smelled like the perfume department at Penney's. No telling what she might say at a moment like this.

Dusty smiled. "Actually, Sylvia gave you a good description, Mr. Wirth. All except for the part about the passageway to hell. The tunnel is collapsed so we don't know for sure where it leads."

Wirth took off his sunglasses and looked Dusty straight in the eyes. "You've found that many dead children?"

"About forty. Most of them are under the age of five, including several infants, but I can't give you an official minimum or maximum until we've fully analyzed the remains. In kivas like this, we often find a lot more skulls than bodies, or vice versa."

Wirth said something to his companion in a language Dusty didn't understand, then turned back to Dusty. "And you really found an old woman who'd been eaten?"

"Well, we can't say that for certain. She was butchered. That is, the flesh was carved from her bones with stone tools, but whether or not somebody threw a little salt on it . . ."

Wirth turned to the unknown man again and rattled off something. Dusty assumed the language to be Arabic. Middle Eastern, at least.

As though he needed privacy, Wirth took his partner by the arm and led him a short distance away to continue the conversation in private.

Steve returned with drinks. He handed Sylvia her Pepsi and asked, "What's going on?" Sweat had cut lines in the dust that coated his dark skin. He used his sleeve to wipe his forehead.

Sylvia whispered, "I think the curtain's going up on the great and powerful Oz."

Steve's black bushy brows lowered. He looked around the site. "I didn't see Toto run by. Who's pulling the curtain back?"

"The guy with ten-thousand-dollar shoes," Sylvia replied.

Dale cocked his ear to the bankers' conversation. "Hmm," he said. "Hebrew."

Dusty's brows arched. "Really? What are they saying?"

Dale listened for a few seconds. "Well, they're talking very low, and I haven't dug in Israel in forty years, but I think Wirth just said *kesef*, which means money."

Dusty watched the men going back and forth, their voices rising and falling. "You mean they're haggling over the price?"

"I would say so, yes."

"How much are they up to?"

Dale listened, then shook his head. "Bigger numbers than I ever needed to know to buy a falafel and a bottle of Gold Star."

Dusty looked at the ground and shook his head. The very idea of haggling over the price of forty dead children left him nauseated. To him, Pueblo Animas was a great American tragedy, like the Gettysburg battlefield, or the Sand Creek Massacre site; it should be treated with reverence and used to teach people the horrors of war. A sour taste rose into his mouth, and Sylvia gave him a worried look, as though she knew exactly what he was feeling.

To lessen the tension, he sucked in a deep breath, smiled, and said, "Yeah, well, speaking of big numbers. When I was digging in Mexico, they only taught us to count to twenty. They were afraid we Americans would get arrested if we had to count to twenty-one."

Sylvia's mouth quirked. "What are we discussing? Imaginary numbers?"

Dusty spread his arms as wide as he could. "Yes, but it's a really big imaginary number."

Steve looked around Sylvia with an incredulous expression. "Even after that event with big Bob Deercapture? I thought you left half of your number sticking to the side of his truck."

"Not half," Sylvia replied. "It was more like a circumcision. You know, a little foreskin—"

"Okay, Sylvia," Dusty said. "Nobody needs *that* many details. I can't—"

"Looks like the bargaining is over," Dale interrupted, and jerked his head toward the bankers.

Wirth shook hands with his friend, and they both walked forward smiling.

Wirth said, "Dr. Robertson, William Stewart, I'd like you to meet Moshe Alevy."

Dale shook first, then Dusty offered his hand, and Alevy gave it a hearty shake.

To Wirth, Dusty said, "Does he speak English?"

"No, but he'll learn." Wirth put a hand on Alevy's broad shoulder. "He's the new owner of this parcel of land. He will likely be spending a good deal of time in the United States."

Dusty's smile faded. He could feel the crash coming. "What do you mean, the new owner?"

Wirth smiled warmly, as though proud of himself. "Well, we have to sign the papers, of course, but in a week or so, he will be."

Wirth and Alevy shook again, both grinning like cats with freshly killed birds.

Dusty said, "Uh, Mr. Wirth, could I speak with you for a moment? Alone."

Wirth looked at Dale, and when Dale shrugged, he gestured toward his Mercedes. "If you can do it in five minutes, Stewart. Mr. Alevy and I have a meeting with our attorneys in Farmington later this afternoon."

"I won't take long," Dusty promised and strode down toward the dust-covered blue Mercedes.

When they stood at the bottom of the rubble mound, out of earshot, Dusty said, "Forgive me, but I thought you told me that this pueblo was going to be the centerpiece for the subdivision, like a park."

Wirth leaned against the blue hood and looked up at the sky. His reflective sunglasses were filled with clouds. "Can you pay me a half million dollars for the ten acres where the pueblo sits?"

Dusty felt a little faint. His fists knotted involuntarily. "That's what he's paying?"

"It is, and I'm lucky I could sell it at all after what you found here."

Dusty kicked at a rock and watched it bounce down the hill. "That's archaeology for you. We're always digging up dirt about people's past, and few appreciate it."

Dale, Sylvia, and Steve had turned away to watch Alevy roam his brand-new archaeological site. He kept picking up artifacts, examining them, then almost tenderly placing them in the exact location where he'd found them.

Dusty said, "Is he an archaeologist?"

"No."

"Hmm. He acts like one." Dusty waited a moment, then said, "Okay, so. Let me get this straight. You're going to sell priceless pieces of our American heritage to a foreigner?"

Wirth's mouth curled into what approached a sneer. "They're not 'priceless,' Stewart. Just very expensive. Besides, people have been doing it for centuries. Remember all of the Aztec golden idols the Spaniards plundered to take home to Europe?"

"As I understand it, that was to help fund the next glorious crusade against the infidels. You know, for God and country, not a new Porsche. Uh, excuse me, a Mercedes."

Wirth straightened, and though Dusty couldn't see the threat in the man's eyes, he could feel it in the air. The hair on his arms stood on end.

"Now, you listen to me." Wirth aimed a manicured finger at Dusty's heart. "Mr. Alevy buys holocaust sites, and he takes special care of them. He protects them for future generations, do you understand?"

Dusty felt like he'd just been punched in the stomach. He stuttered, "No, I—I mean, that's great. If true. Tell me how he protects them?"

"You need to ask him that. But, believe me, there is *no one* who will take better care of your precious archaeological site than Moshe Alevy."

"That's a little vague, Mr. Wirth. Does it mean he wants us to backfill it, to keep excavating, or what?"

Wirth smoothed his hands down his shiny silk sleeves and said, "I'm sure Mr. Alevy will be in contact regarding the details."

Wirth strode vigorously up the hill, and Dusty chased after him, calling, "Wait a minute. Please? Let me talk to you. You told me I could have five minutes!"

TWENTY PACES AWAY, Steve leaned sideways and whispered to Sylvia, "Dusty looks like he's surrendering to the *Federales*. Why does he have his hands up like that?"

Sylvia studied Dusty for a moment, her mind working. "I suspect he thinks it's a lot more dignified than pulling his pants down."

Dale gave them both disgruntled looks and walked toward Alevy, calling out in a language Sylvia didn't understand.

Alevy stopped and smiled.

"Now what's Dale doing?" Steve said.

Sylvia brushed a lock of brown hair behind her ear. "Probably trying to figure out just how screwed we really are."

As they walked away, talking, Dale's face tightened.

Peter Wirth walked back for his Mercedes, and Dusty trudged up the hill toward where Dale and Moshe Alevy stood. Before he got there, Alevy shook hands with Dale and hurried down the hill to catch up with Wirth. Dusty and Alevy nodded politely to each other as they passed.

Dusty sighed. Talking with Wirth had been an irksome experience. The man offered no information and had little interest in the actual archaeology, other than the fat check it was going to bring him. Just the sort of thing he'd expected when they began this project.

A wall of thunderheads was pushing up from the south, eating the blue sky as it came. Beneath the largest clouds, translucent veils of rain waved like gray silk scarves. By dusk, they'd be hip-deep in mud again.

Sylvia and Steve gathered around Dale, asking him questions, and Dusty saw Maureen get out of the Bronco.

As Dusty joined the group, he heard Sylvia ask, "So, should we start packing, or wait for the pink slips?"

Dale shoved up his fedora and scratched the wiry gray hair over his right ear. "Keep digging. He'll need as many artifacts as he can get for the museum he plans to build."

At the same time, Steve and Sylvia shouted, "*What?*"

Dusty peered at Dale over the rims of his sunglasses. "He's building a museum?"

"A good one, William. Right here on site." Dale wiped the sweat from his neck with his sleeve. "It's an interesting story, actually, and with my poor Hebrew I'm sure I only caught half of it."

Maureen joined them, carrying an ice-cold bottle of Snapple peach iced tea in her hand. As she unscrewed the top, she said, "What story?"

Dale tipped his head sideways. "Well, it begins almost sixty years ago.

His grandparents were Polish Jews. They died in concentration camps, along with almost everyone else in his family—cousins, aunts, uncles. Moshe's mother lived only because her father begged a Catholic family to take his daughter and raise her as their own." Dale shook his head. "I think he's visited every holocaust site in Europe, as well as several of the killing grounds in Asia, South America, and Africa. Moshe Alevy genuinely believes that 'In remembrance lies redemption.' "

When Dusty could close his mouth, he said, "So. He really does want to protect this site? You believed him?"

"Very much. He told me that in every religious war, the enemy has three ways of accomplishing its goals: First, they try conversion. If that doesn't work, they use expulsion as a means of getting rid—"

"—Like happened here in the Southwest?" Sylvia's green eyes flared. "I mean, isn't that another way of looking at the mass exodus of the Anasazi during the thirteenth century? The heretics were being forced out?"

Dale studied Sylvia. "Possibly."

Dusty said, "What was Alevy's third way?"

"Annihilation. If you can't convert them, and you can't make them leave, you have to kill them to cleanse the world."

Maureen's dark eyes looked out over Pueblo Animas, taking in the burned roof timbers, the charred walls, the mass grave. "I'd say this kiva, and many others in the region, fall into the last category."

Steve sipped his Pepsi and said, "Good Lord, the things human beings do to each other."

"That," Dale said, and pointed a finger at Steve, "is precisely why Alevy buys and preserves holocaust sites. No matter their location, no matter the culture, race, or religious affiliation, he believes they must be preserved as constant reminders of what we, as human beings, are capable of."

Dusty frowned out at the site. A pair of crows perched on the kiva wall, peering down at the bone bed with bright eyes. "Well, if that's the case, I wish there were more like him. What does it mean for us?"

"For the time being, he wants you to keep digging, William."

Sylvia let out a triumphant whoop and said, "Great! Let's go make dinner to celebrate, then tip a few until the stars come out."

Maureen brushed her hands off on her jeans and a cloud of dust rose. Curls of damp black hair fringed her forehead. "Good idea. Then Dusty and I need to get some rest. We have an appointment at dawn."

Dale smiled and heaved a sigh of what sounded like relief.

Dusty glanced at Dale, and gave Maureen a suspicious look. "What appointment?"

CHAPTER 49

STRAIGHTHORN CONCENTRATED ON his feet as he trotted across the brown sandy soil with brush whipping off his calves.

Something had died inside him. In its place, a murderous rage had been kindled. Like a beast, it lay there next to his heart, waiting for the moment it could be loosed in vengeance against those who had killed Redcrop.

He did not know this new man who lived in his hate-filled body.

Thirty warriors, led by Catkin, trotted in front of him. Browser had barely made it back to Longtail village; the last half of the run he had been supported by Catkin and Straighthorn. When they stumbled into the village, Cloudblower had taken charge of the War Chief.

Straighthorn trotted up the ridge, lungs working as his legs pumped and dust puffed from under his yucca sandals. Half wore the yellow color of Dry Creek villagers, the others, the warriors of the Katsinas' People, wore red war shirts.

Straighthorn lagged a few paces behind the last man.

The trail back to the secret cave led over rolling hills and around pine-covered rock outcrops. Afternoon sunlight glittered from the fallen cones and needles that littered the way. He didn't wish to speak, or look at anyone. The sympathy in their eyes affected him like a knife in his belly.

When they crested the hill overlooking the cave opening, Catkin held up her hand and the war party halted and unslung their bows. Whispers passed through the group as they nocked arrows. Catkin had cut her hair in mourning for Redcrop. Jagged locks blew about her beautiful face, but a terrible darkness lay behind that angry gaze.

She pointed with a straight arm. "Those boulders at the foot of the hill mark the opening to the cave. This morning, there were five warriors there. By now, there may be a hundred. If we are attacked and outnumbered, I want you to fall into a defensive formation, and we'll fight our way out. These warriors are tested and tough. Do not let your attention waver even for an instant!"

Mutters of assent went through the ranks. Straighthorn numbly pulled an arrow from his quiver and slid it into place in his bow. As they started the run down the hill, his heart thudded against his ribs.

Could he stand it? Seeing her face again?

"It isn't going to end here," he whispered, and his throat constricted.

He would be up all night helping Cloudblower prepare Redcrop's body, washing her, dressing her, combing out her hair. She had no family—but him.

The dirt trail, barely four hands wide, curved around a clump of junipers, then dipped, and as they rose up the other side, Catkin called, "I want guards on those four high points. The rest of you spread out! Search the area along the rim and in those trees to the east, then come together at the cave entrance!"

Straighthorn followed ten other Katsinas' warriors as they fanned to the right and sneaked along the canyon rim. Scrubby pines clung to the edge. Far below, he could see his own tracks in the damp sand, and the winding trails cut by other feet. From the looks of it, at least thirty people had crossed that patch of ground.

As the trail veered away from the rim and dipped into a thicket of head-high greasewood, Hummingbird, in the lead, called, "Let's split up and go around it! Jackrabbit? Take Straighthorn and Little Firekeeper and go to the east."

"Yes, Hummingbird!"

Jackrabbit waved to them, and Straighthorn and Little Firekeeper, a youth of fourteen summers, followed him. Jackrabbit slowed to walk at Straighthorn's side. Voles scampered through the brush as they passed, and birds took wing, swooping up into the sky like many-colored arrows.

Jackrabbit said, "I know you and Catkin are supposed to carry the burial ladder back to the village, but I thought that perhaps you might wish me to carry it for you."

Straighthorn bowed his head and stared at the sand. In the past nine moons, they had become good friends. Jackrabbit was trying to spare Straighthorn the pain of staring into her wide dead eyes all the way back. "Thank you for offering, Jackrabbit, but it is something I must do."

Jackrabbit's brow wrinkled. "I heard Catkin say that after we finish here, she is going to send a small detachment to the rock shelter to find the Matron's skull and retrieve our former friends' bodies. Are you certain you wouldn't rather go with that party?"

Straighthorn looked up and met Jackrabbit's concerned eyes. Dust coated Jackrabbit's pug nose and filled in the lines around his wide mouth. "I don't know why Crossbill ordered them brought home. I think we should leave our former friends there to rot. They'll be of more use in the bellies of coyotes and crows."

Jackrabbit nodded. "My heart votes with yours. I still can't believe that they—"

The anger surged, tickled to life. "Believe it! Skink attacked me when I tried to rescue Red . . . my girl. He told me he was going to kill me." They skirted a gnarled lump of tree roots. "Springbank is the one who shocked me."

"He shocked all of us, my friend. When I first came to the Katsinas'

People, our Matron told me that he was their most faithful member. She said he had joined the quest only a few moons after she revealed Spider Silk's vision. We all thought he was a deeply holy man. When he left for days at a time to pray, no one thought much about it. Holy people need the company of Spirits more than ordinary people do."

As they came around the brush, Straighthorn saw Catkin gently place Redcrop's body on the burial ladder, and his steps faltered.

Jackrabbit said nothing; he just stopped beside Straighthorn. When Little Firekeeper walked up, Jackrabbit said, "Go on ahead, Firekeeper. We'll be there soon."

Firekeeper glanced at Straighthorn and nodded. "Yes, Jackrabbit."

Dust puffed beneath his feet as he trotted away. Twenty warriors gathered around Catkin and the burial ladder. They warily split their attention between her body and the surrounding countryside, anxious lest there be an ambush.

Straighthorn watched several men break from the group and duck into the cave. He frowned. Catkin would have checked the cave first and turned to Redcrop only after she'd found it empty.

Jackrabbit said, "I hope they leave some for the rest of us."

"What?"

"The wealth!" Jackrabbit replied with a barely masked excitement. "Matron Crossbill told Catkin to clean out everything and bring it all back to Longtail village. Do you know how much food and clothing we—"

"I didn't hear Crossbill say that."

"I think, my friend, that you had other things on your mind. You were helping Elder Cloudblower with the War Chief when this was being discussed. Crossbill is right. After all the murders committed by the White Moccasins, why shouldn't the Katsinas' People benefit from their treasure? The White Moccasins plundered the ruins of the First People to get it. The Katsinas' People need it. It seems just to me."

Straighthorn narrowed his eyes, jaw tightening.

"You think they are tainted with witchcraft?" Jackrabbit asked. "I heard the War Chief whisper that to Cloudblower."

"I think it comes to us on a river of polluted blood. We are going to live to regret this day. Mark my words, Jackrabbit. We will, and so will the White Moccasins." Eddies of rage trembled his souls.

Hummingbird whooped as he ducked out of the cave carrying an enormous basket of turquoise and jet fetishes, coral beads, and shell bracelets. He held up a copper bell and shook it. As the delicate music rose, warriors crowded around him to look, and a low roar of conversation built. More warriors appeared with baskets and began dancing around as if they'd drunk too much fermented juniper berry drink. Yells and shouts of glee rose.

Straighthorn slung his bow and slipped his arrow back into its quiver.

"Come, my friend. I have more important things to worry about." He took a deep breath to fortify himself and strode for Redcrop's burial ladder.

And the end of a dream.

Catkin stood when she saw him coming.

Straighthorn pushed through the jostling warriors, looked at Redcrop, then his gaze darted and he spun around, crying, "Where is the witch's body?"

Catkin stepped up to him. She stood tall, her eyes shining in the afternoon gleam. Ugly bruises splotched her face and arms, and one of her eyes had almost swollen shut, but she wore the injuries with a warrior's pride. "Gone. The White Moccasins carried Two Hearts away along with the other dead. Ten Hawks, the rest, all gone. Only their blood is left."

A breathless sensation swept through Straighthorn. "But he *was* dead, wasn't he? You didn't find his tracks, did you?"

Catkin said, "No. But they would have carried him. Dead, or alive. He was their leader."

"He must be dead." Straighthorn said, and his ears filled with a loud hum, like a gale rushing through a pine forest. "He was coughing up blood! I—I saw him!"

Catkin put a hand on his shoulder and squeezed until he looked up into her eyes. "I do not see how he could be alive, Straighthorn. I'm *sure* he's dead."

Straighthorn gazed into her confident eyes for a time and felt better. He shoved the fear away and crouched at Redcrop's side. As he took her cold hand in his, the beast inside him cried out. He barely heard the whoops and laughter that surrounded him.

CHAPTER 50

"COUSIN BARBARA TOLD me she would bring Dusty and Maureen out at sunrise, Aunt," Maggie Walking Hawk Taylor said. Tall and slender, she had a round face, with short black hair. "They shouldn't be too far behind us."

"Okay," Sage Walking Hawk said weakly.

Sage propped her cane and took another step. The cool predawn breeze fluttered the hood of her yellow coat and blew wispy gray hair around her deeply wrinkled face. She made soft pained sounds as she climbed the trail. She'd had trouble with her balance since a car accident more than ten years ago. Sometimes she walked fine, other times she staggered like a drunk.

Maggie used both hands to steady her great-aunt's elbow. With each step, the folding lawn chair she carried over her left elbow patted against her hip. It was a cool autumn morning, the temperature around fifty degrees. The faded blue jeans and denim shirt she wore barely kept the cold at bay.

They walked along the western wall of the ancient pueblo toward the circular structure at the top of the hill. The glow of dawn poured through the towering cottonwoods, scattering their path with pale blue diamonds.

Sage stopped and blinked her cataract-covered eyes at the ground while she breathed. She was trembling.

Maggie's grip tightened on her great-aunt's arm. She had promised herself that when this ordeal was over, she would go sit on a mesa top somewhere and give her grief free rein. But not today. If she broke down today, it would make this last morning harder for her aunt.

"Does this seem like the place you saw in your dream, Aunt?"

Sage nodded. "Yes."

To their right, a wall of finely fitted tan sandstone blocks rose fifteen feet into the air. A broad band of green stone ran along the base of the wall, but it looked black in the predawn light.

The Chaco Anasazi had abandoned the giant walled town in the twelfth century. Two generations later, a new group of Anasazi had reoccupied it. The later "Mesa Verde" occupants sealed several entryways, converted many living rooms into storage chambers, latrines, and burial rooms. Though the Chaco Anasazi had carried their trash outside, the Mesa Verdeans used interior rooms for trash dumps, packing them floor to ceiling with garbage. The Mesa Verdeans had done everything they could to minimize the need to venture outside the pueblo's protective walls. The warfare was so intense that by about A.D. 1275, the pueblo had been abandoned again.

Sage turned to look westward where a few of the brightest stars still sparkled. "I flew over it in my dream." The words came haltingly, puffed more than spoken. "But I think this is it. Where's the Sun Room?"

"The way you described it, it sounded to me like one of the tri-walled structures, Aunt. There's one up the hill."

Only twelve of the mysterious circular structures had been discovered in America, and three were at Aztec Ruins in New Mexico. They consisted of two rings of rooms around a central chamber.

"Up there?" Sage pointed a crooked finger. "It's up there?"

"Yes, Aunt."

Sage nodded and took a deep breath.

"Aunt, do you need to sit down for a while?" Maggie started to slip the lawn chair from her elbow.

"No, child. Thank you." Sage clutched Maggie's arm. "I want to go see if he's there."

Maggie frowned. "He? Who do you mean?"

Maggie supported her aunt as she hobbled up the slight incline past the numbered interpretive markers. An orchard filled the hollow to their left, and a modern farmhouse sat against the hills just beyond the tri-walled structure. The scents of dew-soaked brush and damp stone filled the air.

Sage stumbled, and Maggie gasped, "Aunt? Are you all right?"

Sage patted Maggie's hand. "I'm just clumsy this morning. Your grandmother would have said she tripped on a ghost rock, a rock that was here when the ghosts were alive. But I think maybe I'm just not as light on my feet as I used to be. I never have been able to step into other worlds like she could."

Maggie squeezed her aunt's sticklike arm. The elderly woman resembled a tiny hunchbacked skeleton. In the past year she had shrunk in size, and her skin had turned shiny and translucent, as though the cancer had eaten away her muscles and bones.

Sage said, "The man in my dream, he was calling to me from inside a tower."

"Well, there's nothing left up here but rings of stones on the ground, but it was a tower once. What did the man say?"

Sage shook her gray head. "I couldn't make out his words. It sounded like he was talking with a mouthful of cooked squash."

Sage took three steps, breathed, then took two more steps, forcing herself up the hill. As sunrise neared, a purple halo arced over the eastern horizon, and the rolling hills turned the deep rich shade of thunderheads.

Sage stopped, breathing hard, to survey the opening to the tri-walled structure—a break in the outer ring. Interpretive marker number five stood in front of them. The walls were clearly visible as three concentric rings of stones.

Sage lifted a shaking hand and pointed to the opposite side of the structure. "There. That's where his voice was coming from."

Sage turned right and started to walk around the circumference of the structure. Maggie hurried to grab her arm to help steady her steps. When they had made it almost halfway around, Sage suddenly shivered and leaned on Maggie.

"What is it, Aunt?"

Sage bowed her head. For a few seconds, she didn't speak. "Don't you feel him? The desperation? The sadness?"

Maggie frowned at the tall golden grass that filled the spaces between the stone rings. She tried to open her souls to the "other" world, but felt only the cool morning breeze tousling her short black hair. Every elderly woman in Maggie's family could touch the Spirit World. Her grandmother had been known as "She Who Haunts the Dead." Aunt Hail had been called "Ghost Talker," and her aunt Sage was known as "Empty Eyes," because of the way she looked when she was listening to ghost voices. The talent had apparently missed Maggie's generation. Oh, she'd had a few strange experiences, particularly around ancient ruins, and there were times when she sensed something roaming the darkness, but she couldn't say it was a ghost. It might just as well have been a hungry coyote.

Headlights came up the road in front of the Aztec Ruins Interpretive Center, and Maggie heard the low roar of an engine.

"That must be Barbara, with Dusty and Maureen."

Sage looked up. "Hmm? Did you hear something?"

"Yes, Aunt," Maggie half-shouted so she would hear. "A car engine. I saw lights, too."

"They're early," Sage said, and smiled. "Go on. Go meet them. I'll be fine here by myself. I need to do some talking in private."

Maggie unfolded the lawn chair and set it up on the flattest place she could find. "Let me help you sit down first."

She took Sage's arm and guided her to the seat. Sage sank down wearily. Her clawlike fingers curled over the chair arms. "Remind Barbara to bring the cornmeal."

"I will, Aunt." Maggie bent and kissed Sage's forehead, then trotted back down the trail.

When Magpie disappeared behind the giant pueblo, Sage looked down at the stone rings. They had a blurry silver glow, as did the blades of grass that swayed and nodded in the breeze.

"Well," she whispered. "I'm here. Why did you call me?"

Whimpers eddied around her, but it might just have been the wind. She could no longer tell for sure. Each time the doctors gave her chemotherapy, she lost more of herself. The last bout had wounded her souls. She could feel her breath-heart soul—the soul that kept her heart beating and her lungs moving—hanging around her like a ragged old sun-bleached cloth, while her afterlife soul huddled somewhere deep inside, eager to go free.

From her right, the place she'd seen the man standing in her dream, the feeling of sadness swelled, as though it upset the ghost that Sage couldn't hear him as well as he'd expected she would be able to.

"You'll just have to speak louder," she said, and smoothed her arthritic hands over her yellow coat.

She hadn't wanted to take the radiation or chemotherapy. She'd been longing to get out of her sick body for over a year, but Magpie had pleaded with her to try the treatments. Sage loved her great-niece with all her heart. She would have walked through a den of rattlesnakes if it would have made Magpie smile for just a few seconds. Sage had swallowed the poisons and survived much longer than her doctors had predicted. But all the pain and anguish was finally coming to an end. Yesterday, the doctor told her he wanted her in the hospital this afternoon.

Sage gazed out at the orchard. They looked like apple trees, planted in rows. High above them, clouds sailed through the brightening morning sky.

Sage offered a silent prayer of thanks to the *Shiwana*, the Spirits of the dead who had climbed into the sky to become cloud beings. They watched over the living, and brought the blessed rains.

"Are you up there, Slumber? Hail?"

Her sisters, Slumber and Hail, had died a few years ago from the same cancer that was killing Sage. It would give them something to talk about when her sisters came to get her. If Sage could get a word in edgewise. Slumber had been a real talker. Hail had told her once that Slumber could talk a dead rabbit away from a starving weasel.

Sage chuckled, remembering the irritated expression on Slumber's face.

Voices drifted up from the Interpretive Center, and Sage twisted around to look. Barbara and Magpie walked side-by-side, holding onto each other affectionately as they approached Sage.

She smiled. Funny how at the end of life nothing a person had done mattered. Not the things they'd owned, or built. The only things Sage counted were the people she loved. Everything else in the past eighty years had been leaves tumbling in the wind.

A child's voice . . .

Sage turned her good ear toward the tri-walled structure.

"What's wrong?" she asked in concern. "Are you here with the tall man?"

The whispers turned to cries, muted, breathless, as though they strained against tightly closed lips.

"It's all right, child. I'm here. I won't let anyone hurt you if I can stop him."

Magpie and Barbara stopped in front of the tri-walled structure with a blond man, and a woman with a long black braid. Magpie said, "Aunt Sage, I want you to meet Dusty Stewart and Dr. Maureen Cole."

As they walked around the ring of stones, Sage saw it, glowing like a sickly green light around Dusty Stewart. The woman, however, was surrounded by a beautiful blue glow. It fluttered around her like concerned hands.

"Good morning," Sage said. "I see the ghosts haven't got you."

"Yet," Dusty answered, and glanced around uncomfortably. He knelt in front of Sage and said, "Thank you, Elder, for helping us today."

"I haven't fixed anything yet," she said. "You'd better wait to see what happens."

Dusty nodded and backed away.

Maureen knelt in Dusty's place. "Good morning, Elder." She pulled a necklace over her head and gently placed it in Sage's fingers, then she closed her own fingers around Sage's. "This is a gift from my people, the Seneca. It was blessed by our elders. I hope it brings you luck."

Sage opened her trembling hand and looked at the beautifully carved tortoise fetish. She smiled and touched Maureen's cheek. "It's beautiful, child. What's your real name? The name your people call you?"

"Washais," Maureen said, and explained, "it's a drawknife that my people use to carve sacred masks."

Sage stroked Maureen's face. "I'm going to free you, child." She gestured to the Sun Room. "I want you and Dusty to take off everything metal and go sit in the middle ring there. No watches, no silver buttons, no change in your pockets. Kind of like being at the airport."

Magpie had warned them, so they'd both worn sweat pants and sweatshirts, but they sat down to remove their coats and boots.

Sage waved a frail hand to Magpie and Barbara. "Keep the metal outside the circles."

"Yes, Aunt Sage," they said almost in unison, picked up the coats and boots, and hauled them a short distance away.

Short and pudgy, with a big nose, Barbara had a round moony face that always seemed to glow with happiness. As she came closer, Sage could make out her red shirt and blue jeans.

Barbara kissed her on top of the head, and said, "Good morning, Aunt Sage."

"Hello, Barbara. Thank you for bringing Dusty and Maureen out to me. Did you remember the bags of cornmeal?"

Barbara pulled four tiny leather bags from her pocket and placed them in Sage's hand. "They're right here, just as you asked."

Sage fingered them, looking down to make sure she could tell the colors apart: blue, red, white, and yellow. Yes, she was going to be able to do this, just like Magpie wanted. The knowledge made her feel better. She couldn't do much of anything anymore. Not even for herself. But she still knew the sacred ways.

Sage sighed and looked at the three stone rings. Faint whimpers echoed, like standing inside a big seashell. Sage cocked her head. After a moment, she asked, "Is that a little boy? Or a little girl?"

Magpie and Barbara exchanged a look, then took up positions on either side of Sage's chair.

Magpie said, "I'm sorry, Aunt, we don't hear anything."

Sage whispered, "It sounds like a girl to me."

Magpie's forehead lined. "I thought it was a man who came to you in your dream, Aunt Sage?"

"Yes, but ghosts don't always come by themselves. The girl might want to be freed today, too."

It took two tries before Sage could shove out of her chair and stagger into the inner ring to stand between Dusty and Maureen. They both looked up at her expectantly.

"I'm almost ready," she said, and fumbled open the laces on the white-painted leather bag. The sweet nutty aroma of white corn rose.

Sage waited until the first golden sliver of Father Sun's face crested the dark hills in the distance, then she dipped her fingers into the sacred cornmeal and lifted it. As she Sang, she walked forward, sprinkling a path of white cornmeal to the east. Then she followed the path back, tugged open the bag of red cornmeal, and poured a path to the south. The yellow road led west, and, finally, Sage poured a blue cornmeal road to the north—sacred roads for the trapped ghosts to follow to the Land of the Dead.

A luminous haze of meal swirled around Dusty and Maureen, coating their clothing and sticking to their hair, purifying them.

A little girl's laughter, sweet and high.

Sage saw the green glow seep out of Dusty and sail away up the blue cornmeal road to the north.

As Father Sun rose higher, the hills cast off the dark capes of night and gleamed like molten gold. Sage lifted her arms to the sky, then carefully bent over and touched earth, sealing the prayers.

When she straightened up, Sage just looked for a time, not thinking of anything, not wanting anything, just being grateful she was alive to see the morning light.

Finally, she braced her wobbly legs and looked down at Dusty and Maureen. "You can go now. The ghost that was squatting inside you is free, gone. She's running the road to the Land of the Dead. I don't know how that old witch managed to lock a sad little girl's soul in that *basilisco* you had, Dusty, but she was glad we set her free."

Dusty's blond hair shimmered with cornmeal. "It was a little girl who was giving me bad dreams?"

Sage nodded. "I think she knew that some day you'd have sense enough to get cleansed. That's why when she touched your soul, she wouldn't let go."

Maureen reached up to lightly take Sage's hand. In a soft voice, she asked, "Elder, what about me?"

Sage squeezed her fingers. "Every person carries within her a life road that is watched over by Spirit beings. Yours are strong. You have fiery creatures who protect you, Washais. Do you know them?"

Maureen's face slackened. "The *Gaasyendietha,* yes. Thank you for telling me, Elder Walking Hawk." She touched her forehead to Sage's fingers, silently asking for her blessing, then smiled.

Sage patted her hand and released it.

As she hobbled back to her chair, she waved a hand. "Now, I want all of you to go away. I need to sit here by myself for a while." She slumped into the lawn chair and heaved a tired breath.

Sage waited until Dusty and Maureen had put on their coats and boots and started down the trail to the ruins with Barbara and Magpie, then turned to the man who stood to her right, near the outer ring. He was tall, with light brown hair and green eyes.

Sage said, "She's all right now. You've taken good care of her, but you've got to think of yourself. This may be your last chance to get free."

Sage could feel his worry, his love for Washais. She pointed to the north. "That's the way. Go on now. She'll be with you again before you know it."

The blue glow faded, then flared, as if he'd turned to look at Washais one last time.

"Isn't that why you called to me in my dream?" Sage asked gently. "You knew it was time? You were right. It's all right to let her go. Go on. Let her go now. Let her go."

The blue cornmeal at the edge of the ring whirled up in a gust of wind and sailed away with the man's soul, carrying it northward.

Sage smiled and nodded to herself.

MAUREEN SHIVERED SUDDENLY and gasped, feeling as if she'd just been bludgeoned. She braced a hand against the magnificent sandstone wall of Aztec Ruins.

She heard Dusty say, "Excuse me."

He left Barbara and Magpie watching their aunt, and trotted to Maureen. "Are you all right?"

Maureen's throat had constricted; it hurt too much to speak. She shook her head.

Without a word, Dusty put his arms around her and pulled her against his chest. He didn't ask anything else, he just held her. Maureen listened to his heartbeat and the steady rhythm of his breathing.

Dusty finally whispered, "Is there something I can do?"

Maureen disentangled herself from his arms. Dusty seemed reluctant to let her go, but he did.

She said, "Thank you, but I'm all right. I just felt suddenly empty, like a part of me had been ripped away."

Dusty scrutinized her face, then said, "It's probably hunger. I'm starving, aren't you? These cleansings take a lot of strength."

Maureen smiled. "Yes, actually, I am hungry."

"Why don't you let me take you and the Walking Hawks out to breakfast? I know a place nearby with great *huevos rancheros*."

"Sounds good." She forced herself to smile.

"Great. Let me go ask them." But before he left he looked her over carefully again. "You're sure you're okay?"

"Yes," she said, and waved him away. "Go on. I'm just going to stand here for a minute."

As Dusty hiked up the trail, Maureen sagged against the stone wall. She felt like weeping. She was alone for the first time since John's death, and she knew it. She looked northward and her eyes blurred. A pale blue gleam lit the horizon.

"I'll miss you," she whispered, "but I'm glad you're finally on your way."

CHAPTER 51

STONE GHOST STOOD on the burned kiva wall gazing up at the ash-filled sky. Buzzards circled high above. They looked like windblown black leaves against the snowy clouds.

Straighthorn breathed, "I pray I can stay here until the end."

Stone Ghost turned to the youth. He stood barely an arm's length away, but the still autumn day seemed to catch his voice and throw it around the burned village. It had the same effect as a shout.

The mourners who had gathered for the burial ceremony turned to look at him, then murmurs broke out.

Stone Ghost put a hand on the young warrior's shoulder. His buckskin cape felt warm and soft. "You can. Just think about the color of the sky and the birdsong."

"I can't think of anything but her face when she died!"

Stone Ghost squeezed his shoulder. Inside him, he had a wall of faces like that, each one caught in that final moment, each one a silent scream. He said, "I hope you will share my supper tonight, Straighthorn. I knew so little about her, I would like to know more."

Straighthorn closed his eyes, and his jaw clamped as though struggling with overwhelming emotions. "Thank you, Elder. I would like to share your supper."

The people standing on the kiva walls whispered as they handed around baskets of dirt. Jackrabbit reached up for each basket and gave it to Catkin, who silently stepped through the dead, pouring dirt over them.

The pungent scents of burned bodies and scorched walls made it almost impossible to take a deep breath. Coils of smoke continued to rise from the destroyed village and twist away in the wind.

Catkin's small detachment had found Flame Carrier's skull and the bodies of Skink and Water Snake. They had also looked for the little girl. Catkin had tracked the girl for a hand of time, then lost her steps in the rocks. Catkin had also reported seeing the mummy still hanging in the rear of the rock shelter. Since she had belonged to a powerful witch, no one would touch her. No one would bring her home.

That morning, Crossbill had ordered that Skink and Water Snake be thrown into shallow graves. Everyone had watched as Cloudblower placed sandstone slabs over their heads, sealing their souls in the earth forever. They would wail into the darkness for eternity, never able to join their relatives in the Land of the Dead.

Redcrop had been gently lowered into the tower kiva with the burned children, and Cloudblower had arranged Flame Carrier's skull so that her forehead touched Redcrop's temple—that way they could whisper to each other as they always had.

People had been carrying baskets of dirt for five hands of time now. The bodies, and a few small pots of offerings—everything people had left after the fire—were almost covered.

Browser rounded the northeastern corner of the ruined village, and Stone Ghost turned to watch him. He walked as though he had barely enough strength to force his feet to move. Cloudblower had cleansed and wrapped Browser's head wound with tan cloth. The tied ends fluttered over his left ear. Browser's chamber had been completely burned, all of his belongings lost. One of the Dry Creek village warriors had given Browser a clean knee-length yellow shirt to wear. It complemented his red leggings.

Stone Ghost patted Straighthorn's shoulder and said, "I hope to see you at supper," then he turned for the ladder that leaned against the rear wall. He took the rungs down one at a time, wincing at the pain in his knees. When he stepped to the ground, he sighed and headed toward his nephew.

Browser smiled weakly and lifted a hand when he saw Stone Ghost.

Stone Ghost called, "How are you feeling, Nephew?"

As he walked closer, Browser put a hand to his head. "My left eye is still blurry, but Cloudblower says she thinks it will pass. Is the burial almost over?"

Stone Ghost looked up at the people standing on the high kiva wall. "Yes, very close. Catkin has a few more baskets of dirt to pour." He took Browser by the arm. "I would like to show you something, Nephew, if you are well enough."

Browser frowned. "What is it, Uncle?"

Stone Ghost led Browser out into the juniper grove. Ash coated the evergreen branches and lay half a hand thick on the ground. It puffed with every step they took, swirling up to coat their hair and clothing. The entire world seemed to have turned gray. Even Father Sun's brilliance had been dimmed by the ash that swirled in the air.

"There," Stone Ghost said, and pointed.

A hundred hands north of the village, a large sandstone boulder lay overturned. Clumps of damp earth clung to the side that had been on the ground.

"What happened to the rock?"

"Someone rolled it aside, Nephew."

"Why?"

Stone Ghost released Browser's arm. "See for yourself. I found it this morning."

Browser plodded up the hill and frowned down at the square, pole-framed hole in the ground. The timbers were old and brittle. He swiveled to look back at the village. "What is this?"

Stone Ghost hobbled up and eased down onto the boulder. "A tunnel to the tower kiva. I crawled into it right after I discovered it. It goes all the way to the middle of the kiva floor."

Cold panic filled Browser. His heart started to hammer. "You mean you think this is how he got out?"

Stone Ghost nodded. "I think he shoved the last child up onto the roof, so no one would see him leave, then he dug up the door in the kiva floor and ran."

"But how old is this? How could he have known about it?"

Stone Ghost laced his fingers in his lap. "I suspect it was originally constructed over one hundred sun cycles ago, to allow First Man and First Woman to make a grand entrance during ceremonials. Can you imagine them climbing up into the kiva, emerging from the underworlds, as they did in the Beginning Time? The spectators must have been amazed."

Browser reached into the tunnel and pulled out a handful of dirt. "It smells old and dank. I wonder how long it's been since someone used it?"

"Other than two nights ago, you mean? Oh, many summers. Sixty, seventy. Perhaps more."

Browser let the dirt trickle through his fingers. "But Two Hearts knew about it."

"Yes. He probably discovered it when he lived here thirty summers ago. Or maybe he was told about it by relatives who lived here long before that. It's hard to say." Stone Ghost's eyes tightened. He paused for a long while, then said, "Nephew, there is something I must tell you. Do you recall the story I began last night when we were sitting by the First People's spiral?"

Browser nodded with care, as though the motion hurt. "Yes, Uncle. What of it?"

Stone Ghost reached for his nephew's hand. "I would like to finish that story, if you don't mind."

"Go on."

Stone Ghost took a deep breath and very softly said, "My grandmother, Orenda, married the second son of Cornsilk and Poor Singer."

Browser's strength seemed to fail. *"What?"* He sank to the ground with his mouth open. "Are you telling me that I—I am..."

Stone Ghost held up a hand to halt the flood of questions he knew would be coming. "His name was Snowbird. I don't know much about him, except that he was a very gentle man, much like his father, Poor Singer. But despite his peaceful nature, Snowbird was always at war with his older brother. He—"

"Who was his older brother?"

"The Blessed Ravenfire." At the look on Browser's face, Stone Ghost said, "Yes, your dead Matron's father. He was Cornsilk's firstborn. I don't know how it happened exactly, but Ravenfire was not Poor Singer's son. I heard rumors that Cornsilk had been raped. It may be true. At any rate, Ravenfire grew up to hate everything his parents stood for. He hated the katsinas. It was Ravenfire"—Stone Ghost said through a long exhalation—"who betrayed Night Sun to the Made People."

Stunned, Browser murmured, "When did this happen, Uncle?"

"Oh, she was around sixty summers at the time. The great war had just begun."

Browser blinked at the ground. "You are telling me, that I am related to the great Matron of Talon Town? The Blessed Night Sun was—"

"—Your great-great-great-grandmother, yes."

Browser glanced over his shoulder and swallowed hard, before he whispered, "I am one of the First People?"

"*We* are, Nephew."

Browser shook his head as though refusing to believe it. In a strained voice, he asked, "Gods, why are we alive?"

"Well, you were lucky. Your family forced you to marry Ash Girl. She was one of the First People."

"She was..." He seemed to run out of air halfway through the sentence. "Why did no one tell me?"

Stone Ghost shrugged. "If you had known, it would have been dangerous for you. My sister, Painted Turtle, decided it would be better for everyone concerned if her grandchildren never knew the truth." He touched his chin. "That's why you did not receive this tattoo at your birth, Nephew."

"That's the same tattoo the mummy—"

"Yes," Stone Ghost sighed, and his wrinkles deepened. "I'm afraid I know who the mummy is and why she was hung at Aspen village."

"Who? Why?"

"The Blessed Night Sun."

Browser looked as if he'd been gutted. "That's why our Matron struggled so hard to keep the Katsina religion alive? She was related to Night Sun?"

"Well," he tilted his head. "Not exactly. I mean, yes, she was. But because she was Ravenfire's daughter. My grandmother told me that he had brought her up to hate everything about the katsinas. That's why Spider Silk divorced him and ran away. Ravenfire kept their son, Bear Dancer, and I heard that Ravenfire remarried a woman from the Green Mesa clans. I think at the end of her life, Spider Silk was trying very hard to . . ."

"Dear gods," Browser whispered. "That's what Obsidian meant when she said that the turquoise wolf meant I was 'suitable.' " He shook his fists. "That's what Two Hearts meant when he asked me to join them!"

Stone Ghost nodded. "That is also why they didn't kill you at Aspen village, Nephew. There are so few of us now that they must be cautious who they punish by death."

Browser's gaze suddenly darted over Stone Ghost's face. "What about Catkin, Uncle? Is she—is that why they didn't kill her?"

Stone Ghost shifted on the boulder and his turkey feather cape fell open, leaving his chest vulnerable to the cold wind. He shivered. "I truly don't know, Nephew. Perhaps you should ask her."

"No." Browser shook his head. "I won't do that." He placed a hand on Stone Ghost's shoulder. "Uncle, I know it wasn't easy for you to tell me after all the summers of keeping the truth locked in your heart. I am grateful."

"The burden is yours now, Nephew." Stone Ghost patted his hand. "You must decide whom to tell and when."

"I will tell no one, Uncle. The truth is too dangerous. For all of us."

Browser shakily rose to his feet. Cloudblower had been pouring willow bark tea down him to ease his pain, but Browser seemed to be growing weaker by the instant. He squinted against the sunlight. "Is there anything else, Uncle? I came out here to find Obsidian. If I don't do it soon, I'm afraid I won't be able to."

"Go, Nephew. I will wait here for you to return."

Browser nodded. "Have you seen Obsidian?"

Stone Ghost pointed. "I saw her on the river trail a little while ago."

Browser started to walk away, and Stone Ghost gripped his yellow sleeve to stop him. "What are you going to say to her, Nephew?"

Browser shook his head. "I don't know."

"Be prudent. She is more than she seems. *Much* more."

Browser squeezed Stone Ghost's hand, nodded, and walked away.

A BOW SHOT away, two eagles played. The huge brown birds floated on the air currents as though weightless, tipping their wings and chasing each other.

Browser watched them dive over the cottonwoods, then soar down to the river. The scent of the water was strong today, a pungent mixture of damp earth and ash. He inhaled a breath and let it out slowly.

He found Obsidian kneeling beside the Witches' Water Pocket, staring down as though she saw something stir far beneath the wavering reflections of autumn leaves. She had the blue hood of her cape up, shielding her face, but long strands of black hair fluttered around the hood. Her heavily ringed hands rested on her knees.

Browser's feet crunched in the old leaves as he walked up behind her. "Do you see them?"

She hesitated. "Who?"

"The witches who are supposed to live beneath the water."

She expelled an irritated sigh, and answered, "I see only water, War Chief."

He crouched beside her, picked up a golden cottonwood leaf with green stripes, and twirled it in his fingers.

"You weren't at the burial," he said.

She turned and sunlight bathed her beautiful tear-streaked face. Her black eyes shone like the darkest of jewels. "You must wish to question me, or you wouldn't be here. What is it?" She wiped her cheeks with her hands.

He tipped his aching head back to look up at the cloud-strewn sky. The sound of the wind in the branches soothed him. "Did you know about the tunnel?"

"Not until this afternoon."

Browser closed his eyes for a moment and let the sun warm his face. He'd drifted through the day like a man without souls, feeling empty. So many things had happened, he could not take them all in. His dreams had been tortured. He kept reliving the fight in the cavern, analyzing each minute detail. Everywhere he looked now, he saw First People; it was the triangular shape of their faces, the way they held their heads and moved their hands. Even the lilt of their voices. He did not know why he hadn't seen these things before. Perhaps he had, but had thought nothing of it.

Obsidian threw back her hood; it was an elegant gesture, filled with superiority. His own mother had moved like that. And his grandmother. Without realizing it, they had radiated an authority that had ceased long ago.

He squinted down at the trembling heart-shaped golden leaf he held.

"I'm sorry for the way I treated you," he said.

"It's my fault. There are just so few of us now, I was too eager."

"No. It's my fault. Somewhere deep inside I knew I'd seen you before, but I couldn't place where we'd met."

She looked at him from the corner of her eye. "We met nine moons ago when your people came here, Browser."

"Yes," he said, and nodded, "but you look so much like my dead wife that sometimes in my dreams I find myself replacing your face with hers."

She stared at him, then shrugged, as if dismissing it. "I am much older than she was."

"Yes, that's what fooled me."

"Fooled you?"

He nodded. "I always thought she looked like her mother, until I met you." Tiny lights flashed in his left eye, and he had to close it to ease the sudden stunning pain. "I don't know what was w-wrong with me. I should have seen your resemblance, and her resemblance, to Springbank before."

"You think he's my father?"

Browser looked down at the pool. Sunlight sprinkled the water like goldfinch feathers. "*Was* your father. Isn't that why you're crying? You're grieving for him?"

"No, that's not why I'm crying, you fool."

"Then why—"

She whirled around. "My husband died yesterday!"

The wind pulled the leaf from his fingers. It fluttered into the river and bobbed away on the current. "He was the man—"

"*Yes, Ten Hawks!* The gods know I've heard the story often enough today. The girl killed him! Do you understand now why I could not attend her burial?"

Browser frowned and looked away. "It wasn't just her burial, Obsidian. We were burying over forty children, one old woman, and one girl." He looked back and pinned her with hard eyes. "Besides, I thought you divorced him?"

She smoothed her hands over the fine blue fabric of her cape. "That's *why* I divorced him. When he joined the White Moccasins, I knew he would end up dead. I told him so, but he said Two Hearts was more powerful than I could possibly imagine. He told me Two Hearts would lead all of our people back to glory."

Browser chanced removing his hand from his left eye, and opened it. The pain nauseated him. He closed it again. "You didn't believe him?"

"Two Hearts was insane. Everyone knew it." She flexed her jeweled fingers and frowned down at the wealth of jet and shell rings. "Everyone except Ten Hawks."

Browser's thoughts flitted, trying to coalesce into a sentence. "That's why there was no scandal when you divorced. No one knew what he'd done, but you."

"I couldn't tell anyone, Browser, not without risking my own life."

Browser bowed his head. "Yes, I understand now."

"No, you don't. Not really. The White Moccasins operated silently, in secret—until four summers ago, when your Matron formed the Katsinas' People; it gave them a reason to become more bold. Their numbers have been growing steadily ever since. This is not the end, Browser; it is the beginning."

The ties on his bandage flipped in the wind. He put a hand up to keep them out of his eyes. "Two Hearts is dead. A leader's death often—"

"He wasn't their only leader!" Obsidian looked at him as though he'd turned into a rabbit. "There are many more! And he was never the scary one, Browser. It's his daughter, Shadow Woman, that you should be afraid of. Without Two Hearts to restrain her—"

"But I thought you—"

"*Me?*" she blurted. "Shadow is the one who helped him to kill your Matron, not me!"

When she raised her voice, his head throbbed sickeningly. He didn't speak for a time, then, in a hushed voice, he asked, "How do you know she helped to kill our Matron?"

"Because Ten Hawks told me at the Matron's burial!"

Browser thought back to that day. She'd walked the trail with a tall man, and a woman.

"Was she there, too?" he asked.

Obsidian's full lips pressed into a white line. "Yes. She passes where she will."

"So you know what she looks like. Will you help us to find her?"

Obsidian laughed softly at first, then heartily. "If you value your life and the lives of those close to you, do not even try to find her! She will cut you into tiny pieces and serve you to your family for supper."

Browser rose to his feet and concentrated on keeping his knees locked. "You won't help us?"

"I don't know who 'us' is, Browser." Her black eyes blazed. She leaned toward him and the front of her cape fell open. "*Do you?* The one thing I can tell you for certain is that as more and more people convert to the Katsina faith, more will die."

Browser stared at the pendant nestled between her breasts. He swallowed down a dry throat, and said, "That's beautiful. Where did you get it?"

Obsidian reached up to clutch the black serpent coiled inside the broken eggshell. Its one red eye glared malignantly at Browser. "My father carved it for me when I was a baby. Why?"

Her father. Shadow Woman's father.

The same man?

Browser rose and stood gazing down at her for a long while, noting the curve of her jaw, the shape of her eyes and nose, then he walked away through the piles of autumn leaves.

When he reached the river crossing, he saw Stone Ghost standing at the edge of the water, wet up to the knees. The bottom half of his turkey feather cape hung around him in drenched folds.

Browser slowly made his way down the trail to him, and said, "Worried that I might have fainted in the trail, Uncle?"

Stone Ghost smiled. "A little."

Browser locked his trembling knees. "Obsidian knows who the woman is who helped to kill our Matron. She even knows what she looks like, but she won't help us to find her."

Stone Ghost took his arm in an affectionate grip and guided Browser into the river and back toward the village. He waded the current slowly, a step at a time, to keep his balance.

"But you already know what she looks like, Nephew. You've seen her several times in the past nine moons. You just thought she was Obsidian."

Browser halted and peered down at his uncle while memories flashed: Obsidian that day on the trail. Obsidian in his chamber. And many other times when she had seemed to be a different person.

He said, "*Twin pendants for twin daughters?*"

Stone Ghost nodded. "I think her mother lied about her age when she came to the Longtail Clan, hoping no one would make the connection with what happened here thirty summers ago. She told people her daughter had seen seven summers, not ten, and claimed that her other daughter had died. In a very real way, of course, she was dead. Outcasts are dead to their clans." He rubbed his forehead before continuing. "But I think it goes even deeper, Nephew. It seems that each of his daughters has one of those pendants. Ash Girl had one too, didn't she?"

Browser started to shake his head, then straightened. The cold river swirled around his legs. "She told me she'd found it in Talon Town, and that's what she told Hophorn when she gave it to her."

"I think she wished to be rid of it. I can't say why she chose to give it to Hophorn. Perhaps she thought Hophorn was more powerful than the evil creature that lives inside the pendant."

Browser looked back at the Witches' Water Pocket. The pool shimmered.

Obsidian was gone.

"Blessed gods, you don't think... if there is any chance that she was Shadow Woman, I should go after her!"

"No." Stone Ghost tugged Browser back. "This is not the day, Browser. Today, she will kill you."

"Not if I get a war party—"

"She hasn't survived this long by being foolish. If she thinks for one instant that you suspect, she will kill you, me, Catkin, and anyone else you might have confided in, and then she will vanish forever."

They continued walking. Stone Ghost stepped out onto the bank and steadied Browser's arm while he crossed the slick rocks to the sand.

Browser stood on shaking knees and forced himself to take deep slow breaths. His headache had grown almost incapacitating.

Stone Ghost said, "Let me help you back to Dry Creek camp, Nephew. You must sleep and eat."

Browser nodded, said, "Thank you, Uncle," and allowed Stone Ghost to lead him up the trail.

A group of small boys from the Dry Creek camp ran up the riverbank in front of them, laughing and playfully shoving each other into the water.

Stone Ghost turned to watch them, and his turkey feather cape buffeted in the wind, flattening his shirt against his bony chest. "When you are better, I would like you to help me do something, Nephew."

Browser looked at him through one squinted eye. "Crossbill has ordered that everyone pack up their remaining belongings and be ready to leave for Dry Creek village tomorrow morning. This thing you wish to do, can it be done from Dry Creek village?"

"It does not matter where the journey begins. The task will require several days travel, maybe longer."

"Where are we going?"

Stone Ghost tenderly clutched Browser's arm, then gazed up at the ash-coated cottonwoods along the river. The streaks of sunlight slanting through the branches dappled his face and fell upon the water below like flakes of gold. "A place that I am not even sure exists, Nephew. A place of legends."

CHAPTER 52

AS I LISTEN to the children running the river trail above me, I pluck a grasshopper from the stones and use a stick to mash it flat, then I scrape the grasshopper from the rock and put it in my mouth, chewing patiently.

Seven children.

One of them lags behind the others, panting, coughing.

I stop chewing and silently squat on my haunches in the eroded hole in the bank, waiting to see him come into view beyond the brush to my left.

Thin and pale, the little boy staggers more than he runs. He wears the yellow cape of the Dry Creek villagers.

A smile tugs at my lips, and I feel the growl rumbling deep in my throat. I am the Summoning God.

I step back into the shadows, my black eyes glistening, and chew again. But not today.

Not today . . .

BIBLIOGRAPHY

Acatos, Sylvio. *Pueblos: Prehistoric Indian Cultures of the Southwest*, trans. *Die Pueblos* (1989 eds.). New York: Facts on File, 1990.

Adams, E. Charles. *The Origin and Development of the Pueblo Katsina Cult.* Tucson, AZ: University of Arizona Press, 1991.

Adler, Michael A. *The Prehistoric Pueblo World A.D. 1150–1350.* Tucson, AZ: University of Arizona Press, 1996.

Allen, Paula Gunn. *Spider Woman's Granddaughters.* New York: Ballantine Books, 1989.

Arnberger, Leslie P. *Flowers of the Southwest Mountains.* Tucson, AZ: Southwest Parks and Monuments Assoc., 1982.

Aufderheide, Arthur C. *Cambridge Encyclopedia of Human Paleopathology.* Cambridge, UK: Cambridge University Press, 1998.

Baars, Donald L. *Navajo Country: A Geological and Natural History of the Four Corners Region.* Albuquerque, NM: University of New Mexico Press, 1995.

Becket, Patrick H., ed. *Mogollon V.* Report of Fifth Mogollon Conference, Las Cruces, NM: COAS Publishing and Research, 1991.

Boissiere, Robert. *The Return of Pahana: A Hopi Myth.* Santa Fe, NM: Bear & Company, 1990.

Bowers, Janice Emily. *Shrubs and Trees of the Southwest Deserts.* Tucson, AZ: Southwest Parks & Monuments Assoc., 1993.

Brody, J. J. *The Anasazi.* New York: Rizzoli International Publications, 1990.

Brothwell, Don, and A. T. Sandison, *Disease in Antiquity.* Springfield, IL: Charles C. Thomas, 1967.

Bunzel, Ruth L. *Zuni Katcinas.* Reprint of 47th Annual Report of the Bureau of American Ethnography, 1929–30, Glorieta, NM: Rio Grande Press, 1984.

Colton, Harold S. *Black Sand: Prehistory in Northern Arizona.* Albuquerque, NM: University of New Mexico Press, 1960.

Cordell, Linda S. "Predicting Site Abandonment at Wetherill Mesa." *The Kiva* (1975) 40(3):189–202.

———. *Prehistory of the Southwest.* New York: Academic Press, 1984.

———. *Ancient Pueblo People.* Smithsonian Exploring the Ancient World Series, Montreal, and Smithsonian Institution, Washington, DC: St. Rémy Press, 1994.

———. and George J. Gumerman, eds. *Dynamics of Southwest Prehistory.* Washington, DC: Smithsonian Institution Press, 1989.

Crown, Patricia, and W. James Judge, eds. *Chaco and Hohokam: Prehistoric Regional Systems in the American Southwest.* Santa Fe, NM: School of American Research Press, 1991.

Cummings, Linda Scott. "Anasazi Subsistence Activity Areas Reflected in the Pollen Records." Paper presented to the Society for American Archaeology, 45th Annual Meeting, New Orleans, 1986.

———"Anasazi Diet: Variety in the Hoy House and Lion House Coprolite Record and Nutritional Analysis," in Kristin D. Sobolik, ed., *Paleonutrition: The Diet and Health of Prehistoric Americans.* Occasional Paper No. 22, Carbondale, Il.: Center for Archeological Investigations, Southern Illinois University, 1994.

Dodge, Natt N. *Flowers of the Southwest Desert.* Tucson, AZ: Southwest Parks & Monuments Assoc., 1985.

Dooling, D. M., and Paul Jordan-Smith, eds. *I Become Part of It: Sacred Dimensions in Native American Life.* San Francisco: A Parabola Book, Harpers; New York: Harper Collins, 1989.

Douglas, John E. "Autonomy and Regional Systems in the Late Prehistoric Southern Southwest." *American Antiquity* (1995) 60:240–57.

Dunmire, William W., and Gail Tierney. *Wild Plants of the Pueblo Province: Exploring Ancient and Enduring Uses.* Santa Fe, NM: Museum of New Mexico Press, 1995.

Ellis, Florence Hawley. "Patterns of Aggression and the War Cult in Southwestern Pueblos." *Southwestern Journal of Anthropology* (1951) 7:177–201.

Elmore, Francis H. *Shrubs and Trees of the Southwest Upland.* Tucson AZ: Southwest Parks & Monuments Assoc., 1976.

Ericson, Jonathan E., and Timothy G. Baugh, eds. *The American Southwest and Mesoamerica: Systems of Prehistoric Exchange.* New York: Plenum Press, 1993.

Fagan, Brian M. *Ancient North America.* New York: Thames & Hudson, 1991.

Farmer, Malcolm F. "A Suggested Typology of Defensive Systems of the Southwest." *Southwestern Journal of Archeology* (1957), 13:249–66.

Frank, Larry, and Francis H. Harlow. *Historic Pottery of the Pueblo Indians: 1600–1880.* West Chester, PA: Schiffler Publishing, 1990.

Frazier, Kendrick. *People of Chaco: A Canyon and its Culture.* New York: W. W. Norton, 1986.

Gabriel, Kathryn. *Roads to Center Place: A Cultural Atlas of Chaco Canyon and the Anasazi.* Boulder, CO: Johnson Books, 1991.

Gumerman, George J., ed. *The Anasazi in a Changing Environment.* School of American Research, New York: Cambridge University Press, 1988.

———. *Exploring the Hohokam: Prehistoric Peoples of the American Southwest.*

Amerind Foundation, Albuquerque, NM: University of New Mexico Press, 1991.

———. *Themes in Southwest Prehistory*. Sante Fe, NM: School of American Research Press, 1994.

Haas, Jonathan. "Warfare and the Evolution of Tribal Polities in the Prehistoric Southwest," in Haas, ed., *The Anthropology of War*. Cambridge, U.K: Cambridge University Press, 1990.

———, and Winifred Creamer. "A History of Pueblo Warfare." Paper Presented at the 60th Annual Meeting of the Society of American Archeology, Minneapolis, 1995.

———. *Stress and Warfare Among the Kayenta Anasazi of the Thirteenth Century A.D.* Field Museum of Natural History, Chicago, 1993.

Haury, Emil. *Mogollon Culture in the Forestdale Valley, East-Central Arizona.* Tucson, AZ: University of Arizona Press, 1985.

Hayes, Alden C., David M. Burgge, and W. James Judge. *Archaeological Surveys of Chaco Canyon, New Mexico.* Reprint of National Park Service Report, Albuquerque, NM: University of New Mexico Press, 1981.

Hultkrantz, Ake. *Native Religions: The Power of Visions and Fertility.* New York: Harper & Row, 1987.

Jacobs, Sue-Ellen, ed. "Continuity and Change in Gender Roles at San Juan Pueblo," in *Women and Power in Native North America.* Norman, OK: University of Oklahoma Press, 1995.

Jernigan, E. Wesley. *Jewelry of the Prehistoric Southwest.* Albuquerque, NM: University of New Mexico Press, 1978.

Jett, Stephen C. "Pueblo Indian Migrations: An Evaluation of the Possible Physical and Cultural Determinants." *American Antiquity* (1964) 29: 281–300.

Komarek, Susan. *Flora of the San Juans: A Field Guide to the Mountain Plants of Southwestern Colorado.* Durango, CO: Kivaki Press, 1994.

Lange, Frederick, et al. *Yellow Jacket: A Four Corners Anasazi Ceremonial Center.* Boulder, CO: Johnson Books, 1988.

LeBlanc, Stephen A. *Prehistoric Warfare in the American Southwest.* Salt Lake City, UT: University of Utah Press, 1999.

Lekson, Stephen H. *Mimbres Archeology of the Upper Gila, New Mexico.* Anthropological Papers of the University of Arizona, no. 53, Tucson, AZ: University of Arizona Press, 1990.

———, et al. "The Chaco Canyon Community." *Scientific American* (1988) 259(1): 100–109.

Lewis, Dorothy Otnow. *Guilty by Reason of Insanity. A Psychiatrist Explores the Minds of Killers.* New York: Ballantine Books, 1998.

Lipe, W. D., and Michelle Hegemon, eds. *The Architecture of Social Integration in Prehistoric Pueblos.* Occasional Papers of the Crow Canyon Archaeological Center, no. 1, Cortez, CO, 1989.

Lister, Florence C. *In the Shadow of the Rocks: Archaeology of the Chimney Rock District in Southern Colorado.* Niwot, Colorado: University Press of Colorado, 1993.

Lister, Robert H., and Florence C. Lister. *Chaco Canyon.* Albuquerque, NM: University of New Mexico Press, 1981.

Malotki, Ekkehart. *Gullible Coyote: Una'ihu: A Bilingual Collection of Hopi Coyote Stories.* Tucson, AZ: University of Arizona Press, 1985.

———, ed. *Hopi Ruin Legends.* Lincoln, NE: University of Nebraska Press, 1993.

———, and Michael Lomatuway'ma. *Maasaw: Profile of a Hopi God.* American Tribal Religions, vol. XI, Lincoln, NE: University of Nebraska Press, 1987.

Malville, J. McKimm, and Claudia Putnam. *Prehistoric Astronomy in the Southwest.* Boulder, CO: Johnson Books, 1993.

Mann, Coramae Richey. *When Women Kill.* New York: State University of New York Press, 1996.

Martin, Debra L. "Lives Unlived: The Political Economy of Violence Against Anasazi Women." Paper presented to the Society for American Archeology 60th Annual Meeting, Minneapolis, 1995.

———, et al. *Black Mesa Anasazi Health: Reconstructing Life from Patterns of Death and Disease.* Occasional Paper no. 14. Carbondale, IL: Southern Illinois University, 1991.

Mayes, Vernon O., and Barbara Bayless Lacy. *Nanise: A Navajo Herbal.* Tsaile, AZ: Navajo Community College Press, 1989.

McGuire, Randall H., and Michael Schiffer, eds. *Hohokam and Patayan: Prehistory of Southwestern Arizona.* New York: Academic Press, 1982.

McNitt, Frank. *Richard Wetherill Anasazi.* Albuquerque, NM: University of New Mexico Press, 1966.

Minnis, Paul E., and Charles L. Redman, eds. *Perspectives on Southwestern Prehistory.* Boulder, CO: Westview Press, 1990.

Mullet, G. M. *Spider Woman Stories: Legends of the Hopi Indians.* Tucson, AZ: University of Arizona Press, 1979.

Nabahan, Gary Paul. *Enduring Seeds: Native American Agriculture and Wild Plant Conservation.* San Francisco: North Point Press, 1989.

Noble, David Grant. *Ancient Ruins of the Southwest: An Archaeological Guide.* Northland Publishing, Flagstaff Arizona: 1991.

Ortiz, Alfonzo, ed. *Handbook of North American Indians.* Washington, DC: Smithsonian Institution, 1983.

Palkovich, Ann M. *The Arroyo Hondo Skeletal and Mortuary Remains.* Arroyo Hondo Archeological Series, vol. 3, Santa Fe, NM: School of American Research Press, 1980.

Parsons, Elsie Clews. *Tewa Tales* (reprint of 1924 edn.). Tucson, AZ: University of Arizona Press, 1994.

Pepper, George H. *Pueblo Bonito* (reprint of 1920 edn.). Albuquerque, NM: University of New Mexico Press, 1996.

Pike, Donald G., and David Muench. *Anasazi: Ancient People of the Rock.* New York: Crown Publishers, 1974.

Reid, J. Jefferson, and David E. Doyel, eds. *Emil Haury's Prehistory of the American Southwest.* Tucson, AZ: University of Arizona Press, 1992.

Riley, Carroll L. *Rio del Norte: People of the Upper Rio Grande from the Earliest Times to the Pueblo Revolt.* Salt Lake City, UT: University of Utah Press, 1995.

Rocek, Thomas R. "Sedentarization and Agricultural Dependence: Perspectives from the Pithouse-to-Pueblo Transition in the American Southwest." *American Antiquity* (1995) 60: 218–39.

Schaafsma, Polly. *Indian Rock Art of the Southwest.* Albuquerque, NM: University of New Mexico Press, 1980.

Sebastian, Lynne. *The Chaco Anasazi: Sociopolitical Evolution in the Prehistoric Southwest.* Cambridge, UK: Cambridge University Press, 1992.

Simmons, Marc. *Witchcraft in the Southwest* (reprint of 1974 edn.), Bison Books), Lincoln, NE: University of Nebraska Press, 1980.

Slifer, Dennis, and James Duffield. *Kokopelli: Flute Player Images in Rock Art.* Santa Fe, NM. Ancient City Press, 1994.

Smith, Watson, with Raymond H. Thompson, ed. *When Is a Kiva: And Other Questions About Southwestern Archaeology.* Tucson, AZ: University of Arizona Press, 1990.

Sobolik, Kristin D., ed. *Paleonutrition: The Diet and Health of Prehistoric Americans.* Occasional Paper no. 22, Center for Archeological Investigations, Carbondale, IL: Southern Illinois University, 1994.

Sullivan, Alan P. "Pinyon Nuts and Other Wild Resources in Western Anasazi Subsistence Economies." *Research in Economic Anthropology, Supplement* (1992) 6: 195–239.

Tedlock, Barbara. *The Beautiful and the Dangerous: Encounters with the Zuni Indians.* New York: Viking Press, 1992.

Trombold, Charles D., ed. *Ancient Road Networks and Settlement Hierarchies in the New World.* Cambridge, UK: Cambridge University Press, 1991.

Turner, Christy G., and Jacqueline A. Turner. *Man Corn. Cannibulism and Violence in the Prehistoric American Southwest.* Salt Lake City, UT: University of Utah Press, 1999.

Tyler, Hamilton A. *Pueblo Gods and Myths.* Norman, OK: University of Oklahoma Press, 1964.

Underhill, Ruth. *Life in the Pueblos* (reprint of 1964 Bureau of Indian Affairs Report). Santa Fe, NM: Ancient City Press, 1991.

Upham, Steadman, Kent G. Lightfoot, and Roberta A. Jewett, eds. *The Sociopolitical Structure of Prehistoric Southwestern Societies.* San Francisco: Westview Press, 1989.

Vivian, Gordon, and Tom W. Mathews. *Kin Kletso: A Pueblo III Community in Chaco Canyon, New Mexico,* vol. 6. Globe, AZ: Southwest Parks & Monuments Assoc., 1973.

Vivian, Gordon, and Paul Reiter. *The Great Kivas of Chaco Canyon and Their Relationships,* Monograph, no. 22, Santa Fe, NM: School of American Research Press, 1965.

Vivian, R. Gwinn. *The Chacoan Prehistory of the San Juan Basin.* New York: Academic Press, 1990.

Waters, Frank. *Book of the Hopi.* New York: Viking Press, 1963.

Wetterstrom, Wilma. *Food, Diet, and Population at Prehistoric Arroyo Hondo Pueblo, New Mexico.* Arroyo Hondo Archaeological Series, vol. 6. Santa Fe, NM: School of American Research Press, 1986.

White, Tim D. *Prehistoric Cannibalism at Mancos 5MTUMR-2346.* Princeton, NJ: Princeton University Press, 1992.

Williamson, Ray A. *Living the Sky: The Cosmos of the American Indian.* Norman, OK: University of Oklahoma Press, 1984.

Wills, W. H., and Robert D. Leonard, eds. *The Ancient Southwestern Community.* Albuquerque, NM: University of New Mexico Press, 1994.

Woodbury, Richard B. "A Reconsideration of Pueblo Warfare in the Southwestern United States." *Actas del XXXIII Congreso Internacional de Americanistas* (1959) II: 124–33. San Jose, Costa Rica.

———. "Climatic Changes and Prehistoric Agriculture in the Southwestern United States." *New York Academy of Sciences Annals* (1969) vol. 95, art. 1.

Wright, Barton. *Katchinas: The Barry Goldwater Collection at the Heard Museum.* Phoenix, AZ: Heard Museum, 1975.